Although my name is Rebecca, you can call me Becs.

My life is pretty much like that of any other twenty-something, except that the people I hang with aren't human. Years ago, I got my gift (my curse)—the Kiss—which allows me to summon . . . things, including demons.

But no more. I quit, because stupid me summoned a high-level demon on behalf of a client and things went south. I fixed it, but it cost me, and now I owe that demon a favor. And I don't know when he's going to call it in, what he'll want . . .

. . . or what he'll do if I refuse.

Books by J. D. Blackrose

The Summoner's Mark series

Demon Kissed

Demon Kissed

Book 1 of the Summoner's Mark

by

J. D. Blackrose

Jenna —

Be carful seummoning

demons ———

JDBlackrose

Bell Bridge Books

Bell Bridge Books
PO BOX 300921
Memphis, TN 38130
Print ISBN: 978-1-61026-167-8

Bell Bridge Books is an Imprint of BelleBooks, Inc.

We at BelleBooks enjoy hearing from readers.
Visit our websites
BelleBooks.com
Bell Bridge Books.com
ImaJinn Books.com

10 9 8 7 6 5 4 3 2 1

Cover design: Debra Dixon
Interior design: Hank Smith
Photo/Art credits:
Woman (manipulated) © Artycrafter | Dreamstime.com
Symbols (manipulated) ID 30149868 © Samiramay | Dreamstime.com

:Lkdr:01:

Dedication

This book is dedicated to my wonderful family, including the most supportive husband, children, brother, and parents a writer could ever ask for.

Chapter 1

"I WAS FAT-SHAMED by a fortune cookie."

"Did you eat it and show it who's boss?"

I checked my rearview mirror. The black sedan slipped one lane left of mine, but it was still on my tail.

"Rebecca Naomi Greenblatt, are you even listening to me?"

Ah. All three names. Mickey only used them when she was angry, like our mother. My sister often droned on about her latest fad diet or workout, and when she did, I tuned her out, so it was a fair question. Also, she was on speaker, so I raised the volume to hear her better over the traffic.

"Yes, *Mikayla*," I said, stressing her first name, teasing her as only an older sister could. "What did the fortune cookie say?"

I sped up and swerved around the red Jetta in front of me, earning a honk and a middle finger, but the black car still followed. *Damn.* They weren't even pretending to stay hidden now. Who were these people?

"The damn slip of paper said, 'No one looks good in skinny jeans.'" Mickey sniffed to express her displeasure. "And I was wearing skinny jeans at the time!"

"That's not even a fortune."

"Right? My point exactly."

"Maybe try another restaurant next time?" I took a sharp right into a parking garage and zoomed up a down ramp, fish-tailed around the curve, narrowly missing an oncoming dark-green Ford Escape, and circled to the left, heading toward the exit ramp on the far side of the garage. The black car followed but didn't make it, slamming into the Escape. The crunch of metal on metal and loud cursing echoed through the concrete lot.

"Becs? What was that? Were you in an accident? Are you in trouble? It's that damn job of yours, isn't it?"

I touched my neck where my locket used to be, wishing I still had it. Mickey wore a duplicate. "I stopped doing that job, Micks. I work at a bar now."

"You say that, but for some inexplicable reason I can't visit you at this bar. You're still summoning, aren't you? Becs, you almost got killed six months ago."

"I'm not summoning, and things happen to people in all kinds of jobs."

"It's the kind of people you work with, Becs, and you know it. The scum of the earth."

"Worked with, past tense, and they were desperate. They needed help, and I provided it. I'm sorta the only one who can do it, and you know that."

"You don't help. You hand them a shovel so they can dig a deeper hole." Her voice was hot and angry, and I knew nothing I said would make a difference. We'd had this argument a million times.

I sighed. "It wasn't my fault they made bad deals."

Except that one time. That time it was my fault, and it was the reason I gave it up.

My sister didn't believe me, and I couldn't blame her. It was true— she couldn't visit me at my new job. I worked at a fae bar and she, like any other normal, couldn't see the door or find the address.

"Mickey . . . ?"

"Ruthie got her first tooth." After a pause, she said, "Your niece misses you. Even if she's too little to say so."

"I know." I missed her, too. All of them. Even my brother-in-law. "Text me a picture?"

"I will. She's so cute. It's a bottom one." Her mommy enthusiasm cut through the sadness, and I smiled.

"Does she have any more hair?"

"You would know if you ever came by to visit, *Auntie* Becs. When can we see you? Shabbat dinner Friday?"

I squirmed in my car seat. Jonah, Mickey's husband, wasn't my biggest fan. He hid it from Mickey, but we'd had words in private. Mickey didn't believe in the creatures I summoned, such as demons. She was aware some people did believe, but a literal Dante type of Hell with demons wasn't in her personal belief system. She knew I summoned bad things, but that was it. Jonah, however, understood that whatever people believed in, I could manifest and summon, and he didn't want my demon "stank" to come near his wife and daughter. I didn't blame him because he was totally correct.

I owed a powerful demon named Valefar a favor for fixing the mistake that made me walk away from summoning, and I didn't know when he'd call it in. I lived on edge every minute, thinking he'd use the locket I'd given him to prick my soul, get my attention, and trade in his chit.

Part of me hoped he'd never do it. Another part of me wanted him to do it and get it over with. All of me lived in terror of what he'd ask me to do.

For the bazillionth time in my life, I glanced at the symbol on my inner left wrist. The sign of the Devil, some people called it. The protecttion of Satan, said others. The mark of Hell. Most people called it the Kiss. It did sort of look like lips. The top curved like an upper lip, although to me it looked like the outline of a seagull, and beneath it, a "v" shape. Call it by any name you want, it made me one of a handful of people on earth who could do what I could do. I was, or had been, a summoner. I was born a summoner, although I hadn't known it until my thirteenth birthday when the Kiss appeared on my wrist. Mickey had been eleven. I was twenty-eight now, so I'd been living with it for a while.

Mostly I summoned demons, but that's only because I had a lot of New Testament-following, Dante-believing clients. In reality, I could summon anything from any theology, pantheon, or belief system. That was up to the client's beliefs, not mine. Once, using an ancient pair of *wakizashi* swords as a focal point, I'd summoned a particularly unhappy ancestor in the form of a dragon. The Japanese couple had paid a steep price for the knowledge they'd gained, and they'd lost the swords too, because the swords had disappeared with the dragon.

No one asked to summon beings without power, meaning it was all dangerous, so despite wanting to see Mickey and Ruthie more than anything, until I figured out who was following me, I said the only thing I could and hoped that one day soon I wouldn't still be running from my past.

"Rain check?"

I heard my sister's teeth grind together. "With you, it's always a rain check. Ruthie won't know you. You must make the time."

Making the time was easy, making sure of their safety was harder. Jonah had worried for a reason. I could summon a demon or entity without a circle, and while it could never take my soul, that didn't protect anyone else.

If others tried to summon a demon, and it got loose, well, there was literal Hell to pay. If I summoned a demon, all it could do was sit there, negotiate, and have a cup of tea. Until recently, I'd been fine with that, but I was beginning to see things Jonah's way. In addition to Valefar showing up at any moment, some humans didn't like me much either.

Which made me wonder again, who the hell was tailing me?

Mickey would never understand.

"Hey, I hear you. In the meantime, thank the internet gods for texting. Can you send me a pic of our cutie-pie's little face?"

"I will." Mickey sighed. "Speaking of the cutie-pie, she's crying. I gotta go."

"Kiss her for me."

"I will. Love ya."

"Love ya, too."

Hanging up, I slammed the steering wheel with the butt of my hand, blinking to hold back the tears. It wouldn't do to cry because I needed to see where I was going, so I swallowed the lump in my throat and continued. I couldn't afford to be late. I'd stopped summoning six months ago, and that had been my only source of income. I'd blown through my savings despite being frugal and didn't have a nickel to my name. I was damn lucky to have the job at the bar.

I wiped my nose on my sleeve because who had money for tissues? I wondered about the people in the black car, who they were, and what they wanted. Maybe someone had heard I'd hung up my shingle and needed me to summon a power? I'd lost them for now, but I knew I wasn't lucky enough to have gotten rid of them forever. I headed to Joey's for my shift.

Joey's wasn't the kind of place you walked into by chance. A fae bar, you'd only see it if you had magical energies. She enjoyed the company of other paranormal oddballs and the lost and lonely. I fit right in.

I parked behind the bar, hoping the dumpster would hide my car from prying eyes. The only thing to steal was under the hood, and no one would know that by looking at it. If they wanted to break in, I'd rather they didn't smash the window. On the outside, it looked like a red Prius. In reality, it was far older than that. On the inside, it purred like a Ferrari since I'd had Max, my magic mechanic, put a little woo-woo in the hoo-hoo.

My phone dinged, and I checked the text. It was a photo of my sister and my niece. Ruthie smiled with a single tiny tooth in her bottom gum. She lay on her tummy wearing a darling outfit with hearts on it and a red sequined headband with a glamorous pink satin bow. She looked like a baby model in a magazine. My sister glowed with happiness. We looked nothing alike. I had dirty blond shoulder-length hair and green eyes while she had warm brown eyes, and rich, dark hair that reached her butt. I texted back, "gorgeous" with three kissy emojis and ran a finger across their beautiful faces before saving the photo. I held the phone to my heart before putting it away.

I stepped out of the car into the humid air. Smokey Point, Ohio, positioned on Lake Erie, tended toward warm and muggy in the summer, although never too hot, even in mid-July. I'd grown up here and had never lived anywhere else.

I took one step and splashed in a puddle of vomit. A little seeped through the hole in my boot's sole and soaked my sock. As usual. I did my best to ignore it and opened the bar's front door. I stopped to admire the layout of the dim room, full to the brim with customers. Red leather-topped stools lined the center counter, and tables circled the outside. The wood gleamed, lending a natural glow to the bar's interior.

Joey used copper on spouts and rivets, a metal the fae tolerated, gnomes more so than others, a little-known fact she'd once confessed to me after too many ales. I kept that knowledge in my back pocket, certain it was a secret.

Runes covered the ceiling, and the collection of ceiling fans circled alternately clockwise or counterclockwise to dissipate magical energy. I saw demon energy clear as day, and when I summoned other powers, I could see their energy as well, but fae energy eluded me. Joey saw fae magic as smoky purple waves and was teaching me to identify it. She said the fans scattered the energy so it couldn't concentrate into a useful spell, making Joey's a safe space for her guests. We had several bars of this type in Smokey Point. Joey said the rough currents of Lake Erie thinned the barriers and made for an easy access point to get in and out of Faerie.

Joey was only half-gnome, which had allowed her to reach the prodigious height of four feet. Her gnome father gave her hair, lots of it, all over. Long white hair trailed down her back, and dark hair covered her arms, back and chest, peeking out at the neck of her shirt. I had never met her mother but always wondered what kind of human fell in love with a gnome. She was almost a friend, but I didn't have many friends. No one in my former line of work did or should.

She greeted me with a cock of an eyebrow.

"You're late."

"I'm sorry. Had a little car trouble."

"Can't afford car trouble your first week. Get behind the bar."

I did, storing my backpack in a secret hidey-hole behind a wall of liquor bottles so my high-powered, expensive binoculars wouldn't get stolen. I grabbed my apron and served my first round of drinks to a couple of dwarves who gave me a gold coin in tip.

"Joey, what do I do with this?" I showed her the gold coin.

"Ah, that's a good tip in Faerie. They're generous today."

"Can't use it in here in the real world."

Joey flicked her towel at me. "First of all, calling this the 'real world' is fae-ist. Faerie is as real as here."

"Okay, what do I call it?"

"We call it the Slow World."

"Slow World? Why?"

"Time moves differently here. Slower, but sometimes faster. You can never tell."

A pixie in her human height tapped the bar top. "A gimlet please."

I shoved the coin in my pocket and grabbed the mixology binder. "Sure thing. Hang on a minute."

I opened the file, skimming my hand down the page as I searched for the right drink. The pixie's stare bore holes in the side of my head, and I tried not to look at her from the corner of my eye.

Fuck. Gimlet. Something with gin. I remembered because they both started with a "g." I flipped the pages with enough force to make me glad they were laminated.

I looked up at the pixie. "How about I bring it out to you?"

She pouted her pretty lips. "You suck as a bartender. It's only got three ingredients."

I took a deep breath. "I'm new." I'd promised Joey I'd keep my temper, but this bitch was pushing me.

She flipped her hair over her shoulder and pointed at her table. "I'm over there, and you're not getting a tip." She flounced back to her stool.

I measured out the gin when another patron called for a beer, and then two more wanted to see a menu, and someone else requested a whiskey drink, but I didn't hear past whiskey so I didn't know what kind. I handed the menu to the two waiting elves, poured the beers, and then got back to the gimlet.

The pixie obviously couldn't wait because she returned and smacked her palm on the bar. "Did you get that drink made?"

"Yup," I said, forcing a smile, dumping in the lime juice. "Here you go." I handed her the glass and grabbed another for the whiskey drink.

Gimlet Girl spit the drink out on the floor.

"There's no simple syrup in this drink!"

I counted to ten in my head and then said, "I'm sorry. Here, let me fix that." I knew we had a squeeze bottle for simple syrup somewhere.

"Never mind." Her pixie hit team of mean girls sidled up to surround her. It was like high school on steroids.

"Listen, you human freak," said the second-in-command. I recognized her. She was the Gimlet Girl's top hanger-on. The one who secretly resented being the bridesmaid, never the bride, and would slice Gimlet Girl's throat if she could get away with it. Yeah, I had her number.

I stared past her shoulder, biting my cheek, not responding, but I was certain the tic at the corner of my eye gave me away.

Gimlet Girl snapped her fingers. "Forget it. She's not worth it. There are other bars. Sorry, Joey, but you need better help." And just like that, with a swish of their tight derrieres and the eyes of every male—and some female—patrons, following them, the "It Squad" dropped the mic and left.

Joey pulled me aside by my sleeve. "What is so hard about a gimlet?" she asked.

"I'm sorry, Joey. I forgot the syrup."

"Three ingredients, Becs. Three. Can't you count that high?"

"I'll do better."

"Please." But she gave me an encouraging pat on the back.

I hung my head and breathed in and out. *Suck it up, Buttercup,* I thought to myself. *You made this bed of nails; now lie in it.*

Chapter 2

NO SOONER HAD the pixies left than a big guy in a rumpled suit walked in, made a beeline for me, and snapped his fingers at me, as if he were keeping time to a jazz band.

"Can I help you, sir?" I avoided his eyes. There was something about him that made my radar ping. I snagged a rag and wiped the bar top a second time.

"Gregory Adamos sent me."

That made me pause and sent my tummy churning.

I said nothing, but continued pouring a chardonnay for a dwarf, taking pains to get a perfect six ounces. Then I took a deep inhale and tried not to heave the bar nuts I'd eaten a few minutes ago.

Rumpled Suit snapped at me again. Everyone was snapping their fingers at me today. "Did ya hear me, girly? Gregory Adamos sent me. He needs you to summon for him."

"I have no idea, why, of all people, Gregory Adamos would want me, but I'm not summoning any more demons. In fact, I'm not summoning, period."

"Because . . . ?" He drew out the word to make it a question. He seemed truly confused.

The memory froze me in place. The acrid smell of smoke and fire. The demon Valefar's haunting laugh. I swallowed and shook myself back to the present. "I gave it up for Lent."

Rumpled Suit protested, his voice a harsh rasp. "You don't celebrate Lent, Rebecca *Greenblatt*."

"Was that a Jewish joke?" I looked around to make sure no one was paying attention and then leaned in close, getting angry. "I gave it up, meathead, that's all you need to know. Tell your boss I said no. Gregory Adamos is the last person on Earth I'd ever work for again."

I backed away and passed the six-foot fairy with the droopy pink wings a thimble-full of honey mead. "Here, Pinky. Have at it."

"Thanks, Becs," he said, low and sad, as always.

An elf tapped the top of the bar. "Draft beer, human."

I poured and slid it to him, frowning at the sideways glance he cast at Pinky, irritated at the way other fae treated the fairy.

Already off-kilter, I found it hard to keep my patience. I jerked my chin at the elf. "Hey, are you a Vulcan or something? I get my TV shows mixed up with my fae creatures. Anyway, here's your beer. I didn't even spit in it this time."

The elf huffed off.

The suit ignored all of that, opening his arms wide in a magnanimous gesture. "Mr. Adamos says to tell you he forgives you. The past is the past. What matters is that you get results." He sounded like a game show host. He pointed his finger at me. "He wants you and he'll get you. Gregory always gets what he wants."

I pinched the bridge of my nose. Gregory always got what he wanted? Well, wasn't that peachy for him? I wanted my damn locket back and to not owe a Duke of Hell a favor. But I didn't say that. Gregory Adamos didn't know the details of what I'd done to get his younger brother back, and I intended to keep it that way.

"Tell him to summon the freakin' demon himself. Tell him to hire a warlock to make an ironclad circle and he can negotiate to his heart's content. There's one in the area that's been advertising."

"You're the only one with the Kiss," the paunchy rat said, stabbing his finger toward my left wrist, which I covered with a leather band two inches wide and engraved with protective symbols. "This is what you're born to do."

I whirled around, reached across the bar, and grabbed his forearm, pulling him toward me. Joey, who was suddenly there when I needed her, leaned into his back, holding him in place. I couldn't have secured him without her because he was unexpectedly strong.

I inhaled, and one whiff explained his strength and how he'd found Joey's fae-only bar in the first place. That, and with him this close, I could see his skin color. Slightly green.

"Okay, you pissant troll." Plains troll, if my nose didn't deceive me. "I don't know what you're doing working for a cobra of a human like Gregory Adamos, but you should run—not walk, not shuffle—*run* away. My answer is still no. It will always be no and won't change."

Before I'd traded in my locket for Nick Adamos, Nick had been in Hell under Valefar's, ah . . . tutelage. Now, Nick was a grown man who slept with a nightlight and sucked his thumb. Since I'd fubar'd that complicated situation, I'd sworn off summoning, and I meant it.

The troll yanked his arm out of my grasp, pushed Joey away, and stomped out.

"Gregory's an asshole, sending that guy in here for you," Joey said, wrinkling her nose. "What a jerk."

"Thanks for your help."

"No problem. You did well keeping your temper with the pixies."

"Sorry about the elf."

"He deserved it. I don't like when they're mean to Pinky, either. Why don't you take a break? Go sit on the other side and I'll get you a beer. One drink. Relax, then you can get back to work."

"Why is everyone so mean to Pinky?"

She never answered because a necromancer walked in.

"What can I get you at . . . ?" Joey started, stunned. She glanced at the due-south corner of the inner part of the bar, checking the magical sundial that worked, although there was no natural light in the bar. "At eight p.m.?"

Was this an odd time for a necromancer to be awake? I had no idea. I asked myself questions like this every night. Despite having one foot in the magical world, I was learning as I went. Working at the bar was an eye-opening experience.

"Why do you smell like flop sweat and throw-up?" Pinky asked, his voice its usual monotone. I wondered what happened to Pinky to bring him down this way. He'd lost his Faerie-given sparkle. I hadn't asked because it was none of my business and I was certain he would consider it rude, but in a room full of oddballs, he was an outsider. The other fae gave him a wide berth, and I couldn't help feeling sorry for him.

"Yeah, you stink," said Joey, handing me a foamy draft. I lifted it to my lips with a sigh of gratitude and gulped down a third of the pint. The gold liquid slipped down my throat, smooth with the right amount of bite and the welcome smell of hops.

Pinky turned to face me. "You've got vomit on your right boot. You need new boots. Those brown ones are officially holey."

"Maybe when I get a paycheck."

Pinky ignored me and continued. "You're wearing jeans that are worn through at the knees, and I have no idea what your hair is doing. It's amber when you wash it, but now it's some lank, sweat-soaked, limp, brownish dish-rag color. And you should trash that shirt you're wearing. The sweat stains under the armpits will never wash out."

I slugged down the rest of the beer and put my forehead on the sticky bar. "I know, Pinky. I *know*."

He swung his feet back around to the bar, head low, and muttered, "Wasn't criticizing. Just stating facts. Your eyes are green when you're relaxed, and now they're dilated and hazel. That's a sign you are worried or upset."

Joey shot me a look. We'd had a talk about Pinky's sensitivity. His feelings got hurt easily, but darn it if he didn't remember every detail of everything he ever saw.

"I'm sorry, Pinky." I waited until he met my eyes, so I knew he accepted my apology. "I didn't mean to jump down your throat. I am a sloppy mess. I got chased by some mystery men in a black car today, and I stepped in somebody's vomit when I parked my car. And now that guy came in for Gregory Adamos."

"The baby troll's," Pinky said. "I can smell the vodka."

"You can tell whose vomit is on her shoe?" Joey asked, raising one wooly eyebrow.

"My nose is unfortunately excellent," said Pinky. "It's one of the reasons I stay drunk." He saluted us with his thimble of honey mead and downed it in one go.

"Joey, why are you serving minors?" I asked.

"You referring to the baby troll? Baby refers to its size. It was only, what, Pinky? Maybe six feet tall? And it was twenty-five years old. It just hadn't hit its growth spurt yet, that's all. Forest troll. It'll be fifteen feet by the time it's finished growing and it won't be able to fit in here. Came in while it could still clear the fans without decapitation."

Joey nabbed a footstool and raised herself to higher than counter level. "You're stalling. Tell us what happened with the men trailing you."

I told them about the car, leaving out my fortune cookie fat-shamed sister as that was personal and incidental to the story, and waited for them to tell me what they thought.

"No one wants to kill you that you know about?" asked Pinky.

"Not this year."

Joey held up one finger, telling me to wait a moment, and left to fill someone's glass. The guy was asleep at the bar, but his glass was empty, so she charged him for a refill anyway and didn't notice when someone else drank it. His problem. It seemed rude to me, but fae ways, fae bar.

"Do you think Gregory Adamos sent the black car?"

"I doubt it. Adamos sent his goon after me because he's direct and to the point. This is somebody else. My guess? One of the people who called recently demanding my summoning services, who didn't like it when I refused."

"How many potential clients have called?" asked Joey.

I wrinkled my nose, mentally calculating. "Ten in the last month?"

"Is that a lot?" asked Pinky.

"Normal. I'm constantly shocked at how many people want to summon entities."

Pinky drained his thimble. "Any seemed particularly upset?"

I sighed and ran my fingers through my hair, getting stuck as the beer and liquor combined to make my ends a sticky tangle. I yanked them out. "They're all upset."

"Different subject," Joey announced. She leaned in close and waggled her eyebrows—and that was a lot of eyebrow to waggle. "Tell us about the hot guy upstairs."

Pinky narrowed his eyes. "What hot guy?"

I waved his question away. "The guy who lives in the apartment one floor up from me. The top floor. The only floor above me. Whatever. He's cute, I guess."

Joey's eyebrows travelled to her hair line. "Cute? When I stopped by to get you for work the other day, I got a good gander at the guy. By the stars and all that is true, that man is *hawt*."

I gave her a beady eye. "Where did you learn the term 'hawt'?"

"Kids these days. But that's beside the point. The guy has curls you want to run your fingers through. Deep-brown eyes you could swim in. And what he wears? Those tight jeans. That white T-shirt. Muscles flexed underneath that, Becs. You'd have to be blind not to notice." Joey propped her elbows on the bar and batted her eyelashes at me.

I frowned. "Okay, so he's good looking." He was more than good looking, actually. I stopped breathing when he walked by, but I studiously ignored him. I didn't need a man in my life.

"He's gorgeous! His mouth is a cupid's bow."

Pinky stared at me as if he could see through me. I flicked my eyes at him. "What?"

"What does he want with you?"

"I steal his Wi-Fi. He probably wants me to stop doing that."

Pinky shook his head. "That's not it. Has he talked to you?"

"Just to say hi." And once to ask me about my bird feeders. Boy, had I fucked that up. He'd asked me what kind of seed I put in the platform feeder. I tried to utter the words, "songbird seed," to explain that it was important to have "specific feed for finches," and it came out "pacific feed for pinches." I ran away.

"Why would a man that handsome live above a takeout place in the skeevy part of Chinatown?"

Now it was my turn to lift an eyebrow. "Because he doesn't have much money? That's why I moved in. My last apartment was in a nicer part of town."

"A man that beautiful could live with a girlfriend, be a model, find a job as a receptionist on his looks alone. Anyone would hire him. So why's he *there*, where you are?" Pinky scooted his stool too close to mine.

I elbowed him. "Pinky, move back over an inch or two, will ya? Remember what we talked about? Personal space?"

"Oh, yeah. Sorry." He moved but also kept studying me like a gnat, not giving up his train of thought, gnawing at his lower lip, and tapping his fingers on the table. He was like that. Once he got a bug in his brain, he kept puzzling it and working it like a dog with a bone.

"What's his name?"

"Don't know."

"Where does he go during the day?" Pinky asked. "What does he do? What's his profession? What does he smell like?"

"What does he smell like?" I repeated. "Pinky, why would I know that?"

I did know that. He smelled like birthday cake and sex, but there was no way I was telling Pinky that.

"Does he smell like gasoline and oil? Or like sweat? Or maybe like a train after a commute? Papers and coffee? If I smelled him, I could tell you." Pinky nodded sagely. "You should introduce me to him."

"Not happening, Pinky. He's not my friend. He's a guy, upstairs, who so far hasn't said a word about me stealing his Wi-Fi. He sometimes looks like he wants to say something, but he never does, so I'm ignoring him, hoping he never will. That's it."

"What's his password?"

"Genesis."

Joey shoved a glass of chardonnay in front of a dwarf and said, "That's weird."

"No. People use all sorts of things for passwords. What's weird is he doesn't protect it, which is the same thing as asking someone to steal it. He deserves what he gets."

Chapter 3

I CLIMBED THE fire escape to my third-floor apartment and entered through my sliding glass door. I'd installed a key lock with Mr. and Mrs. Long's permission, since the restaurant was usually closed by the time I got home. I didn't want to have to wake them to come through the front.

I stopped for a second to check the feeders for moisture. It hadn't rained, but mold grew in even a little water. I'd check the hummingbird feeder in the morning when I could see better.

I was blind tired, and all I'd gotten in tips was a gold Faerie coin I couldn't use. I pulled the coin from my pocket and dropped it in my bag, letting it sink to the bottom with the gum wrappers, pennies, paper clips, and lint. I placed the backpack in the corner near the door where it always went.

The sliding glass door opened directly into a dining room that I never used. The room housed a table with mismatched chairs and currently bore the weight of dozens of books. It opened directly into the sparsely furnished main living area, but I turned right into the kitchen, with its white Formica cabinets, its cracked sink, and coffee-stained mugs.

I snagged my last clean glass and glugged a full eight ounces of tap water. I promised myself I'd clean the sink in the morning.

No matter how tired I was, one thing that couldn't wait was the trash. My apartment smelled more like soy sauce than usual. Living above a Chinese takeout restaurant tended to do that, but I ate a lot of Mrs. Long's veggie lo mein as well, and the cardboard cartons overflowed my bin. As exhausted as I was, I couldn't sleep with the odor. I knotted the bag, hoisted it over my shoulder, and walked through the main living area to the front door into the hall.

And that is how I bumped smack into my foxy upstairs neighbor, and I mean *bumped*. I was five feet, ten inches, not short for a woman, but my face hit him in the chest. I bounced off those rock-hard muscles and rubbed my nose, blinking.

"What are you doing up at two in the morning?" I asked, my tone more demanding than necessary, but I should have been able to take my garbage out at that hour in peace, and I looked a fright. This was not the time to run into McHottiepants for my first conversation.

"Taking out my trash," he said, gesturing to the double-ply bag on the ground next to his feet. "Sorry I scared you. Seems we think alike." His voice was a bass rumble and steady, completely unlike my whiney one, and he smiled at me as if he'd woken from a restful midday nap in the sun. I ground my teeth at the unfairness and cursed my sticky hair.

"What are the chances?" I said, turning my back to him to get to the stairs. The trash bin was on the side of the building. so we both hauled our bags down three flights and out the side door. He politely took my bag while I held the door, and he threw them into the dumpster.

"Don't you sleep?" I asked, rubbing my eyes, immediately regretting it since I got something slithery and vaguely sesame smelling on my cheek. I wiped that away too, muttering, "Ick."

He pulled me inside the door, closing it behind me, and touched my elbow to guide me up the stairs. For a moment, I wanted to lean in and let him, but then I remembered I didn't even know this guy's name and I wanted to avoid a Wi-Fi discussion. I jerked my arm from his grasp.

"I'm Ash," he said.

"Who cares?" Thank the Lord my mother couldn't hear me.

"The full name is Asher, but my friends call me Ash."

We reached my floor, and, for reasons I never questioned before, he had to cross the third-floor hallway to get to the stairs for the fourth. Old buildings, I guess. Maybe the fourth floor was an add-on? We didn't have an elevator.

"I'm not your friend." I yawned.

That made him laugh, and I noticed he had perfect teeth.

"Be careful, Rebecca. Good night."

"Good night, Asher."

I closed my door, locked it, and fell on my hand-me-down, poop-brown-colored couch. I'd sold all my good furniture. My last thought before I fell asleep was that I hadn't told Asher my name, and I wondered how he knew it.

I got up at eleven, showered, and did all the necessary things to make myself presentable. The hummingbird feeder needed filling, and I sipped jasmine green tea with honey while I watched who came to visit. I was a little high up for robins, although they strutted the grass beneath my apartment, where it bordered the gravel lot, but the blue jays dive-bombed the feeders and when they scattered, the smaller birds came by.

I had a goldfinch, a house finch, and I even had the pleasure of seeing a rose-breasted grosbeak, surprising for July. I sliced an orange in half and scooped a quarter of a cup of natural grape jelly into a bowl and hoped for Baltimore orioles, but again, it was late in the season.

Dressed in workout clothes, I stopped in the restaurant for my breakfast. Kenneth was there, as always. He had a crush on me, which I regretted, but I tried to be nice. At twenty-five he was only three years younger than I, but he seemed so innocent, it might as well have been a decade. I took a deep breath and remembered the manners that had escaped me last night.

"Hey, Kenneth. Mom and Dad in the back?"

Kenneth Long smiled at me and cracked two eggs into a bowl. "Of course. Getting ready for lunch rush."

"Like your T-shirt."

He flashed me another megawatt smile. Damn him. Why was he so perky?

Today his shirt read, "I'm all that and dim sum." He had a whole collection of foodie T-shirts, and I looked forward to reading them each morning, although I wouldn't admit that out loud.

I slung my backpack onto the seat of an empty chair and waited, rubbing my hands over my eyes. My mind turned to Valefar and when he'd claim his favor. As long as he held that necklace, he had a hold on me and could ask me to do something for him. I wanted to get it over with, but the thought of what he'd ask terrified me. Maybe I should move? What if he appeared in this restaurant? Or what if he wanted me to hurt Kenneth or Mr. and Mrs. Long? I couldn't imagine why he would want that, but he could ask for anything to screw with me.

I whispered a prayer. "God, I'd appreciate any help you can toss my way. I don't want to hurt anyone." I touched my leather cuff with its protective symbols.

"Hey, Kenneth," said a male voice.

"Oh. Hey, Asher," Kenneth responded, his voice unusually flat.

Asher slid into the seat across from me. "Good morning, Becs. How are you feeling this morning? We both went to bed late."

Kenneth slid my vegetable egg foo young in front of me and dropped my utensils with a clatter. "Exactly how you like it, no green pepper. What's this about you both going to bed late?" he asked, his eyes narrowed.

"I got home late and ran into Asher taking out his garbage," I said, waving my fork and breathing through a mouthful of egg foo young.

"Thish is good, Kenneth. A little hhhott." I inhaled cooler air into my mouth, but it was too late. I'd already burned my tongue.

Kenneth grinned as he punched me lightly on the shoulder. "You do this at least once a week. How many times do I have to tell you? Give it a minute to cool." He shook his spatula at me.

Turning his back on Asher, he asked, "Did you know they opened a new drive-in movie theater near the Honda dealership? They're having a monster movie marathon, and I was thinking of going to catch the original Godzilla. Maybe you'd like to go with me?"

My stomach sank. He was such a sweetie, and the most sunshiny innocent person I'd ever met. I worried that exposing him to my world was akin to offering a demon a bag of potato chips and a Coke.

"Kenneth, I'm sorry, but no, okay? I can't."

He swallowed and rushed on. "Friday? Saturday? Whenever you have time? They're running the marathon for several weeks. I could show you the schedule if there's something else you'd like to see. We could go as friends, not a date or anything."

"Kenneth, I said no."

His face fell, and I looked away, the egg foo young threatening to come up. I hated hurting him, but I didn't want to date him, and I'd never forgive myself if he became a demon appetizer.

Embarrassed, I shot to my feet and dumped my uneaten food in the trash. I shouldered my bag and backpedaled toward the door. I tried for a quick, if awkward, exit. "Gotta go. Put that on my tab, Kenneth. Thank you again. It was delicious. Asher, hope you have a good day, doing . . . ah . . . whatever it is you do."

I looked Asher in the eye as I said that, surprised by the concern in his eyes.

"Good luck, Rebecca. Be careful," he said.

"Why do you keep telling me to be careful?" I asked. Just as I did so, a customer entered and smashed the door into my lower back. I staggered forward with an *oompf*. Kenneth and Asher both ran forward to catch me, but I stopped my own fall by putting a hand on a chair. The man who hit me breezed by, not stopping.

"Watch it, asshole," I said.

The guy turned. "Didn't see you there. You shouldn't stand so close to the door, chickee."

"You should be more careful!"

The guy shrugged and turned away.

Asher and Kenneth looked at me, silently asking with their eyes if they should intercede, but I shook my head. I didn't want them to save me. Mrs. Long came out to take the man's order but gave me a nod first. She called out to her husband using a Chinese phrase, *a bèn dàn*, that literally translated to "a big stupid egg" but was a way of calling a person an idiot and was their code for, "Add extra peppers; we've got a live one here." I was certain this man would suffer later, but it killed me to be so helpless.

I closed my eyes and counted to ten, pivoted on one foot, and left, ducking under the flashing neon "So Long Noodles" sign in both English and Mandarin. I sprinted to the back, revved up my car, and went to the only place where I could be more humiliated. Since I was a glutton for punishment, I went there at least once a week anyway.

I walked in, stored my stuff in a locker as usual, and made my way to the floor.

Oded, the owner of the Krav Maga studio, and my teacher, pointed to a spot on the floor. "Stand there."

Oded had let his hair grow out from its shaved military cut to a close mass of dark curls, which complemented his dark, deep-set eyes. I'd been training with him for five years, and I'd never seen him without his close-cut beard and mustache, but I noticed a little gray coming in on the sideburns. His Mediterranean complexion made it hard to guess his age. He never discussed his time in the Israeli and then American armed forces, but he carried a weight on his shoulders that he seemingly couldn't put down. He kept his body strong and muscular but also lithe and fast. Skilled in hand-to-hand combat, he was also skilled in weapons. I'd once watched him disassemble and reassemble a Beretta M9 blindfolded in thirty seconds. I learned to watch his clavicles when we fought. He was so good at not projecting his movements that watching his feet or arms was useless, because he moved from the torso, so I watched his neck and shoulders. It gave me a tenth of a second of warning. About five feet, eleven inches, you would think he wouldn't be intimidating, but if he wanted to, he'd make you stammer apologies for things you hadn't done. Other times, he disappeared into the background and you'd forget he was there.

He studied me silently, long enough to make me uncomfortable.

I couldn't take it. "What are you . . . ?"

"Quiet."

Breathe in. Breathe out.

"Why are you . . . ?"

"*Sheket.*"

He'd switched to Hebrew, but the message was the same, so I stayed silent.

"What's going on with you? Your concentration is shot lately," he said, his arms crossed, head to the side. His heavy Israeli accent made his question sound funny, but his eyes, which had seen war and death, dug into my brain cells, dragging the information out.

I cocked a hip and said, "Nothing."

"Fine."

Bam! He attacked my throat, and I parried, coming up inside his arms, pulling backwards at his wrist area to drag him forward while I simultaneously kicked at his groin. Krav Maga is all about defend and attack, then attack and attack until you've crushed your opponent or you've opened up enough of a gap to run.

I opened a gap, but there was nowhere to run.

Oded used his strength to his advantage and moved around to get me in a headlock and then a shoulder hold. I evaded each attempt and got a good elbow strike to his ribs and another to his jaw. We didn't strike hard, and he had pads, but the exertion was real enough. We drew back, sucking in oxygen like we couldn't get enough. The whole encounter took less than a minute.

"Why can't I learn to attack first, not solely defend?" I asked Oded.

"Why would you need to?"

I told him about my experience that morning with the guy and the door.

"Were you seriously hurt?" he asked. "Were you able to walk away?"

"I wasn't injured at all. I left."

"Embarrassment is no reason to get into a physical altercation with a man bigger than you are. What if you attacked and, in self-defense, he'd injured you seriously and called the cops? It would be self-defense on his part, and you'd be hurt and arrested."

"I wanted to hurt him." I paced, my anger forcing me to my feet. "I needed him to pay attention to me. To notice me and to recognize that he'd hurt me. For him to feel the humiliation I felt!"

"Sit." He pointed to a bench, then sat beside me. "You do not need that. You want it, but that is a negative emotion. Learn discipline. Self-control. Calm your emotions and your brain will take over. More power, more possibility."

"Fuck you, Yoda."

"That is the opposite of what I am talking about," he said. "We need you out of your head. Zara!" He called to a female instructor. "Spar more with Rivka, please. Then bag work, a lot of it, and when that's done, planks. Make her sweat. Get her so tired that she can't think."

He was the only one allowed to call me by my Hebrew name, the bastard. I glared at him, but I followed Zara. I'd sparred with her many times before and we were gym friends, but today she had a hard glint in her eye. I knew that if I let my guard down, she'd kick for real.

Smack! An overhead strike to my left arm got my attention.

"I wasn't ready!"

She continued attacking, and I fought back, but I was sloppy, especially because my left arm tingled. "Right," she scoffed. "Because the bad guys on the street are going to ask if you're ready. Come on, you can do better."

"I don't know how." I huffed, squandering air. In real life, I'd lose this fight.

"Act on instinct. Let your mind go. Whatever it is, Becs, you can't let your inner demons let you lose focus."

"If I do the wrong thing, other people will get hurt."

She whipped around me, and I side-stepped enough to avoid an elbow to the ribs, but I missed the shove that sent me to the ground. I landed hard on my upper back, right between my shoulder blades.

Zara stood over me. "You need to rely on your insight. You've got the training. The intelligence and ability. All that is necessary." She squatted in front of me. "Trust yourself."

"I'm having some difficulty with that."

"Why?"

"I don't see a path forward. I'm waiting for something to happen."

"Have we taught you nothing? Standing still is death. Movement is survival."

I lay on my back, breathing hard, thinking that, at the moment, movement was pain.

Oded came by with a broom. "What's this big piece of dirt lounging on my mat?" he teased, brushing me with the bristles. "Go on, get going. Skip the planks."

I crawled to my feet and punched him in the shoulder. He winced for me, a complete act since I hadn't hurt him at all. I appreciated the charade.

I limped to the changing room and took a hot shower to relieve the tightness in my back muscles. I changed into black jeans, a black T-shirt, my brown scuffed, holey boots, and my brown leather jacket, which I wore despite the heat. I buckled my leather cuff on my wrist and smashed a faded blue Outer Banks ball cap left over from a summer vacation on my head and headed to the hottest joint in town.

If standing still was death, then I had to move. Time to see a cat.

Chapter 4

I WALKED AROUND several homeless people hanging out on street corners—more than usual, I thought. Something about it niggled at me, and I stopped, studying the square, in front of a busker singing a passing version of *Mr. Tambourine Man*. A dark unease settled into my consciousness, but I couldn't put my finger on why.

I dropped five bucks into the busker's guitar case. "There's a lot more homeless folks up here than I'm used to seeing. More topside. Don't people usually squat in the old subway tunnels?" Many homeless lived in the tunnels where it was cool in the summer and out of the snow in the winter.

The busker strummed his guitar and hummed a few bars, then said, "The power pushed a lot of them out of UnderTown."

"What power?"

The busker dipped his head to me. "Dark juju, man. That's all I know."

I tried to ask another question, but he shook his head. He crouched, pocketed his money, put away his guitar, and strolled away. I stared at the street again, letting the bad feeling roll over me one more time. Unsure what to do about it, or if there was anything I could or should do about it, I tucked it away and moved on. Truth was, I had enough on my plate. I didn't need to go looking for trouble.

My mom's voice reverberated in my head, "Oh, darling, trouble always finds you."

I continued walking until I got to my destination and one of my favorite places in the city. The library's imposing entrance overlooked the main city square, called Third Central Plaza, named after Third Central Bank, which had originally owned all the land in that area. The bank still occupied a building on one side of the plaza but had long since sold the rest of the real estate to the city. I knew nothing about First and Second Central Banks and for the life of me hadn't found anyone else who knew, either. It was a source of mild frustration.

Made of red brick, it had an arched entrance flanked by statues—

one of a dolphin, to represent curiosity, and one of a ram, for determination. I mocked them when I first heard of these animal guardians, thinking they weren't nearly as noble as New York City's public library lions, but they'd grown on me. The dolphin appeared to swim in the air, and its eyes shone with intelligence. Poised and ready to charge, the ram's muscular shoulders were wider than the base, communicating persistence and strength. The local artist had long since died, but I wished I could tell him how much I admired his work.

"Hello, Dolphin. Greetings, Ram. It's nice to see you today," I said as I entered the main door archway. I always made a point of saying hello.

The lower level looked like any library, with its checkout counter, reference desk, and librarians who wore reading glasses perched on their noses. Sunlight streamed in through the archway windows except for the center pane, where a medium-sized stained glass suncatcher turned the light into rainbows that fluttered to the floor in airy, ephemeral colors. I breathed in the smell of books and magazines, pens and paper, and listened to the chatter of patrons asking for assistance and the frazzled librarians' replies.

"Where's the photocopier?"

"Where can I find the latest book by . . . ?"

"What do you mean I'm fiftieth on the wait list? How many copies are on hold?"

"I can help you log in, if you'll wait a moment."

It washed over me in a pleasant haze, but as much as I liked it there, it wasn't my destination, so I headed to the elevator.

I took the elevator to the third floor, which housed most of the older encyclopedias and dictionaries, including foreign language versions. I never saw anyone on this floor and assumed you could get all the information you needed online these days.

Walking by these books, I inhaled their rich scent and wanted to reassure them they still meant something, but that was silly, right? Books didn't care. Then why did I feel like needed to run my fingers over their spines and murmur encouraging words? Shaking off the sentiment, I stayed on track, covering the length of the room until I arrived at the circular staircase.

I'd found the staircase when I'd asked a librarian if they had anything on demonology and he'd given me an odd look, sat ramrod straight on his rolling stool, and said, affronted, "We do not! While I'm open to study of almost any topic, I'm afraid that's not something we'd allow in *here*."

Judgmental folks threw me disdainful looks, and one woman covered her child's ears before scurrying away. I gave them my best glare and tried not to care, grateful my cuff hid my mark. No one wanted a demon summoner until they needed a demon summoner. We were like injury lawyers in that way. Two-faced hypocrites. I hated them all.

I had been about to slink away when the librarian on duty removed his glasses, cleaning them with his tie, and beckoned me forward with a jerk of his head. He leaned in close enough that I could smell cinnamon on his breath. He'd whispered, "Fourth floor. Take the elevator to the third and look for the circular staircase."

I hadn't seen that librarian since. I hoped my question hadn't caused his dismissal, though I couldn't see why it should have.

The circular staircase had a brass hand railing and precisely thirteen steps. It opened to a hole in the fourth level's floor which required you to jump and use your upper body strength to hoist yourself up to your hands and knees before getting to your feet. It reminded me of a tree house entrance, and I wondered what the American Disabilities Act had to say about it.

As usual, a big orange cat meowed a greeting. "Hi, Stacks," I said as I wiped my hands together to get rid of any dust. "How are you today?"

Stacks, the name indicated by his collar, only occupied the fourth floor as far as I knew, though I supposed it would be no problem for him to descend the staircase given that he was a feline. He was fat, friendly, and well groomed, so someone obviously took good care of him, although I couldn't say who because I'd never seen a librarian at the small reference desk. In fact, I'd only ever seen one other person up here before, and she'd been as shocked to see me as I'd been to see her.

Stacks rubbed up against my legs, and I petted him, as required. He followed me to my regular bean bag chair, and I scratched his chin and dropped my backpack there. I wasn't usually a huge cat person because cats ate my birds, but this guy was the exception.

"Back to the demonology section, big boy. Maybe there's something I overlooked."

I'd read, or at least skimmed, every book in the section, but it didn't hurt to refresh my memory. There had to be something in there that I could use to protect my family and neighbors from Valefar. Something I could use to gain the upper hand.

It was too much to hope to be free of the Kiss. I'd tried everything, consulted everyone. I'd even tried tattoo removal, but it wasn't a tattoo. It didn't matter how many layers of skin we removed. The mark remained. I needed to set my sights on something more realistic, something that could stymie Valefar and give me some wiggle room. I was looking for a technicality. Owing him a favor was one thing, but there had to be limits on it, something that would protect my friends and family.

Stacks accompanied me to the demonology section, purring and intertwining himself with my legs and feet, almost tripping me with every step.

"Quit it," I ordered, which did nothing. I relented, picking him up and cuddling him on my shoulder. I was at the edge of the demonology section and noted that the number of books had expanded.

"Look at this, Stacks. The library added to its collection. I see the usual suspects. *The Lesser Key of Solomon,* both the modern interpretation of Crowley and the Peterson version, of course. These have been invaluable. A separate copy of *Pseudomonarchia Daemonum.* Then we've got: *Demons: The Good, The Bad, The Ugly; The Encyclopedia of Demons and Angels; Demonologia Pro Imbecillibus; Demonologie: The 16th Century Church's Guide (Translated); The Bible's Walk Through Hell; Magikal Evokation: A Primer; Grimorium Malum; What Would the Pope Do?* Oh, and the oddly titled, *The Zohar Cliff Notes.*"

I noticed a few new titles and looked closer. "These look helpful. *A Jewish Guide to Angels and Demons.* And these, *A Practical Guide to Demon Visitation* and *The Demon Rule Book: Summoning and Dispersion.* I'm going to put you down so I can bring these books to my reading spot. Be good now."

I hauled the books to my bean bag and sank into it, pulling a notebook and pen from my backpack. Most of it was the regular stuff. Valefar or Valefor, Malaphar or Malephar, depending on the text, was the sixth demon listed in the *Lesser Key of Solomon.* He was a duke who commanded legions of lesser demons and was infamous for being a thief and teaching humans to steal or influencing them to do so. Powerful, vain, and short-tempered, he often appeared as a lion with the head of a man.

Yeah, he looked like a lion . . . if you thought lions were seven feet tall and muscled like a comic book supervillain from space. His head was indeed a man's face but with golden skin, sharp horns sprouting from his skull, pointy thorns lining his cheekbones, heavy dark eyebrows, and deep-set black eyes lined with kohl. He also wore a mustache and beard clipped close, whose texture resembled a lion's mane more than human hair. He also occasionally sported enormous griffin wings.

He appeared with gold smoke, the smell of ash, and had totally outsmarted me. I'd been drunk and shouldn't have summoned Valefar, no matter how hard Nick Adamos pushed me or the weapons his goons flashed around. I'd been too slow to notice the deal was going sideways when Valefar dragged Nick off to Hell, body and soul. I'd failed my client.

That's when I'd given my locket to Valefar and traded it for Nick. It'd been the right choice at the time, but now I was screwed six ways to Sunday.

I read until twilight, Stacks sitting on my feet, alone in the library. I'd picked up a few interesting tidbits, but no "ah-ha" moments. You needed an iron-clad circle unless you had a Kiss, and very few had one of those. No one had a count of how many were "Kiss Born," but it was believed to be exceedingly rare. I'd known this, but it was interesting to see it documented.

There were a couple of rules I hadn't been aware of. Demons didn't traffic in true love. They also didn't find lost pets, mostly because they found it boring. They couldn't touch children because their souls were too pure and trying to do so would backfire on them in "odde and payneful ways," according to the *Rule Book*. Though I had known children were *odde* off-limits, I hadn't known about the rebound effects if they tried to interact with kids.

"Well, Stacks, I need to get to the bar. Time for work. I wonder if I can check these books out? They're reference books, so maybe not." I slipped my feet out from under Stacks, who took great umbrage and turned his back to me.

Though the reference desk was always empty, I approached it anyway, searching for a bell or other information. A laminated piece of card stock sat in a clear plastic case informing me that if I wanted to check out a book, I could, but I needed to use the old-fashioned card setup since these books were not in the computerized system yet.

I flipped open the inside cover of the first book, and, sure enough, there was a little college-ruled card like I'd used in elementary school sticking out of a small manila pocket. I signed my name and the date and dropped it into a small slit in the desk where the directions indicated. It didn't say how long I could keep the book but the normal library check-out period was three weeks so I figured that would suffice. I took out several.

I placed the books in my backpack and petted Stacks. "Hope your caretaker comes back soon. I hate leaving you alone, but you seem healthy. See you next time."

The cat lifted his hind legs and washed his nether regions. I was dismissed. So long and thanks for all the pets.

Cats. I knew there was a reason I preferred birds.

I exited the library and headed to work, yawning. It had been a long day, but I needed to earn some money, and one fae gold coin wasn't going to cut it. Time to earn some cold hard cash. I drove home first, changed into an all-black outfit including my slip-resistant shoes, dropped the library books on my coffee table, and shoved a peanut butter and jelly sandwich in my mouth to stave off starvation. I snagged a bag of baby carrots and an entire sleeve of Oreos and left via the fire escape, pausing only for a second to admire an oriole who'd come to snack on the grape jelly.

My watch told me I was running ten minutes late. Joey was gonna kill me. I ran out the back door, down the fire escape, and into the well-lit parking lot.

"Hey, Becs!" Asher called to me from his balcony. I didn't have time to talk to him, nor did I want to. I ignored him, started my car, put it in reverse, and—

Stopped.

An evil energy oozed through the cracks between the passenger door and the car frame. It smelled like licorice and smoke—not the good smoke like your uncle's cigar, but the smoke after a fire that killed thousands of people and woodland creatures. It wafted through my vehicle, flowing through the air like a genie from a bottle, tiny diaphanous fingers exploring the space.

I shoved the car into park and leaned back against the car seat, holding still. I couldn't see it well, but I could feel it as sure as I could feel the wind in a rainstorm. If I opened the door, would it pour in? Would I make it worse or could I escape? What did it want? Who had sent it?

I huffed air in and out in shallow, fast breaths, hyperventilating but afraid to breathe in the energy. Sweat dripped down the back of my shirt, between my shoulder blades, and into my waistband. The energy continued to feel its way through the car until I squeezed all the way to my left, unbuckling my seat belt to scoot away from it.

An embarrassing, ungodly whimper escaped my throat. It wasn't demon energy. That I knew what to do with, but it was similar. A tendril touched my right forearm, and it burned cold, so cold. I turned my head, but that tendril climbed my arms, leaving a thin trail of whitened skin until it touched my shirt. It skipped the shirt until it reached my neck and stabbed me again making me throw my head back in a howl of agony as it reached my jaw, probed the tender nerves there and set my teeth on fire.

As I screamed, the energy touched my tongue and raced down my throat. It tasted like death and dying things. Beetles and worms. Graveyard dust and loam. I got a picture of iron and circles, cinders and soot, yellowed nails and broken bones.

I pulled the latch, jumped out, and slammed the door shut.

Shaking like a leaf, I squatted next to the car and wrapped my arms around myself, tears streaming down my face, biting my lip to keep from shrieking. The pain disappeared the second I'd lurched from the car, but the memory of it gnawed at me like a migraine, and my molars ached with it.

Strong arms squeezed me from behind, and I leapt to my feet, using the crown of my head to strike upwards at my attacker's chin, connecting hard.

On instinct, I ran while my assailant was down, getting to the end of the parking lot and the beginning of the street until I turned to see who it was.

"Oh, Kenneth."

Kenneth sat on his butt, feet straight out, one hand to his chin, the other to the back of his neck. Blood streamed between his fingers onto his T-shirt that read, "I Dream of a World Where Chickens Can Cross the Road Without Having Their Motives Questioned."

I jogged back to him and kneeled at his side. "Kenneth, I didn't know it was you. I acted on instinct. I take self-defense, you know? You really shouldn't surprise a girl that way."

He nodded but didn't speak, dazed. I'd hit him hard. I wasn't sure what to do. I thought about calling 911, but I didn't know what kind of insurance he had. I was just about to tell him to stay there so I could get his parents when I heard footsteps.

"Kenneth, here's a towel and an ice pack." I wanted to kill Asher for showing up and interfering because his presence would embarrass Kenneth, but he was helping, and we had few choices. From the look on Kenneth's face, he felt the same.

"Thanks, Asher," I said.

Kenneth held the towel to his chin and the ice pack to the back of his head. I cringed when I saw the split under his chin. "I think you may need some stitches."

"What happened to you? Why were you spooked?" Kenneth

managed to ask, but his tongue was thick, and he gasped for his words. "You were crying."

Great. Spooked, crying. In other words, vulnerable. I couldn't tell them about the death magic. Meanwhile, there I'd been, balled up on the ground, sobbing like a baby, an easy target for Valefar or whatever minion was circling like a vulture with this creepy new energy signature, and Kenneth had walked right into it.

"Come on. You were huddled down as if in pain. What's going on?" Kenneth repeated, sounding stronger. He readjusted his ice pack to his chin. The bleeding had slowed, so the cut wasn't as bad as I feared, and now I was angry.

"It's none of your business. You shouldn't come up behind a woman and hug them without warning." My voice rose a few decibels. "I'm sorry I hurt you but, really, you got what you deserved. That's a sure way to get your balls knocked into your intestines, Kenneth."

His face crumpled, as if I'd run over his puppy. "I was trying to comfort you."

"Well, next time, don't. You're lucky I only split your chin."

Asher studied me, his perfect eyebrows drawn together. "You're not being nice, Rebecca," he said. I knew I was acting horribly, but something evil and terrible had found me in my car, and I didn't need Kenneth or holier-than-thou Asher to be nearby when that evil found me again. Their presence would only increase the body count and add to the red on my ledger.

More importantly, I seriously feared for my own well-being and it was a tad time-consuming staying alive under these circumstances without also worrying about them. I was simply hoping for sane. Sanity would be good.

"I didn't ask for help, and I don't need lectures. You don't even know me, Asher, so shove your judgment up your ass. Now get the hell out of my way. I'm late for work."

Was I being unreasonable? Maybe. But the shit was going to hit the fan, and this was the first salvo. Getting innocents hurt was exactly what I was trying to avoid.

I opened my car door, gritted my teeth, and stuck my hand in, then breathed a sigh of relief. The energy had dispersed, so I got in and gunned it. If I hadn't been peeling out of the parking lot at that exact moment, I would have missed the mysterious black car driving away.

That damn black car! I'd practically forgotten all about it. I was certain it was the same one. It had to be. Pushing Kenneth and Asher from my mind, I chased it down the road, turning left on a red to follow, my pain and fury aimed at the driver of that car. Whoever was in it had to be related to the death energy. Maybe they sent it or knew who did.

I swerved around a dump truck as the black car increased its speed. My car's magic motor let me catch up and pull almost next to him. I caught sight of a hooded figure, most likely male, in the driver's seat, his gloved hands on the wheel. He hit the gas and turned off the main thoroughfare onto a side street, which forced me behind him because the street wasn't wide enough for two and parked cars lined both sides. I tried to stay on his tail, but he sailed through a yellow light. I didn't make it, plowing into a Volkswagen Cabriolet.

Its driver was not happy, and the police were even less so. But it was Joey I really didn't want to face.

Chapter 5

WHEN I WALKED into the bar, I was already upset because I was facing several hundred dollars of tickets, an upcoming court date, and increased insurance premiums. Luckily, my magic car had made it through without a scratch. Pinky accosted me and plastered himself to my side.

"You're an hour, thirteen minutes, and twenty-one seconds late."

"I know, Pinky. Well, I didn't know the seconds, but I knew I was late."

Pinky peered at my face, getting so close I could smell his breath. He'd been drinking mead again. "What happened to your forehead?"

"Step back, Pinky. Too close."

"Yeah, sorry. But what's with the gash?"

I touched my forehead. "I didn't know that was there. I was in a car accident, and I must have hit the windshield. I don't have airbags."

"Why don't you have airbags? Airbags have been standard in all passenger cars since model year 1998 and in all SUVs, pickups, and vans since model year 1999. You have a Prius."

"It only looks like a Prius. My car is ancient. But I have to go see Joey. It's time to face the music."

Joey snapped her gum when she saw me. "You'd better have a great reason."

"Death energy tendrils, the mysterious black car, and I rear-ended a pregnant woman?"

She put down the tumbler she'd been drying, her face hard. "You had me at death energy tendrils. Tell me exactly what happened."

"Hey, Becs. Now that you've shown up, you think you could get me a beer?" a river sprite yelled to me.

"Hold your flow, Ripples. I'm coming. I'll tell you later, Joey. I do apologize. I'll close by myself to make it up to you."

My hands finally stopped shaking once I got working, and I avoided talking to Joey, focusing on what was in front of me. I hustled drinks and sought equilibrium, pulling myself together. I didn't mess up any drink order too badly until Gimlet Girl came along.

She tapped the bar top with one perfectly shellacked index finger. "You." I ignored her. She tapped again. "You. Barkeep."

I looked around. "Are you speaking to me?"

"Yes, stupid. You see anyone else here working as a bartender?" Several trolls and elves tittered. I sent a pleading look to Joey, but she only raised an eyebrow.

I took a deep breath. What had Oded said? Calm your emotions. Embarrassment is no reason to attack. "What is it you want?"

"A vodka gimlet, please. Can you make one correctly this time?"

I smiled at her, my expression fake as a four-dollar bill. Still, I was determined to make it through an interaction with her without incident. "Why, I believe I can."

I remembered the three ingredients and that she'd requested vodka this time, not gin, and poured a perfect drink, handing it to her. "Here you go. Would you like to pay now or open a tab?"

The pixie took a sip of the drink, her posse watching her every move, and grimaced. "You used cheap vodka."

"I used decent vodka. You watched me make it. If you preferred a certain brand of vodka, you could have requested it."

Gimlet Girl struck a pose. "You should have known."

I closed my eyes and counted to ten inside my mind as the rage rose. I smelled smoke and idly wondered what was burning. When I opened them, the bar stools stood empty as every patron had jumped back ten feet away from me. Everyone except Pinky, who pointed to my hands.

"Becs, it's okay. Calm down. She's not worth it."

My hands bled death tendrils. Gray, licorice-scented smoke ringlets of cold death energy leaked out of my fingers and floated through the air, creating a halo around my hands. Joey stayed in the back of the bar but distanced herself from me as far as she could go, pressing herself into the far corner. Only Pinky dared to get closer. He leaned across the bar and stared into my eyes, strange behavior for him because he avoided eye contact usually.

"Becs, look at me. Suck it back in. It's like inhaling but with your whole body. You can do it. I believe in you."

"What's happening to me, Pinky?"

"Magical transference."

"What the hell is that? This is the energy I experienced this morning. It isn't mine."

He recited it as if he were reading an entry in an encyclopedia.

"Magical transference is a component of physics, similar to conservation of energy. Magical energy can't be created or destroyed, merely changed, or in this case, stored. It's magical physics. Not that complicated if you understand the basic rules of thermodynamics and study Einsteinian quantum mechanics, plus Oberon's Rules of Magical Harmony—"

"Shhhh! Don't say his name! You know better," said Joey.

"Oh, sorry." Pinky hung his head and searched the room with a furtive expression.

"Whose name?" I asked.

"The Fae King's. We don't say it out loud. It could summon him, and that's not a good idea."

"I still don't understand."

Joey approached me, her face a rictus of fear. "You're a magical being, one with only a single talent, but magical, nevertheless. This death energy found you and saw you as a well or, in another way of thinking, a storage space, an empty battery. It sank into you."

"How do I get rid of it?"

She shook her head. "That's unknown for now. Right now, suck it up like a straw."

An elf I hadn't seen in the bar before spoke up. "Lass, this is important. I don't know who came after ye with this stuff, but it is deadly. Listen to me voice and remember what Pinky said. Think of taking a deep breath, the deepest breath ye've ever taken, and then take it with your entire body, shrink it in, muscle to bone. Ye have to do it, lass, or we could all die. That kind of energy is a ticking bomb."

I exhaled and let out all my air as Oded had shown me in practice and then took two smaller breaths to center. I stared at the energy floating around my hands and watched in horror as one creepy vine escaped my limited control and reached for Pinky, shooting out like a spark of flame to grab for the closest victim.

The scent of licorice filled the room. Smoke and ash. Beetles and dead things.

"No!" I shouted. "Pinky, get back!"

Pinky rolled off the stool, crashed to the floor, and cried out in pain as he crushed a wing. Every remaining patron scrambled out the door, abandoning Pinky to his fate. Joey swore a stream of cuss words and scurried to Pinky's side, caught him under the shoulders, and dragged him father away.

I grabbed at the tendril with my other hand to tug it back, but all that did was freeze a line of sheer agony on my palm.

"Breathe it back, lass! Ye must!" The elf was the only other one who'd stayed.

I inhaled as hard as I could, but it did nothing. The tendril leaped out again like a puppy realizing he was stronger than his master, but that image gave me a thought.

"Down, boy," I growled. "I am the mistress here."

"Becs, that is the equivalent of magic napalm," Joey said, her voice pitched low and smooth but with a tinge of panic. "Get that shit under control *now*. I can't believe you brought that in here with you."

I swallowed, straining for control. "I didn't bring it in here on purpose. Now, quit jabbering. I'm working here."

I pulled at the strand, sucking it back in like a theoretical noodle, pausing ever so slightly to get more air, clamping my metaphysical lips around it, inhaling until it was back where it belonged. Then I attacked with my mind, all Krav Maga, punching and kicking it repeatedly, pushing it down inside until I found a pulsating box I'd never noticed before. I shoved it in there, closed the lid, and locked it.

I gave the elf, Joey, and Pinky a wan smile and collapsed to the floor, passing out.

When I came to, Pinky handed me a glass of ice water. "Here, you might be thirsty."

Thirsty? Parched was more like it. I downed that water and accepted a new one from Pinky's outstretched hand like a woman in a desert reaching for a mirage. "Where's Joey?" I croaked.

"Here." The half-gnome perched on a stool near the bar entrance. "Waiting for you to wake up."

I stood so I could see her, shaky but on my feet, whispered my thanks to Pinky, and walked around the bar to lean back against it, breathing hard.

"You seemed to recognize what that was. Can you explain it to me?" I asked.

Pinky came to my side. "You said someone attacked you with death magic? Well, instead of killing you, it took a liking to you and grounded into you, like electricity."

"Okay, but what really happened?"

"You ran off all my paying customers," Joey said with a deep sigh. "Tell us what you experienced earlier today."

I told them the entire encounter.

Joey tapped her index finger against her teeth. "Either they were trying to kill you, in which case they did a terrible job of it, or they were feeling you out. One way or another, they most likely didn't expect you to act as a sponge for the energy. Now you've got some of their magic inside of you. I'm certain that's a shocker to them."

She hopped off the stool. "But whatever it is, you've got some potent crap inside of you, girl. I'm sorry about this, but I'm going to have to ask you to leave and not come back until you can get rid of it. That kind of death magic could kill everyone in this bar—hell, everyone on this city block—if it gets out of control. I just can't take that chance."

I rocked back on my heels. "I need this job, Joey. I've got it locked down now."

She passed by me to walk to the cash register, which she opened with a *ping* sound. Pinky stared at me, sadness in his eyes.

"Here," Joey said. She handed me some money which I snatched from her hand, counted, and shoved into my pocket. "This is the best I can do now."

I stalked by her, grabbed my bag and a bottle of beer. "Thanks for exactly nothing, Joey."

"That's not fair, Becs."

"Yeah, tell me about it. It's not fair I got attacked for no reason by a practitioner of death magic. It's not fair I've got a demon ready to ring my doorbell at any moment and I don't know when. It's not fair I can't see my sister or my niece. It's never fair. Nothing's fair. The world's not fair."

"Sounds like you're doing a good job of throwing yourself a pity party."

"Well, I'm having a phenomenally bad day, and no one else is throwing me one."

I got to the door and turned slightly. "Pinky, I'll see you in the park?"

"Yes, Becs. I'll see you there," he said. "But I have one question."

"What's that?"

"Did you really rear-end a pregnant woman?"

"Nah. I rear-ended a middle-aged man. I made up the pregnant woman to make the story better."

As I opened the door, I growled one last thing. "Thanks for the money, Joey. You owe me two hundred dollars more." I slammed the door just in time to hear the glass stein shatter against it.

Chapter 6

I HAULED MYSELF up my fire escape, opened my door, and dumped my bag in its place. I wanted to sleep, but I needed to do something first. I sat at my laptop and, using my stolen Wi-Fi, I ordered Kenneth an apology T-shirt that said, "Spooning leads to forking. Be safe. Use condiments." He'd know who it was from.

I could have apologized in person, but I was a coward. I owed Joey an apology too, but I wasn't anywhere near ready for that yet.

Despite my fatigue, I still couldn't rest, and I didn't want to think, so I cleaned. I scrubbed my kitchen sink until it gleamed, wiped the counters, and polished my fingerprints from the white refrigerator and dishwasher. I removed the burners from the top of the stove and scoured the spilled food. I swept and mopped the laminate flooring. The white with gold marbling was ugly as sin but at least it was spotless. The scent of lemon permeated the entire apartment.

I checked my two African violets for moisture, refilled the hand soap, and when I couldn't find anything else to do, I showered and donned pajamas. Light would break over the horizon in a few hours. I still didn't go to bed but sat on my couch holding a throw pillow to my stomach as if it would ward off the day and hold the death magic in.

Valefar was coming—I could feel it in my bones. But I didn't know if he was related to the death magic or not. It could be my experiences earlier were a precursor to his inevitable visit, or it could be unrelated, in which case I had another problem on my hands.

I tried to think of someone who would give me a job. I'd been friends with a number of people in high school, but I'd let them all drift away, and I hadn't made any real friends as an adult. Maybe Oded would let me sweep up the studio.

Who was I kidding? I might not be alive long enough to sweep anything. I blinked back tears and held the pillow tighter. I had magical napalm inside of me. I could kill everyone if I let this get out of control.

I jumped at the knock on my door and wiped the tears off with the back of my hand.

"Rebecca? It's me. Asher."

"What the hell? Asher, don't you ever sleep? What are you doing knocking on my door at this hour?"

"I saw the light on and your car in the lot. I've been worried about you."

I opened the door and lost the ability to speak. He smelled sooooo goooood—like chocolate syrup mixed with a soupçon of brandy and a touch of spice. The scent zipped to places on my body that hadn't zapped in a really long time and made them stand up and notice. I was surprised my tongue didn't roll out of my mouth.

He must have just showered, and now, there he stood, leaning with one muscled arm against the doorpost, all wet, dark, tousled hair, and big brown eyes in an unbuttoned short-sleeved shirt and low-slung jeans so I could see his happy trail go down into his pants. . . . *Ohmygod, I shouldn't be looking. No, no looking.* But yes, he had that "v" of gorgeous musculature that made me want to drag him into my apartment, lay him on the ground, and nibble him from neck to belly button.

"Rebecca?"

I was off-kilter, so I did what I always did. I countered.

"Do you have a job?"

That earned me a smile. "I'm a host."

"What?"

"I'm part of the host and hostess staff at Giatanos. Wait. Stop. I need to stop saying that. I'm a member of the management team. I've been there several years, and I've worked my way up to management, but I keep forgetting."

Damn, that was a nice restaurant. It served a fusion of Greek and Italian food. He looked the part, too, like a classical Greek or Roman statue come to life. He'd look perfectly appropriate with a crown of laurel in his hair.

He interrupted my train of thought. "Although watching over you seems like a good idea too. May I?" He gestured to indicate entering the apartment.

"No. It's late."

"True, but we're both up, and we're annoying your neighbor."

Sure enough, Mr. Fishbein, my next-door neighbor, stood in his doorway in his bathrobe and fuzzy slippers, glaring at us.

Stepping aside, I let him in.

"Asher, you shouldn't be here. I'm not up to company."

"I'll only stay a moment. I have . . ." He floundered, flipping his hand back and forth, trying to find a word. Finally, he said, "I have something to tell you, but it will sound weird."

Oh dear. I couldn't take any more. Blowing out a breath, I motioned to the couch. "Weird is my specialty. What is it?"

"I'm psychic."

"You're what?"

"Okay, not truly psychic, but I get feelings, premonitions, glimpses, and I've been getting bad feelings about you. Feelings of danger. That's why I've been hanging out near you."

Oh.

I sighed. "Asher, you being psychic doesn't faze me at all. I believe you. And here's the thing—you're totally right. Bad things are happening to me, but I know what to do about them. So thanks for the warning, but I'm okay. But you and Kenneth and the Longs should all stay away from me. In fact, I'm thinking of leaving."

"What? You can't leave. How can I protect you if you leave?"

"You aren't going to protect me, Asher. Why in God's name would you think you should have to?"

He leaned back and threw his arms over the back of the couch like wings. "You can't leave."

"You're not the boss of me."

"Thank heaven for that."

Arrrgh. I rubbed my eyes with fatigue and frustration. Why didn't I ruffle his feathers the way he ruffled mine?

"Look," Asher said, "why don't you tell me what is going on and let me see if I can assist in some way."

I stood and paced. "You won't believe any of it."

"Why?"

"Do you believe in magic?"

He ran his fingers through his hair, hesitating before responding. "Well, I'm psychic, so yeah. Of course, I also had a friend who was a hedge witch."

"Perfect. Do you believe in demons or fae creatures?"

"Never seen any, but I've heard stories, like everyone. That baby that disappeared and reappeared and his mom swore he was different?"

"A changeling," I said.

"Or that story about Bigfoot in Indiana?"

I shrugged. "I can't say I know anything about that one. But do you remember the stories of when the Cuyahoga River caught fire in 1969?" I asked.

Asher gave me a lazy smile and put a foot up on my coffee table. "Only because the Great Lakes Brewing Company makes a beer called Burning River."

I knocked his foot off. "It's a pale ale, to be precise. Don't joke."

He put both feet on the floor and leaned toward me. "I didn't mean to be dismissive. What are you trying to tell me?"

"The Cuyahoga River did burn but not because of the oil slick on the top. Don't get me wrong—the river was horribly polluted. But a demon caused that blaze, summoned by someone who lost control, and it wreaked holy hell to show its power, literally lighting water on fire."

Asher sat back on the couch and crossed his legs. "Go on."

"Have you ever heard of the Kiss?"

Asher pulled at his lower lip, thinking. "My friend, the hedge witch? She once told me that some people were born with a mark that let them summon great powers, like demons and gods and goddesses. It's true?"

"Yes."

He furrowed his brow and leaned in and took my hand. "Tell me what this means. Not generally, but to you. To you, personally."

I removed my cuff and showed him the Kiss.

"We are born to it, and we don't know who gets it or why, and we don't do anything special to develop it, but it comes in at puberty. Mine showed up when I was thirteen, but I've never summoned a god or goddess."

He raised a single eyebrow. "Who do you summon?" he asked.

"Demons. A dragon. I summoned a ghost once, but that was an oddity."

"Why would someone want to do these things? Given my visions, I'm assuming it is dangerous."

"That's a really good question," I said. "It is dangerous. People summon things with power, but some entities are more good-natured than others. Most people want to make a deal, an exchange of a favor for a favor, or information for riches or heirlooms. Sometimes, someone wants something big and the trade is steep, like years off someone's life force, or a piece of their soul."

Asher pulled away and rubbed his hands as if he'd gotten an electric shock. "Demons want that?"

"Absolutely." I didn't mean to, but, for some reason, I spilled out the whole story. It tumbled from my lips, and he listened to it all without interruption. When I got to the part about not seeing my sister and the baby, I cried, and he hugged me, and God help me, I let him and snuggled in closer. It was the first time I'd shared the disaster that was my life with another person.

He sat up straight. "You have *what* inside of you?"

"Death magic."

He unentwined himself and stood to stare down at me. I shivered with a sudden chill.

"Magical napalm, they called it?" he asked, hands on his hips.

"They might have been exaggerating." The lump in my throat sat there, hard and unyielding. I turned my head to play with the throw pillow.

He paced to the sliding glass window and stared out at the bird feeders, mumbling under his breath. He seemed to be arguing with himself. After a few minutes, he whirled around, strode back to me, and bent on one knee to take my chin in his hand.

"It seems my visions have greatly underestimated the danger you are in."

I shrugged. "It's not like you could have known."

"I feel like I should have."

"Don't be ridiculous."

He blew out a breath, sat back down on the couch, and held my hand. Warmth slid back into me like sunrise after the coldest night.

He leaned forward and tapped the books I'd placed on my coffee table. "Now I understand why you have this bit of light reading here."

I poked them with my toe. "Yeah, trying to study everything I can."

"When your Kiss comes in, doesn't somebody, like, explain how to use it? What the rules are?"

"Yes, but my trainer is not . . . around. He showed up and then disappeared." I tugged at my earlobe. "Forget it. That's not something I want to talk about."

"Okay, fair enough. Is there anyone else you can ask? Another person with the Kiss?"

"I've never met one."

"You poor thing. You've been alone a long time."

I didn't want his pity. I moved out of his embrace and sat up. "I've done fine."

He shook his head, and I watched his curls bounce. "You're always so prickly. I didn't mean to imply that you haven't done well. I meant to say that you've done incredibly well without anyone's help. It's impressive. Inspiring."

"Alright then. What about you? I've told you about me. Where are your friends? Family?"

His eyes darkened. "There's not much to tell. No parents. No siblings." He shrugged. "I'm starting over. Like you, I don't want to talk about it. Some things are best left in the past."

"I'm sorry."

"It's okay."

The moon was setting, and the sun would rise in the next thirty minutes or so. I yawned the biggest, most unladylike yawn of my life. A full molar, bad breath yawn that would scare off bears in the wild, but Ash gave me a hug and laid me down on the sofa.

"Get some rest. I'll check on you tomorrow."

"M'kay." My soft afghan from my side chair settled on my body, and for the first time in the last twenty-four hours, I relaxed into sleep. I heard the door click shut and that was all.

Until a sharp pain in my mid-section woke me up and words bellowed into my ears. "Tonight, REBECCA NAOMI GREENBLATT. Summon me tonight."

I rose to my feet like a shot. Valefar had made his social call.

Chapter 7

IF HE WANTED me to summon him, that meant I had time to prepare. He knew I couldn't summon him during the day. But tonight, I'd have to go to my office and call the Sixth Duke of Hell to fulfill my end of a dark bargain, and I had no idea what he'd ask me to do, or what I'd do if it was too awful to bear.

I left my couch and sank into my bed, curling up with my pillow and a stuffed lamb I'd received as a birthday present when I was ten. I fell back asleep, but I dreamt of a desert surrounded by red and purple flames, hissing lava pools, and rows upon rows of minor demons connected by ropes around their waists, all heaving boulders toward a tall city in the distance, each bent at the waist, weeping whip marks on their backs. The sulfurous air crackled with heat and poisonous fumes, but still the demons toiled, their feet burning on the dark-black coals that lined the ground. When one fell, the others kicked him aside, the demon behind him untying him (or her, it was impossible to tell) from the work chain, retying the rope to the one ahead, and a large bird collected the fallen demon, dragged it by the legs down a long rocky walkway that ended in a cliff, and tossed the body over.

Except it wasn't a body. The demon wasn't dead, and it screamed the whole way down. In my dream, I looked up, and up, and high on a craggy cliff stood Duke Valefar in his lion form with his scary human head and giant griffin wings, which should have looked ridiculous but instead terrified me, a halo of red rage and superiority emanating from him like some hellish sonar. The duke looked directly at me, smiled so I could see his corroded fangs dripping bloody saliva, and he mouthed, "Tonight."

I woke with a start, bathed in sweat.

I showered and checked on my birds. Two blue jays. Six robins patrolled the grounds. A falcon shot across the sky. I counted my visitors, filling birdseed by rote, making sure each feeder was full to the top. I gripped the side of the railing and breathed, gradually unclenching my jaw. A bright-red cardinal perched at the top of the large tree next to the building and chirped his distinctive mating call. A laugh burbled up and out of my belly. That cardinal reminded me that life continues and I'd better get on with it.

I mentally reviewed what I needed to do that night. I was surprisingly calm now that the time had arrived. Whatever it was, I'd deal with it. Just in case though, I knew I should take care of a few things. I removed half of the money Joey had given me and placed it in an envelope and addressed it to Kenneth, along with a short letter. I wrote another note and addressed it to Pinky. Finally, I checked my watch. I had enough time.

I cut through the parking lot, then the basketball court, lifting the broken fencing to sneak through. I waved to the guys playing three-on-three and hustled past them so they could continue their game without my getting in the way. It would be nice if the city cleaned up the area, but you had to cross the main street, go east, and head a bit uptown to the medical area before gentrification set in. Once you got the main hospital buildings, you saw the investment. This was the northern part of the hospital's wide-ranging campus called Winter Medical Park. It was twelve city blocks of prime real estate owned by the hospital that had been turned into green space as required by the city in return for favorable tax rates. The one farther south, named Summer Medical Park, was an equally large complex focused on nursing homes and rehabilitation facilities, but I'd never been to it personally.

I often jogged here, and today I got in a good power walk. The clear air and chirping birds made it easy to push my worries away and stay in the moment. A red-shouldered hawk swooped overhead looking for an easy meal. A nuthatch walked down a trunk, defying gravity. A couple of bunnies hopped away as I approached, their fluffy tails in the air. The sun shone brightly, and I envied the moms strolling with their babies in prams and the doctors meeting for quick sandwiches on benches between patients.

I didn't envy the people here for appointments with oxygen tanks and wheelchairs or the elderly with their companions helping them eat or keeping them company before their appointments. I turned my head and focused on the smell of gardenias, which led me to the shade tree garden.

Pinky napped at the bottom of a huge oak tree, curled up like a child, snoozing as if he hadn't a care in the world. I saw him as he was, but he'd informed me that others saw a homeless skater boy with torn painter's pants and a graphic T-shirt.

A sturdy man with graying short hair and a goatee spied me. "He sleeps here every night," he said. "I cover for him, because the cops and social services come through pushing out all the other homeless folks who try to bed down here. He's going to have to go to one of the shelters soon."

"I appreciate you helping him out, Mr. Lincoln. Don't force him out yet. I promise I'm trying to find his family." We'd had this conversation before. "I don't want to wake him. Will you give him this letter for me?" I handed it to him, and he stuck it in his jacket pocket.

"You okay?"

"Yeah, it's probably nothing but better to be prepared."

Mr. Lincoln eyed me. "You in trouble, girl?"

I winked at him. "Always."

"I'm serious," he said, propping himself on his rake.

"I'm a woman alone in a city. It's not a safe situation."

He snorted and slapped at a fly. "Guess not, but don't do anything stupid."

"It's a safe bet I will."

My lighthearted joke didn't go over well. Mr. Lincoln removed his gardening gloves, buying time while he thought about what to say.

He pointed to Pinky. "He won't do well in a shelter. You know that. I take care of him as best as I can, but you're his only other friend that I know of. If something happens to you, he's in trouble. Think on that before you do something reckless." He smacked me lightly on the arm with his gloves. "Besides, I kinda like you."

I touched the back of his hand, feather light. "I kinda like you, too."

I reversed course and headed back home, hands in my pockets, head down, thinking. Damn, that Pinky had slid in right between my ribs into my heart. If I didn't make it, Joey would take care of him. That's what I'd told him in my note—to trust Joey.

Back at home, I ate crackers and peanut butter with tap water. My tummy growled after that paltry meal so when I opened my front door to tape Kenneth's letter to it, I was happy to see a note from Asher.

Meet me tonight at six pm at Giatanos. Dinner's on me.

I'd planned on summoning Valefar immediately after sundown, but facing him on a full stomach had appeal. Besides, it might be the last time I saw Asher and I wanted to see him again. I did a mental inventory. I hadn't heard a peep from the death magic, and I prayed it would stay locked away.

I dressed in black pants, black shirt, and black tennis shoes, read a bit more from my library books, taking additional notes, and when it was time, I drove to the restaurant.

Walking into Giatanos made me stand a little taller, sway my hips, and look for the power brokers in the room. It also made me look over my shoulder for the derringer about to stick me in the ribs. It had that old-time feel that said you didn't have the money to be here and if you did have the money, why were you here and not somewhere else? The hushed atmosphere added to the mystery, and the soft overhead lighting gave the facelifts a lovely glow.

A waiter glided by with a seafood platter, and I almost fainted from the heady smell of garlic. A sommelier popped the cork on a merlot, and the fragrance almost brought me to my knees.

I didn't recognize anyone, but I almost smelled the money and heard the bank accounts snap open and closed. This place catered to the rich and famous. I bet the staff got good tips if they knew how to serve well and schmooze.

"Can I help you, miss?"

A slim man with the perfect blank stare smiled at me from the host stand. I'd expected Asher to be there. Hadn't he said he was the host?

"Uhm. Yes? I'm here to meet Asher?"

"Of course. Let me call him." He picked up a black hand receiver and punched in a three-digit extension. "Mr. Michaels, your guest is here." He waited a moment. "Yes, sir."

He smiled at me again. "Let me show you to the chef's table. Mr. Michaels asked that I get you seated. He had a situation to attend to but will be down shortly."

We passed the bar where three bartenders dressed in white shirts, black pants, black aprons, and black bow ties fawned over perfectly coiffed guests. I realized I looked more like the wait staff than a customer. I checked out the liquor and saw an Irish whiskey that I knew was supposed to be out of distribution and a Japanese whiskey that cost more than I made in my best year. The tequilas were equally impressive.

The chef's table seated two and was at the edge of the kitchen, so I could see the workings of the line cooks, the sous chef, and the pastry chef. The wait staff ran in and out, dropping orders. I loved watching the inner mechanisms of a finely tuned professional kitchen.

A strawberry-blond server with dramatic eyeliner waltzed to my table, eyeing me as if I were a rare animal in a zoo. I instantly went on alert.

"So, you're Ash's guest?" she asked, her gaze roving over my face and chest.

"I'm his neighbor."

"He's never had anyone here before," she said.

"None of my business if he had."

She took a step back and assessed me again. "I don't understand what he sees in you. You're pretty, but you're not all that."

I raised an eyebrow. "Maybe he likes that my boobs are real?"

She lifted the corner of her lip in distaste. "Does he call you his girlfriend?"

"No. He calls me 'baby.'"

Her eyes widened. "I thought you said you were his neighbor."

"And I thought you wanted my drink order. White wine, please. A nice riesling, if you have it."

The waitress's face turned an eggplant color, but she flounced off.

The pastry chef burst out laughing, although her hands kept working a mile a minute. "Ignore Kellie. She's wanted to get into Ash's perfectly ironed pants since the day she met him."

"How long has that been?"

"Long enough. At least six months. I feel confident saying that Ash's ass is safe from her clutches."

I waited another few minutes, taking a good look at the surrounding tables. Even after working at Joey's, I had trouble seeing through fae glamour, but I thought there were at least two tables with fae customers. I let my eyes pass over them lest they notice me staring. I read a table across the room as a man and his mistress. She was much younger than he, and she accidentally swept the white tablecloth aside as she flipped off her high heel. I got a good glimpse of her long leg stretching across the table and her foot reaching his groin. His eyes glazed, and he asked for the check. She giggled.

Asher slid into the seat in front of me.

"Sorry I was delayed. We had some issues with a private party."

"It's no problem. Thank you for inviting me. I can't stay long, anyway."

Ash frowned. "Why don't you have water and breadsticks?"

"Your server didn't like me."

"What? Who is it?"

The strawberry blonde zoomed into view, all business now that Asher was there, carrying breadsticks, water, and my wine on a tray.

"Here you go, miss. Have you decided what you wanted to order?"

"Nobody gave me a menu."

Kellie blushed. "My apologies. I'll get one right away."

Asher sighed. "I'm sorry for the less than stellar service. We've been very busy. Make sure you order two entrées so you can take one home for tomorrow. It's on me."

"No need to do that."

"I invited you, and I insist."

"I appreciate the food, and I wanted to see you." I lowered my voice so the pastry chef couldn't overhear. "Valefar contacted me last night. I am summoning him tonight, and I wanted you to know."

Ash's face turned to stone. "Are you certain you have to do this? You said this was serious, possibly life-threatening."

"Yes."

"You don't seem scared."

"Now that I have to, I'm not. It's time to face the music. I'm ready."

"I'm worried, Rebecca. These beings . . . are tricky and can hurt you with a thought. With a word."

"That's the point. I've got the Kiss. This is what I'm supposed to do, summon demons, spirits, and other nasties. I should tell you about the dragon some time. Look, I got wrapped up in this one too tight, and all I want is to get out of it. I've got to face this now, on my own, and deal with it so I can get my life back."

Ash drummed his fingers on the table, then took my hand, staring at me intently. "You're going to be faced with decisions."

I raised an eyebrow. "Is that a vision?"

He sat back in his chair and studied me. "You could say that. What do you want me to do?"

I drank my wine. Why had I told him? What did I want from him? I didn't speak until a platter of stuffed portobello mushrooms landed in front of me.

"What's this?"

"I ordered appetizers for you. You need to eat."

"They smell heavenly. Veg?"

"Vegan, in fact. I wasn't sure if you ate cheese?"

"Yes, and eggs and honey." But I wasn't certain he understood me because my mouth was full of the most delicious mushrooms I'd ever tasted.

"I'll have the eggplant dip wrapped up for you for tomorrow," Asher said, still studying me. He took a breath and let it out. "Look, I'm glad you told me, even if I can't do anything. It's your job; you have free will and I can't interfere."

"Of course, you can't interfere. You'd only get hurt." I waved my fork in the air. "But I thought someone should know what I was doing, in case. In case I don't come back." I couldn't meet his eyes.

"You think that's a possibility?"

I huffed out a breath. "It's always a possibility." I extracted the paper napkin from under my wine and turned it so I could write on a dry part. I dug into my bag, grabbed one of my many pens, and scrawled my sister's phone number on it.

"Here, this is my sister's number. Her name is Mikayla, but she goes by Mickey. If I don't make it back, please call her and tell her what happened, and that I love her."

"Oh, no!" Asher leaned forward. "You call her. That's not my burden."

"Okay. Stay there." I walked around to his side of the table, and before he could object, I took a quick selfie of the two of us.

"What was that for?" he asked.

"I'm texting it to Mickey informing her I'm on a date and if I'm not around tomorrow you'll know where the body is. I'll be at my office, by the way, at the storage park near the highway. Last unit, second row. Also, please return my books to the library and take care of my birds."

"Becs, this isn't funny."

"I'm not actually going to say you'll know where my body is, don't worry." I wouldn't say it. I'd imply it.

Hey Mickey, This is my friend Asher. He lives on the 4th floor of my apartment bldg. Cutie, right? Gotta do some work tonight. It's a bit of a thing, so I'll catch up later. Love, Becs.

There. That was perfect.

I ignored her text back. *Becs! Are you dating? He's hot. What do you mean, "It's a bit of a thing?" Does that mean dangerous?*

Followed by her second text. *Of course, it means dangerous. You better text me tomorrow!*

I couldn't promise, so I didn't, and because I was a shithole of a sister, I ignored my phone when it rang.

"Ash, since I'm asking you to call my sister if I don't come home, I guess it's okay if you call me Becs."

Ash gave me a half-hearted smile. "Does that mean we're friends now?"

Chapter 8

MY SO-CALLED office was a storage unit at the end of a row of self-storage units in a veritable communist block of self-storage units. It was an acre of concrete, where cheer and love and all things good went to die.

It was perfect for my profession. I drove up, parked in front, and left the car unlocked, leaving my keys inside in case someone had to move it later.

Summoning things that generally didn't want to be summoned, particularly demons, was the antithesis of cheer and love. It was disgust and hopelessness, futility and derision, and I had capitalized on it for money because it was my only talent. Bartending was a developing skill at best.

My storage space had a smart lock connected to my phone, so I swiped "unlock." This newest model also had a steel curtain roll-up door that I could open with my phone as well. Super high tech, and awesome. I'd jazzed up my space by adding some battery-operated lighting. I'd also created a divider to the space so that if you were looking at it from the outside, you'd see two halves. The right half was the client's half, the left was mine.

The client's half wouldn't be used today. I closed the door so no one could see the weirdness that would certainly transpire in the next several minutes.

My side contained a comfy, oversized chair upholstered in a horrible floral pattern from somewhere in the early '80s, a microphone and speaker for talking to the client when needed, and a desk. The desk sat against the back wall, taking up most of it because it was a huge industrial metal beast scrounged from a trash pile, which I'd dragged to my unit on one of the hottest days of the year, because I hadn't been able to pass it up. It had enough drawers for all my contracts, pens, and blood-drawing instruments. Plus the multiple boxes of tissues. There was a lot of crying in summoning.

I'd lined the top with a collection of superhero bobbleheads and my copies of the *New Testament*, the *Old Testament*, *Gods and Goddesses of Asia*,

Old Norse Beliefs, plus extra texts on the Greek, Roman, and Egyptian pantheons and a new collection on Santa Muerte.

Using a stencil I'd made for such occasions, I chalked a pentagram onto the floor. Now that I was here, I was eager to get on with it. I opened a vintage steamer trunk I kept next to my desk and extracted five deep-red candles and placed them at the points of the pentagram. I lit each one, stepped back, and took a deep breath.

Sharp pain stabbed my belly.

"I'm getting there, you bulbous snot rag."

I took a breath. "Duke Valefar, get the hell up here, you arrogant bastard."

Sparks jumped from candle to candle, and gold smoke swirled in the air, blinding me. I closed my eyes, choking on the gold motes that filled the pentagram, coughing until a giant paw patted my back.

"Rebecca Naomi Greenblatt, how good to see you again."

I lurched away, blinking to clear my sight. Valefar sat in the center of the pentagram, although I had no doubt he could leave if he wanted to. He had the body of a lion and his griffin wings, but this time he had the head of an ancient Chinese man with a long flowing beard.

"Changing it up, I see," I said, motioning to his face.

"Oh, this?" he said, tossing his head like a Miss America contestant. "It's a Thursday."

"Do you have underwear with the days of the week on it, too?"

A stabbing pain lanced my head, and I staggered under its force.

"Caution, girl. I have a claw into your spirit." He brushed the beard aside to reveal my locket around his neck.

Regaining my feet, I still mouthed off. "Yeah, about that. I want it back."

He mimicked me. "Yeah, about that. You have to earn it."

"What is it you want?" The headache he'd started settled in for an extended stay, and I sat in my chair as it pulsed in my temples. "Let's get this over with."

He stalked toward me, verifying my theory that he could leave the confines of the pentagram with ease. He sniffed. "What's going on with you, Ms. Greenblatt? You smell different. Have you been a bad girl?"

I leaned back in my chair to get away from him, but his wrinkled face and lion's neck drew closer. By the time I realized that he meant to scent my neck, I couldn't extract myself from the chair and he'd pinned me to it, his huge body hovering over me. He smelled like a mix of cat and brimstone, his body four feet wide, blocking the light in the room.

His human head leaned in and snuffled my neck, his beard brushing my shoulder and arm.

"You've been playing with death magic, Rebecca Naomi Greenblatt. Now, who's been teaching you this, hmm?" he asked as he finally, *finally*, slinked away, sinewy and graceful like the lion he mostly was. "You're holding some powerful illicit devilry inside you. If you don't get rid of it soon, it will eat you from the inside out." He whipped around, shoving his head at me again. "Like cancer," he snarled. "It will eat your cells, dissolve your organs, and melt your body, piece by piece. There will be nothing left but bones, and then I'll get your soul for a promise unfulfilled."

"You can't have my soul."

He sat in the middle of the pentagram and licked a paw with his human tongue. "I could teach you how to get rid of that nastiness, of course. It would only cost you your niece."

Stunned, I stammered out my answer. "You can't traffic in children. I know the rules."

He sighed. "True, but it needn't be now. You could turn her over when she gets older. Say, age twenty-one." He yawned. "There are always loopholes."

"No."

He licked a paw. "Your sister, then."

I shook my head. "You can't have her either. Mickey doesn't believe in you, remember? You're not part of her spiritual belief system. She doesn't believe in a literal Hell."

He laughed, and shivers ran down my spine.

"Normally, that would be true, buuuuuuttt, there's a tiny fracture in your logic." He flicked the necklace. "Her photo is in this locket with yours. So she's tied to it."

"That's not enough." My stomach flipped because it might very well be enough.

Black smoke rose from the ground, and my office shook, knocking books to the floor. "It is enough, and I've got more than that, you puny human. But now's not the time."

"What? What do you mean?"

He pointed a massive claw at my face. "It means nothing. What matters is that you're a pile of magical radiation right now, so you'd better do what I need you to do quickly."

I decided to ignore the magical radiation remark in favor of finding out what he wanted. "And what is it that you want me to do?"

"Gregory Adamos."

I blinked and looked around me, hoping an explanation would mysteriously appear out of thin air on an enchanted chalkboard. Like you'd see in the cartoons or in a comic book.

I got nothing. "Uhm? Gregory Adamos? I don't understand."

"I want Gregory's soul."

Whatever it was I was expecting, this was not it. "I can't give you Gregory Adamos's soul."

Valefar flicked his tail. "I understand you can't get his soul exactly, but you can find out what he covets, and that is effectively the same thing. Then you will summon me in his presence, and I will negotiate for that thing. It will achieve the same purpose."

"Why do you want his soul?"

He roared. A full lion's roar came out of a human mouth, but it was tinged with magical power that needled my nerves and made my eyes water. He smelled like he hadn't brushed his fangs in a millennium. "It doesn't matter why I want it! You will do this thing, or I will find a way to take your soul. And if you cannot do this in a timely manner or if the conjury inside you sizzles your body and brain, leaving you an empty husk, I will take your sister's soul in recompense. DO I MAKE MY-SELF CLEAR?"

I rocked back, punched in the chest with the force of his will, the wind knocked out of me. Finally, I managed to squeak out, "Crystal."

I kept my head down so he couldn't see the fury in my eyes. There was no way he was getting my sister.

"Excellent. I shall talk to you soon."

Poof. With one blast of gold smoke, Valefar, Sixth Duke of Hell, disappeared.

It could have gone better. He'd threatened my sister's soul, told me the death tendrils inside me were the equivalent to magical cancer, and assigned me an impossible task. But still, I was breathing so I counted it as a temporary win. I collapsed in my chair and rubbed my temples.

Suddenly, my phone rang.

"Hello?"

"Becs, it's Joey. Can you come to the bar, please?"

Please? Joey of the broken beer stein used the word "please?"

"What's wrong?"

She spoke in a higher tone than normal, strained and raspy, "There's someone here looking for you."

I sat up. "Who?"

"He says his name's Warlock, and I think he's the guy who put that death magic in you."

"His name is Warlock, or he is a warlock?"

"His name is Warlock, and right now, I'm not clarifying."

"Unoriginal bastard. I'll be right there."

I PUSHED MY CAR'S magic engine to the limit and thanked my lucky stars I didn't get caught. Joey's voice, and her use of the word "please," told me this Warlock might be hurting people, and though I had no idea what I'd do when I got there, I owed it to her to get there fast. With luck, just my presence would shake him off of her, Pinky, or anyone else in the bar.

I didn't like guns, and I couldn't bring that much cold iron in there anyway, so hand-to-hand combat was my only option if I had to fight. But when I parked, I did take a moment to remove my leather wristband and replace it with something else.

I had a special case in my car for two leather caestus I'd had hand-made for me. They wrapped around my forearms, wrists, and hands like boxing gloves, protecting them when I needed to block a punch. But the right one, my main offensive hand, also had small holes in the knuckles into which I could insert a separate leather piece with iron spikes. I did this now. Joey wouldn't appreciate even this small amount of iron, but if this Warlock guy was hurting people—and I could hurt him back—she'd deal. I pulled on a zip-up sweatshirt over my T-shirt. I always kept one in the car, and I pulled the sleeves down over my fingers, so the caestus were all but invisible. I looked like a slob, and any thinking person would wonder why I wore a sweatshirt in July, but I hoped the warlock wouldn't think that hard.

I opened the door as if I were entering the OK Corral, pushing it inward with false bravado to discover a frozen tableau of fae creatures. Their stricken faces said they were anxious. Some appeared more impatient for me to negate the threat so they could get back to drinking than actually worried, but others appeared genuinely concerned. The threat came in the form of an unusually tall, thin man with an overactive sense of Gandalf panache in his gray cloak and staff. His hood fell over his eyes so I couldn't see his face.

I could see the firm grip he had on Joey's neck and the ugly twig he pointed at her eye.

I jerked my chin at it. "Let me guess. Baby chick feather core, two-and three-quarter inches?"

"No. It's much bigger than that."

"I wasn't talking about the wand."

A few fae snorted.

He lifted Joey to her toes.

Joey gagged. "Less chatty-chat, more ass-kicking."

Ass-kicking? Maybe I could snark him to death, but if there was ass-kicking to be done, I was afraid it would be my ass getting kicked. Fun fact: the length of a person's extended arms, from fingertip to fingertip, was roughly the same as their height. Given how tall this guy was, his wingspan alone had me at a huge disadvantage. I could bait him outside, however, and find out what he wanted without endangering anyone else.

I rolled my shoulders and squared my stance, trying to look tough. "I hear you're looking for me. Why don't we go outside and talk about it?"

"Question. How did you survive the death spell?"

"You sent that?"

"Answer! How did you survive it?" He lifted Joey another half inch, and she yelped.

"I absorbed it. It's inside of me."

"Interesting." He scratched his head with his wand, which was far better than having it at Joey's neck. "An unanticipated approach. Not a wise one, long term, but an unexpected short-term solution. I had not foreseen this."

"What is it you want? Why did you send this spell after me?"

"Simple. You're in my way, and I need something you have."

"I don't even know you."

"False."

"What's false? Do we know each other? Have we met? Fine, let's get reacquainted, but outside. No need to involve these folks."

"Agreed. They are meaningless."

The Warlock threw Joey to the side and trained his wand on my face. He stalked toward me, his long legs eating up the floor. I back-pedaled out of the bar, my arms pin-wheeling to keep me upright. I gulped at the ferocity of his focus, and though I couldn't see his eyes clearly under his hood, I glimpsed two fiery red orbs staring at me, unblinking.

On the street, he grabbed my arm and pulled me to him, snarling, "Hold. Don't fight me or I'll take this block down. Don't think I can't do it."

"What is it you want from me?" I asked as he pulled me along. I didn't struggle, but I didn't cooperate, either. I made him work for it.

"Simple. I want your Kiss."

He yanked me harder and steered me several blocks toward one of the old, boarded-up subway entrances. That was when I tensed. This was what the busker meant when he said the homeless had been driven out by the power. It wasn't the power; it was A Power. This warlock had taken over UnderTown.

I remembered a lecture the police had given about personal safety. They said to avoid letting an assailant take you to the second location. Once a kidnapper got you on their territory, you'd already lost. So I knew if I went to UnderTown with the Warlock, I'd be toast.

I pulled from him as hard as I could and almost broke his grip. He drew me closer. I put my hand on his chest and shuddered at the touch of bones without muscle or fat. His sternum shifted and crackled under my touch like marbles in a bag. I winced at the sound.

"Wait. Wait. This is pointless! You can't have my Kiss. We are Kiss Born. You can't take it from me, and I can't give it to you."

He stopped and sighed, speaking as if he were talking to a particularly dimwitted child. "Incorrect. It's taken me years of study, but I can steal it from you. It involves your death, the corruption of a soul, and a couple of other things you wouldn't sanction, but it can be done. Then I get your power and your job."

"You want my job? You can have it! No Kiss required. You're a warlock. Create a circle."

"Can't. I need the Kiss. That's all Gregory Adamos and his ilk respect. Stupid sheep. They don't understand the fundamentals of magic. I can do what you do without the Kiss, but they're fixated on your mark."

"No. I'll back you. I'll tell them all you don't need the Kiss, that you're strong enough as a warlock."

He waved his hand in the air to dismiss my statement. "Immaterial. I've been casting circles since I was a child, but they don't care. However, once I steal your Kiss, it will all be simpler. Besides, the Kiss has so much more potential, and you're wasting it. I will use it properly. I have other needs for it."

"No!" This time I put my back into it.

He was so overconfident that he didn't watch his knees. Though he pulled me, I'd grounded myself pretty well, so I got a hard kick with my left foot to the side of his knee and dragged my foot down his entire tibia to stomp on his foot. He howled in shock and doubled over. Magic users rarely expected a physical attack.

I followed with a punch to his temple with my right fist, letting the caestus' iron spikes dig into the soft flesh. I rabbit punched him twice in the ribs with the same hand, flinching at the unsettling crackling sound that happened when fragile bones break. He finally dropped his hold, bending over to hold his injured ribs, and I twisted out of his reach and cracked his nose with the back of my elbow. He crumpled like a tin can. His hood fell back, revealing his face, and I stood frozen in horror. It was blackened on one side, so dark his cheek looked like charcoal briquettes. The other side was the color of dishwater. He had no eyelids, and the pupils glowed red. His nose and mouth were normal shaped but were an icy blue, as if he had frostbite. A dark, thick, blackish blood seeped from the wounds in his temple. Despite the malformities, something about him tweaked my memory, but I couldn't think why. He'd said we had known each other, but from where?

"Hey! Whatcha doing to that man?" someone yelled, running toward me, phone to their ear. People approached from all over. I had just enough time to reach into his inner cloak pocket, find his wand, and run like hell. I made it to my car and sped away, glancing over my shoulder to see that the Warlock had disappeared and the onlookers stood mystified, staring at an empty space. I did a double-take, because warlock or no, his injuries should have kept him down.

It wasn't until I was out of eyesight that I smelled a faint charring. I'd dropped the wand on my passenger seat, and, luckily, I had real leather seating because the wand was aflame. A fabric covering would be on fire.

I sped up and drove to the park, pulling over in a shady spot. Moving fast, I used a snow shovel from my trunk to scoop the burning wand onto the road, thinking it would burn out. It burned bright for several minutes and then smoldered for another ten until it was particles the size of fish food.

"A self-destruct setting. Handy," I joked, because it was either that or scream. I put my head on the side of my car and took five deep shuddering breaths. Then, reminding myself that sitting still was death, moving was survival, I removed my caestus, cleaned them, stored them properly, and checked my passenger seat for damage, which was minimal.

"You should still clean up what's left."

"Ah!" I jumped, whirling around. "Pinky! Don't sneak up on people like that. Especially me."

Pinky's shoulders slumped. "I was in the bar and followed you to make sure you were alright."

I held my hand to my heart which was beating a mile a minute. "That's thoughtful, but you have to let me know when you are here. You scared me."

"I *was* letting you know—by speaking. That's how I let you know."

"Right, but you have to give me some warning."

"What kind of warning?"

"I don't know. Whistle or something."

He nodded. "Okay, next time I shall whistle first."

"Great. Now, what about the wand flakes?"

"It would be best to collect what's left. Even that could have magical properties. I don't think you should leave it for just anyone to find."

"Can't I scatter it?"

He shrugged. "Dump it in running water, maybe?"

"Okay, I'll take it home and flush it." I scraped up as much as possible with an old popsicle stick and a tissue and shoved it into my cup holder.

The dark park twinkled with fireflies, and its peacefulness settled me after the craziness of the last several hours, driving the adrenaline out of my body. Fatigue washed over me, and I slumped in the driver's seat. Pinky climbed into the passenger side.

"Becs?"

"Yes?"

"Your note made me sad and happy at the same time. It was confusing. You told me you are my friend. That made me happy."

"I am your friend, Pinky." I reclined my seat.

"But you also made it sound like it could be the last time I ever saw you, and that made me sad."

"I summoned a demon, Pinky. I didn't know what would happen, but it turned out okay. I'm still here."

"You have death magic inside you and a warlock after you, so celebrating is premature."

I managed a tiny laugh. "That is an honest assessment."

"Becs, I want to go home."

"Back to the fae lands?"

"Yes."

"Why don't you go then?"

He didn't answer, so I rotated my head to the right to study him. "Pinky, what is it?"

"It's embarrassing."

"You can tell me."

He gathered his wings around him in a hug. It reminded me of a child wrapping himself in a blanket.

"I've forgotten how to go small."

"You're stuck in this large size?"

He nodded, tears in the corners of his eyes.

"Can't you ask another fairy?"

He shook his head hard. "They won't tell me."

"They won't tell you? They know but won't help you?"

He pulled his wings closer to him and rocked back and forth. "They make fun of me. This is something you learn when you are very young. They think I'm stupid."

I was going to rip off their wings.

"You are one of the smartest people I know. I've never met another fairy in the bar, only elves and such. Can any of them help you?"

He shook his head again, and a tear landed on the passenger window. I watched it drip down the surface.

"Can you remember anything?"

"My mother gave me a rhyme to help me remember where the door to home is, but I'm so confused. Will you help me? I can ask you because you said you are my friend." The look he gave me melted my heart. I needed another burden like a hole in the head, but there was no way I could refuse.

"Yes, Pinky, I'll help you. What was the rhyme?"

He sat up straighter and recited.

"Bees, so far they've flown;
No matter how far they roam;
Forever, will find their home."

I made him repeat it.

"I don't know this poem," I told him. "Maybe I can research it."

But not now.

"Pinky, do you need me to drive you someplace? I've got to get to my apartment."

"I'm fine, Becs. I think you are too tired to drive though."

"I'll rest here a moment." My head nodded forward. I'd never been this tired before.

"If the park officials see you, they will give you a ticket. This is not beneficial for you as I understand you've recently acquired several tickets from the authorities already."

I closed my eyes. "Hopefully, they won't see me."

"I can help with that," said Pinky.

"Huh?" I needed to nap; the tide was drawing me under.

My fairy friend opened the door and stepped out. He reached under his wing and drew out a handful of fine powder and sprinkled it on the hood of my car. "Fairy dust, Becs. It will make you invisible and safe for a few hours."

Chapter 9

MAGIC FAIRY DUST hid me until I could make it home safely under my own power. I clambered up my fire escape and dropped into bed until morning, when I woke to the sound of someone knocking on my door. Banging, really. Loud. Irrationally loud banging.

"Wake up, sunshine! It's after ten in the morning, and I know you're in there because your car is in the lot."

"Kenneth, go away." I couldn't deal with him at the moment.

He couldn't hear me from the bedroom.

"I've got orange juice, coffee, and your favorite doughnuts."

I peeked my head out, the sing-song of his voice and promise of fried circular dough covered in sugar weaving a spell.

"I'm eating one . . . ," Kenneth teased.

I hauled my ass out of bed and opened the door a crack. "You have Boston crème doughnuts?" When was the last time I'd eaten? Maybe that explained the nausea I felt this morning. My stomach ached, and acid spurted up my esophagus.

He grinned and pointed to his shirt. "I got your gift and I love it. And yes . . ." He waved a white, greasy bag in front of the door. "Inhale."

I smelled the sugar through the one-inch opening. "You don't play fair," I said with my usual enthusiasm, but my tummy flipped at the scent, and I struggled not to wrinkle my nose in disgust.

I let him in and pointed to the couch. "Sit. Because I actually like you, I'm going to brush my teeth."

I not only took care of my teeth, but I also washed up and put on antiperspirant and fresh clothes. I popped an antacid and two acetaminophens. By the time I'd returned, he'd moved my books, lined the coffee table with kitchen towels, found two plates, and served us each a doughnut, coffee, and juice. He was such a catch for some woman. Not me, but someone.

"How did you get away from the kitchen to come up here and wine and dine me with snacks?"

He dove into his doughnut, a jelly-filled sugar-coated one. He got sugar on his nose and looked adorable.

He squirmed in his seat and jutted out his chin a millimeter, slightly defensive, as if he were expecting his mother to come searching for him any moment. "I took a break. Nothing wrong with that."

"No, nothing." For the first time in my life, I couldn't eat a doughnut. My stomach continued to churn, and I was seconds away from throwing up. I flashed back to the incident with the Warlock and massaged the back of my neck, trying to will the image away.

"Tight muscles?" Kenneth asked.

"Must have slept wrong. It's nothing. How's the restaurant?"

"Oh, it's fine. Introducing a new dish. You won't eat it because it's made with lamb, but we made a deal with the Muslim restaurant in the strip mall to only use *halal* meat and set aside special pots for them. We're making a few special dishes for them, as well. It's helping us pick up business, and we're sending some of our customers there to try new things, too. Win-win."

"That's outstanding. I love it." I cleared my throat and swallowed hard.

"I think everyone got bored with the same old flavors."

I held a hand to my mouth to cover a burp. "Food is always a great way to break boundaries. Once you share a meal with someone, it's easier to see similarities rather than differences."

"Agreed. What's wrong? Why aren't you eating?"

I fled to the bathroom, closed the door with my foot, and vomited gray pellets.

"Becs, you're sick?"

"Kenneth, I'm sorry." I raised my voice so he could hear me. "I ate something yesterday that isn't sitting well. It was so nice of you to stop by. Can we do this another time?"

"Sure. I'm sorry that you aren't feeling well. My mom will want to drop off soup, you know."

"Oh, please tell her not to do that." I panted, my hands on my knees. "I'll be fine."

I dry-heaved, and cold mucus radiating with death energy dripped from my mouth and nose into the toilet.

"Should I stay and help you? Let me get you some water."

Another round of heaving. But this time, the death energy shot out of me in pointed, thorny arrows, tearing my esophagus, throat, and tongue, before flying at the door, almost going through the wood. I gagged up a wad of blood and spit it into the toilet.

"Kenneth, no! Please go home."

"Are you certain? It sounds like you need a hospital. I'm not afraid of ickiness you know. I work in a kitchen, after all. We butcher our own chickens." His footsteps got closer. The arrows quivered and wiggled, worming their way through the wood. I grabbed them with both hands, the thorns pricking my palms deep enough to draw blood. The thorns drank the blood, drawing it in, but continued writhing as if they were going to burst through the door and attack Kenneth. They sucked my blood from my hands, so much so that I barely maintained consciousness. I was fading fast.

I managed to rasp, "Kenneth, please, you need to go."

I choked up a second set of arrows, smaller, but no less deadly than the first. They dropped to the peach ceramic tile and squirmed into the tiny space between the door and the floor. I stopped them with my legs, letting them dig into my calves.

"My dad is a doctor, and my mom has lots of things for nausea. You know ginger is good as well as turmeric, fennel, and licorice."

"Kenneth, please leave!" I shouted as loud as I could, but it was barely a whisper. He heard me though, which meant he was entirely too close to the danger.

He sucked in a breath. "Uh. Okay." Another breath. "I'll see myself out."

Once I heard the door close, I held fast to the death magic thorny arrows and crawled to the peach porcelain 1950s bathtub with them stuck to me like barnacles. I remembered what Pinky said about running water negating the energy of the wand, so I took a chance. Turning on the water with my blood-soaked wrists, I tumbled into the tub, holding my hands under the faucet and letting my legs soak. The arrows separated from my skin and dropped with heavy plunks, sinking like dead weights on the bottom of the tub as my blood turned the water red.

"Nice going, Becs." I mocked myself as I coughed up more death energy. This time it came out as a gas and spiraled to the ceiling. "Be a summoner, they said. It'll be so much fun, they said. No one said anything about warlocks hunting you or giving you magical cancer, or demons threatening your sister. Must have been . . ." I puked another chunk of death magic. ". . . in the fine print." Now I had the magical flu?

Some distant part of me recognized that I needed to stop the bleeding. I reached over the edge of the tub for the bathmat and wrapped my left hand in it, then snagged my towel from the bar and used my teeth to wrap my right hand. I made it out of the tub and turned off the water before flushing the toilet, expecting the pellets to go down.

Surprise, surprise. They didn't.

My phone rang but I ignored it, my head pounding with a combination of fear, blood loss, and death sickness. I found my first aid kit and dabbed at my wounds with hydrogen peroxide. The phone kept ringing and ringing.

I ignored it.

It rang again.

I continued to ignore it, wrapping bandages until I had the wounds covered.

The phone started up again.

"Argh!" I limped into my bedroom and stabbed at the answer button, putting it on speaker. "What?"

"That's how you answer your phone?"

"Mickey?"

"Yes, it's me. Who else? You send me this creepy message yesterday, and then you answer the phone with, 'What?' Rude. What's wrong with you?"

"I'm sorry. I had a hard night. Feeling sick this morning."

"Drink too much?"

"No, really, I'm sick." Despite everything, hearing my sister over speakerphone calmed me, and my fingers worked better. I cleaned the rest of my wounds and patted on an antibiotic ointment.

Jewish mothers can't stand the word "sick." "You want I bring some soup?" she said. "Matzah balls or *lokshen?*" *Lokshen* was Yiddish for noodles, and while I loved matzah balls, good old chicken noodle soup was my favorite.

"I might be contagious. I'll take you up on that soup in a week or two."

"Promise?"

"Promise." If I wasn't dead.

A pause. "Who's this man you're dating?"

"Sorta dating. One date. His name is Asher."

"Oooooh. Asher is a Biblical name. I like. Tell me more."

I'd managed to wrap my wounds in gauze and tape, so I wobbled to the kitchen, holding the phone gingerly between my thumb and index finger. I placed it on the counter and did a mental jig that Kenneth had left the orange juice and coffee.

I knew she'd know, so I asked. "Remind me where is Asher in the *Tanach*?"

"Genesis, second son of Jacob and Zilpah."

"Did you look it up or did you know it off the top of your head?"

"I attend a women's Bible Study every Saturday."

I recalled my Sunday school and Hebrew school lessons. "Right. Asher means 'happy.'"

"*Tov Ma'od.* Very good. Rabbi Schwartz would pat you on the head right now."

"Wasn't Rabbi Schwartz the rabbi who gave out candy whenever you got an answer, right?"

"You remember!"

"I remember the stale candy."

"Hush. Don't be such a complainer. Tell me about this guy."

"He lives upstairs. Asher, I mean. Not Rabbi Schwartz. I don't know him well, but he works at a nice restaurant, and he invited me to dinner."

"Wait." I heard her run water and waited until the faucet stopped. "He invited you to the restaurant where he works?"

"Hmm."

"What?"

"It's just, I don't know. Is that a real date?"

"Don't be so judgy."

"Mikayla!" Jonah called her in the background.

"Oops, gotta go. Jonah needs something."

"Is that your sister on the phone?" Jonah asked. "Let me talk to her. I haven't spoken to her in a long time." He gave her a little kiss that I could hear on the phone. "Ruthie's little friend's mom is outside talking about a playdate. Do we do playdates? Can you chat with her?"

Mikayla laughed. "Sure, honey. Talk to you later, Becs. Love you."

"Love you, too." But she'd left already.

"Rebecca."

"Jonah."

"Hope this little chat doesn't mean you're considering visiting."

"It's nice to talk with you, too."

"Becs, how many times do we have to do this? Your world is dangerous, and I don't want it anywhere near my family."

"They're my family, too."

Jonah's voice was low, but I could hear the anger. "Mikayla and Ruthie are my life, and while I know you care about them, your presence here is unwelcome. If anything ever happens to either one of them, I will make it my business to hunt you to the ends of the earth."

Despite the pain and blood loss, I found enough energy to work up a headful of righteous indignation, and it burned hot. "Jonah, if I ever cause them harm, you won't have to hunt me because I'll either already be dead or I'll show up at your door with a loaded gun so you can shoot me. How's that?"

"It's just that—"

"No. You listen to me. You're a good husband and father, and you're right to worry. The crap I deal with is perilous, and it's the reason I've stayed away. But don't tell me I *care* for my sister and niece. I *love* them just as much as you do."

He exhaled, and I could practically hear him counting to ten. "I know you do."

"Good. Now that we've gotten that squared away . . ."

Without warning, tendrils of death magic swirled down the hallway to the kitchen, making a beeline for me. Before I could dodge them, they flew up my nose, into my ears, and down my throat.

"Unnnngggh . . ."

"Becs? What's wrong? Are you there?"

I collapsed to the floor as the death magic stuffed itself back inside. I gasped for air and managed to say, "Be careful. Keep them close."

I disconnected and dropped the phone, struggling down the hall to the bathroom. The arrows and pellets of solidified death magic were sublimating, turning back into their original gaseous form, joining with the cloudy tendrils on the ceiling. And they were coming for me. The cloud storm of evil knocked me down onto my back, and before I knew it, the entire dose had stuffed itself back inside my body.

I lay in the detritus of my horror of a morning, bloody gauze and towels, wet floor and a broken door, my head on the cool tile, shivering with fever as the joint aches settled in, as if I had the worst flu of my life. My eyes swelled shut as I convulsed, wheezing for air. My legs contracted up to my stomach as I cramped up tight and then shot out straight. I cracked my knees on the old-fashioned peach sink pedestal, but the pain barely registered, and I cried out as every nerve ending burned.

I fell into a red haze of agony. Kind voices at the far edge of my hearing murmured comforting words, but I didn't understand what they said. My body fell into cold water, and I shouted at the assault but leaned into the warmth of being wrapped in something soft afterwards.

"That should break her fever," a male voice said.

"I'll watch her," said someone else. Another man, someone familiar.

A woman's voice interjected. "Make her drink the tea when she wakes. I hung the wormwood at the front and back doors."

A hand brushed my forehead. "I'm sorry I told them, Becs, but I heard you scream."

"It was the right thing to do, Kenneth," said the voice holding me. I let myself drift the rest of the way, feeling safe for the first time in a long time, which was reckless and a great way to get dead. But I was too far gone to remind myself.

Chapter 10

I WOKE CUDDLED against a something firm but soft, on what felt like my couch. Heavenly scents urged me back to relax and made me want to rub my face in the soft blanket twisted in my hands. I yawned, and the burning pain in my throat woke me up with a start.

"Ow!" What should have been a scream came out as a croak, and I shot up only to collapse as a dizzy spell brought me down.

"Shh. I've got you. You've been sick."

"Ash?"

"It's me. Let me help you sit up, and I'll get you some tea. Mrs. Long insists."

The heat rose in my cheeks as I realized that I'd been sleeping against his chest, my body stretched out next to his as he'd reclined on my couch in what had to be the most uncomfortable position. As if to prove me right, he stood and stretched his back, showing a supremely sexy inch of tummy as his white linen short-sleeved button-down shirt rode up, and his back popped a quick one-two-three times. I winced.

"I don't remember much but thank you for taking care of me." It came out as a whisper because my voice was so hoarse.

"You're welcome." He smiled. "I'm getting you that tea."

I didn't have the strength to argue or to ask another question. I leaned back and closed my eyes. I must have dozed because I woke again when he petted my cheek and placed a steaming mug into my hands.

"Here you go. Mrs. Long promises this tea will make you feel better."

"It smells terrible."

"It has herbs in it. Anise, ginger, turmeric. Also, something else I don't recognize, but I'm a little scared of her, so I didn't inquire." He pushed my hair out of my eyes and helped me get the mug to my lips.

"It's hot."

"Stop pouting."

"I hurt everywhere."

"Drink."

I took a sip, and it wasn't bad. "What happened?"

"Kenneth didn't like how he left you and came back to check on you. He heard you scream, so he got his parents. They opened your door. They're your landlords, so they have a key. In any case, they found you on the bathroom floor running a fever. It looked as if you had cut yourself badly, tried to do your own bandages, and fallen. Your phone was there, so we assumed you were attempting to call for help."

"Wait. When did you come in?"

"Stop talking. I'll explain the entire story. I was passing by on my way home from grocery shopping." He pointed to some sacks on the floor with food staples in them—rice, cereal, and what looked like cookies. "My milk, veggies, and eggs are in your fridge." He gave me some stern side-eye. "Keep drinking."

I drank more tea. He nodded in approval.

"You were burning up, so Mrs. Long took charge. For a woman no taller than four foot nine inches, she's terrifying. She sent me and Kenneth out the door and then stripped you down. Mr. Long helped."

"Really?" I grimaced.

"Stop it. I told you not to talk and don't be embarrassed. Did you know he was a doctor in China and she's a trained herbalist? They dumped you in lukewarm water and then immediately pulled you out, redressed you, and bundled you in blankets. It worked. Your fever broke, and then I stayed with you to make sure you'd be okay."

I finished my tea, giving myself space to figure out what to say. I settled on, "Thank you."

"You're welcome. I'm texting Kenneth to let them know you're awake." He kissed the top of my head, and my stupid body didn't know that it had been through a trauma because a sexual thrill trilled down my spine to all the right places. "Down, girl," I murmured.

He turned around. "What did you say?"

"Can I have more tea?"

"Sure," he said, his brown eyes crinkling at the corners. "I'll make you some toast, too. Or oatmeal. Would you like oatmeal?" His black pants rode low on his hips, and I followed them as he walked to my kitchen. Maybe it was being so close to death, but I was suddenly horny as hell. Even the sight of his bare feet was turning me on.

Oh, crap on a cracker. I checked my watch. It was five p.m. I'd lost my whole day. I held a hand over my mouth and breathed into it. *Ick.* That killed any romantic thoughts I had. My breath stank as if I'd been eating nacho cheese and eggs with whiskey all at the same time. And yes, that happened once, so I knew how bad that stench could be. Utterly rank. I checked my pits, and they were equally awful.

I pushed myself to my feet and waited until I knew the room wouldn't shift under them and then shuffled to the bathroom while Ash talked to me from the kitchen.

"Do you know how you got so sick, Becs? Were you around someone who was ill? Was this related to the demon summoning, or have you had so much stress recently that your body is telling you that you need to slow down? And we didn't talk about it, but you are cut up bad. How did that happen?"

I didn't answer.

"Hey, where'd you go?"

I'd made it to the sink, closed the door, and shakily lined up my toothbrush with the squeeze tube of peppermint paste. With a heroic effort, I'd gotten the paste on the brush and had it in my mouth. I sat on the toilet and examined my condition in privacy, deciding that I'd never been more screwed in my entire life. I didn't even know precisely why the death magic flew out of me only to sink back in. Maybe it was just to mess with me, hurt me, and let me know who was boss.

"Becs? You okay? Not on the floor again, are you?" His tone was light, but there was an edge too.

"Need a minute of privacy, Ash, that's all. Feeling better." Total lie. I felt like rewarmed canned soup left out on the table too long. Weak, odious, and distasteful. I washed up and took stock of my life.

I had to discover Gregory Adamos's deepest desire and inform Valefar. I was sick with a magical poison that I needed to get rid of, and the jerk who gave it to me was probably gunning for me extra hard now that I'd beaten him up in front of onlookers and destroyed his woo-woo stick. Well, technically, he'd destroyed the wand, but only because I'd stolen it. Pinky needed to go home, and he'd forgotten how to become small, and he couldn't pass into Faerie when he was so big.

Valefar's demands pressed on me the most, since Mickey was in danger if I didn't solve that problem first. There was no way I could walk up to Gregory and ask him to tell me his most heartfelt desire. On the other hand, Gregory must want something pretty badly, since he'd sent that troll in a suit to get me to summon for him. Maybe the troll could give me some insight?

Then it hit me. One person would know, but it remained to be seen if he'd be in any shape to help or would be willing to do so. After all, the last time I'd seen him, he lay whimpering on the cement of my office, bleeding from both eyes, naked, with whip marks across his back and buttocks and blisters on the soles of his feet. He'd torn his hair out in handfuls, so he was bald in spots, and he'd chewed his nails to the quick. I'd heard that he'd improved physically but still slept with a nightlight, sucked his thumb, and didn't venture past Gregory's front door.

Nick Adamos, Gregory's younger brother, had taken a bad trip to the underworld, almost entirely of his making, but not completely. A sliver of that was my fault, and though I'd apologized and gone to the mat with Valefar to get him back, I'd bet all that I owned that I wasn't Nick's favorite person. In fact, I was probably the last human on the surface of the planet he'd want to see, but desperate times called for desperate measures.

I slipped out of the bathroom and into my room where I changed into jeans and an old tie-dyed T-shirt.

"What are you doing?" asked Ash.

I froze and checked the door. Closed.

"Getting dressed in a fresh outfit. Be out in a minute."

"I can practically hear your brain working. Come out and tell me what's really going on. Let me help."

I opened the door, and there he was, filling the doorframe. I couldn't pass by him if I wanted to, so I lifted my chin, placed a palm on his chest, and pushed, but he didn't budge . . . or even sway. I remained centimeters from his body, enough that I could feel his heat seeping into me, warming me, and whispered, "Are you going to move?"

To my surprise he whispered, "Yes, but first . . ." I met his eyes, confused. He held my gaze as he placed his right index finger on my temple and slowly traced my face and jaw. Then he cupped my neck, dipped his head toward mine, and kissed me. A gentle press of his lips, no more than a second. Maybe two seconds? But in it was a lifetime of sensuality that I wanted to clasp and hold.

"That . . ." I said, swaying into him, but he'd stepped away, hand to his lips.

"Was a mistake."

"Was amazing."

"It shouldn't have happened. I'm sorry." He turned from me.

"What for? Why are you so despondent, Asher? That was nice." I reached for his sleeve.

He kept his back turned to me. "Please, forget it."

"You dropped the best kiss of my life on me, and now you're telling me to forget it?"

"Drink your tea." He walked down the hall, his back stiff.

I stomped into the kitchen. "You're a bastard and a tease."

He shook his head. "I didn't mean to be, but I can't be what you want me to be. What I'd want to be."

"A date? A boyfriend?"

His eyes held a well of emotion I didn't understand. "A lover, a partner." He handed me a fresh mug.

"That kiss says otherwise, but I wasn't asking for either." The tea energized me, going down easier this time.

"It's complicated."

"Everything about my life is complicated."

He rubbed his eyes. "Speaking of which, eat this oatmeal and tell me what's really going on."

I wanted to press him about the kiss, but my sister's face flashed before my eyes and reminded me of what was most important. I'd already told him about Valefar, so adding the new details wasn't hard. I stirred the apple cinnamon oatmeal he'd made me while he processed the new information. He noticed me playing with my food.

"Sorry," I said, remorseful. "It's cold now."

"If you'd eaten it when I made it, it would be warm and delightful."

"I'll zap it. Tell me what you think about Valefar."

"Given what you've told me, the Valefar situation has to be your primary concern. Pinky's is last, unfortunately. This warlock is an unexpected, serious danger. You've never heard of someone stealing a Kiss?"

"Never. I have no reason to believe it can be done, but I totally believe he can make me dead."

"I agree. I'm hoping your recent escape, along with the destruction of his wand, makes him hesitate to attack you again." He nodded at my tea mug. "Mrs. Long says the tea will keep the death magic at bay for a while. She suspected something, she told me, which is why we didn't take you to the hospital."

I frowned. "How did she know?" I turned to place the oatmeal in the microwave.

Ash shrugged. "You know, at this point I'm not asking any questions. She also hung wormwood at your front and back doors, to keep evil spirits away. And I bet there's a Devil Chaser Mask as well. She mentioned bringing one. She said that their scary faces frighten evil spirits from the home."

"How can such things work against death magic?" I brought the reheated glop to the table.

"I think that everything must work on faith. She believes; therefore, it works. Given what you've told me, you know better than anyone how faith and magic intertwine. The herbs are truly medicinal, though. Even I know that. Speaking of faith and magic, where's your cuff?"

I smacked my hand to my head. "In my car."

"Since you believe in it, you should wear that all time. What are the symbols?"

"A Chamsa, an Eye of Horus, Star of David, a Pentacle enclosed in a circle, and a Solar Cross."

"Those sound powerful."

"Becs? Asher? Are you in there?"

"Mrs. Long?" I crossed the floor to open my door. My landlords waited at my threshold. Mrs. Long wore a faded blue housecoat and slippers, and Mr. Long had on his usual tan khakis, white undershirt, and wire-rimmed glasses. Her bun held her gray-streaked hair in tight to her head, and she squinted at me through bright-pink half-moon reading glasses. A bright-red, green, and black Devil Chaser Mask hung to the left of my door. They are rare, and this one must have been worth a small fortune. I knew enough about the Longs not to make a big deal of it, but I wanted to acknowledge their generosity.

"Please, come in. Thank you for taking care of me and for my apartment's protection."

"It is our home, too." Mrs. Long must have weighed eighty pounds soaking wet, but her personality more than made up for it. Mr. Long wasn't much bigger, but he exuded a quiet, calm strength. No matter how busy the restaurant got, he smiled through it all. Now, I wanted to know more about him.

"Mr. Long, should I address you as Dr. Long?"

He smiled with soft eyes. "That was a long time ago."

"Why don't you practice here in the United States?"

"Too many hurdles to get my medical license here, and I needed to support my family. Besides, I like stir fry." He winked and placed a hand on my forehead. "Stick out your tongue," he ordered, and I complied.

"Hmm," he said. "Look up." He pulled at my eyelids to see the whites of my eyes. "Sit. Have you been drinking my wife's tea?"

"Yes." Ash and I spoke at the same time. Mrs. Long nodded with a stern set to her lips.

Dr. Long held my wrist and checked my pulse, frowned, and did it again. He sighed. "Becs, Western medicine cannot solve what is wrong with you. Even Chinese medicine can only do so much."

"I know. I have bad magic in me."

"Who did this to you?"

"A warlock, who, believe it or not, calls himself The Warlock. So conceited."

Mrs. Long sat next to me. "If you get a chance to stop this man, do not hesitate. He is evil."

"I know. He's high on my list, but I have other things I have to attend to first. And I'm running out of time."

Asher grunted, crossing his arms across his chest. What did it say about me that with all that was going on, I sat staring at his biceps? I thought about it for a millisecond and decided it said that it meant I was entirely normal.

Mrs. Long pointed at Ash. "You will help her, yes? She's in no shape to do whatever it is alone."

"Yes, ma'am," he said.

"Uh, no." I stood, fluffed the pillows on my couch, and folded an afghan. "I'm not sure that's a good idea," I said.

"Good, it is settled." She stood, smacking her hands together, as if we'd agreed on something. Mr. Long followed her lead.

"Before we leave, I have something for you." Mrs. Long reached into her housecoat pocket and extracted a red string. "Hold out your arm." She tied the string around my wrist and pulled her hands away, revealing a tiny gold dragon on it dangling from the end. "For good luck and protection. Don't take it off."

"I am honored. Thank you again."

She sniffed. "How you got into this mess, I do not know, but you are unbalanced. Keep drinking the tea. It will give you some time, but you will need to find a way to dispel that which is inside you. It is wreaking havoc with your yin energy. No one can survive this way." She pursed her lips and shot Ash a look. "I'm counting on you."

Ash raised his eyebrows. "I'll do what I can."

"I'm standing right here, people," I said.

Mrs. Long spoke right past me. "She needs her cuff, too."

"Already on it," Ash replied.

"The tea is good hot or cold, so make a thermos to take with you."

"Good idea. I have a big thermos in my apartment that we can use," Ash said.

"Really! Don't you know I can hear you?" I waved my hands in the air.

Mrs. Long chastised me like a small child. "You obviously need supervision if you allowed yourself to get into this fix to begin with. And I hear you don't have a job anymore either?"

"Geez, news travels fast."

"It is to our benefit if you don't die since you owe us rent. Figure this out and get back to work, Becs. Payment is due as normal."

"I left cash for this month!"

"But there is always next month."

She walked out the door, followed by Mr. Long, who waved on his way out.

"Tough cookie," remarked Asher.

"No kidding."

Ash locked the door and rubbed his hands together. "Let's go over the plan, Becs. We've got a demon to beat at Hell-opoly, and I want to be the race car. You can be the boot."

"I think it's Demonopoly, and I'm the Scottie dog."

"Well, where do we start?"

I sighed and sank down in my chair. "There's only one person I can think of who can tell us what Gregory Adamos's greatest wish is—besides Gregory, of course. But I don't think he's going to want to talk to me."

Ash sat back on the couch and crossed one leg over the other, tapping his knee with his index finger, thinking. After a minute, he said, "Maybe he'll talk to me."

Chapter 11

"TELL ME WHAT happened to Nick," said Ash, as we drove to Gregory's house where Nick reportedly lived. Ash drove in his second-hand but nicely maintained blue Toyota Corolla hatchback. I still wore my jeans but had changed into a nicer blouse, red with a dolman three-quarter length sleeve. I'd managed a little makeup to hide the dark circles under my eyes, and small gold earrings. Ash had also changed and now wore dark-black jeans and a short-sleeved, pink button-down shirt with an untuckable hem and a slight pattern to the weave. He was positively edible, but after the discussion about the yummy kiss, I kept that thought to myself. We'd come back to it. Still, that didn't keep me from studying his muscular forearms and sexy wrists and hands on the steering wheel.

I considered his question while I chewed a bite of my veggie spring roll, hoping it would stay down, and pondered how to explain the events of that night. I looked out the window, shame creeping into my mind, thickening my tongue.

"Becs?"

"Nick demanded that I summon Valefar, and I warned him not to, but he had some heavies with him with guns, and I'd been drinking and wasn't at my best. It was a recipe for disaster."

"Why had you been drinking so much?"

"I'd summoned another demon earlier that evening, and it hadn't gone well. Or, rather, it had gone exactly as expected. The client got what he wanted, but the cagey demon knew more than I did and basically tricked this guy out of the last year of his life. It's a long story."

"The client made a bad deal?"

I ate another bite and placed the remainder in the bag, my hunger diminished by the memory. "A terrible deal, but not against the rules. I drank because I was ticked off that I hadn't seen it coming."

"So Nick came along . . . ?"

"Nick came along right after, no appointment, and I was tipsy—okay, drunk—and I was mad at the world. I warned him not to make a deal with Valefar, but he was insistent, and, as I said, he had some bodyguards with him who were packing, so the pressure was on. We summoned Valefar, and Nick got sucked into Hell, literally."

Ash scratched his head. "I don't understand how this is your fault."

I sucked in a big breath. "Because I was so drunk that I didn't get Nick to sign the contract properly, in blood, before we began. That's the first thing. But most importantly, I wasn't paying proper attention and didn't jump in as soon as the deal started to go south. If I'd been sharper, on my game, I could have stopped Valefar from taking Nick alive."

"You don't know that."

"I do know that!" I shouted inside the car, and the sound bounced around, echoing in the small space. "It was all my fault. When Gregory came after me, he was right to do so. The improperly signed contract between Valefar and Nick voided the agreement. I didn't do my best for Nick, and I had to make up for it."

"You traded your necklace for Nick." Ash's voice was low and flat.

"Yeah."

"And, in doing so, you traded a piece of your soul."

"Well, sorta." I toggled my hand back and forth to show it wasn't quite that straightforward. "That's not entirely accurate. I'm not walking around with a chunk of soul missing. I gave him access to it, to my spirit, and a way to reach me, to claim a favor I owe him. It's been a couple of months, and I've been waiting for him to call in his chit, wondering what it would be, and now that I know, I have to deliver."

"And he wants Nick's older brother, Gregory. Did he say why?"

I leaned back in the seat. "He wouldn't tell me when I asked. He's a dick that way."

"Aren't all demons dicks?"

"Believe it or not, some more than others." I paused, thinking, then spoke quietly, trying to get my words right. "I think some of them remember what it was like to be an angel, before they fell."

Asher shot me a look. "You think they still recall their time in Heaven?"

"Eyes on the road, and turn left here." I sucked in a breath. "I think they all remember and miss it. I think it is the whole reason they misbehave in the first place. They suffer, so they think everyone should suffer."

"That can't be," Asher said, shaking his head. He'd gone pale and wiped the back of his neck. "That's just wrong."

"Why? Of course it can be true. You don't know them like I do." I sat up and pointed. "See this turnoff on the left? We're getting closer to Lake Erie. That's where we want to go. I've heard about this property. It should be amazing. We didn't call first, but I'm counting on Gregory letting us in."

"He did send that troll after you. We may get lucky."

The turnoff took us down a private drive which twisted and turned for a country mile. Dense woods lined the road so I couldn't see the lake, but when I rolled down the window, I could smell the water as we got close. The house appeared after a final tight curve, and it was as magnificent as its reputation. A giant brick colonial mansion that backed up to the shoreline, the property featured meticulously maintained front grounds with the brightest green lawn I'd ever seen and beautiful trees all around. A stunning maple and manicured bushes and flowers lined the front entrance, and the driveway led to a three-car garage. I knew from its description in *Exceptional Homes of Ohio* that the mansion featured its own dock, a concrete patio, and an outdoor pool in the back.

"This is gorgeous," Asher said. "Where does he get this money?"

"His legal business is real estate, but Valefar and Nick both indicated he's a Greek organized crime magnate. The business came over with his great-great-something grandfather, who established it with an iron fist here, and, as the older brother, he inherited the position. It's what motivated Nick to seek Valefar in the first place. He wanted power that he didn't have as the younger brother."

"It's still hard to believe." Ash's voice faltered, reflecting his distress. "He sought out a *demon* for power."

"Power, money, and sex, Ash. What else makes the world go 'round?" I couldn't believe he still had trouble wrapping his head around this. "In the end, that's what everyone wants."

"I don't." He stopped the car in the driveway.

"I suspect you are different from most people."

I'd expected security, but no one stopped us from driving up to the house. So there was nothing to do but approach directly and knock on the front door. My knuckles were an inch from the wood when the door opened on its own.

"Ms. Greenblatt and her upstairs neighbor, Asher Michaels, welcome." It was the pissant troll from the bar, still wearing his ill-fitting suit. He'd faded to a paler shade of puce, which told me he hadn't returned to his home lately. "Mr. Adamos was not expecting you, but Ms. Greenblatt, you are on the list."

"You don't look so well," I told him. "Don't you need to return to your family's land every so often? Or at least soak in home soil?"

He smiled a wide, uncomfortable smile. "I'll return when Mr. Adamos says he doesn't need me."

"Or when he allows you to?"

"They are one and the same."

"As you say. You had cameras watching our car and identified us before we made it to the house?"

"If we hadn't identified you, you wouldn't have made it to the house."

We stepped through the double doors into an enormous foyer with light-cream-and-white marble floors, a lit crystal chandelier, and cherry-wood molding handcrafted to highlight the beautifully sculpted archway ahead of us and the grand staircase to our left. Natural light filled the room from glass within the doors and above the balcony. The entire space was undeniably stunning. A faint scent of orange filled the air.

"You mentioned a list?" I asked. "What list?"

The troll hacked a loose cough into a handkerchief. "Pardon me. The list of guests who are welcome at any time. Mr. Michaels is not on it but is recognizable to us, and since he is with you, it is allowable."

"You've gotten kinda formal lately." The troll who'd walked into Joey's had been casual, free-wheeling, almost "New Yawk" in his speech. This guy was practically English butler material.

"It is Mr. Adamos's preference," he said with a wheeze.

This troll would be dead inside two weeks. Mentally, I shrugged it off. Not my problem. I couldn't help it if people, or trolls, made bad deals.

"Is Gregory home?"

"Not at the moment, but I will let him know you are here."

"May we speak to Nick?"

He whirled his sickly face around. "You wanna speak with Nicky?"

Ah. There was the troll I knew. "Yes."

"Nicky's not well, Ms. Greenblatt. Because of you."

"I'd still like to try. I know he blames me for what happened, and he has a right to, at least partly. But I could use his help. Hey, what's your name, anyway?"

"Perrick."

"Perrick, I've gotta talk to Nick. Valefar is back and wants me to do something. I'm looking for a loophole. Nick is the only person who understands what that means."

Perrick turned all the way to face me, and I noticed he was sweating buckets. In fact, he was standing in a small pool of water. "You've got some nerve. You're trying to welch on a deal with a demon, and Valefar to boot?" He shook his head, splattering perspiration in every direction. "You know that ain't gonna work. You might as well find a Hellhole now and jump into it."

"Help me talk to Nick, please."

"What's in it for me?"

Ash, who hadn't said a word this entire time, said, "She'll ask Gregory to let you visit your family."

I poked him in the chest. "Hey! You don't speak for me."

Ash leveled a penetrating gaze at me. "Becs, look at him."

Perrick looked pitiful, and yes, I'd already thought of that. But I didn't like Ash butting in. "It's not what you said, it's that you stuck your nose in my business."

Ash raised his hands in surrender.

I refocused on Perrick. "I will ask Gregory to send you home, or at least let you visit. I can't promise he'll listen to me, but I'll give it a go."

Perrick considered my words as more liquid dripped off of him, soaking his suit. His former paunch now hung limp like an empty camel's hump. He led us to a family room with twin dark-brown leather recliners and a matching leather sectional, and indicated for us to sit. The room contained a wet bar with glass cabinets containing every type of cocktail glass imaginable and a mini fridge with a glass front illuminating champagne bottles. The modern area rug reminded me of a painting I'd seen in a local museum, with a black-and-tan impressionist pattern on a light-gray background.

Perrick heaved a deep sigh. "I'm from the Kansas plains. I had some home soil here, but Mr. Adamos had it dumped into the lake. I can't fly in the condition I'm in, so someone would have to drive me. I need the earth from my birthplace, or this happens." He gestured to his body. "Anything you can do to help would be appreciated."

"Gregory dumped it in the lake? What a shithead. Why?"

"I failed in a mission."

"So he kills you slowly?"

"Maybe you'd come work for him and help me cut a deal?"

I stared at him. "This is because I said no to you?"

He didn't say anything.

Damn. Another person I was responsible for. "I'll do my best, Perrick."

"Then, it's a deal. I'll get Nicky. He's a basket case, but you asked for it."

He sloshed up a back staircase, and I put my elbows on my knees and my head in my hands.

"Ugh. I can't believe Gregory is depriving his right-hand man of home soil just because I said I wouldn't work for him. That can't be it. Why kill his own guy?"

"Because he's a sociopath?" Ash wandered the edges of the room. "I think this is a real Degas," he said in amazement, pointing at a small, framed piece of a ballet dancer. "It's a sketch, not a finished work, but I believe this is an actual original."

"Gregory appreciates only the best. How do you know about art?"

"I had an interest for a while."

"Wow. Forthcoming as ever. You don't share a lot although I've shared everything with you. We need to rectify this." My previous annoyance came rushing back. "Ash, I appreciate your wanting to help Perrick. I do too, especially now. But please don't interfere in my negotiations."

He sat next to me and took one of my hands in his. "I know. I overstepped. I'm sorry."

Well, damn. It's hard to be mad at someone when they say they're sorry then stare at you with genuine puppy eyes of apology.

"Oh. Okay. But we're going to have a talk about sharing. Give and take."

Perrick entered the room from the back. He must have come down an elevator I couldn't see because he wheeled in a figure swathed in blankets, bent at the waist, head hanging low, almost touching his knees. It was cool in the house, but not unpleasantly so, and looking at the blankets made me hot and itchy. Beside me, Ash caught his breath.

"This is Nick?" I asked. It was a stupid question, but still, I thought he'd be better.

"Yup," said Perrick. "This husk is Nicky. I'd say God bless him, but the Devil took him."

"Lucifer didn't," I said. "A demon did. There's a big difference."

"Yes," said Asher. "And it has nothing to do with God."

I turned to him. "Really? You're so in with the big guy?"

"I'm so not getting in the middle of this." Perrick flapped the sleeves of his soaked suit jacket. "I'll leave you with Nick here. Whatever you do, don't make things worse. I'm warning you." Perrick shook a finger at me and backed out of the room.

I crouched in front of Nick's wheelchair. "Nick? Nick? It's Becs.

Rebecca Greenblatt. Do you remember me?"

Nick Adamos once walked into my office with a cocky attitude and a chip on his shoulder. Now, his shoulders couldn't handle the weight of a pretzel. He lifted his head an inch at a time, so slow I heard his vertebrae crack one by one. His bloodshot eyes met mine, and he opened his mouth.

"Nick, what is it? What do you want to say?"

But all he did was scream.

Chapter 12

"OKAY, OKAY! STOP, Nick. Stop! I'm sorry." I leaped back from Nick's chair, wishing we hadn't come.

Perrick slid into the room like a man stealing home base, but I already had my hands in the air to indicate my innocence.

Ash kneeled in front of the shrieking, broken man and whispered to him, petting Nick's cheeks.

"Ash, what are you doing?"

Ash leaned in closer, continuing to whisper, embracing Nick securely until he'd enveloped the wrecked man in a hug, with Nick's head on his shoulder. Within a minute, Nick had calmed, quietly weeping with the occasional hiccup. Perrick and I watched in disbelief.

"How are you soothing him, Mr. Michaels?" Perrick asked. "What are you saying?"

Nick wound his arms around Ash's neck and whispered something into his ear as tears streamed down his cheeks and onto Ash's shirt.

"Ash?" I questioned.

Nick kept whispering, and Ash continued to ignore us.

Perrick moved with care to Nick's side. "Nicky?"

The two stayed entwined, stock still, in their own world. It was as if they couldn't hear us.

"What's Nick saying, Perrick?"

He stroked Nick's hair and crouched to listen, then dropped his head. His voice broke. "He's repeating, 'I'm sorry,' over and over again. That's it. Nothing else."

"What's Ash doing?"

"He's meditating, maybe? His eyes are closed. It's more like a trance."

"They're communing?"

Perrick spread his arms wide, palms up. "Maybe it's some new age stuff with crystals or something?"

"I don't think Ash is wearing any crystals."

"Becs, I have no idea, but if he's helping Nicky, then I don't care. Nick's been such a freakin' mess, I'll take anything." He rubbed his eyes.

"What's Valefar got on you?"

I noticed Perrick had given up all pretense of formality. I liked this version of the troll much better.

"I swapped him a locket for Nick, and now he's using it to get me to do something that I can't tell you. I hoped that Nick could give me insight, but I didn't expect . . ." I motioned to Nick and Ash. I squashed the wisp of guilt I felt at using Nick to get to his brother. I didn't think Perrick would mind, given the circumstances. I didn't know why he was in Gregory's employ, but there was something keeping him here, even when it was clear he needed to go home. Worse, it appeared his current condition was my fault.

Perrick studied me. "You gave Valefar a piece of yourself? That takes moxie."

I turned to stare out the window. "It was the only way I could get Nick back."

The troll made a sound that was a cross between a croak, a grumble, and gastric distress that served as a resigned sigh in troll culture. "Valefar isn't the only problem you have. Remember, Gregory wants you too."

"Enough to punish you. Do you know what for?"

"Summoning a demon, but not Valefar. That's all I know."

"Gregory can't make me. I mean, I feel bad for you, and we'll find a way to fix that, but I'm not summoning anymore."

"He *can* make you. Valefar may have his hooks into you, but it's more than that. You're missing the big picture." Perrick hitched up his pants. "Look, I'm explaining this to you 'cause your boyfriend here seems to be helping Nicky, who I happen to care for, and because you said you'd help me. But you gotta understand, if Gregory hears me talking to you like this, I'll be in worse shape than I'm in now."

He sat on the sidearm of one of the lounge chairs. "Listen up. No one has to touch your soul. There's Mickey to think about. Everyone knows about her, no matter how much you've tried to protect her. I bet Valefar has threatened your sister as well as your own soul, hasn't he?"

I balked at that, unhappy that he'd guessed. "Well, yes. But Valefar is reaching with that particular threat. I'm fairly sure it's against the rules."

Perrick scoffed. "It doesn't matter. Gregory and Valefar have the same tactics. They can simply hire someone like me to *hurt* her. It's not about her soul, it's about her body. Valefar can't do it personally, and Gregory wouldn't, because he has the money to get someone else to do it. But arms and legs break when a baseball bat hits them. I know ten ways to torture someone that don't leave a mark. Gregory and Valefar work the same way. They'll layer enough people between them to create deniability, but your sister or her family will still end up in the hospital or traumatized, all the same."

His words left me cold and berating myself for not having thought of it. I was such a dummy.

"Hunngh." Nick withdrew from Ash, blinked, and wiped his nose on a blanket. Ash retreated, flopping down in the opposite recliner from Perrick, pitching it back, and closing his eyes.

"Nicky, how are you feeling?" asked Perrick.

Nick sat up straighter, and I thought his eyes were clearer, a fact confirmed when he pointed at me and said, "Go away."

Perrick clapped his hands. "Nicky! That's a whole sentence. That's terrific progress. Ash, I don't know what you did to him, but thank you. Absolute magic. Nick, are you hungry? I'm going to take you upstairs and ask the nurse to look after you. Maybe you'll want a shower? Not sure if your legs are strong enough, but you've been getting physical therapy every day . . ." He took hold of the wheelchair and rolled Nick away, prattling on until he was out of earshot.

"What did you do to him?" I asked Ash.

"Nothing."

"That wasn't nothing. He was a screaming mess, and you calmed him down, and suddenly he's intelligible. He recognized me."

"It's touch therapy, Becs. Hugs have healing powers. Prolonged proper hugs, where the hearts are touching, are as close to magic as you'll ever see. I don't think anyone's ever hugged that man. That's what he needed."

"You healed him with a hug?" I tried, but I couldn't keep the skepticism out of my voice.

"Boosts the immune system, calms nerves, and increases serotonin. Just what the doctor ordered, but it didn't truly heal him. That's going to take time."

I perched on the arm of the recliner. "How did you know that was what he needed?"

He opened one eye and smiled at me. "Instinct. But now I'm hungry. I think it's time for us to get out of here. I need good food, and we can review what we learned here today. I know an Italian place that makes the best eggplant parmesan. How's that sound?"

"We didn't learn anything. I'm no closer to figuring out how fulfill Valefar's request, I still have this poison in me, I'm still unemployed,

Pinky's still trapped on our side and can't get into Faerie, and Perrick's dripping wet because I refused to help Gregory. We've achieved nothing. In fact, things are worse." I shoved myself to my feet and paced the room.

Asher pushed the recliner closed and stood, stretching. "We're going to figure it out, come Hell or high water."

"Well, if it's Hell you want, that's perfect, because I have a deal for you." We spun to see a composed Gregory Adamos poised in his doorway, wearing a dark-gray suit tailored to his six-foot frame, barrel chest, and wide shoulders, pale-peach tie loose over a lighter gray shirt, and a pair of what appeared to be genuine snakeskin loafers in a deep burgundy. His dark hair, beard, and mustache gave him a sophisticated air that probably attracted many ladies, especially with his full lips, aristocratic nose, and hooded, pale-blue eyes. Yes, I was certain he was never lonely for intimate company. It had only been a few months since I'd last seen him, but it was still too soon.

Those eyes held no appeal for me. They scrutinized me with cool detachment. I was a thing to be used, bought, and sold. A tool to be exploited, depleted, and discarded. I hated it before, and I hated it now. I wondered if he had ever loved anything or anyone in his entire life. Could he feel passion or tenderness? Was he a machine, broken and frozen inside? When he was four, did he have a favorite teddy bear? Had someone taken it away and told him it was a weakness to want a stuffed animal?

Would knowing that make me feel any differently about him?

No.

Because he'd made choices that led him to this moment, and all he wanted from me was to summon a second demon, even knowing what the first one had done to his brother.

I snuck a look at Asher to see if he wanted to hug it out with Gregory and wasn't surprised to see the answer was no. Ash's face held nothing but contempt for Gregory. It was disconcerting. I'd never seen Ash be anything but kind with anyone. He was caring with Kenneth, me, and even with the nasty waitress in Giatanos. He'd held onto Nick long enough to transfer neurotransmitters or hormones or something. So this expression of contempt and disgust was new. His gorgeous, curly locks suddenly looked lank, and his normally warm, brown eyes flashed with loathing. He widened his stance when he turned to Gregory but crossed his arms. The stance was that of a fighter, but the arms said he was holding back and letting me handle it. I appreciated it.

"I've already told you that I'm not summoning any more demons." I raised my chin in defiance.

"You don't know what I'm willing to pay yet."

"You don't have anything I want."

His brows furrowed. "Then why are you here?"

"Checking on Nick."

He barked out a laugh. "It's been months. Why now?" Gregory yanked at his tie, curled it around his fingers, and laid it on the refrigerator top.

I gave him a one-shoulder shrug. "Feeling guilty, I guess."

Gregory shed his jacket and slipped deeper into the room. I backed up the same amount of distance, not wanting to be any closer to him than I had to be, which made him smirk. Ash stayed where he was, but Gregory took no notice of him.

"I don't believe you."

"Believe what you want. I don't care. Besides, there's someone out there who wants to summon demons for you. You should give him a try. He's been a real pain in my ass, and if you hire him, he'll leave me alone."

Gregory poured himself a drink over ice and added a dash of water. I couldn't see the bottle but from the smell, I guessed it was ouzo. "You mean that warlock fancying himself a summoner? He's a moron. He'll get himself killed the first time he tries."

"He says he can cast a strong circle." I was suddenly desperate for Gregory to hire the guy. It would get the Warlock off my back, and maybe he'd retrieve his magical cancer if I got him the job. The two deserved each other.

Gregory sipped his drink, and sure enough, it was a milky white color. Ouzo for sure.

"You should give him a try." I did my best to sound earnest and struggled to keep the desperation from my tone.

Gregory took another sip and rattled the ice in his glass, dismissing the idea, his blue eyes as stormy as his drink. "He doesn't have the Kiss," he hissed. "I don't deal with amateurs."

"How do you know about the Warlock? Did he offer his services to you? Did you talk to him? I had a run-in with him, and he's powerful." I leaned against the windowsill trying to appear casual.

Gregory swallowed the rest of his drink. "Warlocks are good for curses, bad luck potions, and minor spells. If I need to plan a heist and require a spell to knock out the security system, I get a warlock." Gregory poured another drink and knocked half of it back, propping himself on the edge of the liquor cabinet in a show of false indifference when in truth, he was coiled and ready to strike.

He continued. "If there's a guy making noise in the wrong places, and I want to make sure he has an accident, I hire a warlock. They have their uses, but this guy's out of his depth. He can't do what you do." He raised his glass above his forehead in a toast to my abilities.

Curious, I asked, "What if you want to do more than break legs?"

"I use a gun. Cleaner, simpler."

"Why are you telling me this?"

"Because you are going to summon a demon for me. I have my heart set on something, and I see no other way to get it. You're going to help me." The sun fell below the horizon behind me, and the room darkened as the natural light faded.

Okay, maybe the murdering, venomous, bastard deserved what he got. I hated myself but . . .

"I can summon Valefar. We could do it right now."

Ash shot me a look.

"Not him," Gregory said, swirling his drink.

"Why not? He'll give you whatever you want."

"He's not suitable for what I require. Demons have specialties, and this isn't his."

Summoning Valefar for Gregory would solve my problem, even if it put red on my psychological ledger. "He always answers me. He knows you. I'm sure he'd make you a good deal. You tell him what you want, and poof, you'll have it."

"I told you, he's not the one who can do this for me."

"What if we summon him and he gets you the demon you need, a broker role?"

"What is it with you and Valefar? I don't want him. No. You'll summon someone else."

"I won't."

"You will." Gregory said, dusk shadowing half his face. "You will or I'll send Perrick to Joey's, then to your sister's, and then . . ." He jerked his thumb toward Ash. "Maybe I'll send him to take out your special friend," he said matter-of-factly, as if he were threatening to order a sandwich.

I squared my shoulders. I was getting pretty sick of everyone threatening my friends and family, so I did what I'd trained to do—attack. I let what light there was silhouette me and stepped toward him, my voice low and steady. I, too, could operate in the dark.

"I don't think Perrick will do any of those things. You need to send him home or your troll isn't going to live long enough to pour you another drink."

"Bah. He's being a baby."

"No, he's dying. Get someone to drive him home or whatever contract you have with him will be null and void by way of death."

"I'll take it under advisement." Once again, he spoke with calm indifference.

"You'll consider it?"

"I don't like wasting my best assets."

I scoffed. "If you really had his home soil here and dumped it into the lake, all you've done is prove you're a cold, heartless viper who plays with people's lives. You bang them around until they're bruised, battered, and hopeless, and then dump them like a dead mouse on a rubbish heap. You're a user, Gregory Adamos. The only thing you care about is money."

"You're not wrong," he said, his voice cold, his body taut. "I make no apologies for it. I have an empire to run, and I do it exceptionally well. Perrick!"

The troll appeared from the front hallway. He must have circled back around somehow.

"Mr. Adamos, you should know that Nick is alert and is speaking in complete sentences."

Gregory whirled to face Perrick. "Truly? How?"

Perrick's eyes slipped to Ash, who gave a miniscule shake of his head.

"I think it was seeing Ms. Greenblatt."

Gregory swiveled to look at me. "Really? You are useful for so many things, Rebecca."

He turned back to Perrick, and I detected a slight softening to his face, a tiny relaxation at the corner of his eyes and around his mouth. "Tell Nicky I'll be up to see him in a minute. Please also call his speech therapist. Make an appointment for tomorrow."

"Yes, sir."

"Ms. Greenblatt tells me you're ill and need to go home, because I dumped your soil."

"Yes, sir."

"Too bad. You'll need to stay longer."

"Yes, sir. I'll make do."

"Dismissed."

Whatever joy I'd seen in Gregory's face fled as soon as Perrick departed. "You're the one killing Perrick now. Do what I want and Perrick goes home. Don't, and he dies. His life is in your hands."

"You bastard." My body vibrated with fury.

"I knew my father and mother, so that's not true. But you know the stakes now, Ms. Greenblatt. Figure out your next steps. You can let yourself out."

Chapter 13

ASH DROPPED ME at my door with a quick, "I have something to do." We'd both seethed with rage the entire ride home as we contemplated Gregory's final words, Ash apoplectic at Perrick's condition and Gregory's dispassion. I'd expected vile behavior from the mob boss, but this was lower than even I expected him to go, and now I had Perrick's life on my head, as well. I didn't trust Perrick, but he'd been up front with me about the danger to my sister, and I respected the way he cared for Nick.

My tummy ached as the death magic squirmed and jabbed, so I drank another mug of Mrs. Long's tea and ate a few crackers to go with it. I couldn't sleep, but I wasn't welcome at Joey's bar, so I went to the only other place I knew might still be open.

Oded raised an eyebrow when the doorbell tinkled to announce my arrival. I'd always wished I could do that, raise a single eyebrow. His was a thick caterpillar of an eyebrow, and he could raise it to the sky. Zara tied her shoe, waved, and walked out the back.

Oded grunted. "Rivka, you're late."

"How could I be late? I don't have an appointment."

"Doesn't matter, you're always late."

"Is it okay that I dropped in, or were you closing up?"

"Still open. Go change."

My joints ached, and my head hurt from the events of the day, not to mention the stomach issues. In fact, I was close to throwing up again. But I changed into my sparring clothes, then walked to the center of the mat. Oded examined me top to toe, his head cocked to the side, chin in hand, as was his way when he was thinking. I noticed he'd turned the door's "open" sign to "closed."

"You're not well."

"I'm meh," I admitted. "Been better."

He took a step towards me, and I raised my arms in defense.

"Good instinct, but you can lower your fists. Relax." He placed the back of his hand on my forehead. He stepped closer, and I tensed. "Shh,

Rivka, it's okay," he murmured. He leaned in, and I smelled his soap and shampoo, his skin and aftershave, a mixture that was simply Oded, steady and as immutable as a redwood. With surprising gentleness, he pressed his lips to my forehead.

"You have a fever," he said. "You're sick."

How was I going to explain a magical illness to Oded? His world was about physical combat. Guns. Hand-to-hand. I needed a commonality.

"I'm not sick in the usual way. I know you've seen people under so much stress that their bodies give out, right? They get fever and chills and can't sleep because their jobs are killing them, or they're surrounded by so much negativity that they literally can't handle it?"

"Of course."

"And you've seen people with post-traumatic stress disorder?"

His face grew dark, and he rubbed one arm with the other. "Unfortunately."

"This means you understand that negative energy and emotions can make you physically sick. I can't explain it more than that, but someone bad is trying to hurt me. They've already tried to kill me once."

Oded's eyes opened wide in alarm. "Someone is actively trying to assassinate you?"

"Yes," I replied.

"Have you gone to the police?"

"No. It's hard to explain. When I think about outlining all the things that have happened, I get confused."

"What has happened?"

I blew out a breath. How would I explain this without mentioning magic? "He's followed me in his car, run me off the road, stalked me at my apartment, and attacked me at my workplace."

"That seems like plenty enough to get a restraining order or at least to report him and create a record." Oded took a few steps toward his phone. "I'll be with you when you talk to the cops. You don't need to be afraid. Do you know his name? Can you describe him?"

"I'm not going to do that, Oded."

"Why the hell not?"

"I have my reasons."

Oded regarded me in a new way. Not bad or good, but he was definitely considering his next words.

"Let me get you a towel, and we'll sit."

We sat cross-legged, backs straight. I wiggled on the mat under me, trying to get comfortable.

"Rivka, the law is your friend in this case. Krav Maga is for self-defense, but it cannot protect you from someone running you off a cliff. It can't protect you from a bullet. Why is this man stalking you? Why does he want to hurt you?"

"I don't want to talk about that."

"Okay, but remember that you have many tools in your arsenal. Your foot is a tool. It can be used to kick a man in his balls or kick a door down to help someone escape a burning building."

"I get it. A gun can shoot a murderer as easily as a child. It depends on who you point it at."

"Exactly. The law is another tool, and it is where you should start. Also, a whistle and your phone. And it would be smart if you didn't go out alone."

"I understand."

"You say that, but I don't think you do or you wouldn't resist going to the police. This has me concerned."

I held up a hand to stop before he continued.

"Fine," he said. "Then it's guided meditation time. We need to get your mind clear."

"No punching?"

"Rivka, you're *meshuggenah*. Close your eyes and breathe naturally."

Breathing naturally meant nothing to me at this point. What was that? In and out? Should I count?

"For goodness' sake, woman. Stop thinking."

"I can't." I was whining, and I knew it.

"Try. Listen to my voice. Squeeze your toes, then let them go. Good. Now your feet, curl them in as hard as you can. Relax. Now flex them up and do the same for your calves. Hard, hard, hard. Good. Now relax them."

We did this for my whole body, muscle by muscle, all the way to my face. By the time I'd scrunched my face and released three times, my body was a puddle of goo. The sun was long set, and Oded lit a few low-level amber lights to create a relaxing atmosphere.

"Stay right there, where you are," he said, his voice soft and soothing. "Sink deeper into your mind. There's a path. Do you see it?"

"I see a staircase."

"That's interesting. Where does it go?"

"Down. It spirals into darkness. No, wait, not darkness. There's light at the bottom. A pulsing green light and wind. It howls and smells like the woods, like trees and growing things."

"Do you want to go down it?"

"Yes."

"Then go."

The staircase reminded me of the one in the library as I took the first step. Thirteen steps down, twisting to the right, and then to the right again. I stepped onto a firm surface and was faced with a lush forest on my left and an abandoned cityscape on my right. The green glow emanated from the forest while the wind whistled through the painted bricks and rusted metal of the cityscape. They met at a sharp bifurcation in front of me, as if they'd hit a wall I couldn't see. Behind me they faded into nothingness; there was only the staircase.

Birds chirped in the forest, although I couldn't see them, and when I concentrated, I heard waves crashing in the distance. I smelled the water, too, damp and heavy in the air. While I didn't see any sky, nothing blue or starry, a glow permeated the entire scene.

I stepped forward, and a wedged path opened up so that both forest and city angled away from me until I was in the middle of a triangle, the tip in front of me, the two other corners behind me to the left and to the right. I knew that danger lay within the forest and the deserted city, but I also knew that wonder lay there, too.

Calm and unafraid, I gazed at the apex of the triangle.

And nearly peed my pants when Valefar appeared with an explosion of dust, ash, and crackling flame. He wore a donkey head this time, a visage I'd seen in pictures from some of the oldest demonology texts, and he stood frozen, poised with his donkey jaws preternaturally unhinged, lion paws ready to swipe me down.

I whirled as a gust of shrieking wind drew my attention to the corner on my right where the Warlock manifested with his gray cloak and burnt face, his wand at the ready, death magic swirling around him in stunning gray and burgundy tendrils. The burgundy was the color of drying blood. He reeked like decomposing leaves, and I gagged at the smell. He, too, didn't move.

The *ping* of an elevator announced Gregory's arrival as he stepped out of fog to take his place on the left corner, dressed in his gray suit, peach tie, and snakeskin loafers, yawning as if he didn't have time for this.

"What do you want?" I asked, easily finding my natural state of pissed off in this meditation. "Are you in this together? Working together? Three asshole amigos?"

They didn't say anything. Nothing. Not a damn thing. Didn't even notice me.

"Well, screw this noise. I'm outta here then. This isn't getting me any answers."

A loud *crack* from the forest made me stop. A huge tree fell, knocking other trees down like dominoes, and when they hit the forest floor with a resounding *smack*, light flooded in and I could see the water beyond, whitewater-tipped waves cresting in the distance. Three vines slithered through the new clearing toward each of the cornered naughty, naughty boys. One wrapped around Valefar's ankles, the second around Gregory's wrist, and the third around the Warlock's upper arm, then they bound themselves together in a twist and came to me as one rope, sliding up my leg to present themselves to me. I took the single, entwined rope and studied it, looking from the rope to each of the men trying to hurt me and the people I cared about.

As I thought of my friends and family, figures appeared on the edges of the triangle. My sister and Ruthie. Pinky. Asher. Kenneth. Mr. and Mrs. Long. Oded. Joey. Even Perrick. A couple of other figures I couldn't make out but who seemed familiar. The more I concentrated on them, the more they retreated. When I turned my head to the side, I could see them from the corner of my eye, but when I looked at them head on, they faded.

The bright sounds of a violin made me turn toward the cityscape where shadow shapes danced on the broken sidewalks, their footsteps solid indents but their bodies amorphous. I recognized the step from a traditional folk dance I'd learned in Hebrew school, and when I looked closely, I saw the form of an older woman holding the hand of a middle-aged woman, who gently held the finger of a younger girl. Others danced with them, but their shapes vacillated and flowed with the music. They danced in a circle, one foot over the other, one foot behind, four steps, then four in the middle, stepping over rusted tailpipes, broken strollers, and discarded shoes. Their scarves sailed behind them as they danced and clapped. I could hear a clarinet and a drum along with the violin.

The music stopped, and all three figures, visible but wavy like watercolor paintings in super-heated air, faced me and pointed to the vine rope.

The rope sprouted burgundy tendrils from the central portion in my hand and sped toward my friends along the triangle's edges, grabbing them each at their feet, wrapping them like mummies in swift, efficient motions. I screamed and yanked on the rope, but when I did, Valefar, the Warlock, and Gregory woke from their stasis and eyed me like candy.

"You'll give me Gregory, or I'll take your soul and capture it in this locket," said Valefar, snapping his donkey jaws like a wolf ready to take its prey.

"Death. I tried to kill you and it didn't work, but the death magic will eat away at your insides, and you'll die all the same," said the Warlock, raising his wand high.

"Summon the demon I choose and grant my wish, or Perrick dies as well as your sister," Gregory warned, shaking an index finger. "It's simple. Why do you fight what you are? You're Kiss Born."

My friends and family, even the figures I couldn't see, toppled over, consumed by the vines, their mouths covered, but I heard their desperate muffled cries for help. Their eyes begged me to save them, but I had no idea what to do.

The city's drum picked up again, and the dancers took up the beat. "Wait? What do I do?" I called to them. They didn't answer, dancing away into the distance. "Please! Help me! They're dying."

They disappeared across the horizon.

"Becs . . ." My sister's voice carried on the wind. "Why did you kill me?"

Perrick growled in my ear, although his wrapped body lay yards away. "Good going, Kiss Born. You destroyed Nicky and me as well."

Pinky said nothing, but his eyes burned bright with trust, believing in me right up to the moment when the light in his eyes flickered and died. Tears streamed down my face.

I shouted into the void. "What's the freakin' point of this? Everyone I care about dies at the hands of these three brutes, and I'm holding the magic jump rope that causes it all? I'm at the center, so it's all my fault? If I die or disappear, will that stop it?"

I dropped the vine rope and let it tumble to my feet. It hit the ground and withered, curling up into brown, dry, brittle pieces that scattered into the city's wind. In seconds, the vine rope disappeared, and the music stopped.

Valefar, the Warlock, and Gregory remained where they were, unmoving. The mummified remains of my loved ones rolled over, so their backs were to me.

Infuriated and bitter, I punched frozen Gregory in the nose, shocked when blood spurted, and he punched me back, the hit stinging my entire solar plexus, knocking the wind out of me.

"You want to hit things, Becs? Go for it."

He punched, but I was ready and ducked, then ducked again as he threw with his left hand. I spun into his body, grabbing his left elbow with my right hand, and as I bent at the waist and rolled forward, he rolled with me and took the brunt of my weight and the jagged pain of the roll on his spine. I leapt off him but wasn't fast enough, and he twisted, undulating in the air, catching my ankle. I let him pull me down, punched him again in the nose and then in the throat.

I scrambled off him and ran for the stairs. He was big, heavy, and fast, but I was trained and quick. Knowing I could take him in close quarters with no weapons didn't mean much to me. He'd always have a gun and a flunky, and a bullet was always faster than a fist. Even if I had a gun, and as much as I hated him, murder wasn't on my menu.

I'd learned nothing.

I ran up the stairs, taking them two at a time. The triangle, cityscape, and the trees melted away.

I opened my eyes, and Oded handed me a bottle of water. "What did you see?"

"Nothing helpful." I rubbed my face, adjusting to the light.

"You may not understand it yet."

Now that I sat before him in the real world, the vision seemed ridiculous. "It meant nothing. It's my imagination attempting to make sense of the last few days."

"You try my patience. You're in danger of bodily harm, maybe even *death,* and you won't tell me why. Fine, I can respect that. But you've got to decide how to protect yourself. Your subconscious is telling you what to do. Listen to it."

"My subconscious could be more direct and send me an email."

"Stop whining. You think God gave Moses a map marked with an X? Did Noah get an atlas? No, he got a bird and a twig."

"Moses didn't make it into the Promised Land, Oded, and Noah forgot the unicorns. Not the greatest analogies."

He dismissed my objections. "Not the point. The point is, if you want everything spelled out for you and tied up with a bow, be an accountant. The situation you're obviously in is for people made of stronger stuff."

Lightning flashed and the lights went out.

Oded rolled his eyes. "*Basa!* We lost power. Go home, Rivka. Think on what you saw. I'll get a flashlight." He mumbled to himself. "I think I can find it in the dark." He reached for a wall. "Wait for me here," he instructed.

I remained where he left me. He found his tactical flashlight by feel alone in the cabinet under the cash register and walked me to the door to make certain I got in my car safely.

"Be careful, Rivka."

Chapter 14

I TOSSED AND TURNED that night and woke utterly exhausted. Cranky and miserable, I drank more of Mrs. Long's tea and surveyed my food supplies. Sparse was an understatement. I choked down my last bruised banana and wondered if I could ask Ash to bring me leftovers from the restaurant.

I started my day in a place they didn't allow food, anyway. I paid my respects to the dolphin and ram, petting each on my way into the library, and paid no attention to the first-floor activity. My brain cells didn't care. I took the elevator to the third floor, scrambled up the staircase to the fourth, and hoisted myself over the lip until I came nose-to-nose with a cat.

"Stacks. Good to see you."

"It's nice to see you, Ms. Greenblatt. Glad you found the books you were looking for."

I observed the cat carefully as I got my knees under me, stood, and wiped my hands off on my pants. "Stacks?"

The voice laughed. "Up here, Ms. Greenblatt. I believe Stacks could talk if he wanted to, but so far, he hasn't."

The librarian who helped me find the fourth floor sat on a tall stool behind the information desk.

I blinked at him as if he were a mirage. "I've only seen one person up here before."

"We don't need full-time coverage on this floor, so I'm up here sporadically to reshelve and re-sort books into the proper order. There aren't many visitors into the paranormal and metaphysical." He beamed a sunny smile.

"I'm here to return these books," I said lamely. I was still a bit stunned to see him there. "Where do you want me to put them?"

"Give them to me, and I'll put them away correctly." He smiled at me. "In any case, I'm glad I ran into you."

I handed him the books. "Why?"

He shifted on his stool, and his cheery disposition dimmed. "I wanted to ask you a question." He readjusted his glasses.

"Oooookay, uh . . ." I read his nametag. "Timothy. What is it you want?"

He held out his hand for me to shake, and I was surprised again when I took it in mine and found it was tiny.

"Timothy Moon. Quarter-fae, on my father's side. Here in the Slow World, everyone thinks I'm a little person but I'm really part hob."

"I thought hobs chose houses and families."

He held up an index finger. "I'm only a quarter-hob. I've a wife and eight kids. I found a human to love me, no matter my size, and my kids are normal human size, albeit on the shorter end of things. I indulge my need to keep house by working here."

"I couldn't imagine a better person for the job." Inside I was thinking, *eight* kids!

"Well, thanks!" Timothy jumped off the stool and came around the desk, his head reaching my waist. He lowered his voice. "I hoped I could hire you to summon my grandma."

I shook my head as if I had water in my ear. "I'm sorry. You want me to do what?"

"Summon my grandma. Sure, she's not my grandma really—more like my great-great-great-grandma—but with fae, it's all the same. I'd like to catch up, and I have some family questions to ask her."

I was so stunned at this request, I couldn't speak for a moment. I finally stammered out, "You . . . you . . . want me to summon someone from Faerie? No one has ever asked me that before. It never occurred to me that I could do it."

"Well, why not?" Timothy asked.

I considered my answer before speaking. "I guess it seemed rude? Fae come and go as they please, like the neighbors you can't get rid of, who never invite you over to visit, and you wouldn't want to eat with them anyway."

"I understand," Timothy said, scratching an ear. "But I don't have any other way of talking to Granny."

"Can't you go into Faerie?"

"Nope, can't get small enough with only quarter blood." Timothy scratched the other ear. "But with your help, I could see Granny and get my catch-up. It's been years."

Why was I even considering this? "Look, I'd like to help you, but I don't summon anymore."

His face fell so hard his ears drooped. "At all? I heard about your problem with the demons, but summoning a family member is hardly the same thing, is it?"

Stacks rubbed against my ankles, and as I squatted down to pet him, I came eye-to-eye with Timothy Moon. "What kind of family questions? Does Granny have big teeth and a hankering to eat someone?"

Timothy narrowed his eyes at me. "Huh? No? I'm completing our family tree. I'll show you." He scurried back behind the desk and climbed up on his stool with a documents canister. He popped the top and removed a rolled file which he placed on the checkout desktop. A virtual three-dimensional tree hologram unfurled itself. The trunk grew out of the paper with new growth waving at the sides and top. It was so cool.

"Look," he said, pointing to the image. "It's my genealogy going back ten generations. See the blank spots? I'm filling in our ancestry. I've got the human side complete, but I need assistance on the fae side. It's complex."

It was a literal family tree, branching out just as he said. The human side was direct and understandable, but the fae side involved twigs and offshoots for half-cousins and halflings, crossbreeds, and great-grand-grands, so I understood why he needed assistance.

"I'll pay you. I don't expect you to work for free." Stacks wound around my feet, meowing until I petted him.

Timothy's offer got my attention, given the state of my larder and the rumbling in my empty belly because one semi-rotten banana wasn't enough to stave off my hunger or the eddying death magic threatening to swirl up my throat.

"You said you can't go small. I have a friend, full fae, who has the same problem. Do you know how to help him?"

"Are you sure?" Timothy's tone said he didn't believe me. "That's something all full-blood fae know from birth. How could he forget something like that?"

"He's different."

"I don't know how to teach him, because I can't do it myself. Maybe we can ask Granny. Can't say for sure if she'll assist. You know how fae are. They don't do anything out of the kindness of their hearts."

"What do hobs like? Can I bring a gift?"

Timothy clucked his tongue. "You don't bring a gift. You bring something to trade. Only thing I can tell you is not to offer clothes. Never clothes. Granny likes wine. Something sweet."

I had the perfect item. An unopened bottle at home, given to me as a housewarming gift by a family friend, along with a *kiddush* cup and

Shabbat candles from when I'd moved into my apartment. This would be a fine use for it.

"What if she gets angry and curses my apartment or something?"

"She won't, I promise. And if she's mad, I'll interfere and take the blame. Promise."

I'd never, ever read of a summoner using his or her power to summon a fae, but I had minimal training, so what did I know? I really needed that money.

"Fine, but you're responsible if she's unhappy. I'm guessing the best time to summon a fae creature is at dusk, when the veil is thin. I'll meet you at my office at eight-thirty p.m. Dusk isn't until late today. I'll give you the address." I peered down at him. "Do you drive?"

"Of course I drive. I have a modified car and get around fine." He waved a finger at me. "Don't go calling Granny a 'creature.' She's family."

"My apologies. The best time to summon a fairy grandmother then."

He sniffed. "Much better."

"I'll meet you then, Tiny Tim," I said, handing him my card and gathering my stuff.

"Yuck, that's a terrible name. Insulting. Too Dickens."

"Apologies. What about TT?"

"You're giving me a nickname? Just between us?" He smiled. "I like that."

"Cool. TT, please bring your checkbook, her full name, a focal object, and I'll bring the wine. We do this by the book, with a contract. No shortcuts."

"Gotcha."

I'd have to run home to get the wine, but that coincided nicely with wanting to check in with Ash. I hadn't seen him since the trip to Gregory's house, and for some stupid reason, I didn't have his phone number. Running back and forth between downtown and Chinatown was damned inconvenient, but it kept me from thinking too much.

I climbed the fire escape and let myself in, taking a moment to tend to the feeders. My suet was low, as were the peanuts, but the wood-peckers always had the telephone poles and the big trees. The fledged baby orioles needed oranges and grape jelly, so I put out my last orange and wondered if the Longs would give me another. They sort of hated the feeders though, because of the bird poop on the pavement below, so maybe I'd refrain from asking. I still had a mostly full bag of seed for everyone else, and some dropped sunflowers had sprouted in the grass below, which was nice. The chipmunks gathered the rest and stored them for winter.

A crow landed on the guardrail as I loaded the flat feeder.

"Hey, crow. Bold of you. Almost done. Wait a minute and you can eat."

It dropped something shiny.

"Paying for supper. Not necessary."

I finished filling the feeder, rebalanced it, and stepped away. The crow hopped on to peck at the seeds and steal a raspberry. The gourmet birdseed blend had a few in it, and the birds nabbed them right away. I looked at the shiny bit the crow dropped.

It was an old-time carnival button that said, "Clock's Ticking," with a laughing hourglass in the background wearing a Snidely Whiplash mustache. It was creepy as hell, and I had no doubt who'd sent it.

"Valefar, suck my clock."

The crow dropped its red, juicy prize, croaked, "Heh, heh. Valefar!" Then, it snapped up the raspberry, swallowed it in one gulp, and flew to a tree to watch me where I couldn't touch it.

Sighing, I went inside and ate a bag of stale oyster crackers from months-ago takeout soup and took two ibuprofen. I made a thermos of tea and drank a quarter of it right away, wondering if Mrs. Long had enough ingredients to make more.

I carried my thermos with me up the stairs to the fourth floor, my first visit to that level, since I'd never needed to visit before. Surprisingly, there was only one unit, so I didn't have to guess which one belonged to Ash. I knocked, a polite *rat-a-tat-tat*.

"Ash, it's Becs."

No answer.

"Ash?" I knocked louder.

Nothing. "Great."

I searched for Giatanos on my phone and called the restaurant. A woman answered.

"Hi, I'm trying to reach Asher Michaels. Is it possible to speak to him, please?"

"Who's asking?"

"I'm a friend of his. Rebecca Greenblatt."

"Oh, it's you." I realized it was my jealous waitress, Kellie, my biggest superfan. *Oh. Joy.*

I huffed out an exasperated breath. "Can I please talk to him?"

"He's not here, sunshine. You can't be much of a girlfriend if you didn't know that."

"He's not at his apartment either. Was he in yesterday?"

"You don't know that either? He called in and took a few days off. Said he had something to do."

"He said the same thing to me, but he didn't tell me what or that he was leaving."

She trilled a high-pitched, brittle laugh. "Guess you're not as close as you thought you were. If Ash was my boyfriend, I'd keep him so busy, he wouldn't have the energy to go anywhere . . ."

I couldn't keep the incredulity out of my voice. "Kellie, do you kiss your mother with that mouth?"

"I don't talk to my mother," she sniffed. "I walked out of that crack house when I was twelve."

That made me pause a second.

"I'm sorry to hear that."

"We all got problems, and right now, you've lost your boyfriend. If I find him first, I'm keeping him. If I see him, I won't pass on a message."

"You don't stand a chance, Kellie. You never did." I hung up.

I wanted to feel sympathy for her rough upbringing, but Kellie was a pain in the ass with a side salad of cruel and a fizzy soda of fuck you. I wanted to put her and Gimlet Girl in the same room and watch them duke it out. Of course, Gimlet Girl would snack on Kellie like an appetizer at a corporate party. The waitress wasn't in GG's league. She was a joke compared to the pixie who'd had decades, if not centuries, to perfect the perfect pout and the subtle claw swipe.

I shook my head to clear it. Hunger and magical illness were destroying my attention and slowing me down. I needed to address at least one of them, and there was only one place to go.

Kenneth manned the register, so I got to read his shirt. It read, "Shhh . . . I'm procrastinating," with a picture of a book, a bag of chips, and an imprint of a greasy hand stain on the side.

"Becs! How are you feeling?"

"I'm okay, Kenneth, thank you. A little hungry."

"I'll get you your favorite egg foo young. You need to eat."

"That's nice of you." I lowered my voice. "Can you add this to my tab like last time? I've got some money coming tonight. I'll take care of it when I pay next month's rent."

He smacked me on the shoulder with a hand towel. "I always let you do that. Why are you acting like that's a problem? Also, we added the tea to your bill. Mom says she can send up more if you need."

"I do need more. It's keeping the pain at bay."

"It's not keeping the damage at bay, though. Mom and Dad explained what's going on with you, as much as they could. You aren't feeling it, but whatever is in there is hurting you."

Great, permanent damage, here I come. "But how? Did she mention that to you?"

He avoided my eyes. "I'll get that egg foo young for you. No green peppers."

"Hey, did she add the wormwood to the bill too? And the mask?"

He shook his head. "Not the mask. That's on loan. The wormwood, yes, of course. She's a businesswoman."

Right. Nothing's for nothing, and the wormwood ain't free. Got it. The food filled me up and settled the acid threatening to challenge gravity. I ordered a vegetarian wonton soup to go, grabbed an after-meal mint like any paying patron, stole two oranges from the display basket next to the menus, and snuck upstairs to my place. I put the wonton soup in my fridge and the oranges on the counter, then I sat in a lawn chair on the fire escape, thinking about the summoning that evening.

The crow lay dead in the middle of the platform, its brown eye open and still.

"Oh no." I gathered the crow in my arms. Had Valefar done this? Why would he kill his emissary?

Something hit me on the shoulder and tumbled to the ground. A bright-red cardinal, dead. Another *thunk* on my back. A bluebird. *A bluebird!* I'd never even seen one in real life because I lived too far north. My birder's Facebook group loved to catch the male feeding the female during mating season. I adored those pictures.

Two mourning doves, because they mated for life, plopped next to my foot. Another cardinal, a female this time. Then a shower of orioles, my favorite species, all dead. The male. The female. Three fledglings with their yellow feathers and curious faces, one with a speck of jelly still on its beak.

The shower turned to a hailstorm of stiff, lifeless birds hitting my head, my ears, shoulders, arms, and torso. Robins, starlings, finches, blue jays, red-winged blackbirds, sparrows, and more sparrows. My fire escape filled halfway with lifeless birds, a harsh contrast to the sunshine and blue sky most people saw that fine afternoon. They spilled over through the railings to the ground below.

"Hello. It's my version of *fowl* play. See, I'm as witty as you are."

The Warlock haunted the tree on the side of the building. Standing on the grass at its trunk, he looked up at me. The bastard obviously thought he was funny.

"Why would you do this? What is your endgame, you freak?"

"Amusement. I tried killing you straight out, and it failed, much to my frustration. But I will still win. Eventually, the death spell will end your life, but for now, it's fun to toy with you. It gives me pleasure and endless amusement. I'd have planned it this way all along, if I'd known how."

"You're sick."

"Irrelevant. That's obvious."

The birds came in a deluge until they reached my waist, and I had difficulty gathering my thoughts. My guts roiled at this abomination of nature and life, as my little loves piled one on top of another. The death magic stabbed me in ribs.

The death magic.

Could I?

I focused on it, closing my eyes to imagine it as gray tendrils, and asked it to come up. It resisted, clawing my esophagus, tearing it into strips so blood poured down my throat and out my ears and nose. I gagged and fell back into the gruesome mattress of dead birds, jumping when my head hit the sharp beak of a red-tailed hawk.

"Tut-tut. Are you trying to regurgitate the death magic to come after me, Becs? You think my magic would turn on its creator?" He tapped his foot, seeming to consider this as an academic problem while I retched on the death tendrils expanding in my throat.

"Improbable. Not impossible, but certainly not something I'm concerned about. You keep struggling. The more you hyperventilate, the sooner you'll expire, and I can steal your Kiss."

I tried to find my feet in the macabre lake of feathers and talons, pushing my tiny friends aside to get into my apartment. I gasped for air, patting at the door, finally opening it, letting stiff small bodies drift into my dining room as I fell to my knees and crawled to my kitchen for the thermos. I placed the lip to my mouth and tilted my head back so whatever dregs were in there dripped onto my tongue.

My heart boomed in my ears as it fought, sending wave after wave of frantic compression against my retinas, and my vision blackened as my oxygen-starved brain let go. I tipped another bit of tea into my mouth with shaky, weak hands. With the last of my strength, I sucked in air through my nose.

Suddenly, a dam broke, and the pressure loosened all at once. The death tendrils receded into my stomach, and I inhaled a long, grateful breath. I gulped two big swallows of air, crawled back to my sliding glass door, shut it, and locked it. I caught some dead birds inside, but I didn't care. I didn't want to leave the door open to the Warlock any longer than I had to.

I lay on the carpet, breathing in and out. I'd never been so appreciative to be able to perform this simple act before. Once I'd convinced myself that I could breathe normally, I allowed myself the luxury of a big ugly cry.

For two minutes. I didn't dare take time for more.

Chapter 15

AWARE THAT THE Warlock could still be out there, I crawled to the sliding door and pressed an ear to the glass. I sensed nothing, and when I peeked out, I saw nothing but blue sky and sunshine. Convinced he'd had his fun and left, I picked myself up and attended to the ghastly task of cleaning up the birds, weeping the whole time. Hundreds of little bodies, my winged friends, dead for no reason except for a half-man, half-monster who liked to toy with his food. Warlocks got energy from death, so by killing these innocent creatures, he not only caused me pain, he refueled.

Not knowing what else to do, I stiffened my spine and scooped the birds into large garbage bags, wincing at the flashes of yellow as I counted almost a hundred goldfinches. He'd decimated the local population. Big pileated woodpeckers and the smaller downy ones. Purple finches and warblers. Three hawks and a peregrine falcon. He didn't spare a single species. There was even a gorgeous blue-headed vireo which I cradled for a moment before putting it in the bag, crying anew.

I drove to my office with the bags in my trunk, fresh tea in my thermos, and my other supplies in the passenger seat. Heartsick, I'd taken down all my feeders.

A grassy median separated the storage facilities from the highway. Rarely mowed, the grass grew high and tall reedy plants wavered in the wind. I opened the bags, removed four birds, set them aside, and strew the rest of the birds' bodies across the vegetation, knowing that vultures would come and do what they did, as designed by nature. It was better than dumping the bodies in the trash. Ashes to ashes and dust to dust was the proper way. I had great respect for nature's recycling program. You had to admire the intestinal fortitude of the turkey vulture. They ate things that would kill us and thought they were delicious.

In fact, the first vulture appeared before I'd even emptied the second bag. I held up a finger and said, "Please wait. I have a third one to go."

After the last bag, I surprised myself by standing to the side, bowing my head, and saying *Kaddish*, a traditional Jewish bereavement prayer. It shocked me that the words came to me so easily. I'd said *Kaddish* thousands of times as a child but would have sworn I'd forgotten it as an adult. But no, the words were there.

After saying "Amen," I turned and walked away, letting the natural process begin.

While I was being all religious, someone needed to come around and remind me of the sixth commandment, because while cold-blooded murder hadn't been on my agenda yesterday, it was today.

I let that anger energize me as I cleaned up the candles from my last summoning of Valefar and tidied up the space, sweeping widdershins, and lighting sage for purification. I dug into a case of water and drank a full twelve ounces of straight-from-a-spring H2O, hoping the label wasn't a giant hoax. I needed the cleansing.

I covered the pentagram with a lush forest-green silk bedsheet and held the corners down with sandstone rocks I'd collected on a visit to Nevada. I placed a bottle of Mogen David kosher blackberry wine in the center of the sheet and encircled it with sand I'd collected from the same visit.

I'd brought the wine because I wanted to ask Timothy's grandmother questions about my situation, so I needed to offer something to trade. I also needed to represent myself and my current situation. To represent the city, I placed a doorknob at one corner, a shard of a windowpane in the second, a subway token in the third, and a brick in the fourth, each paired with one of the four remaining bird corpses. I added deep-green leaves from an oak tree to represent the forest.

I then poured spring water into two bowls and added them to the collection in the middle.

Hobs tended the ground and the home. They appreciated growing things and the cycles of Mother Earth. Representing the beauty of plants and the starkness of the desert where the hardy animals and plants thrived seemed right for a hob, and combined with the wine, the spring water, and whatever Timothy brought, I should be able to call to her. My personal additions were a wild card.

When Timothy arrived, he stared at the prepped summoning area in silence for a full sixty seconds.

"It's unusual," he finally said. "Not what I expected. Why did you add dead birds? That's not hob friendly." He wasn't judging, just befuddled.

"It's something I need to ask her about. The magic is a perversion of nature, and I hope she can help me understand it."

"I wouldn't hold my breath on that one, but you never know. My Granny's wise. Let me add my offering." He placed a bouquet of daisies next to the wine.

"We're doing this by the book," I said, repeating what I'd said before. "Contract first, and I've added a 'you are responsible if she's pissed off' clause."

"You're asking her something too."

"Yes, but I never would have tried summoning a fae if you hadn't requested it."

I filled in the elements of the contract. His name, mine, who we were summoning. I handed him a pin, and he dripped a dot of blood next to his name, as I did to mine. I was not going to repeat the same mistake twice. The usual magic snapped into place like a guitar string strummed just right. Timothy shivered as the vibration traveled down his body.

"Wow."

"It's serious magic, TT."

"No kidding."

"Please sit on the other side in the chair."

"I can't sit on this side?"

"No. By the book."

TT did as he was told and climbed into the chair while I closed the rolling door. I lit six white candles, striving for balance, and called his relative forth.

"Mildread Purplefeather Moonshine, great-great-great-grandmother of Timothy Moon, I summon thee as a bearer of the Kiss on behalf of your family member. We offer wine and flowers."

A tiny silver light about the size of a dime appeared and hovered over the wine bottle. Timothy leaned forward in his chair, eager to get a good look. The light grew to the size of a teacup and then a door the size of a doghouse. A female hob stepped through, snapped up the flowers with twiggy hands, held them to her nose, and inhaled deeply.

Hobs are funny creatures, being a little like a sprite and somewhat like a gremlin. They could be good, annoying, or helpful. Most helped around a house, some in farmland, and occasionally they set up shop in a store or other place of business. This one smelled decidedly horsey.

The one thing you absolutely could not do was offer a hob clothing. There was some argument about whether that "freed" the hob from servitude or simply insulted them, but either way, it made them angry.

And an outraged hob was a dangerous hob. I was already praying this one didn't mind being summoned.

Mildread was about a foot tall, and her ears were the same size as her entire head. She wore a red sleeping cap that hung down her back, a long coat with tiny gold buttons, itty-bitty high-heeled shoes, and carried a bag over her shoulder. She smoked a pipe that stuck out past her bulbous nose and pointed chin, and leaned on a cane I didn't think she needed. Her eyebrows were her most spectacular feature, however, iron gray, bushy, and expressive.

"Summoned! Well, that's a first! I must tell me friends."

She looked around, studying the circle. "This is nice! But I can't be stayin' long, ya know. I've got me chores to do, Tim-o-thee Moon. Hey there, Rebecca Naomi Greenblatt, nice to meet ya. Yeah, I know ye name, girlie, don't think I don't. Ye've proven interestin' alright."

She looked around her. "Can I get a soft spot to land?"

Relieved that she seemed happy to be there, I removed the seat cushion from my chair and gave it to her. She settled on it with a happy sigh. "This wine from ye, Rebecca?"

"It is."

"So ye needs somethin' from Granny too, I'm guessin' from the circle?"

"I'd hoped to ask you a question." I sat on the floor cross-legged, so I was at her height. It seemed impolite to tower over her.

"Tim-o-thee!" She called to him over the barrier between them. "Whatcha be needin'? Why ye all the way over there?"

"Becs insisted on it. Said it was for my safety to go by the book," he yelled back. "I'm doing our ancestry and need your help with the family tree."

Mildread pointed her pipe at me. "Smart girlie to keep ye over there. Weird things about, this summonin' bein' one of them. Summonin' a fae." She shook her head, puffed on her pipe, and pointed at me again. "This might cause waves, don'cha know?"

I didn't know, not really. I'd done as my client requested, contract signed proper, and Granny didn't seem too ruffled about it. In fact, the unruffled Granny was rummaging in her bag, talking to herself until she pulled out a rolled scroll.

"Here it is! I'll leave you with this, Tim-o-thee. This autta do it, lad."

I picked up the scroll, unfurled half of it, and walked to the Plexiglas barrier to show it to him. "This good, TT?"

He nodded excitedly and gave me a thumbs-up. "Can I see her for a moment?" The bottom of the barrier was solid wood so he couldn't see her when she was sitting down.

I didn't think she'd like it if I picked her up, but it wasn't a problem. She muttered a word and floated upwards.

"Tim-o-thee, my lad, you're lookin' good. How's the wife and kids?"

"Good, Granny. I have pictures." He hopped off the chair and showed her some photos on his phone.

"Don't understand those gadgets but look at all those babies. So tall! Not hob-like at all, but good to see them grown. Happy fer yer, Tim."

"Thanks, Granny. It's good to see you."

"Now, I'd be best gettin' to Rebecca. She's needin' me, Tim-o-thee. Remember the things I gave ya when them babies be born."

"Each on their twenty-first birthdays. I remember."

"Good."

She settled back down on the cushion. "Can ye open the wine, lass? I have little time and ye be glowin' with pain and perplexity."

I opened the wine—easy to do, since it was a screw top—and handed her the bottle. She swallowed an enormous gulp and smacked her lips. "Max and Henry did a good job with their little company. A'course, they had help."

"Hobs helped make this wine?" I asked, flabbergasted.

"And brownies. Yer think they could create anything this perfect without fae help? Had to keep the clurichaun away. Ha!" She swallowed another gulp. "Ahhh. The good stuff. They make grape o'course, and pomegranate too. That was me uncle's idea."

"Your uncle suggested the pomegranate flavor?"

"More like nudged them along the way. Now, ye didn't call me to discuss kosher wine. What's yer question, lass?"

"Actually, I have two."

"That's cheatin' but I like the wine, so go ahead."

I told her about Pinky.

"He's fergotten how to go small? Ah, the poor lad. I cain't help him with that in perticuler, but I can get a message to his ma fer ye." She leaned forward. "She must be crazy with worrin'."

I almost said, "thank you," but thanking the fae can leave a debt. Instead, I said, "Pinky will appreciate that."

"Now to this other thing." She scrambled to her feet and walked the edges of the sheet. Her ruddy skin blanched at the sight of the birds.

"Who did this?" she whispered.

"A warlock. I'd hoped you'd know how to beat him."

"I've no magic for that, lass." She touched the goldfinch at her feet with her cane, and the scent of hay and cherry blossoms filled the room. "Evil magic, this is." I stared in wonder as she brought the bird back to life and repeated it with the other three.

I held out my hand, and the goldfinch landed on it, letting me stroke its back.

"How did you do that?"

"'Twas unnatural. Didn't sit right."

She cocked her head, listening to something I couldn't hear. "I've got to go. I don't know how to defeat the evil that caused this," she said, gesturing to the birds. "This is death magic, and my magic's about growin' things. But I can say this—follow the path you're on." She gestured to the circle. "Trust your instincts. The forest and the city. It's connected, Rebecca."

"I will."

She studied me a moment, her cheery face taking on a somber countenance. "I guess it's true. A summoner," she mused. "Never thought I'd see the day."

"What do you mean, Granny?" I asked.

"'Tis nothin' fer ye to worry about now," she said. Before I could press her, she took a deep breath and held the bottle to her bosom. "Nice seein' ya, Tim-o-thee!"

And with that, she winked out in a tiny burst of silver light.

I sat cross-legged for a moment, pondering her last comments, but realized I'd not get an answer that way. It was no use guessing. The fae were mysterious creatures, and they said crazy stuff all the time. I'd ask Joey about it later. I stood and opened the rolling door so the birds could fly out and considered the more immediate concerns and her remarks about the forest and the city. How did she even know about it? None of it made sense.

"Hey, Becs. Can I have my scroll, please?"

"Oh, yeah. Here you go." I handed Timothy the scroll.

"I'll write you a check."

I hated taking any money from him since I'd gotten as much advice as he had, probably more, but even a summoner had to eat. "Half the amount," I said instead. "Look at the scroll. Does it have what you need?"

He unrolled fully. "It has everything! More than I wanted. Look at this, we have a centaur in our family tree. How cool is that?"

"Very cool."

"Probably explains why we have so many kids. Centaurs are fertile."

"More than I needed to know, TT."

He laughed. "Here's your check. I made it out for three-quarters of the amount. Sounds like you're in a tight spot, but since you got something out of it too, I had to deduct. Balance, you know."

"Thanks, Timothy."

"Take care, Becs."

I always meant to take care, but I'd stopped promising.

Chapter 16

WHEN TIMOTHY LEFT, I bent to retrieve the first sandstone rock, and—*whamo!*—a familiar gold dust emanated from the daisies in the center of the green sheet.

I slammed the storage room door closed and hopped back, leaving everything as it was.

"Ah, Rebecca, I heard you summoning and considered it an invitation," Valefar said, as he materialized in full lion form, except this time his human head and beard made a reappearance.

"I didn't summon you, as you can see by this setup. Since when do you like daisies?"

"Since they die." He grinned like the maniac he was and touched the center of the flowers with a claw. They withered, turning to powder.

He studied me for a moment, his eyebrows pulled so close they touched in the middle above his nose. "Who did you summon?"

"None of your business."

"Daisies, though. Unusual."

"Why do you care?"

His eyes grew wide, and the tips of his fingers rubbed against one another as if he were enjoying the crush of velvet.

"I smell sweet wine," he said.

"Again, what is it to you?"

"I think you may have done it." His nostrils flared like a horse, and his eyes grew wide. "You did it, didn't you?"

Crap. Crap. Why was he here?

"I don't know what you're talking about. Go away. It's not time for me to fulfill our bargain, and I didn't summon you. Begone."

He blinked and then circled the sheet, smelling each rock. "You summoned a fae."

"It's none of your business."

He steepled his fingers. "Oh, it is. It is. So fascinating." He sniffed. "Almost right. So close."

"What do you mean by that?"

"Aspects of your setup are almost like home. I do love the rocks, how they smell of the unrelenting heat."

I exhaled and rolled my shoulders to let out tension, thoroughly exasperated. "Why are you here?"

"I wanted to make sure you know what's on the line, because I think you've forgotten. This is what could be if you don't, how do you say it? Play ball?" He raised a paw, flicked out a claw, and drew a rectangle in the air which formed a floating movie screen.

The movie looked like an old-fashioned film, complete with burned spots, a shaking camera, and the *shuka shuka* noise of what used to be called "the pictures."

My sister was reading Ruthie a book while sitting on their sofa. I recognized the sofa. I'd helped move it into their house. It was a many-flowered thing that I hated but she loved because it matched the sage-green carpet.

"Where's the duck?" she cooed.

Ruthie gurgled something and pointed with a chubby finger at a yellow image I assumed was a duck but was probably coincidence.

"Good girl!"

The doorbell rang, and I leaped forward to stop her from getting it.

"Oh, no, no, Rebecca," clucked Valefar. "You can't stop what's about to happen."

I reached out anyway, but my hand went through the image. "Don't answer it, Mickey. Don't."

"Mickey, can you get it?" Jonah yelled. "I'm about to take a shower."

"No problem, hon," said Mickey.

The doorbell rang again. Two times, more insistent.

I covered my eyes. "No. No. No."

Valefar ripped my hands away with his paws. "Watch!"

Mickey smacked a kiss on Ruthie's head and placed her in a playpen. "Wait a moment," she called.

"No problem!" came a voice from outside the door. "Your sister Rebecca sent me."

Rebecca. She had to know that made no sense. Friends would call me Becs. *Don't fall for it, Mickey!*

"Becs sent you?"

"Yes, Becs," lied the voice smoothly, fixing its mistake.

I wanted to move, but Valefar kept a paw on my shoulder and I stayed fixed to the spot. I watched as Mickey hesitated for a moment.

She put her hands on her hips and squinted at the door. "Who are you?" she asked.

"A friend who knows what Becs does for a living. She was worried about coming over herself, so she asked me to bring you this gift for Ruthie. Baby's First Birdhouse."

Damn. That was good.

"Oh, that's so like her. Hold on." Mickey checked once more on Ruthie, who was now lying down. She opened the door and smiled at the benevolent man standing before her with a shopping bag.

"Here, let me show you," he said.

"I have a locket like that," she said, pointing to his neck. "Exactly like that. Where did you get Becs's locket?"

"That's what I wanted to talk to you about." He opened the locket, and Mickey shrank and twirled, like a genie swirling into a bottle. She was sucked into the locket, captured there forever, to be a toy for Valefar. The demon quietly closed the door, and that was all.

Ruthie slept on, unaware something evil had changed her life forever. Jonah sang in the shower and, if this had happened in real life, he would come down to discover his wife missing and call the police. With no clues, the police wouldn't find anything, and suspicion would fall on him. Ruthie might wind up in foster care. This all played out in my mind as the last of the movie played with the *snicker-snack* of film reaching its end.

"I want Gregory Adamos, Becs. It's a startlingly simple task for someone with your talents." Valefar came within inches of my face, and I wretched. He smiled, flicked out a serpentine tongue, and licked my face from jaw to temple.

"Hurry. It. Up."

Then, with one flash of gold smoke, he was gone.

When my heart stopped tap dancing and my breathing evened out, I got mad all over again. I wondered if my storage rental contract required me to mention "demon infestation," when I quit this cubicle. I cleaned up the mess and lit sage a second time, but I knew I couldn't clean the space spiritually with the amount of anger I held in my heart, not to mention the death magic in my belly. I would have to return at a more peaceful time.

I folded TT's contract and put it in my bag, vowing to make a copy of it as soon as possible. I'd recently decided to make copies of all my contracts, file one at the office, one at my apartment, and then scan them into my computer.

As I stomped to my car, I answered my phone on the first ring, hoping it was Ash because I didn't recognize the number.

"Where is he?" said an irritated male voice.

"Who is this?" I responded with an equally irritated attitude.

"Don't pretend you don't know."

Seriously, what was it with all the men in my life? I needed some women friends.

"Hey, snowflake, I hate to tell you this, but obviously you aren't special enough to me to have imprinted. Who are you and what do you want? Ten seconds or I'm hanging up."

The man snarled. I disconnected the call.

The phone rang again. I turned onto the street and let it go to voicemail. He tried two more times and left two more voicemails. I was intrigued but not enough to stop until I got to an ATM. I deposited Timothy's check, pulled out forty bucks, and drove to a takeout chicken place. I ordered a sandwich, waffle fries, plus a drink, and ate in the parking lot.

Only then did I listen to the messages.

The first was a hang-up.

The second was too.

The third took a slightly different tone.

"This is Nick Adamos. Maybe I'm going about this the wrong way . . . but your friend helped me, and my mind is back. I'm not great, but I'm . . . here. Perrick isn't though. That's the problem. He's my only friend, and he's missing. Gregory said his life is in your hands. What does that mean? Did you hurt him? Why? What did he ever do to you? I have money. I'll pay you any ransom you want. Call me." There was a moment's hesitation, then, "Please."

Perrick was missing?

Did he run away? Was he too sick to work? Had he died? Did Gregory do something to him?

I munched fries while my mind raced. There was only one place where I could get answers about trolls, and I wasn't welcome there. But screw it—they would help or they could kiss my sweet human ass.

Of course, that was the moment the death magic decided to remind me of exactly why I wasn't welcome, stabbing me in the stomach, back, and chest, as if a star had exploded in my torso. I drank some of Mrs. Long's tea from my thermos and took two deep meditative breaths, forcing the magic down. I shoved it back into that pulsating box, this time imagining the type of lock you'd see on a bank vault. I banged the door shut with a clang of metal and spun the lock.

Worry made me press the accelerator hard, and I was lucky there weren't any cops monitoring my route. I parked, said a quick prayer of thanks to whatever guardian angel looked over me, and rolled my neck and shoulders in preparation. This wasn't going to go well.

I opened the door, chin high, and held up an index finger to Joey. "Before you say anything, I need information I can only get here."

"Becs—"

"Before you chew me out about bringing death magic here, I need to explain the reason why."

"It's not—"

"Perrick is sick and missing, and I have to find him. Can anyone here tell me where he might be? Then I promise I'll go."

"For cryin' out loud, would you shut up a moment?" Joey pointed to a table.

There was Perrick, sitting with each foot and each hand in a bucket, blissing out. He looked like he was getting a mani-pedi at a fine salon but instead of sudsy water, he was soaking in dirt.

"Perrick? Big guy? What's the deal?"

He opened his eyes. "Oh, Becs! Thank you so much. Your boyfriend drove all the way to Kansas and brought me home soil. Look!" He gestured with his elbow to an enormous garbage bag on the floor filled to the top with dirt.

"He's a keeper, that one is," said a smaller, female troll who massaged his neck. "He tracked down Perrick's father to make sure he got the exact right soil composition and drove it back here so Perrick could heal." She sighed and batted her eyelashes. "That's dreamy. I want a man as considerate as that."

"He. Drove. To Kansas?" That was the best I could come up with. "He's not really my boyfriend, I don't think." I wiped the sweat off my forehead and pinched my nose to keep from babbling. "I didn't have anything to do with this. Ash did it on his own."

Perrick opened his eyes, and I noticed his skin color was back to a healthy mint green. "I gave him directions to my family's farm, and he drove out there. I can't believe he did that. He saved my life, Becs. I owe him one."

"I can't believe he did it either. Keep the dirt here at Joey's, if you can. If Gregory finds it, he'll destroy it."

He nodded, and the female troll hung on to his neck for dear life. "Joey already said I could. I'm going to act sick around Gregory too, so he isn't suspicious."

"Be careful around him. That man's a piece of work, and your skin looks better, so I'd try to stay out of his sight." I remembered the reason

I was there. "Now, speaking of suspicious, Nick called, accusing me of hurting you. Can you call him and let him know you're okay? He thinks I did something nefarious."

"Oh, that poor kid. You betcha. I'll give him a ring now."

Joey tapped me on the elbow.

"I'm sorry for bursting in like that," I said.

"You'd better be," she snapped, but she handed me a towel as a peace offering. I followed her behind the bar and stacked dishes.

"How have things been?" I asked, struggling for casual.

"Okay. Can't get good help. The pixies don't like getting their nails wet. The trolls are too big, the elves too high on themselves, and Pinky misses you, although I haven't seen him for at least three days."

"I miss him. Where's he been? I got a message to a fae who will let his mom know where he is. I need to talk to him about it."

Joey lifted an eyebrow. "Really? That'd be great. He's a good kid, and these dinky dicks won't give 'im the time of day." She swung her arm wide to indicate everyone in the bar. "The whole lot of 'em think their shit don't stink."

"Does fae shit stink? I thought it would smell like flowers and honey?" It was a legit question.

"Some drink blood, you know. Everybody's shit stinks. Don't let them fool you. Fairy farts will blow your hair back. Bastards."

"Good to know."

Joey pointed to a customer banging his tankard on the bar in an obnoxious request for a refill. I poured a draft of our cheapest ale, charged him premium, and gave him my biggest smile with an eyeful of boob. He tottered to his table a happy fae.

"Now you're catching on," Joey said. "You didn't know what Ash was doing?"

"I had no idea. He left, saying he had something to do, and that was it."

"You still have that death magic in your gut, don't you?"

I made a vodka gimlet with ease and handed it to the Gimlet Girl without so much as a backwards look. "Still in there. Mrs. Long is an herbalist and gave me tea to control it, but I'm not gonna lie, Joey. It's not good. I'm a danger to everyone in here."

She sighed. "Everyone's a danger these days, 'specially that warlock. Can you believe he poked his head in here the other day? Seemed to be looking for someone. No idea who, and I didn't ask. He actually ordered a drink!" She overfilled a draft and had to clean up the foam. "What gall!

Then . . ." She got a new glass and started over. "Then, he acted affronted when I refused to serve him!"

"What happened next?" I made a Manhattan, poured two glasses of red, and placed them on a tray.

"Buster stood up." She flipped the top on a bottle of beer.

"Who's Buster?"

"Remember that baby troll? He's filled out. Intimidating. A moment, please." Joey added the beer to the tray, hoisted it on her shoulder, and carried it to a table. I cleaned a section of the bar top and poured three thimbles of cider for some wee folk who huddled on the counter around a candle. They thanked me for the cider and tugged their itty-bitty hats down over their ears.

Joey returned and dunked empties in a cleaning solution. "Anyway, he took offense with my refusal to serve him and slagged my sundial."

Sure enough, the beautiful, magic sundial smoldered in place, burnt to a crisp. An exquisite piece of enchantment destroyed because that overgrown, magical, murderous toddler had decided to throw a temper tantrum.

Joey approached me, her mouth set and eyes tight at the corners. "Find him, Becs. Find him and kill him. For all of our sakes."

"He thinks he can steal my Kiss."

She grabbed a tumbler, dropped three ice cubes in it, and held it to her forehead. "That's the stupidest thing I've ever heard."

"My opinion as well. I wonder who hit him on the head as a child?"

"This warlock's particularly bad. None are good, but some stay in the shadows and don't interfere in people's lives too much, or they charge an arm and a leg for magical workings and do okay. Most don't have much power, needing to drop a circle to do anything requiring the manipulation of real magical forces. This one's got a chip on his shoulder and the power to do something about it. No one likes the combo."

"What I want to know," the wee one wearing a pointy orange cap said, "is why Oberon doesn't take care of him? A number of the 'homeless' are fae who live here year-round, and the Warlock's taken over the tunnels, pushing everyone out. Oberon's still got a responsibility to take care of us, and he's got enough juice to fry the Warlock's ass."

For some reason that made me laugh. It wasn't the language I expected out of one so tiny.

"Don't let Joey hear you say the Fae King's name. He might show up."

The tiny man slurped his cider with a disbelieving snort.

You've been in the tunnels?" I asked.

"Aye," he said, standing up to his full four inches. "Name's Jimmy, by the way. This here is my twin, Rin." He pointed to the wee one in the yellow cap. "That ugly one there in the striped cap and the straggly beard is Trick."

Jimmy cleared his throat. "What you need to know is that the Warlock doesn't notice little folk, so he doesn't see us comin' and goin', but it stinks down there so we can't stay. He's an odd one, no doubt about it."

"Aye," said Rin. "Smellin' up the place with his dark magic and castin' circles. Mutters to himself like a right nutter, too."

The third of the trio, Trick, stroked his beard and nodded. "Talkin' to a wraith, he is. Bad magic."

I poured them each a refill. "Tell me about the wraith. What exactly is it?"

Trick toasted me with his cider and stroked his beard again, milking the moment.

"The wraith?" I prompted.

"A trapped, tortured spirit," he replied.

"Trapped where?"

Rin piped up. "We don't know, but the Warlock said something about camphor. Maybe he has a rash?"

"Or something wrong with his lungs?" said Jimmy.

Trick smacked them both in their chests. "What's wrong with you two? He didn't say 'camphor.' He said 'vapor.' He was talkin' about the steam around the summoning circle's rocks."

Steam?

"The summoning circle involved fire?" I asked, drumming my fingers on the counter. The wee ones bobbled with the vibration, and Trick tipped over.

"Aye, lots of it," said Jimmy, keeping his cap in place with a hand.

Camphor? Vapor? I stopped drumming and bent to look them in the eye. "Could he have been saying 'Valefar?'"

Rin snapped his fingers. "That's it! That's the word. I knew he didn't have a rash."

Well, sit on a stick and turn me sideways.

Jimmy stood and wiped his hands on his pants. "But as I was sayin' before, I still think Oberon should get involved. It's time. More than time. Overdue. What's that lunk doin' all day in Faerie? Tell the high and mighty king to hop over to the Slow World and give us a hand. We want our accommodations back. UnderTown belongs to everybody."

A she-elf left a table in the far back and stepped up to the counter to get a drink. She was tall and lithe, and utterly gorgeous, with enormous eyes that tilted up at the outer corners. I'd have remembered her if I'd seen her before. She resembled every fantasy drawing of an elf in every card game everywhere. She shushed the small fae. "That's twice you said his name. Don't be bringin' the big O into it. You know better, wee one. Don't say it thrice."

The big O? Now that was a lot to live up to.

Joey harrumphed as well. "What is it with you? Naming the one who shouldn't be named? I've no reason to want *his* attention in my bar. That's more power than I can handle. And every time you mention his name, he hears it."

The death magic flipped in my belly, and I knew it was time to leave, but I had to ask. "Are you saying you can summon Ober. . . I mean, the king, just by saying his name?"

The she-elf's companion, a handsome elf with a Vandyke beard, stepped out of the shadows, followed her to the bar, and took a long pull from his draft. The intensity of his eyes pinned me in place. "Aye, lass, merely by mentionin' his name, he might appear. Best not to do it a'tall. Nobody wants to garner the attention of the king. Best to stay uninterestin'."

"That's for sure," shuddered Joey.

"I'll keep that in mind," I said. "For now, I've got to go."

"Remember what I said," said Joey. "That warlock is a bane on everyone's existence. On magic's existence, itself. You have to find a way to kill him, Becs. I know it's not fair, but this burden seems to have fallen on you. He's involved with your demon."

I walked toward the door, cursing to myself. "Great, first I'm an outcast, now I'm the chosen one. For cryin' out loud, somebody pick their cliché."

"Lass!"

One foot out the door already, I turned to squint at the elf with the vandyke beard. "Yes?"

"The magic didn't kill ye, though it should've." The elf stayed in the back, hidden so I could barely see his profile.

"So?"

"Magic sometimes has a mind of its own."

"What does that mean?"

I didn't get an answer because a light whistle next to my ear made me jump. Then, a voice said, "I think that's up to you."

"What the—!" I lost my balance, and the door slammed behind me. "Pinky! What are you doing here?"

"Hoping to see you. I whistled first, like I promised."

Right. I'd asked him to whistle first, and he'd taken it literally. I had no room to complain because I should have seen that coming. His wings hung lower than before, and dirt streaked his cheeks and chin. He was also noticeably thinner.

"Have you eaten?" I asked.

He shrugged. "I usually eat at Joey's, but I don't like to go there now."

"Why?"

He shrugged again.

"Come on, let's go."

I led him to a small diner, relying on his natural camouflage. "People will still see you as a washed-out skater dude, right?"

"Yes."

We sat at a table for two with the typical ketchup, mustard, salt, pepper, and omnipresent tin napkin holder, plus the little jelly rectangles. I loved those. I snitched a few strawberry ones and tossed them into an outer pocket of my backpack.

"Okay, Pinky. Order whatever you want."

"Nothing with meat." The fairy turned green at the thought of it. "Something with fruit?"

The heavy-set waitress flipped her pad over, chomping gum, but she gave Pinky a kindly smile. "Son, you look like you could use something to fill that growing body. Whatcha want? Burger? Fries?"

"He's vegetarian," I replied. "How about oatmeal with berries and honey?"

She smacked her gum and nodded. "I'll bring walnuts and a large glass of milk, too. I assume you aren't vegan since you're ordering honey, right?"

"That'd be great. Thanks," he said.

"No problem. You want anything?" she asked me.

"I'll wait and join him for dessert."

She grinned. "Good choice. They're all homemade."

I turned my attention to Pinky. "Why aren't you going to Joey's?"

"It's embarrassing." He scratched behind his ear. "The other fae don't like me, and Joey can't protect me all the time."

"What do you do all day?"

He perked up. "My job."

"You have a job?"

"Yes, that's the reason I'm here. My job is to help the fruit trees grow. That's what I do all day. I talk to them and work the soil and make sure they're healthy. I can't help all of them though. Some are too damaged."

"You're a . . . fruit fairy?" I coughed into my hand.

"Yes! Exactly."

"That's an important job."

"That's what my mom says, but I haven't seen her for a long time. I miss her. The other fae laugh when I say that's my job, but I don't know why. What's funny about making fruit grow?"

"Absolutely nothing. I love fruit. Maybe you should say you're a fruit tree arborist. That sounds more technical."

"Hmm. That does sound more sophisticated. I'll try it."

The waitress slid an enormous bowl of oatmeal in front of him, along with the toppings. I showed him what to do, and soon he slurped down the whole bowl. She also provided the obligatory rolls and butter, and he ate all of them. I motioned for him to drink the glass of milk, which he gulped down.

"I talked to a hob, Pinky."

His eyes lit up. "I like hobs. They're helpful. Well, unless you make a mess of their farms, homes, or vineyards." His eyes clouded. "They can get very angry."

"This hob said she'll tell your mom you're okay and are looking for a way home."

"That's nice. I'm sure she's worried."

"Do you think you could be looking in the wrong place? The park is really big."

Pinky furrowed his brows, upset by the question. "I've looked evv-evv-everywhere. Thhisss hasss the appple tttrees." He rocked in the booth, more agitated than I'd ever seen him, and I'd never heard him stutter.

"Calm down, Pinky. Like I said, we'll figure this out. What are your instructions about your work here?"

"Meddddical ccccampus garden. Frrrruit ttttrees because I'm ggggood at them. Help and go hhhhome. I haven't gggone home in a long time. All I want is to gggo hhhome."

The waitress rushed to our table. "What's wrong? Are you hurting him? What are you doing to upset him?"

"I'm not doing anything. I'm trying to help, honestly. Can I talk to you a moment? Pinky, I'll be right back."

I pulled the waitress to the side. "What's your name?"

"Betsy."

"Betsy, this boy is homeless, and I'm working on that. Is there a way I can open a tab so that he can come in here and get something to eat whenever he needs?"

Betsy wrung her hands, looking back and forth. "I don't want to get in trouble, but I hate to see him so distraught. I'll talk to the manager. We'll figure it out. Poor kid. Tell him he can use the washroom in the back to clean up."

"Thanks. Can you bring two apple pie slices?"

I returned to the table, and Betsy brought the desserts immediately. The sugar helped Pinky calm down.

"Pinky, I can't have you sleep at my apartment because the Warlock attacked me there yesterday and it looks like he may be in league with Valefar. Are you safe in the park?"

"Mr. Lincoln looks after me."

"Okay, good."

Betsy crooked her finger at me from across the diner.

"Hold on, Pinky." I walked to Betsy but kept an eye on Pinky.

Betsy's cheeks flushed with anger. "The manager won't let me open a tab for you, but tell him to come to the backdoor tomorrow at five p.m. and I'll give him something."

"That's kind of you."

"Kindness got nothing to do with it. Basic dignity, that's all it is." She glanced in her boss's direction. "Schmuck."

It was funny hearing the Yiddish, but the use was right. What was it going to take to get people to do the right thing for Pinky? Why did everyone look at him and see someone less than deserving of respect?

I pushed the rest of my apple pie in front of Pinky, and he dug in without taking a breath. Spoon to mouth, spoon to mouth. I regretted not getting ice cream to go with it.

"Pinky?"

He nodded, head down, concentrating on his food.

"The waitress who served us? The waitress that gave you milk and bread?" I emphasized that part because bread and milk meant something to fae, and I needed to remind him of it. It worked because he looked at me. I had his attention.

"She is going to meet you at the back door tomorrow." I pointed to it. "At 5:00 p.m. Can you meet her here at that time?"

He returned to shoveling the last of his pie but nodded.

"Good. She'll give you more food, and please make sure you eat it. You need to keep your strength up. Then, go back to the park, sleep, and stay hidden. We're going to figure this out, okay? I promised. And I keep my promises."

Pinky sat back in the booth, his stomach extended as if he'd eaten a basketball. "Okay. I'm so tired. And lonely."

This broke my heart. I wanted to jump in and fix everything immediately, but thoughts of the Warlock, Valefar, and Gregory crowded my mind, and I knew that I had to get those creeps out of the cheap seats of my brain first.

"It's important that you keep under the radar, Pinky. Use your dust if you have to."

"I will, Becs. Thanks for the food."

"Let's go out the back so you know where to meet Betsy later."

I asked Betsy for a plastic bag right before we left, which I shoved in my pocket. The back door led to an alley with a dumpster and smelled awful but had the benefit of being out of sight. With Pinky fed and Perrick sorted—the latter thanks to Asher—my mind was free to go on the attack. I planned on talking to Oded again. He was good at thinking strategically, and maybe he could help me understand my vision. There had to be something there I could tease out, a clue to find.

I jumped as something tickled my foot. Pinky watched the creature scuttle away with an air of mild academic interest.

"That rodent is a Norway rat. They're common around here, especially near food dumpsters. Did you know that they can live up to two years and produce up to one hundred young?"

"That's fascinating. Pinky, could I borrow a handful of fairy dust?"

He crossed his arms and jutted out his chin. "Whatcha gonna do with it? You're going to do something dangerous?"

"It will be less dangerous if you give me some dust."

"What is it?"

"Pinky. Please?"

He crossed his arms tighter and squished his eyes together.

"Okay, fine." I blew out a big breath. "I'm sneaking into the tunnels to learn more about the Warlock. I think he may be tied to Valefar somehow."

Pinky opened his eyes wide. "That would be bad."

"Yes. That's why I need to be invisible, so I don't get caught."

Pinky lifted a wing and motioned for my plastic bag. He shook out a cup full or so of dust. "Be careful."

Why did everyone say that to me?

Then Pinky threw his arms around me in a brief, almost not there, awkward hug and disappeared.

Chapter 17

SNOOPING WAS AN honored pastime, especially when life and limb were on the line.

The entrance to the Warlock's lair—big eye roll—appeared unprotected, which meant that it wasn't. I needed a guide.

I thought for a moment about what I was about to do. I wouldn't have tried it if I hadn't successfully summoned Mildread Purplefeather. I could always try asking them face-to-face, but I didn't have time to go all the way back to the bar, and they might have already left anyway.

Squatting in a shadowed corner out of the breeze, I placed a few grains of Pinky's dust on a tissue and whispered the wee ones' names. I made the summons a polite request to which they could say no, but I made sure to add, "I have fairy dust here as payment."

Pop! All three little men appeared and huddled in the corner so no one could see them.

"Whatcha want?" asked Jimmy, as he shoved fairy dust into his pocket. All three snatched up the fairy dust as fast as possible.

"Guess the fairy dust is a good offering?"

"Being invisible at times is useful," said Trick. "But we ain't promisin' you anythin'. This is payment for comin' at all. Fae aren't dogs that come when you whistle, you know."

"I understand and am willing to offer something else in trade for what I want."

"Well, what is it you want?" asked Rin as the last of the dust went into his shirt pocket.

"I need you to guide me into UnderTown to the place you saw the Warlock. I'll make us all invisible so he won't see us, but I'll get in there faster if you tell me where to go. And I know you can see the traps."

The three chattered among themselves, their voices so high-pitched it hurt my ears and registered as a teeth-rattling squeal.

"Well?" I asked before my ears bled.

"We'll help you, but we want something in return," said Trick.

"What?"

"A home," said Rin.

"A what?"

"A home," repeated Trick, as if I were deaf. "We've been driven out of UnderTown, and in any place we go aboveground, a fox or bird tries to eat us. We want someplace warm and safe. We're cold even in the summer, and the winters here are awful."

"We want to live with you." Jimmy took off his cap and held it to his heart, his fuzzy hair blowing in the wind. He looked like he was about to cry.

"Oh, no, you can't live with me. That's impossible."

"We're tired, Ms. Rebecca," Rin said. "A warm, safe place then. Please."

Everyone needed a home. How could I turn them down? "I'll find you a safe and warm place to live. I promise you that."

Jimmy and Rin high-fived each other, but Trick narrowed his eyes at me. "Pinky swear you'll follow through on your end of the bargain."

I held out my pinky, which was a million times bigger than theirs.

"No, no, no!" said Trick, stomping his tiny foot. "I mean, promise on your friendship to Pinky. That's a promise you'll honor."

Wow, these guys knew how to bargain.

"I promise, on my friendship to Pinky, that I will follow through on my end of the bargain . . . if you do your part now."

They nodded, their faces solemn, and said as one, "We so swear."

Somewhere in the distance, a bell tolled. A fae bargain made and acknowledged.

"I need info, and I need your help to get it. You've been in the tunnels before and have seen the Warlock's workspace."

They nodded.

"We'll be invisible thanks to Pinky's dust, but you guys can point out the wards along the way and help me avoid them, right?"

"That's my job," said Trick, pointing to his chest with his thumb.

"Alrighty then."

I blew pixie dust over all three of us and approached the door. The "caution" tape was already ripped off the entrance to what once was the Carmel Street stop, but when I jiggled the handle, the door was locked. Such a simple thing, and I was already stymied.

"I got this," said Jimmy. "Locks are my thing. Hold me up next to the keyhole." Jimmy and Rin sat on my left shoulder, Trick on my right. Jimmy tight-roped down my arm and stood in my open palms. He produced a tiny toothpick and stuck in in the lock, humming and hawing.

"Can you open it?" I whispered, hoping no one could hear me.

"Just a minute, lass! Don't pressure me while I work." He jiggled it some more. "Hmm, that's it . . . right there . . . a little left . . . and done!"

The door swung open, and Jimmy ran up my arm to my shoulder looking pleased with himself. Rin gave him a fist bump.

"Thanks, Jimmy. That was awesome."

Noxious fumes filled the entranceway, and we stood to the side for a full minute letting the air clear out before we ventured in, closing the door behind us. Even letting that initial reek out didn't help the overall air quality. We walked down the stairs to the platform with its nonfunctioning ticket machines and jumped the turnstiles. I removed my keychain from my bag and pressed the tiny little button on my mini-flashlight.

"What's the use of being invisible if you're gonna use that thing?" asked Trick.

"What's the use of coming down here if I fall off the platform and break a leg?" I responded. "Which way?"

"Follow your nose."

I sniffed, and it was obvious. I sat on the side of the track and flipped to my belly, then jumped down, being careful not to hit the first rail. The wee ones had gotten off my shoulders and scampered down on their own. Once down, they asked me to pick them back up, and they resumed the ride.

Keeping the light only a step or two ahead of us, I put my back to the wall and crept along the northbound tunnel. The air grew thick with the stench of rot and, as we got closer, smoke. We picked our way around all kinds of debris. Paper bags, boxes, plastic wrappers, discarded clothing, a broken umbrella, a mattress, a stool, a hand-crank radio, and lots of water bottles. The detritus of life—and of the people who'd fled when the Warlock moved in.

What we didn't encounter was more of a concern. There were no rats. No rodents of any kind. Thinking about Pinky's comments about the common Norway rat, I had to wonder, what had happened to them all?

Jimmy retched, as did his twin, and even stout-hearted Trick gagged. "Breathe in through your mouths," I said. "It's supposed to help."

Terrible advice. Warm, regurgitated cider dripped down my back.

"Sorry, Becs," whispered Jimmy. "I couldn't hold it in."

"'S okay," I managed to say, not doing much better myself.

"Stop!" said Trick. "Ward."

"Where?"

"Turn off the light."

I did, and we plunged into darkness. Trick ran down my arm and swung to the ground, and I froze in my tracks, not wanting to accidentally step on him. A moment later a pale-blue sigil floated in front of me like a spider's web, reaching from one side of the tunnel opening to the other. Trick tugged at my pant leg, and I scooped him up.

"A barrier," whispered Trick in my ear. "A catch-me ward."

"Can we disable it?"

"No, but you see that wide spot in front of us, on the left?"

Sure enough, there was a gap on the left side. "If I kneel, I can crawl through."

"Exactly, but don't hit the webbing," Trick warned. "It will let him know someone is here. We'll go first."

Trick, Rin, and Jimmy jumped through with no problem at all. Like they'd said, the Warlock didn't consider wee folk a danger. With flashes of every spy movie I'd ever seen going through my brain, I crouched and duck-walked to the gap, then kneeled, placed my hands far in front of me, ducked my head, folded my chest down as if I were doing downward dog, and slithered my way through.

We waited on the other side. No alarms. Nothing happened. We'd made it.

A low light emanated from up ahead, so I kept my flashlight off. We progressed slowly so Trick could keep an eye out for more wards. Maybe six feet farther, the ground became mushy and uneven. It felt like I was walking uphill, and then it became impossible to go farther because I was sinking down into this shifting mass. When my hand touched it, I jumped to the middle of the tunnel, ripping out my flashlight and turning it toward where I'd just been.

Dead rats. Dead mice. Dead everything.

I'd wanted to know what had happened to the rats? Well, here they were. Hundreds of them, lining the sides, tumbling out onto the tracks.

He'd killed them all, just as he'd killed my birds. What was it with this guy and helpless little animals?

The wee men asked if they could climb in the pockets of my knapsack, and I motioned for them to do so. I'd hide my head too, if I could. They'd gotten me here. I couldn't ask for more.

Low grunting drew me closer to the light, and after another fifty paces, I emerged at another stop. I stayed low in the tracks, but the Warlock was up on the platform. The smoke and wind blew in a widdershins circle, indicating a summoning. A croaking voice, so low I could barely hear it, came to me on the casting currents. Quietly as possible, I grabbed a discarded lawn chair and stood on it so I could peek over the edge.

The Warlock stood in front of his casting circle, burgundy and orange light swirling counter-clockwise, fire licking at the figure within, and the demon, or what was left of it, looked like a ghost torn at the seams.

The demon ghost, a wraith, spoke first.

"Can't last much longer, Derrick. The bastard's thrown me over the ledge so many times."

"Understood. I will get you back. I promise." The Warlock's voice was hoarse but vehement.

"She will not help you."

"No. But I'm not asking her this time, Father. I'm taking. I asked her once, in high school. She turned me away." He paused. "She wouldn't help anyway, if she knew what I've done."

Panic hit the wraith's voice. "Valefar comes. Drop the circle."

The Warlock broke his circle, and the fire extinguished on its own. I ducked and hid from sight, but it was too late.

"Who's there?"

"Run," said Rin, from my backpack. "Go back the way we came."

I flicked my flashlight on and ran down the tunnel, but I could feel the Warlock behind me.

"Hurry," said Rin. "Run faster!"

I didn't answer and tried to run faster, but I caught my foot on something and landed flat on my face, sending white shocks of pain through my body. Three little men climbed over me and tugged at my hair.

"Becs," said Rin. "Get up. Please. Up. Up!"

I heaved myself to my feet, the wee ones swinging in my hair, grabbed my backpack, and kept moving.

Rin tugged my earlobe. "There. To the left. You see that round door marked 'Security?'"

I nodded.

"Open it."

I did as he said and clambered inside. I turned to close the door and saw the Warlock's fingers curled around the edge, prying it back.

"Leave it, Becs," Rin urged. "Crawl!"

Woozy from my fall, I crawled, but I knew I wasn't moving fast enough. The Warlock's voice chased me in the darkness.

"Father. That's my father you saw, Rebecca. He's trapped in Hell, but I will get him out. With your Kiss."

Panting, I managed to shout over my shoulder. "What did you mean you asked me in high school? If I had known about your dad, I might have helped you."

His voice grew closer. "I *tried* to ask. Derrick Vance. Does that name sound familiar? I asked you to help me. I tried to get you alone so I could explain, but you refused."

Oh my God, that little dweeb who drove me crazy in high school was the Warlock.

"Dude, I didn't know your *science project* was making a deal with a demon to release your father from Hell!"

Rin whispered in my ear. "The tunnel splits. Turn right. Then there's a slight drop."

I turned as he said and fell down a trash chute into a commercial garbage container.

"Remember what you promised," Trick said. He and his brothers stood on my stomach to make sure they had my attention. My stomach gurgled and they swayed, arms out, but stubbornly stayed in place.

"Give me time to handle this mess, and I'll find you a warm, safe place to live," I said, as I picked pasta out of my hair. I couldn't even smell anything by this time. My brain was so overloaded, it had super-fried and shorted out.

At least I didn't hear the Warlock behind me.

Chapter 18

I'D BEEN DAMN lucky that dumpster was full. My landing, while humiliating, was soft. My three co-conspirators winked out of existence with another firm warning that they'd be back to collect on my promise, and I scrambled out of the dumpster, still invisible, and limped to my car.

I'd left Betsy with a twenty to pay for Pinky's food and promised I'd drop off more, although she'd protested, saying she'd be throwing out the food anyway. I returned to my car filthy, smelly, and bruised, but feeling pretty good. I'd made sure Pinky was fed, Perrick had home soil, and I had a little money in the bank.

I mean, there were a few negatives, but a girl couldn't have everything. Three garbage bags of dead birds. The Sixth Duke of Hell had *licked* me. Death magic in my innards. A homicidal warlock, who apparently held a grudge from *high school*. Gregory Adamos thought he was all that and a bag of chips, and I apparently needed to buy a toasty dollhouse.

But—from a certain point of view—I'd made progress.

I pulled into my parking space and ran up the back, opened the door, and locked it behind me. The garbage smelled horrible, and I knew I'd have to take it out the side. Why did I always do that?

I dragged the garbage out into the hallway and again ran into the stunning pectoral muscles of my upstairs neighbor, as if he hung outside my door with his trash, waiting for me to come out.

"Hi, Becs. Whew! That garbage really stinks this time. How long did you let it go?"

"Do you have a camera or something in your apartment that tells you when I'm tying up my trash so you can rush right down here and bump into me?"

"No, but it would be within my rights, given that you've been stealing my Wi-Fi for months."

Oh.

"You spying on me isn't equivalent to me *shnoring* off some Wi-Fi," I said.

"*Shnoring?* Is that Yiddish?" We both bounced our trash bags down the stairs.

"Yeah, to sponge off of, to freeload."

He opened the door at the bottom of the steps. "I'm not spying. I only got home a little while ago."

I motioned for him to keep holding the outside door, and I grabbed his bag and took it to the dumpster. I threw it in, then mine, and wiped my hands on my pants. "Yeah, about that. Thanks. I saw Perrick today. Did you really drive all the way to Kansas, find his creep, and bring back soil?"

He tilted his head. "A group of trolls is a creep?"

"Yup. A flock of geese. A herd of sheep. A creep of trolls."

"Hmm. I didn't know." He ushered me in before him, then closed the door and headed back up the stairs.

He fluttered his hands in the air, trying to find the right words. "I became furious when I saw Gregory treating him so badly. I knew you didn't want me to interfere, but I had to do something. I'm sorry I didn't tell you, but I thought it was best, so you'd have deniability if asked. I didn't tell my co-workers, either. I took the time off, drove all the way there, used Perrick's instructions on how to find his family—uh, creep—explained the issue, and they gave me the dirt. I brought it back as fast as I could."

"How did you get in touch with Perrick?"

"I called Gregory's work number, and Perrick answered."

"Smart."

We reached the third floor, and Ash followed me to my door. "Uh, Becs? You have a lot of mail on your doormat, and that garbage smell is clinging to you."

"I know about the mail. Kenneth drops it off for me. I always forget to collect it."

"Some of these letters look important." He picked them up.

"Let's go inside and see what they are. I need more tea and a shower." My stomach was reminding me of my priorities, and my mail wasn't one of them.

"Here," Ash said, handing me the envelopes.

"Hold on." I made the tea as quickly as possible, but even waiting for the water to heat was taking too long. I dumped two teaspoons of sugar in a mug, added the tepid water with the tea, and gulped it down in three long swallows and then put the kettle back on to actually boil.

"I want to hear about everything that you've been doing and how you're feeling, Becs," Ash called from the other room. "But I think you need to look at some of these letters."

"Let me wash up first."

A quick shower and a change of clothes later, I had my second cup in hand and was studying Ash as he rifled through my mail, his back to me. He was so beautiful. He'd pulled his hair into a loose pony at the nape of his neck. It should have made him look feminine, but his broad shoulders and narrow waist negated that impression. He wore low-slung jeans, a white T-shirt, and an open blue button-down short-sleeved shirt. He'd kicked off his tennis shoes, now nicely muddied after tromping around the Kansas plains. I was glad to see he was human, after all.

The teapot whistled, and I made my second mug, blowing on it because it was now too hot. I placed the mug on a bookshelf to cool. Acting on instinct, I came up behind him and hugged him, my cheek to his back, sliding my hands under his blue shirt and clasping them around his waist. I inhaled the scent of him and closed my eyes. He smelled of vanilla and cinnamon, and he was warm and wonderful. He made me want to curl up in his arms and go to sleep.

He clutched his hands to mine, gripping them tightly as if he didn't want to lose them and dropped his chin to his chest. Slowly, he turned in my arms and embraced me, nuzzling the top of my head with his chin, whispering words I didn't understand but didn't need to know.

I moved my head to gaze up at him, and he stroked my cheek with the back of his right index finger, bringing his left hand to hold the back of my neck. I closed my eyes, and he kissed my eyelids, then laid soft, butterfly kisses down the side of my face before his lips hit mine.

I drank from him as if I were dying and he was life itself. For a moment in time, there was nothing but us, the feel of our bodies together, his heat, my need, our hearts and breath in synchrony. I bit the edge of his lower lip, and he groaned into me, pulling me tighter against him, and I let go of his waist to entwine my right hand in his hair, something I'd wanted to do from the moment I'd met him. It begged for my fingers, and I used my grasp to deepen our kiss, something I wouldn't have thought possible, but somehow it happened. My left hand slid up his back so I could play with his muscles, and I rubbed the heel of my hand between his shoulder blades.

His left hand gripped my neck harder with increased urgency, and his right cupped my breast, playing with my nipple. I panted with need, wanting more, wanting it now.

"My bedroom," I said.

He pushed me away, his eyes large, and brought his hands to his mouth. "We can't."

I couldn't believe what he was saying. "Why?"

"Not . . . it's not right." He blinked furiously, as if clearing his brain. "We have to focus. You need rest, and we have to concentrate on what's happening to your body. We don't know if the death magic can spread, or what will happen if you're intimate with someone. And what if Valefar senses you with . . . with . . . me. This can't happen."

Without so much as a backwards glance, he dashed out the door, leaving me hot, horny, and embarrassed as hell.

I shambled to my bedroom, stripped, and dressed in my most faded pj's. Humiliation burned through me. I curled up in bed hugging a pillow to my stomach and mentally cursed myself, thinking how stupid I was to show my feelings. I made a vow to avoid my upstairs neighbor at all costs. I'd even disconnect my Wi-Fi, because who needed him anyway? I dove under the covers and pulled them over my head like a turtle, trying to hide my embarrassment from the world, although no one was looking. I hadn't even told him about the Warlock.

Eventually, I calmed down and logic prevailed. He'd returned my kiss with equal fervor. He hadn't rejected me. He'd been afraid. Concerned—and he was right to be.

What had I been thinking? I should concentrate on the death magic, the Warlock, and Valefar. And though I yearned for the safety and pleasure of an Asher cocoon, he was completely correct that I had no idea if the death magic could infect him, and I didn't want Valefar to feel my attraction to him. The demon would use it against me, the way he was using my love for my sister and niece against me already. It was time to woman up and solve these problems so I could get on with my life, whatever that was going to be. Only then could I determine if Ash would be a part of it.

I cuddled an old teddy bear and flipped on my left side. I kicked the covers off and rearranged them, but still, sleep didn't come. I decided I might as well do something useful, so I turned on a light and gathered my mail. The first envelope was the reminder that I owed two hundred dollars for speeding. The second, a reminder that I owed two hundred dollars for running a red light. *Ugh.* I was in for four hundred dollars? Oh, no, that wasn't all. I knocked my head against the wall. I opened a third envelope to discover I owed another two hundred and fifty dollars for reckless driving. Six hundred and fifty dollars. I had to wonder if going to court and paying court fees would be worth it. The only reason to go would be to reduce the number of points on my license. I decided I'd have to attend when I looked up the possible number of points. Wow, my insurance rate was going to take one hell of a hit, and I could forget all about accident forgiveness. That had been used up during the small Max "abracadabra-ing my car" incident, of which we do not speak.

I also marveled at the speed at which the Department of Motor Vehicles had mailed me these citations. They were unusually on top of things.

I shuffled through the rest of the mail, tossing the usual marketing. Somebody wanted me to get a fantastic set of knives. Somebody else offered me a deal on a television set, a new roofer was in the area—useless, since I lived in an apartment—and the *halal* place offered a discount on falafel. Coupons for a grocery store, an offer for ten tango lessons—now that was interesting—and a fabulous "buy one, get one free" deal on support hose. I chucked them all except the falafel.

The last was a white linen envelope with no return label, but the address appeared to be handwritten. I knew that could be mechanically created, so I doubted it was real. I debated tossing it for a millisecond but then decided to open it, just in case it had anything to do with the car accident. I hoped it wasn't another ticket.

It was worse. The man whose car I'd hit had hired a law firm and was now suing me for five hundred thousand dollars for medical bills, as well as pain and suffering. How was this possible? The accident happened four days ago!

Walter Hart, a founding partner of Hart & Wells Litigation, wrote to inform me that this poor individual had experienced severe impairment to his spine and neck, resulting in everything from migraines to hip pain, for which he had to seek treatment from several private hospitals. He had been unable to work, and his family, including his four children all under the age of ten, were in danger of losing their home, car, and other worldly possessions. His wife had fallen ill from the stress and was unable to work as well and had taken a leave of absence from her position as a nurse practitioner at the local pediatric medical center.

What? He hadn't also lost his loyal golden retriever and his pet cat? His goldfish hadn't died?

It took me exactly one minute and fifty-three seconds to discover that Gregory Adamos sat on the board of Hart & Wells Litigation. That rat bastard muck-sucking sneak. It probably explained the speed of the DMV as well, as I was certain he had fingers in every aspect of governance.

I was so damn tired. I tossed the letter aside and laughed out loud. My day had been ridiculous. If I wrote it in a novel, no one would believe it.

I lay on my back and checked my phone. I debated sending an "I love you," message to Mickey but didn't. Doing something like that in the middle of the night to a Jewish mom wasn't a good idea. That was reserved for your last words as the plane goes down. I propped the phone up on my nightstand so I could see it from my bed and adopted my most comfy position.

Valefar wanted Gregory for some unknown reason.

Gregory wanted a demon to do something for him but didn't want Valefar.

The Warlock wanted my Kiss and my job. He also needed to free his father from Valefar and had a personal ax to grind.

The key had to be Valefar. He was the only consistent element in this daisy chain of despair.

I focused on the death magic. Why did it keep coming out of me and then going back in? Was it trying to escape but couldn't? Did it want to be released? The elf in the bar had said that magic sometimes had a mind of its own.

What if I could make a deal?

Chapter 19

ONCE I'D GOTTEN the Kiss as a young teen, sleeping became a contact sport. A lot of creepy-crawlies want access to your hindbrain, and they use nightmares as a highway to Hell, or Gehenna, or Sheol, or Hades, the Netherworld, Niflheim, or Avernus. Your choice of name. It was a pick-your-own-menu kind of restaurant. A little from column A, a smidgeon from column B, then add in an ounce of whatever humiliation your teenage brain had experienced at school that day, and voila!

I had nightmares that nightmares were scared of. When monsters dreamed, they didn't have dreams this bad. Bogeymen slept more peacefully, and they carried hockey sticks and chainsaws with them.

One of the first things those who were Kiss Born learned to do was shield. It was critical to our very sanity. My meager training had started with this lesson, and by now, it was automatic. Usually.

Not tonight. Tonight, someone was in here with me.

I couldn't explain it while awake if I tried, but we've all experienced it. Waking dreaming. I was out like a light. If anyone had walked into the room, I wouldn't have noticed and I'd appear fast asleep, dead to the world. But inside my head, the battle for my body and mind raged.

It started as a Shadow, menacing, lurking, and stalking me wherever I went. I turned, and the Shadow was there. I couldn't see it head on, only when I looked at it sideways, out the corner of my eye. It flitted in and out of my perception, and I tried to ignore it, but the Shadow toyed with me. I ran faster and slowed down. I took refuge in a green space and it retreated, but when I felt safe and moved, it found me again and winked. The Shadow was patient, like a cat, and persistent. It had all the time in the world.

Correct. You aren't waking up.

Indeed, I wasn't. I tried to move, to tell my body to wake up, but I couldn't.

I swallowed hard and reminded myself this was a dream and that once my body finished REM, I would wake up. I always did.

Hopeless. Not this time.

I told myself not to listen to it. The Shadow lied, just like the tooth nightmare monster who tore my teeth out when I was thirteen, discarding them on the bathroom tile floor like lost dice from an old Dungeons and Dragons game. That monster had laughed while I bled from my gums and swallowed my fear, mumbling through mouthfuls of dripping, bloody saliva that, "This isn't real. It can't take my power."

It lied like the wraith who'd visited me two years later at age fifteen, demanding I let it into my house to murder my family.

It didn't get through, though. I stopped it.

Liar. What about the specter?

I trembled with fear. That was the one monster, the only one, I wasn't sure about. I thought I'd stopped it, but I held a sliver of doubt. I may have only pushed it away. The neighbor's baby boy got sick that night, very sick. He hadn't died, but the grandfather had, and I'd always wondered if the old man had sacrificed himself instead. I'd never known for certain.

Hypocrite. You know the truth.

It didn't matter. What was done was done, and it was a long time ago. I was young and only partially trained. I'd sought forgiveness for that and was right with myself and God.

Fraud. To make it right, you have to apologize to the person you wronged. How can you do that with a dead person?

Go away, Shadow. You know nothing.

Fool. I know everything, and soon you will, too.

It's time to wake up. Come on, body, let's go.

Nothing happened.

Quaint. It's laughable you don't understand yet. You're stuck here forever—in between and nowhere. I'll be interested to see who visits a Kiss Born. My deepest wish is to have the Kiss, and I will take it from you. In the meantime, I wonder what you dream about. Guess I'll get to see.

The Shadow withdrew, and only then did I recognize that he spoke with the Warlock's crazy speech pattern. The Warlock—*damn him*—had opened the door to my greatest nightmares and invited himself for a sleepover.

Accurate. I'm interested in something. And since you invited yourself into my space, now I'm invading yours.

What?

Contract. You have a signed, executed contract in your bag.

So?

Mine. I'm taking it. Have fun.

How is this possible?

Easy. I'm dream walking, and your mind is mine tonight. I can do anything I want mentally, including rifling through your brain to see what you carry with you, where you are right now.

Whoosh! I fell down a hole in the floor, my hands flung out to the sides, my mouth opened in a wordless scream, and the walls closed in tighter and tighter until I couldn't breathe . . . .

The specter roared in my face only an inch from my nose with fetid breath, laughing at me. "I killed the grandfather as he begged for mercy, and I'll be back for the child's child. Every other generation, doomed because of you." I gasped . . . .

Then I swallowed a mouthful of hornets that clogged my mouth and stung my throat. The rest crawled into my eyes and laid eggs, which burst open with babies that crept up my nose and . . .

The tooth monster loomed in front of me with enormous bloody pliers and cackled, "Open wide" and reached into my mouth to extract my molars . . . .

And when my teeth fell out, I tried to push them back in, but the wraith wrapped its cold arms around me and whispered in my ear, "Open the door and you don't have to feel anything anymore. I'll take them, not you. One short twist of the doorknob." I screamed, my teeth in my hands. . . .

And my sister ran in to help me, but before I could warn her, the wraith leaped for her face, smothering her right before my eyes while I shrieked. But no one came to help us, not my mother, not my father, no one, no one, no one, no one . . .

Fascinating. No mother. No father. You and your sister, abandoned against the horrors of the night. There it is. The key to what makes you tick, Rebecca.

Shut up, Warlock.

Alone. So alone. I know you, now. What you're afraid of in your heart.

The Warlock withdrew, but still, I couldn't wake. My body lay frozen in bed, while my spirit lay in the in-between, the nothingness, the space of dreams and nightmares, where the monsters and leviathans lived, trapped. I swam in circles looking for a way out, but sharks surrounded me, and when I considered swimming through them, I suddenly developed an injury on my side that trailed blood in the water.

I reached toward a light and sank when an anchor tied to my leg weighed me down. I swam down toward a tunnel and hit a glass wall. I thrashed this way and that, desperately searching for a way out, losing air, until a glass coffin with a hole for my face clapped around me, and I banged my hands against the glass to get out. I floated to the murky top, where a giant eye studied me. I dragged in a breath and sank. This repeated every sixty seconds, enough to keep me alive but imprisoned in a sea of fiends who batted me around like a cat toy.

Time lost meaning as I bobbed to the surface and sank again.

I waited, certain I'd wake, turning inward, counting to one hundred, then one hundred again, tuning out the hallucinations of my dreams, reminding myself that as soon as the light came on, they couldn't hurt me.

The leviathans laughed uproariously at this thought and proved it to me by lifting me to the sun and letting me burn.

I screamed, and the creatures below handed me to the creatures of the sky, birds with razor-sharp talons and beaks, who ripped out my liver and ate it like they'd done to Prometheus and chattered to me while they did so.

"We haven't had fresh meat in ages," said one.

"Good to see a new one," said the second.

"I'm definitely hallucinating now," I panted. "But why does it hurt so much?"

"Because it's real," said the first giant bird, an eagle, but not like one I'd ever seen. This would have been an eagle if it had copulated with a bald giraffe. It had a long neck and legs and wings to match, but no feathers. "You're stuck in the middle, not here nor there, where night-mares exist, pushed out of your body to exist with us."

"I'm dying."

"No," said the second, tearing a long slice from something inside me. The piercing of my insides made a loud painful pop, and blood spurted in the air like a tiny geyser. But once she tore the tissue, I couldn't feel it. I wondered how I still conversed at all.

"No," the second repeated. "I'm afraid you're not dying. You can't do that here." She winked. "You're going to have to wait until someone saves you."

A red thread on my wrist twanged, catching my attention. What was that? It pulsed and drew my attention to a gold glow that emanated from my wrist which grew bigger and bigger, like a balloon. Before long, the gold dragon from my bracelet filled my vision and stared deep into my eyes.

"Are you waiting until someone saves you?" it said to me. "No one is coming."

I groaned in agony as the birds reached what felt like my intestines.

I squirmed as hard as possible to get away from them, but I was tied down, hands above my head, feet stretched out.

"Lay still!" the birds said.

The dragon flapped a wing and spoke in my mind. "Waiting for someone to save you is a sucker's game. Standing still is death. Moving is survival."

The dragon was right, and I was tired of this shit.

"Hey, Eleven Spices."

Two ugly bald heads with long hooked beaks lifted themselves out of my abdomen, pieces of my guts dangling from their beaks. "You talking to us?" croaked the first one.

"Well, I'm calling you Extra Crispy. She's Eleven Spices, but it's all the same. Try my stomach. I ate some delicious eggs before I fell asleep."

"Yeggies?" said Extra Crispy.

"Since you invited us," said Eleven Spices.

The two gargantuan bald, literally, eagles sidled closer to my head, the smell of bird poo clinging to their backsides, making me retch. They tore my skin another two inches and dove into my stomach like kids on Christmas morning, or, like what I'd always thought kids looked like on Christmas morning. What they looked like on TV, anyway. What kids did to presents on Hannukah. Let's go with that.

Minus the excruciating pain.

And the blood.

And the death magic.

I felt for the death magic, but it was awfully quiet. I took a chance and spoke to it in my mind.

Was this what you were meant to do? Kill someone from the inside out over a long period of time? Watch them suffer at the hands of a black magician?

The death magic shifted in my gut, like in-laws faced with an uncomfortable question at Thanksgiving.

You haven't beaten me yet, and you're not going to. But you can't escape, either. I'm offering a job. Come work for me. Be a weapon where it matters. Death is dispassionate, right? It comes to everyone eventually, but magic can work for good or for evil.

The magic squirmed again, but it listened.

You can't be neutral any longer. You must pick a side. Your purpose is death, but your magic involves some free will. I can sense it here in the Nightmarescape. Help me. Please.

A few beats of hesitation, then the death magic responded to my will, and when my new tormentors tore into it, the magic tore back, piercing them through the throats, pinning them to the rock. I ordered a shard to cut through my binds, and after it did so, it returned to my hand shaped as a fine hunting bow.

I stood, fully healed. The rest of the death magic circled above my head and settled as arrows in a quiver on my back.

Every eye in the Nightmarescape turned to me.

I nocked an arrow and took out my old tooth monster in one shot with a second hitting the wraith dead center immediately after. Both fractured into a million pieces and disintegrated into dust.

"Will someone kindly show me the way out?"

A bloodsucking tentacled creature pointed with one long, wriggly arm toward an exit that I could now see. I walked through it, made sure it was closed securely behind me, and crashed into my unmoving body.

I opened my eyes and found myself on my bed, able to see, breathe, and swallow. My death magic arrows lay on my bed next to me with the bow, but I could not move my body.

Don't panic.

My body didn't get that message. My heart pounded in my ears, and my eyesight grew dim, but I still couldn't move. Inside I was screaming, but no sound came out.

I'm going to die. I'm going to die right here, and Valefar and the Warlock will win, and I'll never see Ruthie or Mickey again. Pinky will be trapped forever.

Forever, forever, forever.

The words echoed through my mind like a bullet train, and all I could do was follow, inside mewling like a kitten, outside still as a stone.

Until the funniest thing happened. I became aware that I had to pee.

I *really* had to pee. My bladder was close to bursting, and suddenly I had the urge to laugh, because when you gotta take a leak, you can't focus on anything else.

I gulped air and let out a sigh of relief that I'd made it out of the Nightmarescape and then did an internal high-five that my gamble with the death magic had worked. I looked at my clock and noticed I'd missed a call. I didn't recognize the number.

Now, what to do about my body.

Extreme sleep paralysis was understandable, given the circumstances, I reasoned. I rolled my eyes to my phone and could see it was early. No one would be looking for me yet. What I needed to do was convince my body that I was awake or relax and fall into regular sleep so I'd be rested in the morning. Since I knew that second option was unlikely at the moment, I focused on the first by running through multiplication tables, but that didn't get me far because I sucked at math.

I mentally reviewed the drink menu at Joey's.

I practiced counting to ten in French, Spanish, and Hebrew. The pressure on my bladder continued to mount.

I mentally pictured the best routes to get through the city. After an hour without moving, I stopped worrying that the Warlock would come to the apartment to dispose of my body and I wouldn't be able to defend myself and started worrying that he'd come and I'd have embarrassed myself.

The phone rang again, and it was the same number as before. Stupid robocalls.

More time passed as I waited for the sleep paralysis to wear off, proving this situation was magic-induced. Sleep paralysis usually lasted only a few seconds. Pressure built against my lower stomach until I wished I'd leak, just to relieve it. The sun lifted higher in the sky, and my phone rang, but the caller didn't leave a message.

Kenneth knocked.

"Becs? You in there? I see your car is in the driveway. Did you hear the news? You must have by now. Anyway, stop downstairs when you can." He hesitated, shuffling at the door. "I'm really sorry."

Hear the news? What news? Sorry for what?

The phone rang a third time from the same number, and this time, the caller left a message. Now I was aggravated and needed to know what was happening. I concentrated on my death magic arrows and found they didn't respond as well as they did in the Nightmarescape. But they did respond. I urged one of the arrows to inch out of the quiver and it did, a wiggle forward, then another.

Come on, you damn thing, poke me in the toe. Make it hurt.

A text flashed across my phone. "The studio burned to the ground. Sorry to tell you this way. Tried to reach you. Oded is in the hospital. Zara."

The arrow stabbed me in my foot, and I leaped out of bed with a roar.

Ash banged on my door. "Becs? What's wrong? Let me in."

"Hold on!" I dove for the bathroom and did my thing, to my vast relief. Then I hobbled to the door, yanked it open, and waved Ash in. I dialed the phone with my other hand. "Zara? It's Becs. What happened? What do you mean, Oded is hurt?"

"Oh, Becs, I tried to reach you. I called but you didn't answer.

Someone set fire to the floral shop next door to the studio. It spread to the gym, and Oded was inside. The firefighters found him, but he inhaled a lot of smoke and suffered serious burns on the right side of his body. He's in a special burn unit. It's touch and go right now."

I sank to the ground.

"Becs?"

Waves of despair rolled over me, and I barely found my voice. "I'm coming. What hospital?"

"Don't come to the hospital. I contacted his family. They're flying in." She sobbed, so different than her normal tough-girl attitude.

I didn't understand. "Is the flower shop gone, too?"

She blew her nose. "Yes, but luckily no one was inside the store."

"I'll meet you at the studio in two hours." We hung up. I took a deep breath and wrapped my heart in fury and disbelief.

I held up a finger to Ash who'd stayed respectfully quiet during the call. "Stay there."

Returning to my bedroom, I took a moment to think. Oded, close to death? How could this have happened? I leaned against my bedroom door, trembling, tears sliding down my cheeks, and I choked down sobs I didn't want Ash to hear. I wiped snot away with my pajama sleeve and shuddered in a deep breath.

Sitting on the edge of my bed, I brushed my hair in long strokes, starting at the crown and going down to the tip. I brushed my whole head, staring out the window, and kept brushing the front while I thought of Oded—how he'd taught me self-defense, how he'd told me to slow down and speed up at the same time. "You're going fast in the wrong way, Rivka," he'd say. "Move swiftly but with purpose."

I tried to imagine what kind of person would set fire to a flower shop.

I remember Oded kissing me on the head and how he found his flashlight in the dark.

I remembered his hands, strong and capable.

And the more I thought about it, the more things didn't add up.

I got dressed and returned to the living room. I'd almost forgotten Ash was there, but he'd waited. He stood with his hands in his pockets staring at the ground. "I'm sorry about Oded," he said, his voice soft. "He's strong. He'll make it."

"Can you see that? Is that a vision?"

His mouth twisted, and he shook his head. "No," he admitted. "More like a wish." He ran his hands through his hair. "I have to tell you something." He held up his phone. "I just read that the police are treating it as a crime scene. There's strong evidence that it was arson."

I bristled with anger. "So Zara was right. Someone set that fire?"

A low whistle emanated from the fire escape. "Becs, it's me. Oded's hurt."

"Pinky?"

"Can I come in?"

"Of course."

Pinky's wings dragged on the floor, but at least his cheeks weren't as gaunt and he looked like he'd eaten. He eyed Ash suspiciously, sniffing as if he'd done a line of coke, but I ignored it. When he came close and almost snuggled against me, I lifted my arm and gave him a swift hug. To my surprise, he leaned into it and held on for a moment.

"Asher, this is my friend Pinky. Pinky, this is Ash."

Asher cocked his head and rubbed his thumb along his lip, squinting at Pinky in a way that made me think he saw through Pinky's glamour. But when he spoke, he said, "Nice skateboard."

"Thanks. Nice suit."

"Uh?" Ash patted his chest and pockets, raising his eyebrows in confusion.

Pinky mystified me. Ash looked hot in his black T-shirt and black joggers, but he absolutely wasn't wearing a suit.

My shoulders slumped, and I rubbed my eyes. "You are two of the most confusing men I've ever met. And I know a demon, a warlock, and a mob boss."

Chapter 20

EXHAUSTION AND sadness kicked in, and my patience went out the window. "Oded is injured, and I don't have time for weirdness. Not from either of you." I shifted my gaze from Pinky to Ash and back again. "Understand?"

They each made sounds of agreement but didn't look at me directly.

"Let me explain. I've been locked in a bout of sleep paralysis for hours because the Warlock sent me into the Nightmarescape. The death magic has agreed to work for me, by the way, but now it's a bow and set of arrows, which I don't fully control. And let me repeat, Oded is lying in a burn unit. So whatever odd things you want to do and say to each other, do it on your own time."

Both Pinky and Ash looked at me, completely losing interest in one other, frowning as they each mulled over what I'd said.

Ash wrinkled his nose, hesitating as if it pained him to ask, but he finally settled on, "Can you repeat all of that?"

Pinky whistled. "Becs? I think fast . . . but that was too fast for me."

"No time. I'm meeting Zara at the studio. I want to see what remains of it myself. I'm not standing still any longer."

I talked, walked, and announced, "Keep up," as I went to my kitchen to scrounge for something to eat. I found an orange and started peeling it as I ran through the details of my nightmare again, this time including the tooth monster and the bald eagles.

"You named them Extra Crispy and Eleven Spices?" Ash asked.

"That's what you got out of all of that?" I looked at him in disbelief.

"The monster tore your teeth out?" Pinky exclaimed, fingers in his mouth to check that his teeth were still there.

"Losing teeth is a common nightmare," I said. "I shouldn't have told you the details. I distracted you from what matters."

"It's great that you got the death magic out of your body." Asher crossed his arms and leaned against the kitchen doorframe. "Fantastic. I don't understand the part about a 'Nightmarescape,' but the no 'magic cancer' in your gut part is positive."

"Yeah," I said with my mouth full, orange juice dripping down my chin. Pinky handed me a napkin, and suddenly, I broke down into tears and sank to the floor. I'd been through a lot in the Nightmarescape and then fought the sleep paralysis. Waking to discover my friend and trainer had been caught in a fire was just too much.

Neither Pinky nor Ash seemed to know what to do. Pinky didn't look me in the eye and kept handing me napkins. When he ran out of those, he furnished me with tissues. Ash rocked from one foot to the other and settled on stepping by me and getting me a glass of water. Tears ran down my cheeks too, mixing with the orange's juice, and the combination must have been particularly horrible, but I didn't care.

The man and the man-sized fairy waited me out.

When it looked like I was winding down, Pinky scooted behind me and hugged me, wrapping his wings around me. It was the sweetest thing. He wasn't a toucher, so I knew this took effort from him, and I appreciated it as the unique level of trust it represented.

Ash sat in front of me, held my hand, and lifted my chin. "Becs, you are the strongest person I know. Every piece of that is torture, and yet here you are, still standing. Well, sitting, but surviving. I can't imagine going through so much in so little time."

I sniffled. "Thanks."

Pinky laid his head on my back and didn't say anything. He didn't have to. I blew my nose, honking like a goose, and gathered my tissues. I separated from the guys and threw my dirty stuff in the trash and washed my hands. They took the hint.

"Let's see those arrows," Ash said.

"Yeah, and you could use a shower," said Pinky. "You smell like spoiled cheese."

I laughed despite everything.

I brought them into my bedroom and gestured to the bed. "There you go."

"What are you talking about?" asked Ash.

"The quiver of arrows and the bow on the bed," I replied.

"I don't see anything," said Pinky.

I picked them up, balancing their heft in my hands. "Here."

Neither of them could see the weapons formed from the death magic.

"Oh, this is Wonder Woman stuff. I don't have an invisible airplane, but I've got invisible arrows. Now, if I could learn how to use them. I can feel their power, but they aren't obeying me the same way they did in the Nightmarescape. It's almost like they're on the wrong vibration."

"There may be something to that, but before examining it closely, I'd recommend cleaning up like Pinky suggested," Asher said. "We'll give you some solitude."

"You go. I have something to say to Becs that's private," said Pinky.

"What is it?" asked Ash. "You can say anything in front of me." Asher angled himself between me and Pinky, his chest vibrating in an almost growl.

Pinky pulled his shoulders back, and his wings lifted, but he didn't look Ash in the eye. "I said, it's private," he insisted.

"Go on, Ash. It's fine," I said, pushing on his shoulder.

Ash narrowed his eyes. "I'll be just outside that door if you need me."

Once he was certain Ash had walked out, Pinky whispered, "Becs, Asher doesn't smell."

"What do you mean?"

"He smells like nothing."

"I don't understand."

"Everybody smells like something but not Asher. He's a blank space. I've never met anyone like him before, and when I first looked at him, I thought he was wearing a white suit."

"What do you see when you look at him now?"

"Black T-shirt, pants, normal stuff. But he can't hide his lack of smell. He's a null." Pinky tapped his nose. "I don't know what to make of it, but it's like he's not there."

"That's so weird, and . . . alarming."

Pinky bounced up and down. "You do believe me, don't you?"

"I do, Pinky, of course. I know how good your nose is. I'll think about what it means."

"Okay. If you promise."

"I promise. Go on and wait for me. If you're uncomfortable around Ash, wait for me outside."

I washed my hair with my favorite tea tree oil shampoo and slathered it with the coordinating conditioner. While that set, I lathered on a lavender body scrub and relaxed as I inhaled the scent. My shower ran hot, and the water sluiced down my back, relieving the tight muscles in my shoulders. The steam billowed around me, and I breathed it in, comforted that I no longer felt the stabbing pains in my midriff from the death magic. I wept more for Oded, and the tears mingled with the shower water. I let the tears flow, and as I wiped my eyes a moment later, the scent of my bath products made me consider Pinky's words.

Something about Ash made me want to lick him like an ice cream cone, but I had to face the fact that I knew nothing about him except for where he worked and that he claimed to be clairvoyant. No info about where he was from, why he lived here, or who his other friends were. He held me close then pushed me away, and while he smelled delicious to me, Pinky's sense of smell worked on a different level. I didn't know if it was a fae gift or an individual quirk, but he experienced the world in smells, the same way a bloodhound did.

I made a decision right then and there. Whatever was up with Ash, I didn't need that trouble in my life. I had plenty as it was, and I trusted Pinky's nose. Something about my situation with Ash didn't smell right, and I'd been kidding myself by ignoring the obvious.

I dressed in black jeans and a black button-down shirt before throwing my hair in a ponytail and donning my Outer Banks ballcap. I opened my door and yelled, "I'm coming." I hoped Pinky and Asher hadn't killed one another, either by fighting or simply staring each other to death.

Bam! Bam! Bam! A jackhammer pounded the far corner of my bedroom, and both of my companions skated down the hall's wood flooring, shoving one another out of the way like roller derby players, to get to my bedroom faster than the other. Pinky whistled loudly, and Asher clapped his hand to his ear.

"What is that noise? Is that a gun?" yelled Ash, elbowing Pinky into the hall closet.

"Becs, are you okay?" Pinky asked, ducking under Ash's elbow and slanting his body into the room first.

"Relax. It's a woodpecker. A pileated woodpecker, and they are huge. I'm glad to hear him. I thought the Warlock had killed all the birds. He's on the telephone pole next to the building. If we go on my fire escape you may be able to see him." I had to raise my voice to be heard because the woodpecker was really going to town.

"Oh, that's okay then," said an oddly sullen Ash.

"Birds are good," said Pinky, a slight perk to his wings.

I ignored Ash's subtext and nonverbal communication because frankly, I didn't care. I was happy that Pinky got pleasure out of the bird and didn't have time to soothe Ash's feelings. He was jealous of Pinky for some reason, and I got the feeling he thought he was going to bust in and save me from some big bad attack and be a hero. And yet, it was only a bird. Ego, much? Not my problem.

Men. Boys. God help me.

"I'm going to meet Zara. If the two of you want to come, you're welcome, but I don't expect it. You're both sweet to worry about me, and I appreciate you comforting me earlier. I need to worry about my friend with the woman who knows him best."

"I've got to get to the restaurant," Asher said. "I'll catch up with you later." He gave me a look that told me he wanted to say more, but with Pinky present, he wouldn't. I nodded and he left, casting one last look back at me and my fae friend.

"I am sorry your friend is hurt because it makes you sad, but he's in the hospital. He either gets better or he dies and you put him in the ground, and that's the end, right?" asked Pinky.

"Yes, Pinky. That's about it."

"Humans get hurt and die all the time." He scratched his head and looked confused, as if he hadn't considered this before.

"Yes, we die."

"Will you die?"

"One day, but not yet."

"I don't want you to die."

"I won't, for a while," I said, trying to reassure him.

"How do you know that?"

He had me on that one. "You're right, Pinky. I don't. But I'll be careful and try not to."

I gathered my invisible bow and arrows, thinking it was better to have the weapon with me than leave it at home. I tried to extract an arrow from the quiver and was utterly unsuccessful. Even invisible, it seemed dangerous to leave the death magic at home in its new form. I threw the bow and quiver over my shoulder and walked to the back door, where I also nabbed my backpack. Pinky slid down the fire escape railing all the way to the bottom.

"Maybe I need to go with you, to keep you safe," Pinky said, frowning.

"Don't you have trees to tend to?"

"Yes," he said, but he didn't look happy about it. "Some crabapples developed Venturia inaequalis."

I had no idea what that was. "Go do your job, Pinky. Let me meet with Zara and think about Oded." Tears filled my eyes just saying his name again, and worry filled my heart. I couldn't imagine how much pain Oded had to be in. I hope they had good drugs. "It's the middle of the day, and I'll be with another person. Nothing will go wrong.

Remember to get food from Betsy later."

He brightened. "She gave me cake."

"She's a very nice lady."

I had enough time to drop by the diner and give Betsy more money for feeding Pinky. She insisted it wasn't necessary, but I wanted him to get full meals, not scraps, so I chose meals he'd like, and she promised she'd order them to go and ensure that he got fresh fruit as well. That being done, I looped back toward home, taking different roads this time until I got close to the studio.

I parked three blocks away and walked the rest. I checked to make sure I had tissues and noticed Timothy's contract. The Warlock had indeed rifled through my mind while he'd trapped me in the Nightmare-scape and had examined this contract.

Though a psychic connection, he'd left a physical mark—a smeared black thumbprint that smelled like rotten fish.

I vowed to get this evil out of my life.

Smoke tinged the air, and crispy leaves floated down from the trees, disintegrating as they touched the pavement. The odor intensified as I got closer until I ran into yellow crime scene tape stretched across orange cones blocking the entrances to both businesses. I was so tired of smelling burnt things.

You'd think brick shouldn't char, but bricks have a surprising amount of water in them, so they expand and crack. The outside brick stood partially intact, tarp covering the fragments of the flower shop where the fire had started. The windowpanes lay broken in a thousand shards in front of the shop's remains. The studio's front inside wall listed toward the sidewalk, black and sooty, hanging on as if by its fingertips. The firefighters had removed the wooden door and boarded the entrance, nailing a "Danger: Keep Out" sign to it.

The scorch marks most likely told a story to experienced investi-gators, but to me it signaled nothing except that a huge part of my life had been torn away, and unbidden tears streaked down my face yet again. When I wiped them, my hand came away black and gritty, just from the grime in the air. I wiped my eyes with the back of my hand, impatient with myself for crying all the time. There had to be an end to the well of tears my body could hold. I used one of my tissues to clean my hand and threw it in a trash can at the corner of the street.

I spied Zara faltering up the block from the other end, her usual power and grace suffocated by her grief. I met her halfway and embraced her, the two of us holding each other in mutual heartache.

"Did you know that Oded made me part owner six months ago?" Zara asked.

"I didn't."

"There's insurance. We can rebuild if we want, as soon as he's back on his feet."

"Knowing Oded, he'll definitely want to."

She stared at the broken building. "We're dating, but his parents don't know. I can't go in and see him."

"I didn't know that, but it doesn't surprise me."

She shook her head. "It's complicated. I love him, though. Maybe I'll tell them. He's intubated and can't talk."

"I don't think there are any rules with this kind of thing. You should let them know."

"I can't understand why he got hurt," she said, the first signs of anger in her voice. She turned to me, her eyes flashing with resentment. "He didn't do anything wrong. He didn't deal with organized crime, or money laundering, or anything evil. He got caught in the crossfire. He didn't associate with the wrong people. None of that misconduct should have touched him."

Organized crime?

"Wait? The flower shop was a cover for organized crime?"

She nodded, wiping away grimy tears with her hands. "Oded said it was money laundering. He suspected it but didn't have enough proof."

Was this fire part of Gregory Adamos's syndicate?

"I'm sorry, Becs. I didn't mean to unload on you. He's your friend, too. Come on, let's go sit somewhere. You look cold. Let's get out of this smoke and go somewhere sunny."

I was warm enough on the outside, but my mind had stuttered to a halt and was now filled with static. What if Oded had associated with the wrong person? Only that person was me?

Zara wrapped her arm through my elbow and guided me away. "The craziest thing is that there was a witness who said the fire burned normally but then, a tornado of gold dust flew out of it. The guy was drinking, so the police aren't taking him too seriously, but he insists that while there was the normal fire like you'd expect to see, gold dust sailed into the sky as well. It makes me wonder if they used an accelerant that caused a chemical reaction. I don't know how long it will take for the fire investigator to come back with a report."

The static in my brain tripled, and a horde of bees joined in.

Luckily, Zara didn't notice. "My thoughts are all jumbled together, and I don't know what to do first. I need to notify everybody who practices at the studio, but I'm so worried, I can't think."

I gestured to a bench, and we both sat.

I swallowed and gathered my wits. "Who else works with you?"

She ticked off five names.

"I'm assuming they've all been notified?"

She nodded, then pulled a tissue from her jacket pocket and wiped her nose. "They keep wanting to know what they can do to help, but I don't know what to tell them."

"Do you have a registry of all the studio members?"

"Yes, I have back-ups in the cloud."

"Good. Ask them to send a notification to everyone. Tell them you'll let everyone know about creating a fund later, when we know what Oded will need, for physical therapy or whatever. People will want to do that."

"That's a great start. Thanks." Zara gave me a one-armed hug. "I'm going to talk to his parents now. They need to know the truth."

"They'll love you, just as he does."

Chapter 21

ZARA AND I separated after one last hug. I drove to the library, my mind working at a million miles per hour. I patted the dolphin and ram and headed to the reference section on the first floor. Timothy worked at the main desk and waved hello.

"Hey-ho, Becs. What can I help you with on floor numero uno?" He gave me a conspiratorial wink.

"I need to research the ownership of a building."

"Do you have the address?"

"It's the floral shop that burned down, so I'm sure we can find it in the news."

"I heard about that. Terrible." He banged on his keyboard. "Right-o. Here it is." He skimmed the article in the business section. "It says here it is owned by Floral Connection, Inc."

"Who owns Floral Connection, Inc?" I asked, leaning my elbows on the counter.

"Probably the best way to figure that out is through tax records, and that's going to take some digging. Who do you suspect?"

I lowered my voice. "Gregory Adamos."

His eyebrows leapt off his forehead. "Seriously? The Adamos family is no one to play with, Becs. They've been in the game for decades. It's a widely known secret."

"What's their company name?"

"I've seen it on signs for some of the big buildings downtown, including the new casino."

"Ugh. I'd forgotten about that. What's it called? Three Arrows Casino?"

"That's the one. Three Arrows Casino, developed by Adamos Enterprises. They kept it simple. Their symbol is the three arrows of Artemis. It's all explained on their website." He Googled it and turned the monitor so I could see. "See here? It's in the 'About Us,' section. *'As a tribute to our Greek heritage, we use the three arrows of the goddess Artemis.'* You

157

can see the logo with a longer arrow, then a medium-sized one, then the smaller one."

Arrows. Interesting, but could be coincidental. I'd kept the invisible arrows, bow, and quiver locked in the trunk of my car.

"Do you mind tracking it down for me? See if they own the building through Floral Connection?"

Timothy's smile turned sly. "What do you have to trade?"

That little bugger. He was still part fae. Bargaining was part of his nature, and he'd feel an imbalance if we didn't trade something of equal value.

"One free call to Granny?"

He grinned from ear to ear. "Done and done."

"Thanks, Tim-o-thee. Call me later?"

"You bet."

I left the library and sat in my car, unsure of what to do next. My whole body ached with sadness and anxiety. On one hand, I was convinced my involvement with Valefar and Gregory Adamos was somehow responsible for Oded's situation. On the other, the fire *could* have been accidental, which would mean I was reading too much into things.

My head spun with confusion and fatigue. Too much had happened in such a short time—and all of it traumatic. And the person I'd turned to last time to help calm my mind was unavailable, possibly because of my actions.

I didn't trust Asher because I knew he wasn't telling me the truth. Perhaps he wasn't outright lying, but he was keeping secrets from me.

Pinky complicated my life, although I'd help him the second I figured out how.

And on top of all that, I was no closer to fulfilling Valefar's requirements. Or Gregory's. And the Warlock? He was the worst.

Everything was falling apart.

The phone rang. With a sigh, I answered it. "Hello, Becs here."

"It's Nick Adamos."

I almost didn't recognize his voice—his tone was so wobbly and high-pitched. "Nick? What's going on?"

"Gregory found out about Perrick's home soil. He's forbidden Perrick to get it, and he's locked Perrick in the house. Gregory told me to call you, so you'd know. The reprieve is over. The clock on Perrick's life is ticking again."

"Dammit! What is it that Gregory wants? What demon does he want me to summon?"

"I don't know."

"Well, if you want to save Perrick, you need to figure that out. I'm sorry for what you went through, Nick, but it's time to step up. Start digging."

I hung up, opened the door, and removed the death magic bow and arrows from the trunk. I must have looked stupid to anyone watching me, since no one could see what I had in my hands. I tried pulling an arrow from the quiver but couldn't remove it. I tried pulling back the bow string, and it wouldn't move. Frustrated, I threw the bow and quiver on the ground. An arrow immediately sprang from the quiver, notched itself in the bow, and shot itself directly into my right shoulder, releasing tendrils of magic—not death magic, but something painful and itchy. My shoulder froze, worthless, as the magic spread down to my fingers, immobilizing my dominant right hand.

Great. It hadn't killed me. But it *had* told me who was boss.

I retrieved the bow and arrows from the ground with my still-functioning left hand, muttering an apology, then returned them to the car and reclined against the car door. How had the situation gotten so much worse in the last fifteen minutes?

Bing! A text from Mickey.

I love this outfit!

What outfit? Texting with one hand sucked.

This sleep set for Ruthie with the birds on it. Didn't you send it?

The text came with a picture of Ruthie in an adorable two-piece pj set, white, with orange and black orioles on it. I recognized it as a set from Baltimore I'd looked at before. Somebody, Valefar or the Warlock, had hacked my computer browser.

I didn't send that. Don't let her wear it!

What? Why? Who sent it?

Can't say. But it could be dangerous. Throw it out. Better yet, burn it! I was so slow texting with one hand, and my heart was bursting with urgency.

*I hate your job. You said you'd given it up, but you haven't. Have you? Well f*ck you, sister. Don't contact me until you're done.*

Mickey never, ever cussed. Even this half-swear with the asterisk was more than I'd seen from her since the one time she'd done it in high school, felt terrible about it, and swore it off.

Please don't say that. I've got to get out of one situation, then it's over. Promise.

That's what you always say. Now Ruthie's involved? In danger? Jonah's right. Go away.

Mickey, I'm so sorry.

Mickey?
Mickey, please answer.
I'll make this right, I promise.
Nothing. No answer.
Now, everything had truly fallen apart.

Chapter 22

I DROVE HOME at a snail's pace, using my one good arm. I checked my surroundings before I got out and, not sensing the Warlock, slung my backpack over my shoulder, left the arrows, bow, and quiver locked in the trunk, and once again sprinted, or in this case, lurched with haste, to my door. I threw myself inside and locked the door behind me.

I reviewed the notes I'd taken from the library books, looking for any clue to help me take down Valefar, anything I'd missed. I pulled down another book from my own bookshelf as well. I couldn't write with my left hand, but I tore sticky notes from a pad and bookmarked pages that I wanted to remember. Demons wriggled around the rules all the time, but the more I read, the more I realized that if you stood firm, they had to capitulate.

My phone buzzed in my pocket, and I dug it out with my good hand, dropped it, and had to dial Timothy back.

"Hey TT, sorry about that."

"No worries. Why so glum? You sound terrible."

"Nothing important. I'm sad about Oded, that's all."

"The man who was hurt in the fire? You knew him?"

"Yes, he's my friend."

Timothy let out a breath. "Why didn't you say so? We'd have worked out a different deal."

"I don't mind calling your granny, TT. She's fun. What did you find?"

"I tracked this down through court records, can you believe it?" His voice revved up as he got excited. "The whole strip mall had tax problems, and in the 1990s, there were three lawsuits against the owners."

"Who were the owners? Gregory Adamos's company?"

"No, this is the interesting part. His competition, Andino Trading Company, another Greek conglomerate, owns that building, as well as many others in town and on the West Coast. Adamos Enterprises owns most of its buildings on the East Coast. Here in the Midwest, they clash and fight over real estate."

"I've seen their logo. It's the NTC in stylized Greek columns like you'd see on ancient ruins." I paused, wondering what this meant. "Thanks for the information, TT."

We hung up, and I pondered this new development. Could Gregory have set fire to his rival's building and hurt Oded by accident? Or did he hurt Oded to get to me and his rival's building was an added bonus? And why was gold dust, Valefar's signature, involved?

My head spun in multiple directions, and I almost ignored the phone when it rang, but in the end, I answered.

"Becs? It's Nick."

"What did you find out?"

"I'm not sure what it means."

"Tell me anyway."

"No. You come here, and I'll tell you then."

"You want me to drive out to your brother's mansion? Because that went so well last time?"

"I'll tell you what I know only when you bring home soil for Perrick. Gregory is out for the evening, so the coast is clear. No home soil, no information."

Such belligerence. I could practically hear him sticking his chin out, begging me to punch it. Still, he was very different from the swaggering young man who'd walked into my office and demanded I summon Valefar for him.

I shook my head. "What if other staff spy me and tell your big brother that I was there? And if Perrick improves too much, Gregory will know that someone brought him home soil. The whole thing could backfire on you and on Perrick."

"The staff is loyal to Perrick. Everyone likes him, and no one wants him to die. Bring enough to help him hang on. The gardener will hide it. You have to do this. Bring *everything*, dammit."

I was losing my patience. "How bad is Perrick? He had soil just the other day. And by the way, you could be a little more grateful. Ash got that dirt for no reason other than he couldn't stand seeing someone in pain. He spent his vacation time, used his own gas, and drove out there to get the home soil for a perfect stranger because he's a nice person, so slow your roll because I'm ready to hang up and let you deal with it on your own. I'll tell you where I believe it is, and you can get it yourself. You may just have to leave your house."

There was a beat while Nick gathered himself. "I'm sorry. You're right."

"Much better. Thank you. That wasn't so hard."

"The thing is, I don't think I *can* get it," Nick said. "Perrick says it's at a place called Joey's. He says I can't see it, since I'm a plain vanilla human." He muttered something I couldn't hear, and then said, "I hate being human; it's so boring."

"You're the only vanilla human I know of that's aware that Joey's even exists, so consider yourself lucky. Most humans don't know that trolls are real, Nick, much less have them as stalwart friends, so you've got a leg up on everyone else. Come to think of it, after what you've been through, if someone showed it to you, you may be able to see Joey's now."

It was true—Nick was demon-touched. I didn't want to tell him, but the scars wouldn't completely heal. He'd have a hint of darkness in his soul forever. He'd feel it at night when the moon disappeared behind the clouds, when it was raw and bleak, when he sat on the beach at the edge of the sea and acknowledged its vastness. The heat of Hell would break through the crevices of his soul, but it wouldn't warm him. No, it would leave him colder than ever, more bereft. He'd fight depression, and psychiatrists would tell him he needed to take medication and focus on the positive in his life.

They wouldn't ever believe what he'd experienced. What he knew. What he *feared*.

But I didn't tell him any of that.

"How much time do you think Perrick has?" I asked.

"A few days, at most."

"Damn."

"Does that mean you're coming?"

"I'll get there as soon as I can."

Motherhumpin motherflucker. This is the kind of super crap, which is bigger, better, and worse than regular crap, that I didn't need right now. I'd thought Perrick's life was off my responsibility list, but no, of course not. Because someone up there, I raised my one good index finger to the sky, thought my life was a joke. Gave me a Kiss that I didn't want or need, put a friend in the hospital, tied me to a corporate mob boss, a demon, and isolated me from my sister.

The rest of my complaints burst forth out loud, and I yelled at the ceiling. "Oh! I forgot! What else? Death magic! Thanks a whole lot for that too! You also burdened me with a psychotic warlock who has access to my dreams and infected me with death magic. Not to mention dead birds! Perrick! Pinky! Wee ones! And did I forget to add that I can't move my right arm right now? It's totally unfair. People say we never get more than we can handle, but I'm feeling a tad overloaded right now. What did you ever give me to help?"

"Who are you yelling at?" came a concerned voice from the other side of the door. "Is someone in there with you?"

"Ash?"

"Yes, let me in."

With the grace of a sea lion on land, I hauled my ass up from the couch and opened the front door.

"What do you mean you can't move your right arm? What did you do to yourself?" he asked, pushing his way into the room to stand there looking at me with his hands on his hips. "Is it the death magic? I thought they were out of you."

"Yes. No. Wait, stop. I thought you were at the restaurant."

"I left early. Why is your right arm hanging like that? You look like you got Novocain in your bicep."

It sounded stupid even to my brain. "I got mad at the death magic bow and arrow set, so I threw it on the ground, and it shot me."

He blinked at me a few times as he absorbed what I said. "And . . . why did you get mad at the arrows and bow?"

"Because I wanted to nock one and shoot it."

"At anyone in particular?"

"No. At a tree."

He pinched the bridge of his nose. "You wanted to shoot a death arrow at a tree?"

"I was upset."

"Clearly." He stifled a laugh by biting the inside of cheek. He tried to hide it, but I saw. "What did that tree ever do to you?"

"Nothing." I fidgeted like a naughty kid sent to the principal's office.

Ash rubbed both hands over his face. "Becs, you have to have faith. I have to believe that magic misused has a tendency to turn against the user. That's why you have the arrows in the first place, right? The death magic turned against the Warlock."

I rubbed my shoulder and made a face.

"What else happened?" he asked.

I caught him up, including the visit to the tunnels and the Warlock, but I didn't forget Pinky's warning that Ash was an olfactory null. I didn't tell him my suspicions about Valefar and Gregory's involvement in the arson at the flower shop.

"So," I said, finishing up, "it's good you came by because we need to get to Gregory's with home soil for Perrick or Nick won't tell me what he learned. Besides I think Nick will like seeing you. You're his bro or something now."

"My head is spinning with how much trouble you can get into when left unsupervised. Let me change out of my work clothes. Stay here and don't do anything, okay? Don't move. Don't even think about moving." He took a step toward the door but stopped and turned to me. "Where are the arrows?"

"In the trunk of my car."

"I wouldn't leave them unattended."

"I've only got one good arm, and no one else but me can see them."

"Point taken."

He jetted upstairs and returned dressed and ready in record time.

"That was fast." I grabbed my keys. "Okay, let's go. I'll drive," I said.

"You only have one hand."

I glared at him.

He held up both hands in surrender. "Okay, okay. Don't get another ticket though. I saw those envelopes."

Ugh. The tickets and court date. Another thing to deal with, but not now.

I took a chance. "Do you, by any teeny-weeny chance, have any more of that soil in your car?"

"No, I gave it all to Perrick."

"Okay, you can drive, but follow my directions. This is going to look odd."

Ash followed my directions to a T and didn't say a word when I told him to park in a lot next to the diner where I'd eaten with Pinky. "I'll be right back," I said.

"Wait, I'm coming with you."

"You can't."

"It's a diner; of course I can."

I sighed. "No, the soil isn't here."

"He stored the home soil in the alley?" Ash got out of the car and looked around. He could see all the other establishments on the street, but he couldn't see Joey's. "Certainly not at the Irish pub, the coffee house, or the pizza joint?"

"No, not there."

"The sushi restaurant?"

"No, not there. Come to think of it, I've never eaten there. We should try it some time."

He ignored me and kept looking around. "Where then?"

I walked around to his side of the car. "It's confidential."

"I got the soil for him. Doesn't that mean you can trust me?"

I tried not to let my attraction to Ash get the best of me, but damn the boy was cute when he fretted, and despite Pinky's assertion, he still smelled like birthday cake to me. "It's not that you can't be trusted."

"Well, what then? Is your arm working yet? How are you going to drag a bag of dirt here by yourself with one arm?"

A reasonable question. My arm tingled, as if it were waking up after napping on it wrong, so I thought I'd get back feeling and function shortly. But in the meantime, it hung like a ham hock in an Italian butcher shop window.

"I'll figure it out. Stay here. Please."

Maybe it was pheromones, but my resolve weakened like tissue paper in a thunderstorm. I leaned in for a hug, and when he caressed my jawline with a feather-light touch, I closed my eyes and enjoyed that too.

Sue me.

I clomped down the alley in my worn boots, my backpack over my shoulder, and wished life gave me more Asher and less Warlock. More Mickey and less Gregory. More Granny and less Valefar.

Of course, thinking like that was what led to bad deals.

Joey gave me the beady eyeball and skipped the preliminaries. "What's wrong?"

"Perrick is locked in Gregory Adamos's house unable to get to his home soil."

She grunted. "Wondered why I hadn't seen him."

"I'm bringing some to him. How do I get to it?"

She jerked her thumb toward the storage rooms. "Perrick's still a bit of a dick, being an enforcer for Gregory Adamos, you know?" She hesitated for a moment. "Why are you going through all of this trouble to help him?"

"I'm doing it because I need Nick's help and he's friends with Perrick. That, and I don't like seeing people suffer if I can help it. Don't tell anyone."

"Your secret is safe with me." She zipped her mouth shut. "So Nick's talking to you?"

I wiggled my hand back and forth. "Talking is a strong word."

Joey laughed. "The soil is in the back." She jerked her chin at me. "What's up with your arm?"

"Shot with a death magic arrow."

She blanched. "Who shot you, and why aren't you dead?"

"The bow and arrow shot me, and it was to teach me a lesson, not to kill me. I tried to misuse it."

"Ah. Fae objects have a way of doing that, too. You idiot. You got the death magic out of you and it transformed into a weapon, but you . . . what?"

"Tried to practice with it by shooting a tree."

"A tree!" Joey looked at me as if I'd said I tried to shoot a newborn babe. I guessed trees were like that to the fae.

She smacked her forehead with her palm. "You're lucky it didn't shoot you somewhere the sun don't shine, cupcake. A tree, indeed. I'm shocked the death magic took a liking to you."

"We had a heart-to-heart in the Nightmarescape."

She grabbed a stool, sat on it, poured herself a shot of vodka, and downed it in one go. "This has gotten too complicated for me."

"You're not even the first one to say that to me *today*. Hell, I can't follow half of what's happening, and I'm the one living it." I rolled my shoulders and noticed the right one moved. That was promising. "Look, I'd love to tell you everything, but I need to get to Perrick."

"Help yourself. Near the wine."

Joey's storage area was neatly organized with boxes of labelled red wine next to the cooler stone cellar for the whites, magicked of course, to the exact temperature required to keep the wine at its freshest. The liquor sat in boxes in a different room, depending on the type, and the other stuff needed—glasses, rags, and what-nots—lay on shelves. What made the rooms special was that they were as big or small as Joey needed. She never ran out of space, and she never needed to go to the far back to get what she was looking for. The walls appeared to be dug out of fresh dirt, but when I touched them, they were cool and dry, as was the floor. To an inspector, they'd look like normal tavern storage areas, but if you could see it, there was a haze of purple fae magic at the edges. I couldn't see it naturally, but Joey had explained it to me and lent me a little magic so I could see through the glamour and always get what we needed up front.

It astonished me every time I went back there. It simply never got old.

I found the home soil next to the red wine exactly as Joey said and realized that Ash was correct to wonder how I'd move the bags since they were heavy. I required assistance, but I couldn't call Jimmy, Rin, and Trick again since I didn't have a warm place for them to live yet.

I took a chance, closed my eyes, my back to the shelving, and spoke out loud.

"It would be lovely if I had a small bag and a trowel so I could move some of this dirt into a bag I could actually carry."

I kept my eyes closed for about sixty seconds. Hoping, I turned to one of the sets of shelves and, sure enough, a small burlap bag and a trowel lay on the bottom shelf. I opened the outer pocket of my bag and found two of the strawberry jellies I'd taken from the diner next door and left them in their place. You couldn't acknowledge brownies openly or they'd leave, but a thank-you gift was acceptable.

Not having use of one arm made things difficult, but I used my teeth to hold it open, and once I got the bag half full, it propped up on its own. I spit dirt from my mouth, silently cursing Nick, Perrick, Gregory, and myself for being in this situation, and then got to work, filling it the rest of the way. I placed the trowel back on the shelf, noticing the jellies had disappeared, and heaved the bag over my shoulder. With a nod to Joey, I walked back to the car to find Ash pacing the alley.

"Could that have taken you any longer?"

"Whoa, cowboy, I'm working with one arm, remember."

"Oh, I do remember. That's why I offered to go with you."

"If I wasn't so exhausted, I'd tell you that you're adorable when you're flustered."

He took the bag of home soil from me and put it in his trunk. "You think I'm adorable?"

"If my friend hadn't been hurt, if I had use of both arms, if I didn't have to face down a demon, and if a warlock wasn't trying to kill me, then yes, I might say that."

He backed out of the space while I leaned his passenger seat back to rest. "Adorable is good," he said, sounding somewhat mollified. That was the best he was going to get out of me, so I was glad it made him feel better. *Again, men.*

The ride to Gregory's gave me time to think, and I was glad Ash drove. "You know, Ash, I keep thinking that Valefar's specific challenge to me was to find out what Gregory's deepest desire is."

"Right, because he believes that if he knows what that is, he can tempt Gregory into a deal."

"Exactly. What chutzpah! But what if Gregory won't make a deal? What if Gregory refuses to deal with Valefar, no matter what?"

"You know Gregory wants to make a deal with a different demon, correct? Some other demon he thinks can help him better?"

"Yes, but I don't know which one. If I did, that could tell me what he wants. Demons have specialties."

Ash snorted. "Do they actually, though? I mean, demons are demons."

I opened my left eye specifically so I could roll it at him. "Don't be dense. Didn't we already have this conversation? Demons have distinct temperaments. I'm sure angels, if they exist, have different personalities." I laughed at the thought. "I mean, what if Michael is a drill sergeant and Gabriel is nitpicky about his wings and Raphael doesn't like to go barefoot?"

Ash pressed his lips together, and when he opened them, he wheezed out a sound that might have been a laugh but could have been a cough.

"Change of subject," he said. "What if this isn't enough home soil for Perrick?"

"It has to be enough, at least for now. We can bring more later. Besides, even though Nick said the gardener would hide it, there is every chance in the world that Gregory will still find it. Especially if Perrick improves too much."

"Why can't we steal Perrick away and secure him somewhere safe?"

"Who uses phrases like 'secure him'?" I threw Ash a look, but he didn't see it because he kept his eyes on the road like a good, safe driver who'd get an insurance discount. "Gregory has some kind of hold on Perrick. He can't leave or he would have by now. We could make things worse if we steal him away."

"Do you have any idea what it is?"

"I haven't a clue what he's got on Perrick. Maybe Nick does. The two of them are tight." It was a hot night, and the car was stuffy. "Can you crack the window?"

Ash let a little air in. "If we could figure out what he's using for leverage and remove that, Perrick would be free."

"I'll get right on that after I take care of all the other stuff on my plate."

"You're not interested in helping?"

I couldn't deal with his judgment. "Of course, I am. Why do you think we're driving over there now?"

"To get the information you need from Nick."

"Well, yes, there's that. But also to help Perrick, now, and to help free him from Gregory, later."

"Gregory must have something big. Perrick's had a hard time."

"Pulleease. People make bad deals. It happens all the time. I know better than most."

Ash drove down the long lane that led to Gregory's house, and I prayed that Nick hadn't set us up. Gregory had top-notch security, and, as evidenced by our last visit, cameras lined this lane so that he could see us coming.

Once again, I smelled Lake Erie past the heavily wooded trees and heard the crashing waves. Some people clung to the bad images of the lake, but those people could stay away. Beaches called to me, and some of the hidden ones were the best places to sink my toes into the sand, or in between the pebbles. Lake Erie boasted a ton of rocks. High tide, low tide, you never knew what you'd find on the shores, and if you lived here, you knew where to go to get the coziest spots. Many people, like Gregory, had private beaches, a dream I'd had since I was young.

One day, I promised myself, I'd have a house on the lake.

In the meantime, I enjoyed the sound of the water through the trees and appreciated the planned beauty of the manicured front lawn as well. I hoped Gregory took a few minutes every day to appreciate what he had, but I doubted it. He was always chasing something more.

Ash must have had the same thought I did about the possibility of a setup because he seemed wary, looking right and left, checking the trees and windows. When he popped the trunk to get the bag of home soil, I slipped the bow and arrows over my right shoulder, leaving my backpack on my left.

"I can't see it," Ash said, "but I can see the indentation on your shirt. That's peculiar. Also, your arm is moving."

Huh, so it was. "That's cool." It had healed on the way over, and I hadn't noticed.

"Hurry," came a shout. Nick stood in the open front doorway on his own two feet. "Bring the home soil. I'm afraid it may be too late."

Chapter 23

PERRICK WAS BACK to puke green and lay prone on a bedroom floor sweating buckets, clothed only in extra-large bath towels strewn strategically across his body. The bedroom was bare bones with wood floors, one window without shades or curtains, and an open, empty closet. The only item of interest was a smelly sleeping bag bunched into the far corner with a large tumbler next to it. I wondered if that was where Perrick had been sleeping.

Nick opened the burlap bag and squatted next to his friend, gently inserting Perrick's right hand into the soil.

It worked like a light switch. Perrick gasped, like a man coming up for air from the depths, and rolled to his side, barely missing giving us an eyeful, and slid his other hand into the bag as well. He immediately stopped sweating, and his breathing eased. I'd never seen a troll so deprived of home soil and hoped to never see it again. I'd never gotten that close to seeing a troll's niggly bits either and was disappointed because I'd heard they were something to behold. I was slightly ashamed of thinking that, so I didn't mention it to Ash.

While Perrick responded to the home soil, it was clear that this was life support, not a cure. He required the full bags to heal completely, and this tiny amount wasn't going to do more than pull him back from the brink. I no longer had any concerns that Gregory would notice that Perrick was suddenly well. He'd have to be looking hard to notice an improvement, and Gregory didn't care enough to spot the difference between mostly dead and not-all-the-way dead.

"Thank you," Nick said, motioning us out of the room and turning off the lights. "This will help him sleep, and when he wakes, he'll be better. Do you think you can get one more bag? He'll use up the energy in this one pretty quick."

"It's only been a day and a half. Why's he doing so poorly?"

"I don't know. I thought he was doing better. Gregory gave him an assignment, and it was going well. He seemed happier."

"I can get another bag, but bringing it here is the hard part. I don't want to run into your brother." I studied his face. He had more color, and his eyes were clearer. "You seem better," I said.

Nick held out his hand to Ash, who grasped it in this two-handed thingee I've seen men do when they didn't want to hug. "Thanks to this guy. I don't know what you said to me, but you really broke through. I'm not well, but I'm not a vegetable anymore, either."

"Can you meet me somewhere in town? I can get more soil to you that way," I asked, prodding him to look my way instead of worshipping my neighbor. Ash was my crush—he didn't get to be anyone else's.

Nick released Ash's hand and shuffled back two steps, motioning us to follow him down the stairs to the main room we'd been in the first time. He propped himself up on one of the chairs, leaning awkwardly, and drummed his fingers on the leather. "I'm not ready to go outside," he admitted. "I'm scared to leave the house. I'm up and walking on my own now, which is a vast improvement. Thanks to the therapy they did on my legs while I was out of it, I didn't lose too much muscle and have been able to regain strength fast. But leaving?" He shuddered. "I can open the door and look at the driveway."

Once again, I flashed back to the supremely confident man who'd stormed into my office demanding I summon Valefar and compared it to this shell who stood in front of me now. And I remembered my part in his downfall. Shame crashed over me so hard, I almost lost my footing.

"I understand, Nick. I didn't mean to push you. It's my fault you suffered like you did. I'm so sorry. I don't think I said that to you before, at least not when you could understand me. I didn't do your contract right, and you paid the price."

I forced myself to look Nick straight in the eye when I said it, facing the man I'd harmed, recalling what I'd been taught as a child. If you didn't genuinely apologize to the person you'd hurt, repenting to the Divine later wouldn't do you any good. The other part of this rule stated that we had a responsibility to apologize three times, as long as we were sincere, and if that person couldn't forgive us, that was okay—we could stop after three. Luckily, it looked like I didn't have to try more than once.

"We were both at fault, Becs. You tried to warn me, and I didn't listen, being an arrogant fool intent on one thing and stuck in my own greed. Besides, I didn't play fair bringing armed security with me. I paid a price, and I understand you have, too."

"What do you know of it? What do you remember of my bargain?"

It was uncomfortable talking about this part with Nick. He didn't need to know, but I caught Asher's eye. He gave me an encouraging smile and, for some reason, looked proud of me.

Nick rubbed an eyebrow. "Valefar wanted something of you. What did you promise him to get me out?"

"A favor, and I'm trying to fulfill it without hurting anyone else."

"What's he have on you?"

I picked at my cuticles. "A locket." I took a deep breath. "It has my sister's photo in it."

Nick rocked back on his heels. "Ahhhh. I understand. You're caught two ways. Both my brother and Valefar are threatening her."

"Everyone uses her as leverage because they know I love her. She's not speaking to me at present."

"I'm sorry to hear that, but it may keep her safer."

I turned and walked to the window. "Maybe."

Ash spoke up, quietly. "This is why Becs needs to know why your brother wants to summon a demon."

Nick straightened. "I don't like Gregory, but I won't sell him to Valefar."

Ash kept his voice low, the way someone would talk to a frightened animal. "Not to sell him to Valefar, but to understand what his greatest wish is. Why does he need a demon? What's he need so badly? If we could figure that out, maybe we could get the leverage we need to help Perrick and trick Valefar."

Nick shook his head violently. "I won't give my brother up to a demon, especially not Valefar."

I turned around. "I'm not giving him to Valefar."

"No offense, Becs, but that's not enough," Nick said, a note of apology in his tone. But his voice was firm, and I couldn't blame him. I didn't have the greatest track record where Valefar was concerned.

"I won't let Valefar have him," said Ash.

I stared at Ash. How did he dare make such a promise? We'd already had this discussion. I whirled on him. "You can't make promises for me, Ash. You have no say in this. Nick is going to have to take me on my word."

"I believe Ash."

I swiveled to stare at Nick. "Ash works at a restaurant. He's a kind man who helped you out. But keep in mind that a friend of mine says he's an olfactory null, so he's got some mojo I don't understand. But one thing is for certain—keeping demons at bay isn't his job. He can't make this promise to you, Nick."

Ash rubbed the back of his neck. "What do you mean an 'olfactory null'? I don't smell? You're always sniffing me."

I blushed all the way to the tips of my ears, and my chest got hot. "Well, yeah, you smell good to me."

He gave me a lazy smile. "How do I smell to you?"

"Is this really the time?"

"You're the one who brought it up."

Nick's head swiveled back and forth, watching us.

The weight of my backpack and the bow and arrows started to annoy me, but I didn't put them down. "Fine. You smell like birthday cake. Satisfied? But Pinky says you don't smell at all. You're an 'olfactory blank space,' as he put it, and his sense of smell is insane. He can smell two-week-old leftovers before I open the refrigerator. He knows what I ate for breakfast *yesterday*. If he says you don't smell right, I believe him."

Ash cocked his head and considered this, rubbing his chin. "Fascinating."

"Great, Mr. Fascinating. In the meantime, don't go butting your head into my business and making promises you can't keep."

Nick cleared his throat. "So, hey, I don't understand a word of what you're saying except that the two of you want to fool around and should probably work that out on your own time. Meanwhile, I want to help, but I'm not risking my brother's life."

"Can you tell me which demon he wants to summon?"

Nick drummed his fingers some more, still uncertain. Footsteps on the stairs drew our attention, and Perrick, still green but breathing better, entered the room.

"Nick," Perrick said, "tell them."

Nick ran to his friend's side. "How are you feeling?"

"Better." He nodded at Ash and me. "Thanks."

"No problem," I said. Ash said, "You're welcome."

"Nicky," Perrick said, sitting hard in the lounge chair where Nick was. "I can't do this any longer. I tried with your brother, but the second I did something he didn't like, he hurt me again. He always has this hold on me."

This was a chance to ask my question. "Why don't you leave, Perrick? It's not like Gregory could stop you physically. I know trolls are stronger than they look."

Perrick leaned back in the chair and shut his eyes. "I have a son, a half-breed. Half-troll, half-human. He's able to pass as human. Takes after his mother." Talking this much left Perrick winded so Nick took over.

"Perrick's son plays basketball at college, and Gregory found out about it. He threatened to out him if Perrick leaves."

I couldn't believe Gregory's gall. What a putz. "Most people don't believe in trolls, or in fae in general. What could 'outing' him possibly do?"

Perrick wheezed, "Even a hint of scandal could cause him to lose his scholarship. You know Gregory's influence as much as anyone. He wouldn't even have to use the word 'troll.' He'd start a rumor that Simon uses drugs or human growth hormone or something similar, and that would be the end of it. He'd be drug tested to death, his eligibility called into question. Social media attacks. They'd go after him. I can't risk it." He hesitated. "I should have been smarter. I thought I could make it better, and I tried, but it didn't work." He blushed and looked away.

"Your brother is a piece of craptastic work, Nick."

Nick hummed in agreement. "I wish I could say you were wrong. Still, he loves me in his own twisted way. He kept me alive and provided therapists. He never abandoned me."

I hoisted my backpack which kept slipping down my arm. It was hard to balance with things on each shoulder. "Low bar. Did someone neglect him as a baby? Lock him in a dark room?" I muttered.

Nick scoffed. "Sort of. You never met my mother."

"Your mother was evil?"

"Oh, yeah. I know you think my dad had to be the patriarch and the businessman. No. In my family, it was my mother. Dad was an artist. Mama was Maleficent. I'm surprised you haven't heard any stories about Marianna 'Mimi' Adamos."

Asher held up an index finger. "Wait, but what about your last name?"

"Dad was American and modern. He took Mama's last name. It was part of the deal. He got endless funding for his art projects, and she got someone who looked the other way when it came to business and the way she raised the kids."

"Didn't he care about you two?"

Nick motioned us onto the couch and got Perrick a glass of water. I slipped off the arrows while his back was turned hoping he wouldn't notice my odd movements with the invisible objects.

He continued standing, holding a bottle of water for himself, although he didn't offer us any. He seemed lost in thought, remembering his childhood.

"Mama and Daddy met in college, and, believe it or not, it was love at first sight. Daddy adored his aristocratic Greek socialite, and she loved his dreams. Papa, my grandfather, didn't like it, but when Daddy agreed to change his name and made it clear he wanted nothing to do with the family business, my grandfather agreed to it. My grandmother—we called her Yiayia—wanted grandchildren and thought Mama was already too old at age twenty-eight." Nick smiled as he recalled the story.

"Dad loved us in his own way, but his first love was Mama, his second was his art, and we came third. When neither of us showed aptitude for painting or sculpture, he lost interest. Gregory and I preferred sports, and Mama encouraged competition. We celebrated hard-won victories, trophies, and clear-cut wins. Losses and beatings were ways of life and lessons learned."

Perrick spoke without opening his eyes. "Sounds like some troll families."

"Gregory concentrated on being the best, and as he got taller and bigger, it was easier. I was always smaller, and since I was younger, too, I never caught up. He took over the business after Mama's death, and I resented it. I thought I wanted it and the power that came with it."

"So you came to see me," I said.

He sighed. "And started this whole mess."

Asher tapped his lip with his forefinger. "Gregory modelled his whole life after his mother?"

"Oh yes," said Nick, grimacing. "Mimi Adamos terrorized the East Coast and this part of the Midwest. She ruled with an iron fist, stilettos, and the crowbar to match. She made us who we are. I didn't see it until later, of course. All boys love their mothers, and I ignored the stories. I didn't understand why the teachers and administrators of our private school treated us with such deference. Now I know they were terrified."

He took a swig of water. "I do remember wanting to be friends with this pretty blond girl with the biggest green eyes, and her parents wouldn't let us play together. We snuck around anyway, as much as one can in fifth grade. They withdrew her from the school and sent her to public school to separate us. They were scared of Madame Mimi."

"Was she into real estate like your brother?"

Nick wiped a tear I didn't think he realized he'd shed. "Gambling was her game. Casinos on the East Coast, bringing them into the Midwest, and then—*bam!* She struck paydirt with racetracks."

"Horses?"

"Sure, but any racing, really. Motorcycles, drag racing, stock car. She saw the future in owning a lot of racetracks. She didn't care who or what raced in them, only that she owned the tracks."

Even Ash had to admire it. "Genius investment."

Nick snorted. "Absolutely, and all of those sports are dangerous. Easy to hide a death or two or perhaps arrange for an injury if someone gets uppity."

"Your mom sounds like a peach," I said.

"I didn't see it until later, but Gregory got his eye on the game early."

"Your father stayed out of all of it the whole time?"

"Yes. Basically, he ignored us, kept painting, having his shows, and loved Mom, no matter what. Happy in his routine and ignorance."

"Who looked after you?" Ash asked.

"A series of nannies, mostly. I can't remember their names, there were so many. At first, Gregory and I had each other, and then we drifted apart."

Ash gazed at him, a soft expression on his face. "That must have been lonely."

Nick finished his water. "It wasn't great."

"We've got to go. You promised me something to help me understand what your brother wants, what his wish is." I pointed to Perrick. "We did our part. You've got to give us something."

"Tell them," Perrick whispered. "We've got to end this."

Nick squinched up his face, as if trying to stop himself from spewing. "I don't know exactly what he wants, but he wants to summon a demon name Zepar. Does that help you?"

"It gives me something to go on," I said. "Much better than nothing."

"How do I know you won't feed Gregory to Valefar?" he asked, crushing his water bottle in his hands.

"Because I said I won't."

"Not good enough."

"That's all you get, Nick."

Ash shook his head. "No, it isn't. *I* said we won't."

I flushed red. "Once again, whatever your deal is, you don't get to promise that." I grabbed my backpack, hiding behind those movements so that I also retrieved the bow and arrows, then left the house and stalked to the car.

Ash followed, only stopping to say, "We'll try to get more home soil, Perrick."

I raised my voice. "You don't get to promise that either, Ash. Stop writing checks you can't cash."

Chapter 24

THE DRIVE BACK to our apartment building flew by because I was thinking about the demon Nick mentioned. I refused to talk to Ash, afraid I'd lash out at him for continuing to guarantee things he had no business discussing, much less promising to fulfill.

He knew how I felt about it, so raising the issue yet again was a waste of time. But that didn't mean Mr. Birthday Cake didn't want to talk about it.

"Becs, I think we should talk about—"

"No."

"I mean, shouldn't we discuss this demon—"

"No."

"Maybe I can help?"

"No."

"Why?"

"Because you're doing the equivalent of making bad contracts, and I won't do that ever again. Have you not learned anything from my story? You're making bad deals by promising things you can't promise and getting Perrick's and Nick's hopes up." I rotated in my seat as much as my seat belt would allow. "Honestly, why should they trust you? What have you ever done to earn that trust?"

"I helped Nick."

"Yes, you helped Nick. But God knows why or how that happened. You won't explain it to me."

Ash started to speak. He got out a noise, but I shushed him.

"Don't start. I know, it was listening or good eye contact or whatever mumbo jumbo you want to throw at me, Mr. Does-Not-Have-A-Smell. Get over yourself."

"I got Perrick's home soil."

Arrrgh. I hated when he had a valid argument. "Okay. They trust you. But you can't handle demons, so stay out of it."

"Why do you trust Pinky so much?" Ash's voice hitched.

"Because he's always been honest with me, which I don't think you have. That's why. I'm a skeptical human being by nature, and as of this minute, I've decided to be more skeptical. It's better for my life expectancy."

We pulled into the lot and parked. I leaned into the back for my things, climbed out, and I was so pissy, I didn't check for the Warlock. Luckily, the Warlock wasn't present, but Kenneth was.

Ash called after me. "Becs! Wait. Come on. Let's talk about this."

"Bah!" I stormed up my back stairs, managing not to give him the finger. My mother raised a lady.

Ash tried to follow, but Kenneth interceded. "I don't think she wants to talk to you now, Asher." Was there a note of smugness to Kenneth's voice? I thought so.

I fumbled for my key while Kenneth teased an irritated Ash. I finally opened the door and let myself in.

I collapsed on my sofa, sputtering with laughter. The world was ending, and the men in my life continued to act like little boys. I inspired such mature behavior. Some big bad summoner I was. Whatever or whoever was responsible for giving me the Kiss was probably humiliated right now. *See, big mistake. Big, big mistake. You can take it back right now*, I thought. *Feel free.*

I removed my bracelet and stared at my Kiss hoping that maybe it would disappear, but no such luck. I hadn't expected it to, but it was worth a try. I placed my bag and the bow and arrows by the back door and scrounged for something to eat. I found a can of chicken noodle soup next to the dishwasher tabs. I had no idea why it was there, but it was only three months out of date. So dusting it off, I decided it had to be edible. Preppers saved soup for longer, and they stored it next to cleaning supplies, right? Figuring it couldn't kill me, I dumped it in a microwave safe bowl, nuked it to hellfire hot, grabbed a spoon, and returned to my place on the couch.

Zepar. I'd summoned him once. Another Great Duke of Hell. Twenty-six legions, I believed. Zepar's powers veered a few particular directions, but he was best known for taking ahold of a woman's free will and affection. It meant someone was in grave danger, and I needed to figure out who that was.

An internet investigation on Gregory didn't find anything important. Staged gossip magazine photos of him in a bespoke suit accompanied by a model or a television actress popped up on a simple search, but nothing past that. If he had a social media account of any type, I couldn't find it. Remembering what Nick had told us, I searched racing magazines, including horses, race car, greyhound, auto racing, and even kart racing, and while I saw mention of the Adamos brand, all were devoid of any images of Gregory himself. He had flunkies who appeared for him wearing three-piece suits and titanium watches that could feed the homeless of several major cities with no problem.

I dug back further and still nothing. He'd disappeared off the society pages as well.

He went out, because he'd been gone for the evening when we'd arrived, and I assumed he socialized for business as well as pleasure. My bet was at his own club. He'd be safe there. Of course, there was no way I was getting in there on my own. I'd need an entire new approach and expertise I didn't have, plus someone who knew the ropes.

I sipped my soup and ran through the people I knew. Zara might have worked, but it was inappropriate to ask her now. She was at the hospital most of the day, anyway.

Who did I know tangentially? Did I have friends of friends that I could ask? People who owed me favors after summonings?

Then it hit me.

Oh, no, no, no.

She was perfect.

Did I know her real name?

What would I owe her? I broke out in a cold sweat thinking about it. It would be a big ask, and she'd hang it over my head for a long, *long* time.

Then again, in just one night, I could possibly find the answer to this question. A simple reconnaissance mission. She'd be a perfect disguise. No one would notice me. Holy cats, could this work?

What time was it?

I still had time. I could make it over there and ask. My pride would take a hit, but a life hung in the balance, I was certain of it.

Chapter 25

JOEY'S FANS MUST have been working overtime that night, dispersing fae energy up and out the vents in the ceiling, because the bar was hopping with fae of all types, many I hadn't seen before. I didn't ask because it was rude, but three ladies lounged in a baby pool, which was new for me. As soon as I walked in, Joey heaved a sigh of relief, threw me an apron, and told me to make them three Salty Dogs. I had to look up the recipe. Grapefruit juice, gin, and coarse sea salt.

I hadn't expected to work tonight, but it played into my hand, so I hid my backpack in its normal spot, slipped right in, and made a point of rounding the tables. One woman was sitting by herself, and the other fae nearby gave her a wide berth, even moving their high tops several feet away. I wasn't sure I should approach, but she was in the bar, so I asked her what she wanted.

"Can I get you anything?" I stood back, wary. Her entire vibe screamed witch.

"Did you park here, dearie?"

"Yes."

"Was my house in the lot?"

"Your house?"

She waved me off. "I'll take a Shirley Temple."

I made a quick Shirley Temple, avoiding the eyes of others in the place who were staring at me as if I'd lost my mind and thought about what she said. I hadn't seen anything weird in the lot but I had heard . . .

. . . clucking.

I made two Shirley Temples with extra cherries.

"These are on the house." I mentally smacked myself. Making an "on the house joke," to this particular witch? *Idiot.*

"Oh, thanks, that's nice of you, young lady. What's your name?"

"Don't have one." I hurried off as fast as my feet could carry me.

No way was I going back. Two drinks would have to do. I fled to the bar and nudged Joey. "What is *she* doing here?"

"No feckin' clue! I couldn't believe my luck when you came

through the door. She doesn't know you, so I figured you'd get around to her, get'er the drinks and maybe she'd leave. Why she isn't sitting in a similar establishment in Russia, I do not know."

"Can't anyone tell her to leave?"

"Are you mad? Of course not. Baba Yaga goes where she wills and sits where she wants. She and that chicken-footed house of hers. She'll stay until she's damned good and ready to leave. And even if she offers, I'll nae be takin' a cent from her." Joey shuddered. "So wanna tell me why you're here? Not that I'm not grateful, seein' as how I need you and all, but I know you aren't here 'cause you had a premonition about the witch."

"Can we go to the back for a moment?"

Joey placed her hands on her hips. "Seriously? Becs, look at this place. We're five elves deep at the bar, and the mermaids in the pool are waving their glasses."

I snapped my fingers. "Ah ha! I thought they were mermaids."

"Mermaids are soooo much better than selkies."

"Why?"

"Selkies want all their drinks on the rocks."

"Wait." I slid my eyes toward my boss. "Was that a joke?"

Joey flashed me a grin. "Come on, what is it you want?"

I had to raise my voice to be heard over the din, but at least there was little chance we'd be overheard. "What's Gimlet Girl's name?"

"Who?" Joey refilled three drafts faster than I could count to three. I helped on the refills too, taking care of some dwarves. Those suckers could really slurp down chardonnay.

"You know, the pixie squad leader over there."

"Laurel? Why do you want to know? You hate her."

I opened a bottle of riesling for an elf wearing a fine dress of dark-green material with detailed embroidery and poured a generous glass. She lifted an eyebrow at me, and, rather than arguing, I poured another ounce, held out my hand for payment, and rang her up right away. I recognized her kind. Nobility. If I let her run a tab, she'd leave without paying.

"Believe it or not, I may need to ask her for help."

Joey whistled. "Ask her for a favor? That's painful. She's going to need an equal favor in return, you know. I'd hate to owe her. What can you offer her?"

"What do you think she'd like?"

"Jewelry, baubles, high-priced clothing, otherwise known as

nothing you can afford. A luxe vacation. If you were a man, well, then you'd have options. She adores sexual favors, but she only swings one way. How's that hot neighbor of yours? Would he consider fulfilling the bargain for you?"

"No! That's not on the table."

"Kenneth's cute. Maybe she'll take him. She likes innocents."

I snapped her with a towel which she ducked easily. "Joey, how can you suggest something like that? She'd eat him up and spit him out like yesterday's chewing gum."

"I'm giving you options."

"Ugh. This is awful. I have no choice but to go into the lion's den."

"Before you do this ridiculously stupid thing, get the mermaids another round."

"Fine."

Three Salty Dogs and an appetizer of chips and clam dip later, I approached my nemesis, Gimlet Girl, with a freshly made drink and a smile plastered on my face.

"Laurel, do you have a minute?"

Her look of surprise couldn't be faked, and her squad's sudden shocked silence said it all.

"I brought a gimlet. Peace offering."

"Did you spit in it?" she asked.

A reasonable question. "I didn't. Thought about it, but no."

"Why are you talking to me?"

I held out the drink, but she didn't take it, so I placed it on the table and shook the condensation from my hand.

"I need a favor."

She laughed, hard, and her squad laughed harder. When she could breathe, she tossed her long blond hair over her shoulder. "You . . ." She pointed at me. ". . . need a favor . . ." She turned her finger toward her chest. ". . . from me?"

"I'd like to come to an arrangement. I'm already regretting approaching you, so don't make me ask again."

She wiped fake tears from her large blue eyes. "Boo hoo. That's fine. I don't want to know what you need because, regardless, the answer is no. Go on about your merry way, human trash." She flipped her hair again and turned her back to me.

"If humans are such garbage, why do you hang out with us so much?"

"I didn't say all humans were, just you." She revolved back around, her head canted. "Wait. What about Gregory Adamos? I find him quite interesting, although unequivocally unappealing."

"I didn't say anything about him. How did you know that?"

"I picked it up from your thoughts."

I backed up several steps, guarded. "You read my mind?"

She let out a huff of breath that blew the front of her hair up. "I can't read minds, but I pick up strong thoughts. You're going after him."

"He's a total wanker, and I'm searching for some information on him that I can't find through my normal channels."

She studied me through slitted eyes. "You'll get no argument from me on the wanker part. Okay, color me intrigued."

"I need you to get me into his club." Laurel gave great blank face. I got nothing out of her, so I barreled on. "I need to observe him in a place he believes is safe. I don't want to hurt him. Trust that I'm not going to do anything precipitous in such a public place." I crossed my fingers behind my back and hoped she couldn't read that thought. "I want to watch him and see who he hangs out with. He's hiding something important, and I need to know what."

"Why?"

"He's threatened my sister's well-being if I don't do what he wants."

She snorted. "Your sister's life? Coward."

That surprised me. "I wouldn't have thought you'd care."

She raised one perfectly arched eyebrow and gestured to her posse. "Sisterhood is my life. I know you don't think much of us, but these girls are my family. Pixies live in female units. Threatening a sister is something I don't take lightly. That smarmy bastard doesn't understand bonds like that and doesn't value them. Doesn't he have a brother?"

I nodded.

She clicked her tongue. "Isn't his brother the one you . . . ? Oh, yes. I heard about that. Is what he wants from you in retaliation for what you did to poor little Nicky?"

"Believe it or not, no. And you should know that 'poor little Nicky' wasn't always the incapacitated victim he is now. He strode into my office and demanded I summon a demon, complete with an armed enforcer, in case I had other ideas."

Her girls listened attentively to our conversation but didn't interrupt. "Also, I want to straighten something out. I understand sisterhood perfectly. I hold nothing against you except that you bullied me like a queen bee at prom over my gimlet skills for no reason. What did I ever do to you? I was new to bartending, and you were a bitch."

Her squad collectively inhaled an offended breath.

She pierced me with a serious mean-girl stare and then studied her nails. "I don't like your attitude."

"I don't like yours either, but can we do business?"

"Tell me what you're looking for."

"I can't tell you too much." I held up my hand palm out before she got huffy with me. "Don't get your tail all bushy. It's for everyone's protection. But I can say that I think a woman's life may be in danger."

She squinted at me, and I got the feeling she was reading the tea leaves again. "You think Gregory's got his eye on someone else's side piece, and he's going to try to take her by magical means to be his."

She'd hit the nail on the head, but I didn't say anything. Damned mind-reading pixie.

"Hold on, please. Please stand over there." She pointed to a spot a few feet away, and I hovered there like a dog on a leash, resenting every second. But I bit my tongue and bore it because it I couldn't think of a better option.

I snagged a couple of napkins from a table and wiped the grime from a small window in the corner of the bar where I waited. The windows in Joey's were tiny four-paned squares, enough to let in a little sunlight or to acknowledge the fading day and rising moon, but most customers never gave them a passing glance. The quiet, ominous darkness outside punctuated my concerns. Streetlights turned red, orange, green without cars, and the other businesses had either long closed or were ushering customers out for the night. Tiny twinkling lights overhead caught my eye, and I studied them, uncertain what they were. I thought they might be reflections of the streetlamps in the windows or some other trick of the eye, but no, they were real. And as I watched, I realized they drifted in the same direction—south.

South.

Well, wasn't that a thought? I filed it away.

A snap drew my attention.

"I've decided to help you."

I chewed the inside of my cheek to keep from mouthing off. I'd asked for this.

"We need to discuss terms," Laurel said with a toss of her mane.

"Naturally," I replied through gritted teeth because she was going to drag this out and make it as uncomfortable for me as possible. "Let's make sure you understand what I want. I don't want you to do anything other than get me into Gregory Adamos's nightclub as soon as possible, on a night we believe he will be there, with enough glamour that he will not recognize me so I can observe him. That's it."

"The glamour is the hardest part," she said, tapping her fingernail to her teeth, circling me like a shark. "It must be believable, and you give off a certain aura . . ."

"Yeah, an aauuura," said her main wannabe girl, drawing out the word like last season's *Vogue* editor. I wanted to hiss at her like a cat, but I held back because I was an adult. Also, I needed this to work, and there were nine of them and only one of me. The odds weren't in my favor if we got into an epic girl fight.

"I can do it," Laurel said, ceasing her observations. "I know how, but you're going to owe me a favor."

"What kind of favor? I don't like open-ended bargains."

"Too bad because I don't need anything from you right now." She crossed her arms under her chest, pushing her generous bosom up farther. It was an unconscious action, and she did it by reflex. Her posse adopted the same pose, following her every move like lemmings. It was super creepy Stepford wife stuff. *Ick.*

I racked my brain for any other option. Unspecified favors to the fae were the magical equivalents of landmines. In fact, an unspecified obligation was part of what got me into this position in the first place, although being indebted to a demon did have a different, undeniably evil flavor. I didn't get evil vibes from Laurel—simply self-serving, egotistical, and venal ones. I would live through those.

"The favor must be equal in energy expenditure. It cannot go above or beyond in time or emotional commitment. Like for like."

"Agreed. Imbalance isn't good for either of us. It doesn't sit well in my tummy." She winced and rubbed her mid-section at the thought. I'd heard that this was literally true. Fae suffered imbalance as physical illness and wouldn't feel right until they corrected it. It also meant she wouldn't let the favor sit too long. That made me feel a little better about the situation.

"It's a deal," I said, and I knew the moment we struck the bargain because a tiny flick of unease set in between my shoulder blades, one I was certain wouldn't go away until we'd fulfilled the bargain on both sides.

"Where is his club, and when do you think he'll be there? It has to be soon. I'm running out of time." I realized I hadn't expressed my urgency earlier and worried that she'd bail on me for technicalities.

She scrunched her pretty eyes shut, thinking. "Tomorrow evening he'll be there. It's not easily found, but I can get us in. Let's meet here first, and I'll do the glamour. Nine p.m., so you'll be there before he is and can stake out a good spot. Oh, and you're paying for my drinks, naturally. Dress sexy."

"What time will he arrive?"

"Ten-ish."

"Got it." I had one last question. "What's the club's name?"

Laurel settled on her stool, her back to me. She looked at me over her shoulder and said, "The Three Arrows." Then she turned her attention back to her friends, and I was dismissed.

Chapter 26

I'D ALWAYS HEARD that you should wear leather if you wanted to make an entrance.

It was hot as hell to wear, though. Sticky. I loved it as a jacket, but pants were a gamble. I'd gone with pants and regretted it after twenty minutes. My white V-neck blouse stuck to me too, and I quickly threw my hair into a high ponytail. I'd left it down for sexy points, but I was too damn sweaty to keep it that way. And I'd done my makeup super sexy with a lot of mascara and a full-on smokey eye. I didn't recognize myself, but I was club worthy.

We met at Joey's and traveled to The Three Arrows together—me, Laurel, and her crew trailing behind. Laurel made me promise not to say a word but to follow her lead.

First, she'd given me a few lessons.

"Can you stand sexy?"

"I don't know what you mean?"

She cocked a hip out, threw her other leg backwards, and pouted. I'd seen her do it before but never tried to imitate it. So I gave it a shot.

"No, no, no. You look constipated. That's not going to work. Can you look sexy demure? Like this?"

She stood straight, both feet together, boobs out, head down with her hair over one eye. The other eye looked straight at me, shy and coy.

"I don't know. Here goes."

Whatever I did, it was a complete fail.

"Stop it! Don't do that. Just. Don't." She pinched her nose. "Girls, what do you suggest?"

One of them said, "What about the 'tough cookie?'"

Laurel perked up. "That could do it. Becs, do this. Hip out, head at an angle, and adopt a 'screw it' attitude. It's simple."

I knew that one! *Bam*. I added a sneer. Extra points.

"Drop the sneer, add some lip gloss, and you'll be good. But remember, don't say a word." Laurel said a few words of mumbo jumbo, and a light veil of magic settled over me like a fine mist.

"There," she said. "That will last long enough to get you in, but if anyone recognizes you, the veil will lift."

"Good enough."

Someone threw me an unopened tube of gloss with a dismissive, "keep it." I slathered it on and followed Laurel to the entrance where there was already a long line. The bouncer looked us up and down. Each pixie adopted their best pose. Laurel led the assault.

"Hey, Chris." She sidled up to him and whispered something into his ear. Since I stood behind her, doing my best "tough cookie," I was at a good vantage point to notice her hand slide up the back of his thigh and around his hip. He blushed and swallowed but otherwise didn't move.

"Who's the new girl?" he asked.

Laurel gave him a sideways glance. "Becs, come and meet Chris."

I viewed this as an acting exercise and did my best pixie imitation. I caught his eyes and smiled, letting my eyelids drop halfway, and touched the tip of my tongue to my top lip. I approached, rolling my hips, and caressed his bicep with my hand. "Hi, Chris. It's nice to meet you. I'm . . . new."

"Hmm. Where were you before this?"

I waved my hand as if it were of no importance. "Some podunk town. No place in nowhere. You understand." I pressed into his side and let him feel how small I was compared to him. He had to be at least three hundred pounds, most of it muscle. He must have enjoyed the feel of my body, or at least the view down my blouse because he gave me a tight squeeze.

"You'll do. Go on in, ladies."

And that was that—we were in. Laurel and I took a two-seater high top in a corner where we had a good look at the whole club, including the roped-off upper level, which was empty, and the rest of the posse spread out strategically.

The Three Arrows vibrated with a high-intensity vibe, dance music blaring, hot men and even hotter women grinding on the dance floor. The bartenders moved with slick efficiency, and I admired them with green-eyed jealousy. It smelled like sweaty bodies and liquor, but every so often, I caught a whiff of lilac, which I realized they pumped in from the vents above to cut down on the stank created by so many people in one place. I barely noticed the bouncers, except for the obvious ones stationed at the door, because Gregory only hired the best. Not muscle-bound weightlifters, these bouncers glided with the grace of practiced martial artists. I had no doubt they could remove a rabble rouser imperceptibly, so no one noticed or even spilled a drink.

Gregory's club functioned with exquisite precision.

"The bartenders pour each drink at exactly the same number of ounces without looking," I remarked to Laurel. "A perfect one-ounce shot. An exact four-ounce wine. They had to have been trained and tested multiple times to get that level of accuracy."

"That's Gregory for you. He's a stickler."

"He must pay well."

She scoffed. "He doesn't. Bottom dollar, in fact."

"Then how does he get people this good?"

She rolled her eyes at me. "How do you think?"

"Of course. He has something on everyone."

"Bingo."

"That's a stupid business practice. No one is loyal to him."

"Doesn't matter." She pointed to a man entering from the back. "Because that man is, and if he's here, Gregory is as well. They'll go upstairs."

"Oh. My. God. I know that man."

His name was Carl. He'd come into my office when Nick had first asked for his favor. He looked exactly the same—tall, big—but like the bouncers, he moved like a dancer. Shaved head, goatee, and mustache, he scanned the room looking for something or someone, then reversed course and exited. Three minutes later he re-emerged, this time with the man of the hour in tow. A man and a woman accompanied Gregory, and they proceeded up the stairs to the private balcony area. A lovely server wearing fishnet stockings, a bodysuit, high heels, and a top hat, followed them to take their drink orders.

"Do you know who the couple is?" I asked Laurel.

"That's the mayor of Smokey Point and her husband, Becs. Oberon's balls, don't you know anything?"

"Hey, I don't pay much attention to politics. And aren't you supposed to avoid saying the Big O's name?"

"I don't believe in that nonsense." She stared hard at a beautiful man dancing without his shirt. "And, from what I've heard, calling him the Big O is hardly true."

My mouth gaped, and I flapped my hands as if waving away pesky mosquitoes. "For the record," I announced to the air, "I had nothing to do with what she said."

"Oh, don't be silly. I'm going to dance. I did my part and got you in here. You're on your own now." Laurel slithered to the dance floor where the shirtless dude waited, turning toward her like a hypnotized snake. The rest of her posse convened on the dance floor like runway models on the catwalk, and I was left to my own devices.

I hadn't given her the promised cash for her drinks, but before I could run after her, a waiter wearing black leather pants and a black leather bandolier that crisscrossed over his bare chest twice in an "X," stopped at my table. "Can I get ye a drink?" he asked, batting his eyelashes.

His lilt was on point but absurd in this setting. I eyed him suspiciously. "What's with the Irish?"

He laughed. "I thought it'd be funny," he replied in a perfect, flat Midwestern accent. "I heard your pretty companion say something about Oberon, and I decided to bring out the brogue. My mom raised me on Irish mythology, and it seemed amusing. All I want is your drink order."

"Sorry, I'm superstitious sometimes. A glass of chardonnay, please."

He blanched. "Chardonnay? Really? With those pants and that blouse?" He leered like a professional. "You know you want something stronger, and my phone number."

"Fine. Tequila. Suavecito Reposado if you have it. Straight, with a single lime, and no offense, but I'll skip the number."

"Too bad. We could have rubbed leathers together." He sallied forth to get my drink, or to harass other women. Either was fine with me. I couldn't think of anything more painful than rubbing leathers. A gunshot wound would hurt less.

A change in the music drew my attention to the dance floor. The up-tempo vibe switched to a slow song, and couples of all shapes and sizes—not to mention a few threesomes—swayed to the more mellow ambiance. I lifted my eyes upwards. The mayor supported herself on one elbow and spoke urgently into Gregory's ear. He listened attentively while the mayor's husband flirted with the waitress in the fishnets and scarfed down an appetizer. He appeared totally at ease and unperturbed by his wife's close connection with Gregory and didn't bat an eye when Gregory patted the mayor's hand and motioned for a second waitress to bring something edible for the two of them.

I didn't know how to interpret this, but my instincts told me to stay still and observe some more. There was something I was missing. By all rights, it appeared to be a business meeting, even if it was in a club late at night. Suits and ties for the men, a tailored suit for the mayor. She carried a bag large enough for file folders and motioned to it occasionally.

The waitress brought a bottle of wine and two platters of pasta. The mayor shook her head to decline the wine, which made Gregory frown, but he relented and poured himself a glass which he then didn't touch. The two of them continued to talk, heads together.

My tequila arrived, plus a glass of water, served by a pretty waitress. It looked like my bandolier-wearing waiter had departed for greener pastures.

"Suavecito. Slice of lime. Want a tab?"

"No, thanks." I slapped down a twenty. "Keep the change."

"Yes, ma'am."

I'd been "ma'amed" and spent a third of the cost of a bottle for one ounce—a banner evening. I sipped this drink slowly, drawing it out. I must have done a good job, too, because the waitress passed by me several times, eyeing me for another order, but I shook her off.

"Watching everyone's favorite crime lord?" Asher asked as he slid into the chair next to me.

I gaped at him before I found my voice. Since he'd recognized me, I knew my pixie glamor disguise was totally trashed. "What are you doing here? How did you know I was here?"

He pointed at the dance floor.

An unfortunately familiar strawberry-blond head bee-bopped to the music with a friend wearing a tangerine dress that offset her dark skin to perfection. The two caught a lot of male, and female, attention.

"Kellie?"

"And Aster, her friend, also a server at Giatanos. They heard Laurel say your name to the bouncer, which caught their attention since it is unusual. They said you looked different at first but then they recognized you. They seemed to think I should know where my 'girlfriend' was and that she was sitting at a nightclub drinking alone."

They'd seen through the glamour because of my name. Well, that didn't work.

"You told them I wasn't your girlfriend, right?"

Asher smiled. "Nope."

"This counts as stalking." I sipped my water.

"No." Asher shook his head with a cocky smile and threw his arm over the back of his chair. "This counts as going out for the evening with two friends and running into a third."

"Really?"

"Absolutely. Pure coincidence." He signaled the waitress. "I'll have what she's having."

"You don't drink tequila."

He smiled again. "Sure, I do."

I snorted and tapped my finger on the table. "Prove it. What is your favorite tequila?"

"I like all kinds."

"Gold is the best, don't you think?"

"Absolutely."

"No, you dumbass. Gold is the worst. You know literally nothing about tequila. Why are you pretending you drink it?"

"Because you like it, and I want you to like me," he said, loud enough for the people at neighboring tables to hear us, even over the music. One of the women formed a heart with her hands over her chest. I leaned down to "adjust" my shoe and flipped her off. She startled, offended, and gave me the finger back. The behemoth man next to her looked like he was going to get up and beat me to a pulp, but she stopped him with a "she's not worth it," wave of her hand.

Asher continued talking, unaware of the drama happening behind him.

The waitress dropped Ash's tequila on the table and waited for the cash, which he handed over.

"Give it a whiff," I said. "Smell it and I'll explain what you're experiencing while I keep an eye on Gregory."

"Don't swallow it?"

"No, you heathen," I said, not looking at him but watching Gregory continue to consult with the mayor. "Breathe it in."

"What am I smelling?"

"This is their Reposado. It has a woody scent." I glanced at Gregory. "What do you think he's talking to her about?"

Ash hadn't looked up and was still staring into the glass. "I think the tequila is talking to its lover about what she means to him even though he can't tell her all his secrets."

"What? No. Very poetic, but no." I snapped my fingers in front of his face. "Head in the game, please. I'm referring to Gregory. Look up there. He's been speaking to the mayor for half an hour with her husband present. They're very . . . chummy."

Ash blinked at me, then followed my hand to the balcony to observe Gregory and the mayor. "He does appear to take what she's saying seriously."

"More than that, look how he touches her arm every now and then."

"Oookay." He sniffed his drink again. "She doesn't react when he does that, right? So what's the problem?"

"She doesn't seem his type, does she? She's attractive but not gorgeous. Gregory is rich and powerful and fairly good looking. He could have any woman he wants. And this is the one he wants to steal away?"

"You think he's good looking? He's not all that." Ash wrinkled his nose.

"He's got a vibe. Lots of women go for the barrel-chested, big-shouldered thing."

"I don't see it. As you said, though, maybe it's more of a power thing. She is the mayor." Ash took a tentative sip of the tequila.

I waited while he closed his eyes and swished the tequila around in his mouth then swallowed. When he opened his eyes, I said, "Okay, tell me what you taste."

"Something sweet."

I chucked him on the chin with a wink. "Spot on! Cherry, in fact. We'll make a tequila drinker of you yet."

"Gee, thanks, teach." He took another sip. "Why are we watching Gregory Adamos play footsie with the mayor?"

"I'm trying to get inside his head."

"Whoa." Ash jerked his chin at the back entrance. "Who are they?"

A stunning African American couple walked in arm in arm, owning the room, appreciating that eyes turned to them and perfectly comfortable with it, expecting it as if it were their birthright. Maybe it was. Ash and I watched them glide up the stairs to the balcony where Gregory rose to his feet to greet them. She wore a sleeveless sheath dress in emerald green, and he wore a perfectly cut suit with a white shirt and a tie the same emerald as her dress. A few people said hello to them on the way in, but the woman's smile didn't reach her eyes as she acknowledged their greetings. The man shook hands more freely, but he kept close to his wife.

"Hold on for a moment." I shuffled out to the dance floor, elbowing my way to Laurel who was still dancing with the half-naked guy, her head thrown back, their bodies entwined.

"Hey!" I tapped her on the shoulder.

She whirled around, shocked, and when she saw me, her eyes narrowed. "I'm working here," she hissed.

I held up my hands, innocent. "One last question and I'm done." Without moving my body too much, I darted my eyes toward the couple who'd just walked in. "Who is that on the balcony with Gregory?"

She reached behind her to caress her man—ahem, her mark—with one hand and keep him occupied. "At least pretend to dance, stupid," she said to me through gritted teeth and a fake smile. I swayed a bit and tried to look like I was there for a good time. Laurel's boy toy was fooled. Reaching around her to grab my hips, he sandwiched her in the middle, his glazed eyes on her neck, as if he wanted to nibble that beautiful expanse of skin. Boy, was he going to be surprised.

In a practiced, masterful move, Laurel lifted her arm, ostensibly to brush back a lock of hair but used the motion to hide her swift look at the balcony.

"You don't know who they are, either?" She whistled. "You need to get out more, or at least watch the news. That's Terrence and Jordana Beale, power couple extraordinaire. She's an investment banker, and he's a hotel magnate."

"I wonder what business they have with Gregory?"

"They're the high society elite, even if Gregory is a goon underneath the façade. Now, that's the end of my involvement. Girl's gotta eat."

I thought back to what Joey had taught me about pixies. I tried not to say it. I really did, but, damn it, she was around a lot of humans. "Laurel, no killing."

The pixie reacted better than I thought she would. She gave me a curt nod and simply said, "I know the rules."

I left her and the pixies to it. They hardly ever lost control nowadays, Joey had told me, but vampire legends had started somewhere, and the truth wasn't what most people thought. Dracula's brides had been pixies. Dracula had just been the cover story.

Ash glowered at me when I returned to the table. "Who's the pretty boy fondling your hips."

"Laurel's dinner," I replied. "Where's my tequila?"

"I drank it. You're right. I like the cherry notes and the smooth finish."

"A vanilla, almost caramel aftertaste. Did you get that?"

"I did."

"We'll bump you up to the *añejo* next time. The finish is chocolatey."

Gregory stood as the Beales reached the balcony, and he kissed Jordana's hand, which she accepted like a queen at her coronation. Gregory stared at her with an intensity that she either ignored or didn't notice. Terrence and Gregory exchanged handshakes—not friendly ones, but not as if they were enemies, either. Business, I decided. They've probably known each other a while, but trust only went so far. I couldn't tell what Terrence thought about the way Gregory watched Jordana.

The mayor greeted the Beales with deference, a sell-out. Her husband ordered another drink and pulled out his phone, his presence totally ancillary to whatever was occurring.

The Beales sat across from Gregory, and the conversation began. Pleasantries at first it seemed, but then more aggressive, with the mayor seemingly playing referee. Despite this, Terrence seemed to enjoy himself and threw his arm around Jordana while she nudged her chair closer to his. He absently caressed her naked arm while they talked, and every once in a while, flashed her a special smile.

Gregory noted the smile and appeared uncomfortable with the display of affection. To cover his discomfiture, he walked to the balcony to survey his club's dance floor. Though Ash and I were far away, and the club's lighting made it unlikely that he could see us, I turned my head to the side, and Ash did the same. I pulled a play from Laurel's book and let my ponytail down so I could run my fingers through my hair and hide my face.

"Can I get you another drink?" My Midwest-accent-bandolier waiter returned, his attention focused on Ash this time. "Tequila for you both?"

"Absolutely," Ash said. "Can we try the *añejo* this time? Do you carry it?"

"Of course. This is Smokey Point, Ohio. We always have Suavecito here. It's a great brand with local connections."

"Good. We'll have two. Straight."

"No lime this time, please," I said.

The waiter's perfect timing did more to hide us than my hair trick, and by the time I turned my attention back to the balcony, Gregory had returned to his table. Their waitress arrived with more drinks and food, and while the table got sorted, Terrence lifted Jordana's hand to his lips. She gave him a shy smile that was totally out of character for the ice queen privilege she showed everyone else. It was remarkably sweet. At one point during their meal, she used her napkin to wipe a speck off of his suit lapel, and Gregory coughed into his napkin.

These two were obviously very much in love. And from Gregory's reactions, I could tell he hated it and wanted Jordana for himself.

"Ash, she's not picking up on it, but I think the beautiful Mrs. Beale may be in serious danger."

Chapter 27

ASH LEANED CLOSE enough that I could smell him, which I found both exciting and distracting, as well as odd, given what Pinky had told me.

"Danger? In what way?" he asked. "What can we do about it?"

I indulged myself by breathing him in and then placed one hand on his shoulder and another on the sticky table, then pushed him gently away. "We do nothing, at least not right now. You go home in your car, and I leave in mine. We'll figure this out in the morning."

Ash leaned back and threw an arm over the back of his chair, glancing toward the balcony. "She's not in imminent danger?"

I shook my head. "No, I don't think so. I think Gregory's got a thing for her and means to use a demonic contract to get her to fall in love with him and lure her away from her husband. That's why he wants to summon Zepar. He specializes in making women fall in love with men."

"A demon can do that? That's a shitty thing to do."

"It is, but that's why she's not in danger right now. He needs me to summon the demon."

Even in the nightclub's dim atmosphere with the flashing dance floor lights I saw his color rise, and I'd never heard him use the word "shitty" before. Ash drummed his fingers on his thigh and looked ready to jump out of his chair.

I observed him sitting there, his hair beckoning my fingers, his deep-brown eyes filled with concern for a woman he didn't know. He'd come to the Arrows after work, wearing his dark slacks and white shirt, but he'd rolled his sleeves up at the wrists displaying a few inches of sexy, muscled forearm. No tie this evening. He must have left it in the car, and its absence left a bit of dark chest hair peeping out at the neck. He was long and lean, and when he reclined in the chair, he looked like a Greek god. As he blew out a frustrated breath, all I wanted was to cuddle into his arms and lick the pulse in his neck, work my way up his jaw, and kiss his lips, whispering that it would be okay, and drag him under until he thought about nothing else but me.

Whoa. I needed more tequila.

Scratch that. I needed less, much less. Cold water would be better . . . even thrown over my head.

The DJ switched the music to something I recognized, a pop hit that I liked. Couples from every table ran to the floor to get their jiggy on, and I thought, *why the hell not?* So what if Gregory saw us? It wasn't a crime to be in the club. We'd paid for our drinks, and damn if I didn't want to dance with the gorgeous man next to me. Maybe shagging him senseless was a bad idea at this point, but dancing could still be fun.

I hesitated, unsure how he would react. He'd followed me here, but we'd had our ups and downs, not to mention trust issues, to say the least.

Ah, screw it.

I got to my feet and walked around the table. Ash watched me, his gaze tentative. In return, I let him see my uncertainty as well. I held out a trembling hand and didn't hide my vulnerability, letting him see me, no bravado.

"Dance with me?" I asked.

Delight lit his eyes, and a slow smile took over his face. He reached for my hand, his eyes on mine, and growled, "I thought you'd never ask."

As he led me to the dance floor, he grasped my other hand, and electricity sizzled up my arm when he touched my fingers. While it scared me, I vowed not to fear it so much that I missed something special.

I closed my eyes and let the music take me, feeling Ash across from me even when we weren't touching. I raised my arms above my head and floated with it, dropping my head back, moving my hips with the beat. I bit my bottom lip as I imagined Ash grabbing me in front of everybody, kissing me with abandon, making me his, and I wished he'd do it so much that for a moment, I thought he just might.

I opened my eyes, gasping for air because the fantasy was so real, and found him staring at me, totally still in the middle of all these undulating bodies.

"What?" I said, knowing he couldn't hear me.

He stalked toward me, his eyes on mine, placed both hands on my waist, pulled me to him, and crushed my lips with his. Every inch, every centimeter of my body went up in flames, my lips and tongue battling his while my fingers tangled in his hair, tugging him closer. He held me close enough that I felt his hardness against my belly, and I ached to have him inside me. I rubbed my body against his, and he slipped his hands to my head, holding it in place, asserting his dominance. Teasing more, I pulled his hips closer and bit his lower lip.

"If you do that again, I won't maintain enough control for us to get home, angel," he said, dragging his mouth from mine, panting ragged breaths into my ear. "Please? Let me take you home?"

"Yes. I'll meet you there."

He played with a strand of my hair. "No, let me drive you."

I moved closer to nip his ear. "We came in separate cars," I said and stepped back, still holding his hand so that our arms stretched between us. "Don't worry. I'll be right behind you."

He bobbed his head in agreement, stepping away while holding my hand for as long as possible. "Drive fast." He reconsidered his words. "Wait. I saw your driving tickets. Be careful."

I blew him a kiss. "I'll be on your heels. I promise."

Ash melted into the crowd toward the front door, leaving me in the middle of the club. I shook myself out of my reverie and hurried to the table where I'd stupidly left my backpack, a dumb move in a crowded club. My bandolier-wearing waiter saw me and waved me down.

"I held your bag for you, lass," he said with a wink.

"Oh, thank you! I'll even forgive you the cheeky Irish accent."

He motioned for me to follow him to the back where the wait staff stored their stuff. He dug through a pile of discarded purses and shoes, and other whatnots that people left behind. "I saw you dance with your boyfriend and figured I should protect your bag for you. Lots of nefarious people around you know." He tapped his nose.

"It was stupid of me to leave it. I appreciate it." I said, taking it from him.

"Love! It makes you do stupid things."

"I think we're far away from love."

He shrugged, his bandoliers lifting a centimeter from his shoulders as he did so. He was quite muscular, in a lean, predatory way. "Sexual attraction then. It's all good. I say take what you can and enjoy it."

I grinned. "That's what I intend to do. Good night, and thanks for keeping my bag safe."

"Have a lovely night, fair Rebecca. Remain interestin'." He gave me a small bow.

I walked to a small parking lot off the main road where I'd left my car when it occurred to me that I hadn't told the waiter my name, but then I remembered that I'd paid by credit card. Of course, he knew it. If I could get back into the club on my own, I'd see if I could find him again and ask him what he meant by "remain interesting."

The wind chilled the deserted concrete street, and the one street-lamp flickered in the dark, a cliché horror movie setting if ever there was one. Nevertheless, I was so excited to get home to Ash, I didn't hear the footsteps until they were right behind me. If I'd been a dumb blond movie star, I'd be dead at the hands of the masked cinematic villain, slashed to death because of my own stupidity.

"What were you doing in my club, Ms. Greenblatt?"

I rotated slowly to face Gregory.

"Dancing."

"I didn't see you arrive, but then suddenly, there you were, on my dance floor. You and Mr. Michaels were quite passionate, snogging your faces off."

"Is it against the law to visit a disco?"

Gregory whooped, threw his hands in the air, and twirled in a circle, a funny move coming from a tough mobster. "Who says disco anymore?"

An empty plastic bag blew down the street and got tangled at my feet. I kicked it away. "I'm old-fashioned, I guess."

He crossed his arms, his suit jacket straining over his chest. "Why were you spying on me?"

"I wasn't, Gregory. I was snogging my boyfriend, like you said." I held my keys ready. They made a good weapon.

"You expect me to believe that you simply wandered into *my* club? Of all places?"

"Yeah, that's what you should believe. No need to bring any muscle with you." I squinted at the wavering shadow behind him, letting Gregory know I saw his thug.

Gregory touched his chest in surprise. "What? I didn't bring anyone with me." He glanced over his shoulder, but he was looking the wrong way. The streetlamp lit a figure slightly off to my left, the one I'd thought was Gregory's body man. The figure posed, angled between Gregory and me, throwing an oversized shadow on the wall.

It took me too long to recognize who it was, and by the time I figured it out, the Warlock had two handfuls of glowing magic ready to toss at both of us.

"Illumination. It dawns, I see," the Warlock said in his whiny voice. The wind picked up, and a drizzle of rain fell. I wondered if the Warlock's magic was waterproof.

"What are you doing here?" I asked, mentally calculating paths of escape. I couldn't call him Derrick. He'd morphed into this inhuman thing, and it made me feel better not to think of him as a boy I once knew. "Haven't we said all we needed to say to each other? It's totally you, not me. This relationship isn't going to work, mainly because you're a murderous, psychotic lunatic."

"Hilarious. I'm here to finish you off, proving to Mr. Adamos here that I'm the better talent. And then, I'll need your body. Sorry, not sorry."

Gregory scoffed. "You don't have enough summoning talent to tie her shoes."

"Unfortunate. I'm taking over this town, supernaturally speaking, and you were going to be my best client. It's too bad you didn't understand that."

"I see you two have a lot to talk about, so I'm going to take my leave," I said, drawing the Warlock's attention to me, giving Gregory time to reach under his suit jacket.

Pfftt. Pfftt. Gregory drew his gun and shot the Warlock twice in the chest. The Warlock's magic evaporated, and he stumbled to the ground. I hightailed it to my car and opened my trunk where the death arrows rocked hard enough to shake the vehicle. *Okay, arrows, I'll give you a try.* I grabbed them and ran back to the Warlock and Gregory.

As I feared, the Warlock wasn't dead, not by a longshot. The bullets merely annoyed him, and he was up and fighting, throwing a ball of glowy magic at Gregory's head.

Gregory ducked, and the magic cannonball hit the bricks behind him, turning them into slag. The crime boss got off another shot, which abraded the Warlock's arm but didn't slow him down for a moment.

I extracted an arrow from my quiver, shaking with the thought of what I was about to do, bent to one knee to steady my aim, and let the arrow fly.

My shaft missed the Warlock by a mile. He smirked and flicked a look in my direction.

Quick as blink, and before I could nock another arrow, the Warlock swirled his hand in a half circle, called up a tiny eddy of burgundy magic, and shoved it at Gregory's torso. Gregory went down hard, still breathing but out of commission. He appeared to be paralyzed.

"Stupid. Gregory, you fool," the Warlock said as he strode toward me. "We could have been friends. I offered you my services, once this miserable human was out of the way and I rescued my father. But you had to go ahead and shoot me. I had plans for you, but you've ruined everything."

I dropped the bag, arrows, and bow and kicked them out of the way, realizing I didn't have enough skills to use them efficiently. I decided to go on the offensive with what I knew, drawing him away from the death magic arrows, not wanting them to get into his hands.

I ran directly toward him and got him with a left upper cut to the chin, but he was ready for me. He took the hit well, and I wondered if he had a pain amulet because it had to hurt being hit like that and yet he shook it off like a Labrador coming out of a lake. It sure hurt my hand. He snagged me by the back of my blouse and tossed me to the ground, ripping my shirt in the process. The fall knocked the wind out of me, and I lay there for a moment with the weight of the world on my chest. He took the opportunity to kick me in the ribs, and I rolled to get away, but he still connected, and the pain shot through my body like lightning. I rolled farther and forced myself to my knees, gasping for air.

"I freakin' liked this blouse, you homicidal maniac," I said, panting and holding my ribs with my bruised hand.

"Curious. What did you shoot at me, Becs? I didn't see what it was, and all I see with my eyes is your beaten up, lousy bag." He sniffed like a hound on a fox's trail. He stalked toward my stuff, and I couldn't stop him, my ribs aching with every breath. The Warlock raised his hand, palm down. "Bizarre. My senses tell me there is something here, something familiar. What could be over here that you're so intent on hiding from me?"

No. No. Not the death arrows.

He patted my bag, picked it up, opened it, and emptied the contents on the ground. My crap fell everywhere—a hairbrush, my wallet, a pack of gum. A pair of sunglasses, a bunch of loose pennies, nickels and quarters, several pens, a hair tie, hard candies, my library card, and a travel toothbrush. He shook the bag one more time, and the gold fae coin I'd gotten as a tip fell out. It rolled and fell on its side, coming to a rest when it bumped up against the invisible quiver.

I got to my knees, and blood dripped from my nose and mouth to the wet concrete. I wiped my face with the back of my hand.

"Fascinating. What's this?" The Warlock patted the quiver.

I crawled a foot, then another.

He manifested a golf-sized ball of burgundy magic and held it in my direction. "Stop."

I stayed where I was.

The Warlock closed his eyes and concentrated, furrowing his brow, holding his free hand over the bow.

I remembered Ash's words. *"You have to have faith, Becs. Magic misused has a tendency of turning on the user."* I had to trust those words were true. Had to trust in my power and that the death magic had allied itself with me for a reason.

"Alchemy. Camouflaged death magic, perhaps?" He sniffed like a dog scenting a fox. "I don't know how you've done it, Becs, but I think you've curdled my magic, souring it to me. I'd torture it out of you, but I don't have that kind of time."

"You're right. You don't." Gregory's voice was audible but weak, unlike the piercing crack of his gun as he took one more shot at our momentarily shared enemy. The bullet hit the Warlock just below the left shoulder and whirled him around, making him stumble and cry out. Blood spurted from the wound, and his left arm hung limp, useless. He staggered toward me, nonetheless, determined to finish me.

"Bastard!" The Warlock threw his magic at the mob boss without looking, missing his head by inches. "You'll regret that, but Becs needs killing first. I'm so sick of you both," he snarled. He readied another magic blast.

I forced myself to stay down, letting him come closer, and as his knee came within arm's reach, I snapped out my right hand in a hammer fist and connected directly with his kneecap, ramming it backwards. It hurt my hand badly too, but it was worth it to hear his grunt of pain and to watch him collapse. His fall placed his nose close to my fist, making it easy to hit him square in it. It was enough to knock him on his keister, and he finally crumpled the ground as his blood drenched the blacktop.

I wasn't going to wait around to get magicked again. I climbed to my feet, faded back, snatched my bag, and quickly gathered its contents. I picked up the bow and arrows and fled to my car. The rain fell harder then, and a large group of squealing people rushed out of the club toward their cars. I assumed Gregory would call for help. And Carl would find him eventually. But if he didn't? Well, I'd check the obits in the morning.

Chapter 28

ASHER WAS PISSED.

For all my promises that I'd be right behind him, that I'd be careful, I came home late with a torn blouse, bruised ribs, battered hands, and not in the mood.

"For once, Becs, for once, couldn't you do something the easy way?" he asked, handing me an ice pack for a bump on my head I didn't know I had.

"The Warlock started it," I said, wincing.

Ash sank into a chair and put his head into his hands. "You attract trouble like a magnet attracts metal shavings. I've never seen anything like it."

"On the plus side," I said, trying to be the optimist in the room, "the Warlock didn't get a hold of the death magic quiver, and no innocents got caught in the crossfire. I should have run away when I could have and let Gregory fight him alone."

"I know you hate the guy, but surely you don't wish him dead."

I gave Ash a baleful stare. "It would solve a problem."

"And open up more. Who would take over his operation? There'd be blood in the streets."

I lay down on the couch, shaking off my shoes. "Eh. Who made you such an expert at mob boss politics?"

Ash let out a wry laugh. "I've watched the *Godfather* series something like eighteen times." He removed his shirt, folded it into a small pillow, and placed it under my head. It said something about how awful I felt that I could only muster up a small wolf whistle at the sight of his abs.

"Ash, if I haven't told you lately, you are one freakishly gorgeous man."

He kissed me on the head. "And you are one freakishly beautiful, intelligent but frustrating woman who has a knot on her head, a black eye, bruised ribs, swollen hands, and a fat lip. I'm going upstairs. I programmed my number into your phone. Call me if you need me." He rubbed a lock of my hair between his fingers and brushed my cheek with his fingers. "Get some rest. Here's two ibuprofen and some water."

At least, it was one way to finally get his number.

Despite feeling like a platoon of Marines had used me as a punching bag for basic training, I huddled on my couch, satisfied that the Warlock hadn't been able to get his hands on the bow and arrows. They'd truly aligned themselves with me, and that made me happy, or at least, re-assured, even though my aim had been seriously off. I wondered if they'd let me practice with them now. I swallowed the pills Ash left me, struggled to find a comfortable position, gave up, resigned myself to being uncomfortable, and finally fell asleep.

The dream's undertow took me right away . . . .

Back at the triangle of cityscape and forest with the sea in the background. Valefar made a big entrance complete with flashing sparks, gold dust motes, and a black top hat like I'd seen on the waitress at The Three Arrows. He rolled his eyes upwards. "I'm lovin' this hat," he remarked and did a four-footed soft shoe ending with jazz paws.

The *ding* of an elevator announced Gregory's arrival, but this time he sat in a brown leather lounge chair, feet up, ice pack on jawline. "It's been a hard day," he said, by way of explanation.

The Warlock stepped through a wormhole of silver and burgundy magic, snapping his fingers to close it behind him, swirling his cape. I couldn't see his face because he wore his hood like the Grim Reaper. Playing the part to the hilt, he snickered like a B-movie villain and clapped a glass of wine into existence. "You rang?" he asked. Then, looking at me and Gregory, "You two look rough."

I gazed down at my body and discovered that my injuries showed also, visible because I wore a short white T-shirt. My face ached as well, and when I touched it, I became aware of my swollen eye. I followed Gregory's lead. "Tough day."

"Tsk, tsk," Valefar said. "You mortals shouldn't get into such scrapes. You can't survive them."

"Isn't he a mortal?" I asked, jerking my thumb at the Warlock.

"Certainly," Valefar responded, "and, he's—how do you humans say it?—'under the weather,' as well, but hiding it better under the creature-of-the-night ensemble. You two did quite a job on his knee and shoulder. Well done."

I no longer knew if this was my dream or a shared vision. Pinpricks of awareness tickled my neck, warning me that it was real.

"What is this about?" I asked.

"Whatever do you mean?" Valefar asked, his eyes wide.

"Who's yanking my chain?"

"Oh, my dear Becs, this is your dream. You've summoned us here. You're the summoner, after all. You are the only one with the power to do this." Valefar waved his arm with a flourish.

I'd summoned them? Unconsciously? They were actually here, wherever here was?

That was new.

Gregory pursed his lips. "You mean a part of me is here because Becs summoned me? This isn't my dream?"

Valefar cackled. "Oh, poor Gregory. Not in control at all, and he hates it."

Gregory flexed his biceps and cracked his knuckles. "Send me back. Now. This isn't part of the deal."

I showed him my teeth. "We don't have a deal. You ordered me to do something, and you're blackmailing me into doing it by threatening my sister and Perrick. You're a cruel organized crime boss, so if I'm in charge right now, you can sit there and stew."

"And you," I said, turning to the Warlock. "You're a two-bit hack of a snow globe Santa magician who can't even kill me correctly. You can't steal a Kiss, dumbass. I didn't know you had a personal issue with Valefar, but it seems to me that you need to work that one out for yourself. I'm completely and totally done with you."

I whirled to face Valefar. "As for you, Sixth Duke of Hell." Valefar raised one eyebrow and bowed with his top hat. "You have a hold on me because I did the right thing to make up for my mistake. I don't think your hold on me is as potent as you think it is because I aided someone in need, someone you took in a shaky contract. I voluntarily entered a verbal agreement to save someone else, not a written contract for my own benefit."

Valefar's gold dust dispersed, and he growled deep in his chest, his normal human's head disappearing in a flash, replaced by an enormous lion's head, the top hat popping off and rolling away. He roared, showing me his slimy fangs. I stood still, letting his furious bellow wash over me and reverberate through the vast nothingness of the dreamscape.

"One word. Mouthwash."

The Warlock gasped at my defiance.

"Now, I want answers. The flower shop was owned by Gregory's number-one rival. Gregory, did you order its destruction?"

Gregory pulled another ice pack from the ether and placed it on his knee. "No, I did not. Why are we having this discussion?"

I paced. There was another answer here. I just knew it.

"Valefar, a witness saw gold motes, your trademark, flying out of the fire. Did you have anything to do with it?"

Valefar didn't answer.

"By your silence, I'm going to guess the answer is yes."

"Not directly, my dear Becs, as you know. I don't get involved directly in anything."

"You granted a favor."

Valefar conjured a gold and ruby throne. "That's my nature."

The Warlock commented, "I've heard that the Andino Trading Company has had several serious losses in the last six months." I stared at him, and though I couldn't see his face, something about his stance made him appear smug.

"Not my doing, although it has been fortuitous," Gregory said. "It's been my pleasure to see it happen. I've been vocal about my dislike for my rivals, and I assigned an employee to monitor their business assets and report back to me. It's been amusing to see them suffer losses, generally speaking . . ." Gregory trailed off.

"What is it?" I demanded. "Who is watching? Who knows what you want?"

"Someone who wants back in my good graces," Gregory said. "That's all I'll say." His face turned stony.

Valefar whistled a jaunty tune.

The Warlock tapped his foot as he waited for me to figure it out.

Gregory looked . . . embarrassed, as if he'd admitted too much.

The truth hit me like a two-by-four.

Oded was sitting in a burn unit because of the three of them. A mistake. An accident. A by-product of a contract gone wrong. And I'd been helping the wrong person.

I had one more question. "Gregory, are you stalking Jordana Beale? Tell me or I'll find a way to keep you here." I didn't think I could do that, but it was a good threat.

The mob boss studied his feet. "No, I'm not." He looked up. "That's the truth."

Not her, but what she represented. I saw it now. "I'm putting the three of you on notice. Consider this my one note of warning. Do not fuck with me again."

This time, I snapped my fingers, and woke on my couch. I'd been betrayed. I folded the blanket, placed it over the back of the couch, and crept into my bed, pulling the comforter to my chin, falling into a dreamless sleep.

I awoke to the head-banging woodpecker and considered petitioning the city to move the telephone pole to another location on the property. Then I remembered that I owed the city hundreds of dollars in moving violations and thought better of it.

"Alright, Mick Jagger, I'm getting up, you stupid bird." Actually, I was grateful we had a woodpecker his size left after the Warlock did his death mojo, but it would have been nice if he'd waited another hour to get his meal. I also wondered, if there were so many bugs inside the pole, how long could that thing stand up?

I hauled myself out of bed and into the shower. Checking my phone, I saw the forecast called for a hot one with high humidity. I donned a sleeveless tank but still wore jeans. I didn't do shorts, not since seventh grade when Scott Plotkin told me I had fat thighs. Some things stayed with you.

I needed to think about something else for a while, because my heart was heavy.

I made some jasmine tea, cracked a window, plugged in a fan, and opened my computer to do some research. Pinky belonged to the Summer Court, *that* I knew, but my experience with the fae only extended to what I'd seen in Joey's bar. The Winter Court and the Summer Court weren't necessarily good or bad. They each had their fair points and their ugly ones. For example, fairies like Pinky might look pretty, but not one had helped him return home. Lovely, delicate beings to look at. Mercenary, back-stabbing, heartless, little vermin in real life. Pixies like Laurel, also Summer Court, drank blood but would give you a night to remember. On the other hand, I'd met a tundra ogre once, Winter Court, and he'd been solicitous and a great conversationalist. Turned out that he was a voracious reader. It wasn't his fault he slobbered.

Watching the tiny lights fly south from Joey's window had spurred an idea. I searched the hospital campus map, both the one nearby and the rehab and nursing home campus to the south. Both had gardens. The one close to me, the Winter Medical Park, was twelve city blocks away, and Pinky worked in its gardens. The one to the south, named the Summer Medical Park, was an equal twelve city blocks away. I'd been told once that the city named the Winter Medical Park campus after a wealthy family whose last name was Winter, but that appeared to be incorrect, or at least, misleading.

The truth was more forthright than that. The entrances for each court lay in different gardens, and Pinky was in the wrong one.

I couldn't wait to tell him.

I still had no idea what his rhyme had to do with getting home but when we got to the garden, we could figure that part out. This had to be the answer.

I forgot about my tea, grabbed my bag, slipped into my sneakers, and raced down the fire escape, immediately sweating. *Ick.* But it didn't matter. I had good news for Pinky and a plan I needed his help with. I cut through the basketball court, the heat from the concrete seeping through the soles of my shoes even though it was still early in the day, then picked my way through the uncut grass on the other side and made my way to the nicer side of town and the park where Pinky worked and slept.

Food trucks lined the streets near the medical campus, and I stopped at one to get two fresh-squeezed lemonades. The sweetness and lemon flavor burst on my tongue with such brightness that I sighed, wishing I had another one as soon as I sucked mine down. But I kept the second one for Pinky.

I found him flitting, as much as a six-foot-tall pink man with wings could flit, from apple tree to apple tree.

"Pinky, I'm glad I found you."

He didn't look surprised, as if he expected me to show up. "Becs. What do you have?"

"A lemonade. It's for you. Would you like it?" I held it out, letting him come to me. Even though we'd touched a number of times, even hugging, I never knew what mood he'd be in, and I always let him initiate any contact. Today, he took the cup without thinking, although he frowned at the straw.

"Straws are bad, Becs. Plastic cups are bad for the environment too."

"I know. But I bought this on the way over, and this is what they had."

He sipped the lemonade and screwed up his face, holding the cup back out to me. "Hunnnnnh." He shook his head fast, back and forth. "No. No. No."

"Too much?"

His face still squeezed tight, he nodded.

"I understand," I said gently. "Let me take that from you." I'd wanted to surprise him with something delicious, but strong smells and tastes weren't always good for him. At least he hadn't thrown it on the ground.

I removed the straw, opened the top, and drank the rest myself. Pinky stared at the ground, unsure what to say. That was actually awareness on his part. Months ago, he'd have run away and hidden.

"It's okay, Pinky. I wanted another glass anyway. Don't worry about it."

"You sure?" he asked, his eyes looking past me to somewhere else.

"Yes, I'm certain. I've figured something out, Pinky, and I'll need your help to fix it as best as I can. Then, I think I know how to get you home."

His eyes popped open wide, and he made eye contact directly. "Really?"

"Really."

"Okay, what do we do first?"

"Let me tell you what I know."

I explained everything to Pinky. He frowned, rocking up on his toes. "That's not fair."

"No, it isn't."

"We can't make Oded okay again?" he asked, continuing to rock back and forth.

"He'll heal," I said with more confidence than I felt. "And we'll make them pay for hurting him."

"Pay in money?"

"No. I mean, we'll make them feel bad for injuring him."

"They didn't hurt him, Becs. They burned him. That's different, isn't it?"

"Yes, Pinky, it is. We'll make them feel really, really bad though."

He thought about it. "I don't think they can feel bad enough."

"Me neither."

We sat still together.

"After that we'll visit the summer garden?" he asked.

"Yes."

He crossed his arms, hugging himself, and tugged at his wings, thinking. I let him, staying quiet. After a minute, he nodded. "Okay," was all he said. But it was enough.

Chapter 29

I WALKED ASH through it too, and he'd agreed to his part, just as disgusted as I was.

Ash sighed. "You can't help it . . ."

I nodded. ". . . if people make bad deals."

It was all connected, as my vision intimated. It would have been nice if the vision had been clearer, but as Oded told me, all Noah got was a bird and a twig, not a map with an X.

It was time to enact the plan for real. Pinky and I parked about two miles away from Gregory's property, so it would take forty minutes to reach the border of his lot, given that we'd be sneaking in along the shoreline. It was getting dark, but people were still out trolling the beach, enjoying the last of the summer day's rays. Warm and lovely, it would have been the perfect day to indulge in the feel of sand beneath my toes, and I wished all I'd had to do that evening was relax with Ash on a blanket. But obviously, that was not to be.

Pinky sprinkled me, my knapsack, and the quiver and bow with fairy dust. I didn't feel different, but when I looked in my powder compact's mirror, my image was gone. I touched my face.

"You're still here, Becs."

"No one can see me, but can they sense me heat-wise? Will I trip infrared?"

"I didn't think about infrared. You should have mentioned it. You think Gregory has that?"

"Dunno but seems like something he'd do. What about motion sensors?"

"Most definitely." Pinky bounced on his toes. "We'd need my Uncle Sal to avoid that. It's too complicated. I'm sorry."

"It's okay. Not your fault. You have an Uncle Sal?"

"Sure, don't you?"

I thought about it. I didn't have an Uncle Sal, but I had an Uncle Sol, which was practically the same thing. Damn, the fairy had a point.

"You did great. Thank you. I appreciate your help." I took a deep breath. "Well, nothing for it. Let's get going."

In addition to the public beach areas, we had the trickier job of avoiding people relaxing on their private beaches. Also, a couple of dogs gallivanted around, and they weren't fooled at all by our invisibility since they could smell us just fine. One particularly persistent mutt almost got us.

"What's Rocco barking at?" We could hear the owners from inside their bungalow, which was larger than most normal people's houses.

"He's seeing ghosts again."

"Damn dog barks at anything that moves. Come on in, boy. Don't get skunked again."

I was sneaking up on Gregory's estate because I had to set the scene for our meeting without him knowing. Ash would get there as well and occupy him while I finished getting the party ready in the back. It was all about timing, at this point. The dog was messing things up.

"Go on, Rocco, hurry up. Go home," I whispered. Pinky and I backed into a pine. Needles poked me in the back, and sap seeped into my hair. I smelled like a Christmas tree.

Rocco barked louder.

"What is it with that dog?" came the female voice from the house.

"I'll go get him," said the male voice.

For cryin' out loud.

The dog, who was wet from lake spray, ran right up to us and rubbed his head against my leg and begged me to pet him.

"Nice doggy," I said, my voice low, petting his furry mop of a head. He wiggled his butt, excited by the attention, jumping on me to lick my face. I struggled to keep my balance.

Ugh. Now I smelled like wet puppy.

The dog barked, brought me a stick, and dropped it at my feet, panting hot, happy breath.

"I can help, Becs. I speak Canine. Throw the stick." Before I could say anything, Pinky yipped and ran into the dog's path, bowing down like a dog who wanted to play. I threw the stick, Pinky retrieved it, and he and Rocco started a game of tug of war. Rocco delighted in playing with this new pink dog. Pinky dropped the stick, and the two chased each other through the sand, rolling in it with glee. Pinky moved fluidly on his hands and knees, so much like a pooch that anyone looking would have only seen one friendly dog cavorting with another.

Pinky never ceased to amaze me, but I couldn't stand there and watch. I had to take the opportunity he'd given me and get going, even if it separated us and put a kink in the plan. I fervently hoped he caught up later.

I struggled through the sand, tripping over the flotsam and jetsam that washed up on the shore, particularly on the inlets hit by high tide. I picked my way through the driftwood, trash, and the endless rocks that made the ground uneven and perilous. Lake Erie waves crashed on the water's edge, drowning out my voice as I whispered, *"Don't get caught. Don't get caught."*

I must have repeated this a hundred times as I approached Gregory's estate, the last fifty feet or so crouched down, feeling with my hands for any trip wires or obvious signs of border security. I didn't feel anything, but as soon as I worked my way up from the beach and stepped onto the grass, strobe lights raked the property, and klaxon alarms rang across the lake into the dusk.

I froze. *Shit. No. No.* I couldn't be found now. I needed more time. And privacy.

Gregory's voice rang out across the property. "Perrick! Who's there? Find out, now."

Perrick replied, "Yes, sir," in a thin, reedy voice. The troll lumbered onto the yard, lurching with every step, pointing to the sides with his hands, directing other flunkies to check the perimeter. They each brandished a weapon. I didn't know how Perrick would react if he found me there. Would he rat me out, loyal to Gregory, or support me, given that Ash and I tried to help him?

The back yard was huge—this wasn't a normal house but more of an estate. The dock was down an incline next to the boathouse, and I was on the far left side of the yard. The lap pool sat closer to the house, directly across from where I hid. Nearer to the mansion was the large porch with the sitting area and firepit. The firepit was my goal.

One of the guards scoured the area where I stayed concealed. I scrunched down next to a bush, praying Pinky's razzle-dazzle dust stayed true and I remained invisible. The guard walked past me, and I breathed a small sigh of relief until he doubled back and stood right in front of me, sniffing like a golden retriever. He leaned forward, nostrils flaring.

Was he part fae?

He stepped one foot closer, and I didn't dare move but I sucked in my belly and held my breath, shoving my bag and the arrows behind me. His leg was two feet from me, and when he swayed his head side to side like a snake, he sucked in air through his mouth, circulating it through his nose, scenting me like a . . . like a . . .

. . . cat.

I'd never met a were-cat or a were-anything before, but I assumed whatever it was had an excellent sense of smell.

"Perrick!" The were-whatever summoned the plains troll to where I sat, scrunched into a small, still ball, barely breathing.

"I smell something here although I don't see anything."

Perrick sniffed too, his eyes narrow.

He squatted, his thighs shaking with the effort given his infirmity. "I smell wet dog."

Rocco had left his mark.

"There's something else underneath it. Human."

Perrick sneezed, and a great glob of mustard-colored mucus landed on my cheek, and I sat immobile letting it roll down my neck in slow, gelatinous rivulets. I closed my eyes and pressed my lips together forcing myself not to react although I swore revenge on Perrick if I lived through this. My stomach roiled as the troll got within centimeters of me, and I had to hold myself still to keep from screaming at his green, putrid face.

Perrick inhaled deeply, and I saw the moment he recognized my scent underneath the wet dog and pine smells. His pupils dilated, and he patted the grass in front of me, bumping my foot. He halted then patted me again.

"Nothing here. A dog passed through, that's all. Let's go."

So he'd chosen not to betray me.

A few minutes later, the alarms silenced, and the lights returned to the normal glow of the yellow border lights and pretty ones that illuminated the pool and patio. I blinked, sucking in air as if I'd run a four-hundred-meter sprint.

No time to waste.

I scurried onto the lawn, across the great expanse of grass, to the firepit next to the patio. I placed my bag on the ground and noticed it was visible. I checked my hands and arms, and they were too. The fairy dust had worn off. Time to get moving.

I had decided the firepit made a natural circle, providing a symbolic enclosure that Gregory, the Warlock, and anyone else would believe contained the demon inside. In truth, it meant nothing. The only thing holding the demon would be my will.

Risky. Absolutely everything could go wrong. It was the most precarious thing I'd ever done.

Everything probably would go wrong.

But I couldn't back out now.

I extracted five blood-red candles and placed them on the brick border of the fire pit to form a pentagram and sprinkled some gold and black party glitter I'd purchased from a local craft store inside the pit.

The strains of a violin floated on the breeze, coming from the upstairs windows of the house. The deeper sounds of an oboe joined in, then a clarinet, and horns. I didn't recognize the piece, but I was far from an aficionado. I hadn't realized Gregory liked classical music.

I thought I saw a car come up the road, so I crept around the side and watched Ash park in the front.

Ash hauled a bag from the trunk. "I brought home soil for Perrick. We're here to do what you want, so give these to Perrick before he dies."

Gregory said something unintelligible, more of a grunt than an actual sentence.

Exasperation crept into Ash's voice. "She'll be here soon. We came separately. Why should you care? Helping Perrick is good business. He's going to die, and you'll lose your main enforcer. Don't you want him hale and healthy and ready to browbeat people again?"

Gregory sneered and spoke louder this time, clear as a bell. "Perrick's proven he's already willing to do anything to impress me. He doesn't need your soil. We have some here."

"Are you giving it to him?"

"In small doses."

"You're no better than a drug pusher," Ash said. "Fine, give it to him or not, I don't care. Becs called earlier and said she's willing to summon whomever you want. I'm here to watch her back."

"I'll bet you are," Gregory said. "Watch her back I mean." He was silent for a moment, and then, in a completely different tone, he said, "You really love her, don't you?"

Ash mocked him. "You wouldn't know what love is. Why do you care?"

That's the point, I thought. *That's the whole point.*

I rushed back to complete my setup. I lit the candles, thankful there wasn't a lot of wind, so the flames held steady.

Next, I went to the side yard, halfway to the house, and created another circle with six silver candles, the closest I could get to gray. I lit a burgundy candle and dripped dots of wax between the silver candles to create a circle and then lit the six candles. I placed a dead robin in the center of the circle. I'd found it under the tree next to the apartment, and I didn't know if it was one killed by the Warlock's death magic or one that died by other means, but I'd shoveled it into a bag and tied it to the strap of my backpack. Happy to have it out of my possession, I wiped my hands off as I left it there, disgusted that this was an appropriate offering.

Next, I texted the final player.

With a single sentence, I summoned the Warlock, who appeared in the circle of silver candles, confused, and royally ticked off.

"What? What am I doing here?"

"I summoned you."

"How? You can't summon me!"

"Funny. Seems I did, and you're here because I want you here. Now stay, watch, and listen like a good boy, until I let you out. Maybe you'll get a chance to help your father. Or you'll die. I can't say which way this will go."

I put an effort of will in it and clicked the circle closed.

"Trapped? You can't contain me in a circle!"

"I thought I couldn't do a lot of things, but it turns out I can do more than I thought I could. If you're so powerful, work your way out of it. I'll be back, by the way. This is temporary."

I left the bow tucked into some shrubbery at the corner of the patio where I could grab it later. I needed less to carry but didn't want to leave the arrows. An invisible bow seemed safe. An arrow was still a pointy stick. I took a deep breath and walked around to the front of the house.

It was showtime.

Chapter 30

I MET GREGORY and Ash in the same room we'd been in before, with the leather loungers and love seat. Gregory glided to the small fridge, popped a bottle of champagne, and poured three glasses, offering us each one. We both declined.

"Your loss," he said. "This is a lovely vintage."

"We aren't celebrating," I said, taking my place at the corner near the first lounge chair. I kept my knapsack and arrows on my shoulders while Ash leaned on the windowsill, looking nonchalant.

Gregory scented the air. "Why do I smell smoke?" He cocked his head. "And do I hear someone yelling? Perrick!"

I held up my hand in a placating gesture. "No need to bother Perrick. I've set the stage for a demon summoning. The yelling's nothing. Trivial. That'll be clear in a few minutes."

His eyes narrowed. "You have five minutes to explain. Are you going to give me what I want?"

"You haven't told me specifically what it is you want yet."

"No, I haven't." He crossed his arms and studied me, his eyes suspicious.

"Well . . . ?" I asked, rotating my hand to tell him to move it along. "Are you going to tell me or make me guess?"

"I want you to summon Zepar."

I nodded. "I know."

Gregory guzzled his glass. "You know? Then why did you ask? Who the hell told you?" He snapped his fingers. "Could have only been one person. That traitor." He raised his voice, hollering up the stairs. "Niiiiccck! You son of a bitch!"

Ash made a *tsk, tsk,* sound. "He's really not the son of a bitch here, is he?"

Gregory shot Ash a hard look. "I suppose you mean I am. Well, we both are. Our mother was a class-A bitch. Where do you think I learned everything I know?"

Ash frowned. "Then I'm sorry for you."

Gregory scoffed. "What are you? Some kind of naive special butterfly? I live in the real world. I'm grateful to my mom for showing me how to survive."

"How exactly did she do that?" Ash asked.

Gregory downed one of the glasses of champagne he'd poured for us and pointed at Ash with the empty glass. "You want to know? Here's an example. When I was seven, I had two puppies. She told me I could only keep one. She made me choose. It was the most heartbreaking experience of my life."

"Please don't tell me she made you kill the other puppy," I said. I didn't think I could take that.

"Funny you should ask," Gregory said. "She took the puppy outside but made me stay inside. She revved the car, and I heard the puppy squeal in pain, and then I heard a resounding crunch. She told me she ran over the puppy with the car, and I believed that she'd killed that puppy and it was my fault. She made me live with that guilt for ten years."

Gregory's throat worked, and he touched his tongue to his lip before continuing. "A housekeeper told me later that she didn't actually kill it. She gave it to the chauffeur, and the puppy lived out its life and died of old age."

I brought my hand to my mouth, unable to hide my revulsion. "That's evil. What a terrible thing to do to a child."

Gregory shook his head. "Wrong! It was the best thing she did. She taught me what it was like to make a life-or-death decision."

Ash spoke softly. "Children aren't ready for that kind of choice."

"Fuck you. What do you know?" Gregory replied, lifting the third glass.

I shrugged at Ash. None of this mattered. Maybe he'd been badly damaged by his parents, but he was still responsible for his choices now.

"Gregory, what is your most expensive bottle of champagne?" I asked, perusing his collection.

"This one not good enough for you? I have a Krug Vintage Brut 2006 which goes for a pretty penny."

"Perfect." I retrieved that exact bottle. "We have a fire going and the elements for a summoning. Let's get outside and get this over with."

Before Gregory could say another word, I walked out the sliding glass door to his patio, keeping my bag on my shoulder and my invisible quiver of arrows on the other.

I called to Ash. "Remember, stay back, okay? No matter what happens, this isn't your fight. Stay hidden."

Ash raised his hand in acknowledgment. More music emanated from the upstairs windows, another orchestral piece, as if we had a soundtrack for the evening.

"What are you doing?" Gregory sputtered when he saw the firepit with its red candles and gold glitter. "Is this how you summon Zepar? Quit playing around!"

I whirled on him. "I'm done playing, too. Glad we're on the same page." I placed the champagne bottle in the middle of the fire pit and said, "Valefar, Sixth Duke of Hell, I summon thee."

Gold dust, gold motes, the smell of brimstone and ash. The lion body, griffin wings, and, this time, the original head with the dark eyes, close-cut beard and mustache, thick eyebrows, and horns and fangs. He'd come to do business.

Gregory hissed and went for my neck but stopped when Valefar materialized fully.

"This is an outrage!" Gregory was all but spitting. "I don't want Valefar. I asked you to summon Zepar."

"I know what you want," I said. "At first, I thought you wanted me to summon Zepar so you could negotiate for Jordana Beale to fall in love with you. Zepar's specialty is making women fall in love with men, after all. I saw the way you looked at her at The Three Arrows."

"Ah," breathed Valefar. "Finally, something I can work with. Let me help you, Greggie-boy. You know I can make that happen."

"That's not what I want, and if I did, I wouldn't ask for it from you, Valefar," said Gregory, his face flushed with embarrassment and fury. "I admit, it's a form of torture watching Jordana and Terrence together, but only because I want what they have, what my mother and father had."

I nodded. "I know. I didn't at first. I watched you at the club. Your face gave you away, your anger, your jealousy, and your lust on display. You coveted her."

"I don't covet her. I covet what they have."

"I know that now, but it took me some time to figure it out."

Valefar gleamed with excitement. "Tell me what it is, Becs. Fulfill your contract."

Gregory backed away three steps from the demon, head down, not meeting the demon's eyes. I turned to Valefar and told him the truth.

"Gregory wants to find his soulmate. He wants true love."

Valefar's wings burst forth in an expanse of fiery heat, flinging pendulous lava globules into the air which fragmented into tiny scorching volcanic tears that rained down onto our bodies, burning our hair, faces, and arms. I ducked and shoved Gregory out of the way, but he still gasped as Valefar's flames branded our skin.

The lava hit coals in the firepit, and the entire pit and the concrete around flushed with fire like a volcano, molten rock running down the concrete in rivers of hot, scorching death. Some raced down the carefully cultivated grass, destroying it in mere seconds, until it reached the swimming pool, superheating the water to steam, evaporating most of the water in a blur of fog.

A figure stepped through that fog while I was down on all fours urging Gregory to keep breathing in the hazy, hot air. It took me a moment to realize the figure was Ash. He appeared untouched and uninjured and backlit by the moonlight; he spoke with a confidence that belied the situation.

"Stop it, demon. Cease this nonsense at once."

I shook my head to clear it and darted to him. He may have some newfound confidence, but I still needed to protect him. "Ash, what are you doing?" I grasped his wrist. "It's too dangerous. You can't be here, remember?"

Ash gently pulled my fingers from his arm. "It's fine, Becs." He pointed at Valefar. "You know the rules, demon."

Valefar's gold dust flared high into the air, and his eyes flamed red. Sparks flickered outward, and I feared that his wrath could set fire to the whole estate, all the way to the boat house. Maybe even Lake Erie. Wasn't this exactly how Lake Erie had burned before? I shivered at the thought that I could be the second person to cause the legendary Burning River.

Valefar glared at Ash. "You can't meddle," he said, spitting toxic fluid that landed on the ruined grass around him where it sizzled, leaving tiny fires that burned unaided, dancing in the night.

Ash spoke again, his voice calm and steady. "The rules stand as they are."

"Ash!" I pulled him behind me. "What are you saying? How do you know this? I mean, I know these details, but how do you know them?"

He took hold of my hand and squeezed. "I read the books on your table, too."

He had? When?

Valefar gestured with his arms, hurling flames in our direction that missed us by a fraction. "It matters none. You can't interfere if a bargain is to be made. They enter freely."

Ash's smile would have cut glass. "But what Gregory wants, you cannot give," Ash said. "There's no interfering in true love."

I raised my hand. "How about a consolation prize?"

Valefar snapped like an annoyed teacher in an eighth-grade classroom. "What do you mean? Your neck is still on the line."

"Technically, it isn't. I only promised to discover Gregory's deepest wish, which I did. The fact that you can't use it to tempt him is on you, not me."

"Shut up, summoner. You may have gotten me on a technicality, but that doesn't mean I'm letting you off scot-free. I'm a demon. I cheat."

"You already have someone in your clutches. Isn't that right, Perrick?"

Perrick walked out of the house, eyes downcast, refusing to look at me, holding a sheaf of papers in one hand, his phone with my text in the other. Nick stumbled out behind him.

"What does she mean, Perrick?" Nick asked.

Valefar let out a hearty laugh. "Nick! How I've missed you!"

Nick flinched and hid behind his troll friend. "Perrick? What's happening? What does Becs mean?"

Perrick swallowed. "I made a deal, Nicky."

Quietly, I snapped my fingers, releasing the Warlock from his circle.

Nick's mouth dropped open, and he rushed to Perrick's side. "What do you mean? You made a deal with Valefar? Of all demons? With him? After all I've been through? After all you've seen? Why? For God's sake? Why?" Nick grasped his friend by both shoulders. "What kind of deal did you make? Tell me."

Perrick looked at his feet. "I asked for the power to make Gregory's business wishes come true. When Gregory expressed an interest in seeing the Andino Trading Company's money laundering business blow up, I made it happen. I bragged to Gregory about it, thinking it would make Gregory happy and he'd let up on me. He was still pissed that I didn't get Becs to come work for him. I was just looking for a win."

Nick stood frozen, blinking at what Perrick had just said. "It didn't make Gregory happy though, did it?"

Perrick shook his head.

"Because it's never enough, Perrick. It will never be enough."

Perrick scuffed his shoe on the concrete. When he spoke, his gravelly voice was hard to hear. "It backfired. Gregory was furious because a man got hurt and the cops came looking. He didn't care so much that an innocent life had been affected, mind you. He just hated that it had brought the heat, exactly what he didn't want."

"So he deprived you of home soil to punish you? But why did you get so sick so fast?" asked Nick.

"Oh, he gave me soil," Perrick said, looking off into the distance, his hands fisting the papers.

"I gave him soil from another creep's farm," Gregory said, his voice matter-of-fact, as if he hadn't just admitted to attempted murder.

Nick, Ash, and I could only stare at Gregory. Nick was the one who spoke. "You poisoned him by giving him another family's home soil? You're truly a monster. Congratulations. You've outdone our mother."

Gregory gave his brother a hard stare. "I didn't know about the demon's deal. All I knew is that he brought the cops sniffing around our business. And don't lecture me about our mother. Nothing could outdo Mimi. I learned at her knee, and you know it."

"The injured man is my friend, Perrick," I said. I squeezed my hands into fists and dug my nails into my palms to keep from completely losing it.

Perrick seemed to shrink in on himself. "I know," he rasped. "I'm sorry."

"That's not enough," I said, my voice equally harsh as I held back tears.

Valefar couldn't have cared less about my emotions. He clapped his hands with glee. "Sorry it worked out that way, Perrick, but you know better than anyone that a deal's a deal. It's the way the cookie crumbles. Nick, isn't that right?"

Nick turned to his tormentor. "Shut the hell up, Valefar! You have no hold on me anymore!"

Valefar blinked. Nick Adamos, his plaything, his victim, was fighting back. He'd proven he wasn't so broken after all, that Valefar wouldn't win when the points were tallied, that Nick would recover and move on, scarred, but victorious in the end.

I liked seeing Valefar off balance. I gathered myself, burying my emotions about Perrick and Oded for another time. Right now, I needed to be strategic. I remembered what Laurel had taught me and adopted my best "tough cookie" stance. "Guess he told you, Valley. You don't own Nick anymore."

"Oh, shut up, Becs," snapped the demon.

"Not completely in charge, and he hates it," I said and whistled a jaunty tune I learned from Pinky.

The demon sulked until he remembered.

"I still get Perrick's soul."

"Really?" I asked. "I suspect that's not true. Where's the contract?"

"It's crystal clear," Valefar huffed.

"Let me see it. Perrick, is that what's in your hand? You brought it like I asked?"

Perrick shuffled over to me and handed me the contract, then he scooted away from me as fast as he could. I flipped the pages open and scanned them.

"See, Nick, Perrick made this deal with Valefar to impress your brother. He wanted to protect his son, as well as have unlimited access to his home soil. It was an idiotic move, but people do stupid things for love, and he made a bad deal. He may have caught a break though." I skimmed the second page. "Just as I thought, Valefar. You didn't get his soul for this. You got a favor."

"What?" Valefar stood in the conflagration, eyes furious.

"Perrick called the Warlock to summon you, right? The Warlock's an amateur, so he used a contract he stole from me while he held me captive in the Nightmarescape, but he didn't look at it too closely. He stole a favor-for-favor contract. You don't get Perrick's soul. You get one favor in return. You didn't read the fine print, and you made a bad deal. I can't help that."

Valefar looked absolutely gobsmacked. It was delightful. I reminded myself to be careful with the next part, so I kept my voice low and slow.

"Here's the thing. I know the Warlock's deepest, darkest wish, and he's skulking around the perimeter of the yard right now. I gave you Gregory's deepest wish, but you can't do anything with that. Maybe you can do something with the Warlock's."

Valefar sniffed the air while Gregory whirled his head around trying to see where the Warlock was hiding.

Valefar smiled. "I smell him. That loser. He can't make a proper contract, and he can't even kill you, of all people."

"Gee, thanks." I resented that remark. Hey, I had *some* skill.

"Oh, no offense," said Valefar.

"Offense taken."

"That's your choice."

Great, Valefar had a therapist.

A red dot appeared on Gregory's chest. The crime lord froze.

The Warlock called out, "Warning. That's not my gun, Ms. Greenblatt, but it does belong to a paid consultant of mine. He'll pull the trigger if I ask him to."

The Warlock had phoned a friend. That was a wrinkle I hadn't expected. I should have confiscated his phone.

"Resorting to non-magic means, I see?" *Crap*. I'd wanted him here, but I hadn't expected him to learn and adapt. He'd seemed like such a blockheaded, one-tool idiot. My pulse throbbed, and my mouth dried up, but I had to play it cool.

"You misunderstand me, Warlock. I congratulate you! I've never gotten one over on Valefar, and here you did on the first try. Well done. But, as a summoner, for your long-term health, I figure you might want to handle this situation among friends. I'm your backup, not your enemy. This is your moment to negotiate for what you really want," I called out.

The Warlock stepped into the light, and the tableau was complete. We stood in a triangle, like in my dream. Behind Gregory, lush woods with water behind the trees. Valefar in dust, fire, and ash. The Warlock, next to the house, the city in the distance, not where I could see it, but there, nonetheless. Violins and clarinets played in the background. Asher was present, as well as Nick and Perrick. My sister and Ruthie were in my thoughts. And I was in the middle, connecting them all.

For all my bluster, I felt as helpless as I had been in my vision.

A drum joined the music, echoing the pounding of my heart.

In my dream, my loved ones died, mummified by the magic of my enemies, their backs turned to me, their lives forfeited because I couldn't figure out what to do.

I racked my brain. In the vision, I held the rope vines, not Valefar or Gregory, and not the Warlock. I needed to tug in the right place, in the right way, and they should fall like dominoes. That was what my dream had been telling me.

At least, that's what I thought it meant.

Still, it was a lot of guesswork.

Ash put a hand on my shoulder.

A lot of faith.

The Warlock shook me out of my reverie.

"Disappointed. Stay where you are, Ozzie," the Warlock said, speaking to the mystery man with the gun. "It seems I made a mistake with the contract, but I won't make such an error again. As you can see, Ms. Greenblatt . . ." He pointed to the dot on Gregory's torso. "I'm a quick learner."

He crossed his arms over his chest and lifted his chin in a show of false bravado, and walked around the Duke of Hell, as if inspecting a car.

"Elegant. I like the way you used the fire pit to create the circle. It's refined. I appreciate well-designed magic. You seem comfy in there, Duke Valefar."

Valefar bowed his horned head so that his fangs almost hit the ground. He dripped saliva that further scored the concrete with deep burn marks, but it was a bow of a kind, and anyone might have thought it was a sign of respect, if they hadn't seen the flashing, calculating eyes.

The Warlock sneered at the demon's swagger. "But," he said, holding up an index finger, "refined as this may be, it is weak. Look at all this flame escaping the confines of the perimeter. I held the duke in a much stronger circle before, and in the future, I will again."

The Warlock displayed his ignorance. Valefar wasn't bound at all. He stood within the firepit, but the circular stones didn't represent a magical boundary of any type. I held Valefar by my will and my will only. The Warlock had once again exposed his inexperience, and Valefar's wide grin reminded me of a shark approaching an unsuspecting tuna. I handed Ash my backpack and the other burden I carried so that both my arms were free, and rolled my neck and shoulders to get loose. Ash accepted them without a word.

Valefar gave the Warlock a baleful stare. "You can try, Derrick Vance. As you well know, I already hold your father."

"Liberation. Release him. He is of no use to you."

"Why should I? You know what he's done? Should I tell everyone here?"

The Warlock shook his head. "Unnecessary. It is of no concern now. Let's make a deal. Something you want for my father."

"I want nothing you can give me."

I interrupted. "Did you know, Duke Valefar, that Derrick's greatest desire is to have been born with the Kiss?"

Valefar upped the wattage on his evil smile to level "nuclear." It was so malevolent I staggered back a step.

Valefar raised an eyebrow. "Maybe we could consider a trade? I can make it worth your time. I'll give you the power to summon across *dimensions*. Across space and time. What you can see and experience is far more that this measly world, more than Hell itself." Valefar gestured around him. "Do you really think this is all there is? There are worlds out there to explore, and I can give you those. For yourself or your father? What do you say?"

Valefar sat in an invisible throne made of gold motes and waited. I breathed in and out, even, focused, preparing.

Derrick moved closer to him. "Dimensions?"

Valefar smiled wider. "Truly."

The Warlock stood stock still. "Vow. Vow you'll release my father."

Valefar didn't respond, but his smile grew wider.

I hesitated, sweat dripping down my back, making my hands clammy. A sudden lump in my throat made it hard to breathe and concentrate. I knew how dangerous the Warlock was, but now I was faced with Derrick, a man with a father already in Hell under Valefar's thumb.

Did I want to be the cause of another generation's fall? Could I kill a human? When he'd walked into my dreams and invaded my thoughts, I had no problem destroying him. But now? Even though he'd tortured me, attempted to kill me, slaughtered innocent creatures, and threatened the lives of others, could I be his judge, jury, and executioner? He'd done it all to free his dad. Did I have the right? Tears pricked my eyes at the thought of making this choice.

He was a *person* and a *son*.

I had to try to stop him now, even it meant denying Valefar. I couldn't repeat what I did with Nick. I had to try.

I put all that emotion into my plea. "Derrick, order your man to stand down. Tell him not to shoot Gregory. Please. I'm begging you. Things are going to turn out badly if you don't. Look around you. You need to step back from the brink. Don't kill Gregory and don't make this deal. It will harm you irreparably."

The Warlock sneered. "Ludicrous. You poor deluded girl. Killing Gregory is all in the plan. It's ticking off a box for me. Then, you're next."

"Be reasonable. Stop this madness. You can't steal a Kiss. Maybe I can help you get your father back, but don't listen to Valefar. He's a demon and a trickster."

Derrick scoffed. "Obviously. I will not give in, you witless girl. I'm well aware of who Valefar is."

Derrick lifted his hand and blasted me with an orb of fiery burgundy and orange magic that seared the sky with an ear-splitting scream. It came so fast and furious that I didn't have time to run or duck, only to hold up my left arm in a useless, stereotypical, instinctive protective move to cover my face and head, while I turned to my right and shielded the arrows with my body.

I detested that I was going to die in front of Valefar.

I hated that I wouldn't be there to help Pinky.

I loathed that I'd never see my sister or niece again.

Everything and everyone had been motivated by love, and still, it came to this. Gregory wanted true love. I loved my sister. Perrick loved his son. Even Derrick loved his father. And yet, we were all about to die.

Ash leapt to my side and pulled me out of the way, but he was too slow to yank me completely out of the magic sphere's path. It still hit my arm, and I expected it to encase my limb in death magic and spread to my whole body.

Except that it didn't.

The magic hit my leather cuff, and the protective symbols flared to life. Each symbol burst forth from the bracelet and together formed a circle of transparent white light with a radius of about six feet. If the circle was a clock, the Solar Cross took the twelve position, the Star of David occupied the three spot, the Eye of Horus held the six, the Pentacle the nine, and the Chamsa took the center.

The disc beamed a protective shield and blocked the burgundy and orange enchantment, reflecting it back to its owner, who caught it in disbelief.

And to top it off, the outline of a gold and jade dragon burst forth from my other bracelet, soared into the sky, and hovered above the shield, its wingspan over twenty feet, its mouth open, ready to spew fire. I'd have to thank Mrs. Long later.

"Why? Why are you always so difficult?" Derrick raged and threw it again.

My shield rebounded the sorcery, deflecting it harmlessly, giving Ash time to drop my backpack and hand me the bow.

Furious, the Warlock tried again, and this time, the dragon dashed down and swallowed the magic whole.

Ash slapped an arrow in my hand, and in one smooth motion, I aimed. The bow and arrows worked with me now, moving with no resistance, and I knew when I released, my aim would be true.

Valefar snapped his fingers. "Stop allowing yourself to get distracted, Derrick. She's nothing. I'm offering your father's freedom. I'm offering you power. Alchemy. Answers to mysteries you haven't even wondered yet. Why still piddle with these mere humans?" Valefar leaned forward, catching Derrick's eyes. "I don't think you understand the uniqueness of your position. This is a one-time offer. Your father will wither away in Hell tonight if you don't agree."

The Warlock raised his hands to cast. "No. You must think me stupid, demon." He took a single step backwards and pointed to Gregory, who hadn't dared move this whole time.

"Ozzie, take your shot," he ordered.

"Noooooo!" I yelled.

"Yes," he ordered.

"Then, I'll take my shot too," I said, my heart breaking. But he left me no choice. With no more time, I let my death arrow fly.

Multiple things happened at once. I angled my shield to protect Gregory. The death arrow hit Derrick in the shoulder where it met his neck. Derrick cried out, slumping to the ground. Valefar grabbed the weakened warlock around the middle and held him to his torso, wrapping him in a binding of gold motes that braided into a thick rope. Derrick struggled, howling and bucking, but the death arrow sapped his strength. I watched in a combination of guilt and horror as Derrick realized that the end was near. Valefar couldn't take him alive, but dead was another proposition. Derrick turned his head to me and wheezed, "Blight. I curse you, summoner."

A sickly green needle of power, cold as the first frost of winter, hit me in the chest and spread like lightning over my skin before it fizzled and evaporated. I shivered as the bitter chill left my body.

"What was that?" asked Ash.

"His last attempt to harm me," I replied. "It's nothing."

I hoped.

Valefar ripped Derrick's shrieking, damned soul away from his body, sent up a tornado of gold dust, and disappeared, leaving the Warlock's pale, battered corpse behind.

Gregory ducked to avoid the anticipated bullet, but with my shield protecting him he was never in peril. In actuality, Ozzie never got a chance to take the shot. The dragon found him sleeping in the bushes covered in pink fairy dust.

Both dragon and shield returned to their bracelets as soon as the danger passed.

"Derrick never signed a contract with Valefar," I said, as we stared at the burned circle surrounding the fire pit. "I don't know if Valefar can keep him there. It's not binding. He kidnapped him."

"He didn't take him alive. Derrick died and was bound for Hell anyway, as a result of his prior evil deeds. You can't help it if people make bad deals," said Ash.

"He died because I killed him, Ash."

"To save Gregory's life."

"I'm not sure it works that way."

"I am." He hugged me close with one arm, and I breathed in his scent and soaked in his body heat. I was still cold from Derrick's curse.

"Hey, look." Ash bent and swept his hands in the ashes, extracting a glint of gold. "Valefar abided by your agreement." He opened my palm and placed the metal into it.

I couldn't believe it. I opened my locket, and Mickey's photo stared back at me, but instead of my photo, there was a picture of a lion's paw print. I peeled it out and crushed it, tossing it into the fire pit's ashes. "Bastard."

"Does this mean he still has a hold on you?" Ash asked.

"No. It means he has an adolescent sense of humor."

Chapter 31

MRS. LONG SQUINTED over her half-moon spectacles at Trick, Rin, and Jimmy as they shifted from foot to foot on the counter, their caps in hand.

"You'll work in the pantry? Let us know when we are low on supplies and keep things nice and tidy?"

"Yes, Mrs. Long!" Rin and Jimmy said.

Trick added, "That's the deal. We always live up to our bargains."

Mr. Long came out from the back with the coolest, multi-level doll condo I'd ever seen. Barbie could eat her heart out.

The three men's jaws dropped open. Jimmy practically drooled. "That's for us?" he asked.

Rin, the excitable one, hopped up and down until Trick placed a hand on his elbow. Trick, ever more suspect, crossed his arms and harrumphed.

"Climb in," said the gentle Mr. Long.

"They keep the pantry neat or out they go! I don't care if it is snowing," Mrs. Long warned, shaking an index finger as she followed Mr. Long and the wee folk to the back. "Or they pay rent."

I grabbed Pinky's hand, winked, and said, "Let's be on our way."

We drove to the Summer Medical Park campus.

"Bees, so far they've flown. No matter how far they roam. Forever, will find their home."

There it was. Pinky's rhyme. His memory. Right there in wrought iron, above the entrance to the pollinator's garden. Pinky slept in the North Medical Park garden and had never paid attention to the southern campus. Typical for Pinky, who had a tendency to miss obvious things, but it didn't matter.

"What does it mean, Becs?" Pinky asked, eyes wide. "I don't understand." He bounced on his toes, his face red.

"I think this is the entrance you need to get back to Faerie." I spoke in the calmest, lowest voice I could, trying to counter Pinky's rising anxiety.

He bounced to the fence and banged on the iron, burning his hand with a sharp hiss of pain at each moment of contact. "I. Want. To. See. My. Mom!"

"Hey, fella! Stop hitting the fence. Okay? Whatcha doing? You're hurting yourself." The head groundskeeper for the southern garden rushed forward and tried to grab Pinky's hand, which was a big mistake.

Pinky flailed his arms at the thought of being touched by a stranger and accidentally backhanded the groundskeeper, who fell to the ground. I ran to the poor man's side and helped him up, but he was already bleeding from a small cut to his forehead. He reached for a walkie-talkie at his side to call security.

"Please don't," I said, begging him to listen. "He's not dangerous. He's upset and not always in control of his emotions. He doesn't know his size and strength. Please. Mr. Lincoln in the Winter Park knows him well."

The man took a hankie from his pocket and held it to the bleeding wound and watched Pinky walk in circles, talking to himself. Despite the pain he must have been in, he nodded. "I have a nephew like that," he said. "Can you calm him down?"

"Give me a moment."

"Pinky." Pinky didn't hear me.

"Pinky." Louder this time.

"Pinky!" This time he looked at me.

"It's okay. I'm going to help you."

Tears welled, and he wiped his nose with his arm. "This is the place, Becs. I can feel it, but I can't get in."

"Oi! Big guy. Move it!"

Pinky and I whirled around.

"Who said that?" I whispered.

"Me!"

I narrowed my vision to a spot next to Pinky's shoulder and when I closed one eye—and squinted—I could make out a tiny yellow man with wings fluttering in the air. "Your big fairy is blocking the entrance. Tell him to shrink or move on, girlie!"

"Wait! He's at the entrance? I'm right? This is how he gets in?"

"Well, duh. He's holding up the queue. Some of us would like to get home for dinner."

Sure enough, if I squinched my eye almost closed, I could see a long line of fairies, one after the other. All hovering there, some tapping their feet. One even looked at his wrist, as if he were checking his watch after a long day's work and needed to catch a train.

"This is fabulous. Pinky here is my friend, and he's forgotten how to go small. Can you help him?"

The little yellow fairy scoffed. "What do you mean he's forgotten how to go small? No one forgets that."

I pressed my lips together to keep from squashing the man-bee like a bug and said, between gritted teeth, "Pinky has, and he's suffered for it. Please help him."

"Aw, shit. Fine, if it will move things along." He crossed his arms and his eyes gleamed. "It will cost you."

"You mercenary mosquito fuckwit. What do you want?"

Pinky's hopeful face fell, and I stroked his arm to calm him down, glad he accepted the touch.

"Whaddaya got?" The line of fairies behind him grew longer, and a few shook their tiny fists at us. We didn't have much time.

What did I have? Pinky tugged at my sleeve, looking at me imploreingly. I couldn't let him down.

I snagged my knapsack from my back, twisted it around and dug deep into the main pocket. Where was it? I felt around with my hand, tapping the bottom. It had to be here. When had I last seen it? Ah, when it had rolled out on the sidewalk during the fight with the Warlock. I felt it and pulled it out, but it was a train token. *Damn. Wait, wait.* There it was! I extracted the gold fae coin I'd gotten for a tip with a flourish and showed it to the yellow fairy.

"How's this?"

His eyes gleamed, and so did all the eyes from all the fairies in line behind him. One even whistled.

"That will do nicely. Pinky, put that in your pocket and you'll give it to me on the other side," he directed.

Before I handed it to Pinky, I said, "Promise me that this will also pay for you to get him home to his mother. Say it before every fae in this queue."

Despite being a complete asshole, the yellow fae's face sobered up. "I promise."

Pinky accepted the coin with reverence. "Thank you, Becs." He threw his arms around my neck and gave me a sloppy kiss on the cheek. "I love you."

"Aww. Go on, now."

The yellow fairy flew to Pinky's ear and whispered something. Pinky's eyes lit up. "That's it!" He whispered something back and *whizzt!* He shrank to the same size as the other fae, waved, held the yellow fairy's hand, and *bzzt!* He was gone. The rest of queue followed suit in a manner of seconds.

I was alone.

Except for the groundskeeper, who winked at me and said, "It's rush hour around here. Everyone wants to get home." He ambled off while I blinked at his retreating back.

I turned to the empty space where Pinky had been, wrinkling my nose to keep the tears from falling.

"I love you, too," I murmured into the dusk.

Epilogue

ASH STROKED BECS'S shoulder in the early morning light, enjoying the stillness. He blinked at the rising sun and exhaled, letting his anxiety go. What was done was done. He'd made a choice, and he wouldn't regret it.

Becs's burns were healing on the outside. Her hands looked better, and her black eye was down to a greenish yellow, but he didn't know how she was faring on the inside. He could read her fairly well, but she was skilled at keeping things hidden. It was a necessary skill after all she'd been through, and he didn't have the heart, or the permission, to tell her what was yet to come.

A loud banging startled him and woke her. He kissed the top of her head and whispered, "It's the woodpecker, remember? Nothing to be afraid of. I've got you."

It was a testament to her fatigue that she cuddled against him and settled back into sleep. He held a hand over her temple and pushed a threatening nightmare away. Giving her a night's peaceful rest was the least he could do. He couldn't stay, no matter how much he wished to. His time with her was over, and despite his best intentions, things had gone dangerously awry.

He'd broken every rule when it came to Rebecca Naomi Greenblatt, and he'd heard the whispers and mutters from the more conservative of his brethren, but what he'd done last night was forbidden, and he'd have to answer for it. He glanced at the clock. He still had time for a few more glorious moments.

He kissed her neck and breathed her in, enjoying her scent. She smelled like apples and honeysuckle, and something sultry beneath. He inhaled. Sandalwood, maybe? The mix was a complex blend that was distinctly her, and by all the rules, he should be immune. But he wasn't, so somebody had obviously made a mistake. They couldn't put all the blame on him. He'd been drawn to her from the moment he'd laid on eyes on her, from the moment she'd first stolen his Wi-Fi.

He ran his hand down her waist and over the swell of her hips, loving the feel of her curves. He feared this would be the last time he'd experience the physical sensation of human flesh, and he wanted to savor it. He spooned her and pulled closer, relishing the feel of his skin to hers.

Of course, his was a suit.

The buzzing in his brain grew louder, until he couldn't ignore it. He stood, naked, pointed a finger to the sky to say, "one moment, please," and found a note pad. He deftly folded the paper into an elegant origami guardian angel and placed it next to her pillow, hoping she would understand. Staring at her with tremendous sorrow in his heart, he stroked her cheek.

"I've kept her body safe. But have I broken her heart? Have I, in my selfishness, caused her more harm?"

The buzzing swelled, insistent. In response, Ash raised his arms to the light . . . and was gone.

To be continued . . .

Acknowledgements

First, I'd like to thank Joe Lynch, RS, MPH, Program Manager at the Cuyahoga County Board of Health for his assistance in understanding rat living preferences and colony sizes. I could have guessed at that little detail, and maaaaaybe no one would have noticed, but Joe was kind enough to help out and make sure I got it right.

Thank you, William Owens, Ph.D., Ohio University for help with the Latin translation of the fictional book titles.

I absolutely must thank Darin Kennedy, Patrick Dugan, Leslie Gould, and James P. Nettles for reading the first drafts, listening to me kvetch my way through, and brainstorming titles. My little secret library is the key to my success.

I'd also like to thank the Thursday Ladies—you know who you are—who force me to sit, butt in chair, fingers on keyboard, and make words. Also, The Writing Tribe, Authors' Roundtable, and the Cajun Sushi Hamsters. Writing is a lonely business. You make it less so.

A huge thank you to Debra Dixon and Brenda Chin, for believing in this book and series and making my words better. And another massive thank you to John Hartness, friend, author, and all-around good guy, although he'd prefer that not be public knowledge.

About the Author

This is J. D. BLACKROSE'S first series with Bell Bridge Books. Previously, she's published *The Soul Wars, The Devil's Been Busy,* and the *Zombie Cosmetologist* novellas through Falstaff Books. Her short stories have appeared in places such as *Third Flatiron* and *Curiosities,* as well as her own collection, *Seder in Space.* She's always lived in her head and is often accused of not listening. To make up for it, she's mastered the art of looking interested.

Follow J. D. on:
slipperywords.com,
facebook.com/JDBlackrose/
and twitter.com/JDBlackrose.

9 781610 261678